TRUE BLUE
CONFEDERATE

STATEN M. RALL

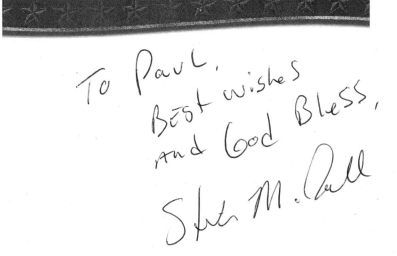

To Paul,
Best wishes
and God Bless,

Staten M. Rall

★ ABC BOOK PUBLISHERS ★

I owe my gratitude to you, Kim Benton, my editor, who read, believed and worked miracles in me as a writer and a person. You loved and nurtured this work through many months. Without you, it would not exist.

More than a creative director, you are a true friend for life. — S.M.R.

True Blue Confederate is work of fiction.
Names, characters, places and incidents are the products of the author's imagination or are used fictitiously. Any resemblence to actual events, locales, or persons, living or dead, is entirely coincidental.

All Characters in this novel are fictional, or are the author's rendering of a Historical participant. The 'Order of Command' pages in this book contain names of the actual participants. All maps are the author's rendering, and for clarity, some unit names and commanders have been omitted.

The Battle of Tazewell map was created especially for this writing, and is as close to accurate as available information will allow.

Any inaccurate information and omissions are the fault, or the design of the Author.

ABC Book Publishers, Inc.

www.abcbookpublishers.com
www.trueblueconfederate.com
www.statenrall.com

Library of Congress Control # 2013939122

ISBN 978-0-9893796-0-1

Original Cover design: Ryan Schinneller
Cover photo By Jennifer Mengel

Printed in the United States of America

ACKNOWLEDGEMENTS ★

Thanks to my parents Frederick and Lucinda for passing down their love of history through books, sightseeing and many trips to Grandma's house. I owe much to my father's German Heritage and military career. My mother's habit of reading stories to me as a child inspired my imagination and without her example, this book would not exist.

Special thanks goes to my cousin Andrew Hall, who read my twenty-five page short story and said, "This would make a great novel." I had no idea of the effort it would take to complete such a lofty venture.

For their expertise and kindness, I will always be grateful for Robbie Crawford, an avid re-enactor and uniform specialist, and Jennifer Mengel who photographed the cover image.

I am indebted to Mr. Ben Bennett of Tazewell who answered my phone call in 2010, and eight months later, shared with me the great spectacle of the Cumberland Gap and a real insider's tour of the Tazewell Battle sites. Without you, my knowledge of this event, and map would be incomplete.

Unending appreciation goes to my brothers, Jefferson, and Raoul for encouraging me through months of editing, and rewriting. Thanks to my nephew Charlie and niece Aneliese for your reassurance. May God bless my employers, Greg & Pat Givens for their patience and restraint amid my creative moods.

Thanks to the generous souls who sheltered me on the road as I traveled - My friends Chris and Mary Effinger, John and Tisha Gay, John and Christine Pickett. Including my cousins Matt & Tracy Hall, Andrew & Amy Hall, Billy & Marion Joseph, and Charles & Laura Joseph. I must thank cousins Will and Kayb Joseph, for the wonderful stay in Chattanooga during my research trip to Tazewell.

For additional wisdom and insight I thank, Chris and Hannah Flynn, Ann Imburgio, Dr Cecil Taylor, and Dr. Vickie Hunt's class at Northwest Florida State College. Appropriately, all praise to God and his son Jesus for salvation, renewal, and creative blessings.

TRUE BLUE
CONFEDERATE

Staten M. Rall

MIDDLE TENNESSEE &
CUMBERLAND GAP REGION

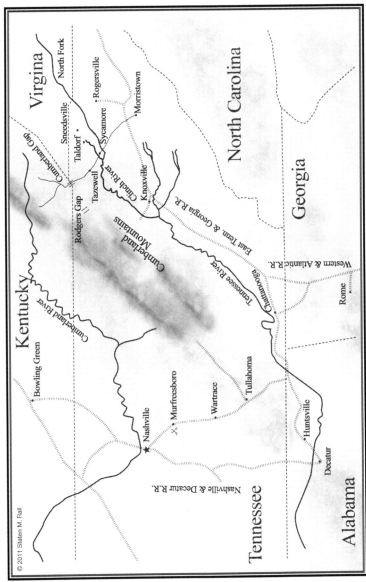

© 2011 Staten M. Rall

PROLOGUE ★

My Dear J.B.,

Nashville, Tenn. July 8ᵗʰ, 1862

I have been directed by your mother as of late, and always, to write greetings and news from your family here in Nashville. I apologize for my lack of correspondence, but as you know, for a time I had to be selective with my outgoing mail. Having yielded to the occupation of our city by the Northern forces, since February of this year, it is only after many months, that I renew my trust in the postal service.

As for the news, the occupation places first. Nashville has become the Union's storehouse. Acting as the perfect Yankee, General Buell posts his orders around the city and parades troops in all quarters. Every wagon, cannon, caisson, and mule that the enemy possesses is parked amid the town's open yards. Where pleasant parks and grassy playgrounds once stood, there are now open pens for hogs. More repugnantly, Union forces have packed downtown with every pleasure known to exist. I dare not tell you what.

They keep a close watch on me, as I have supplied the Southern Army and before that, was a delegate to the Secession Convention. But for want of certain food items and dependable news, we live by wise means and much thrift.

My son, I regret to inform you that the Union commissary department procured our cattle yards in March. I felt that loss deeply, as I staked our whole lot on the breeding grounds and ranch. The cut in our family budget will not harm your two young sisters. Little Eliza is the jewel of our lives; she's learning so much every day and cheering us during these times with her writing and alphabet. She will be five in August. Cassie is growing up too fast and has grown the prettiest long brown hair. She misses your protection and care, and your vibrant readings of Dickens and Poe. She asks if you have received any of her letters. She has only three from you, so my son, you must do better, for your sisters and mother. Please know, if combat or maneuver has restricted you from your literate duties, I err. Voulez-vous envoyer d'autres lettres?

Some cheer came lately, thanks to General Forrest's raid on Murfreesboro last week. He rescued our patriots from jail, and the hangman, then, retook the town for our side. Much pride and promise has arisen here for daring General Forrest.

If he can do this with one detachment of cavalry, surely Generals Bragg and Smith can come to our aid here. Why does this not happen instantly? They flurry around the state like angry bees but do little. Shiloh achieved nothing but to shatter our Army, as you know, and now Memphis has fallen, too, on the 6th of June, and the base at Corinth, Miss. has been abandoned.

Tennessee is lost, except in the east, where you are, my son. Damn the retreating generals, a pox on them, I say.

Rumor and speculation as to the fate of the South is ever changing, but citizens here are strongly governed by purpose and remain loyal in all their efforts. There is still quite a bit of manufacturing here, done in the open for our armies. And who profits? The Federal marshals and generals who have been assigned to police our activities.

The more corruption I witness here in Nashville, the prouder I am of you and your service. I am glad our local captain allowed you to join the regiment in the field, late as you were. I only pulled a few strings to obtain your papers. Thank your Lieutenant Weston, also.

It is evident your duty at the Cumberland Gap has added to your manliness and ardor. Congratulations on earning your corporal's stripe.

I believe our most Honorable President Davis is ignoring the Tennessee front. General R.E. Lee has fought off a vast Army from the gates of Richmond, so it is obvious where the eyes of President Davis rest for now.

Has anyone produced more war goods than Nashville and its surroundings? No one. This city, this state is vital to the Southern efforts. We have coal, iron, wheat and factories to refine them. Thus, my heart laments, perhaps because of my business losses.

I know your love of books and I author one here, just for you. Please read this, as you must, to your comrades and say a hearty hello from Nashville and "the delegate." Perhaps the news from home will entice them toward fervent action in the field!

I anxiously wait to hear how you have used your intellect and ideal education to influence and arouse the warrior in that rabble you grew up with. All those youthful summers on cow ranches endeared you to the lower orders of boyhood companions, but that learning can aid you in leading them as soldiers. J.B., you have all the sense God has ever given me, so please look to caution and obey Colonel Rains. He is the best, I hear.

With love from your mother, Cassie, Eliza and me. God bless you and the Army you serve.

Your Father,

Jack Lyhton

CHAPTER 1★

STONES RIVER BATTLEFIELD
DECEMBER 31, 1862

As the overcast sky brought its first hint of rain, the littered battlefield writhed and moaned in the pall of gathering dusk. Bodies of men and horses lay strewn about the winter grass and cedar forests, shrouded in smoke and mist. It was a cold, gray New Year's Eve, and growing darker.

Confederate Sergeant Jon B. Lyhton rushed through a cedar grove, bounded over rocks and slowed to a walk. Stepping cautiously into a wide, littered clearing he scanned the opposite tree line. The failing light of dusk refused to locate the east or west, front or rear. Jon knew he was lost in the middle ground.

His heartbeat thumped in his ears and blended with the crackling echoes of musket fire rebounding among the trees. Being so turned around, he could not distinguish the authors of the distant fusillades. He panted like hunted game on the run, tired and thirsty. Discovering nothing familiar ahead of him, he slapped his rifle stock in frustration and turned back toward the tree line.

Jon felt the fatigue he had been ignoring all afternoon tugging at his will, burning his muscles. Dragging his mud-heavy shoes, he veered into the woods and stopped to take a few heaving breaths. On impulse, he reached for his canteen. Gauging his reserve, he shook the tin drum. It was near empty. "Damn it, sure as the day,"

1

he mumbled.

Moving further into the trees and away from the sound of the guns, he slowed to a walk, and then sat down on a grassy spot near two large rocks. *Can't rest too long*, he thought. *I must find the regiment before the darkness stops me.*

Earlier that day, around noon, he was with the regiment, when as forward skirmishers, Jon and his platoon attempted to pick off Union artillerymen who had pinned them down behind a rock and rail fence. Along the Nashville Pike, the Yankee cannons were massed together, firing directly at the exposed Confederate charges, repulsing wave after wave of assaults. For extra cover, the Union gunners used the elevated cut of the rail line running parallel to the road. They brought up as many rifles and cannons as they wanted without much resistance. Jon's skirmishers enjoyed little success, mostly firing over the gunners' heads.

As Jon was loading his rifle for another try, the platoon's leader, Lieutenant Weston, ran up behind him. "Recall the skirmish line away from that damned cannon fire! Colonel Gordon does not want to test those guns anymore!"

Jon looked ahead to the body-littered ground and affirmed the order. He checked the deportment of his men ahead and saw a section of the company separated from the rest as they took heavy rifle fire from several directions. "I'll tell Lawsen!" He yelled. Instantly, Jon jumped up and raced towards the imperiled position. Yankee bullets sparked the stone and slapped the wood fence with a frightening rhythmic cadence as Jon found cover behind the low barrier.

The skirmishers were huddled together, not spread out as they should have been. Jon found his friend, Corporal Lawsen, and nudged his arm. "Hey Paul, who's covering your flanks?"

Jumping in surprise, Lawsen turned around. "Oh, J.B., it's you, thank God!" The corporal took a long look to the right and then to the left, scratched his four-day beard and moaned. "Well, I'd say those trees are covering our right... and those rocks yonder, uh..."

"Enough, I get your point!" yelled Jon. "Lieutenant Weston said to leave this horrid place now. Get them up and running; those guns are going to tear us up!"

Like prophecy fulfilled, cannon balls blasted large sections of spiked branches away from the treetops. Live iron rounds hit the earth and rolled to a stop, fuses hissing like snakes. The balls exploded amidst the retreating Confederates as the Federals rained in more rounds, displaying their aiming skills with solid shot and a few explosive case shot for visual effect.

The noise rattled teeth and bloodied ears. Jon and his men ran like mad rats into the woods as they slammed into trees and tripped onto hard, cold rock. Scattered, the soldiers ran to and fro through the smoky confusion between the lines and soon began to shoot at each other in blind surprise. Jon hid for a time, then roamed, stepping cautiously around the next tree, as the woods became a death trap. Eventually exhausted, his wandering brought him to the spot between the rocks.

As Jon lay resting, he noticed the sweat from his panicked sprint had turned into chilled dew. He sat upright, not knowing how long he had rested or even if he had slept. Shivering, he stared into the woods as the darkness poured into the surrounding trees with the fog and the pale, pungent battle smoke. Voices of the wounded and dying rose up to the treetops and hung in the motionless chill. The mournful cries falling over Jon sounded like the haunting pains of many suffering ghosts, or soon-to-be apparitions. "Damn the dark and the cold," Jon whispered.

He knew the night freeze was coming. It would surely be a bone-snapping, wet cold. Only a few more minutes of faded light remained, then the night would engulf everyone into the obscure and frozen world after battle. The enormity of the day's events fell upon him like the ever-present rain. He had never been lost from his regiment, nor had he fought in such massive a battle where thousands of men moved over miles of ground. Even the confusion was grand.

With a shiver, Jon fastened the four remaining brass buttons on his tan, single-breasted uniform coat and thought about what a mess the garment had become in such a short amount of time. It had not been long since he received it as a gift from his family, as he left home for the regiment with an older militia-style coat.

As for the loss of the buttons, Jon hoped one day he could tell them the story, in his unique animated style, perhaps next summer when the war would be long over. It would not be a story he would soon forget because his first action of the day stood as high achievement in the realm of soldiering.

His regiment, the 11th Tennessee, along with seven more brigades, crossed Stones River the day before, preparing for the New Year's Eve dawn assault. The morning fog hid the gray and tan formations, some of them six-men deep, sweeping across the riverside farm fields, cedar groves and high brush. When they had crossed the east-west Franklin Road, their red flags were finally spotted by the Yankee pickets, cooking breakfast in an open clearing.

The rebel yell broke the morning calm as birds exploded from the cedars and rabbits raced into their holes. To the few Union men who stood long enough to see it, the effect was overwhelming. The Confederate wave swallowed up the forward lines of blue pickets and their breakfast like an incoming tide. Whole encampments melted away under the gray wave, washing clean the spoilt land of their ancestors.

Torrents of Union soldiers retreated into the woods and formed temporary lines to stave off the flood of yelling rebels swarming over their camps like so many shrieking ravens. The 11th Tennessee had waded into a stand of cedars and rushed a Yankee company sniping from a large clump of boulders. At close range, the marksmen emptied their rifles, shooting full of holes the first dozen rebels to reach them. With no time to reload, most of the outnumbered Federals retreated, but the remaining bluecoats braced themselves for the clash.

The Confederates hurled themselves over the rock and blended into the blue company, each man pairing up to fight his own foe in a close, personal struggle, clubbing, gouging, kicking, and swearing.

Before he could pick out a target, a Yankee soldier charging blindly into the melee upended Jon. The collision severed him from his rifle, and he scrambled to regain control of his bearing. This was nearly impossible, because the man clinging to him was rather large and strong. Jon's canvas haversack tore at the flap as the attacker pulled at him with crazed intent.

The man's face, bloodied with a fresh wound, winced with spite and his eyes foretold future acts of violence. He had a claw-grip on Jon's coat, as he lifted him cleanly off of the ground and slammed him back down. The force of the blow dazed Jon, who was no weakling himself and had outlasted several large cousins at wrestling. Reaching around the man's large arms, Jon felt a holstered bayonet and pulled it out, but before he could use it, the enemy lifted him up for another thrashing to the ground.

This pounding was worse than the first and as the blow forced air from Jon's lungs, his eyes blurred and watered. He had dropped the bayonet and molested the ground to rediscover it, only to see it flash in the hands of his enemy. He reached in sharp angst for the man's face, his fingers slipping on the blood and cold sweat. The sharp prong of steel went up in the man's hands when in one instant, over Jon's face appeared the silver blur of a rifle muzzle jabbing straight into the huge man's thick chest. The brawny yank shrieked in pain as he was pushed away.

Jon, still in some degree of concussion, rolled over to his rifle and swung it around towards the large man. What he saw captivated him. His friend Martello had the Yankee stuck on his bayonet. As

Martello pulled the Yankee by his own rifle, it reminded Jon of a fisherman's pole overwhelmed by a sizeable fish. Martello fired his musket. The shot echoed into the trees and brought an end to the Yankee's struggle, as he fell back hard to the ground.

Jon heaved for breath, looked around and saw no immediate threats. All surrounding combat had ceased, and the sounds of soldiers shouting or running after shouting soldiers, prevailed through the wet drizzle. Men reloaded as they bit cartridges and pulled ramrods, filling the space under the trees with the sounds of sliding metal.

Much relieved, Martello helped Jon to his feet and they both stared at the dead Union man, larger than most. Jon rubbed his sore arms. "That big bastard was mad and determined to let me know it!"

"Pick someone you can whip next time, J.B.!" Martello exclaimed.

"That bull picked me, I'm obliged to say," said Jon. "Thank you kindly for interrupting."

Jon's friend was the shortest man in D Company, but possessed wide shoulders and thick legs. Sometimes Jon called him "Leonardo" because of his dark Italian looks. The two barely had time for a congratulatory address before First Sgt. Hillford yelled commands for the troops to redress the lines.

Lieutenant Weston rambled by, wide-eyed and pirate-like, with his sword drawn and pistol smoking. His smile burst through his mustache and goatee. Punching Jon's arm, he said, "*Bon travail, mon ami.*" A neatly cut, butternut uniform, trimmed in sky blue, fit his angular frame perfectly, all the way down to his long boots. His square jaw set, he nodded approval and then bolted away to direct scattered troops to the colors.

As D Company gathered prisoners, Jon noticed that the massive hands of the Yank had ripped the top three buttons from his coat. "Drat, I'll freeze before the New Year," he said, trying to pull the gap together.

Martello inspected the rent garb. "Aw now, you'll get a chance at one of those fancy Yank overcoats soon."

The first fight of the day had been a quick one. The Union men had never intended to hold the perilous position, but only bought time for more organized units to form lines of resistance. Jon's jocular tone with Martello masked his heightened nerves. For Jon and the 11th Tennessee, the survival mindset had banished personal fear, and the anxiety of the massive battle was tripled by more killing than they had ever seen.

As the company's victorious deed faded from Jon's mind, the soft drizzle of rain turned into a cold shower of steady drops, tapping the surrounding boulders. After many hours without food, hunger began to disorient him. There had been no time to think about much, but now isolated from the large troop formations, his thoughts ran by with no clarity, like the lost men running through the woods, with no aim. The ringing in his ears lent a disturbing quality to his aloneness and he jerked his head around, hearing false voices and orders shouted. He fixated on the company; the men had done well today, the platoon was mostly intact, his friends. Weston had led well, but where was his mentor and comrade now? How can he continue, and what if he were to be a prisoner? The land grew dark, and there was no way home.

Jon's train of thought had no direction and he shook off the confusion. Knowing he would have to get up and try to find the main Confederate line, he loaded his musket, assuming he may run into the enemy, hidden in the dark.

* * *

STONES RIVER

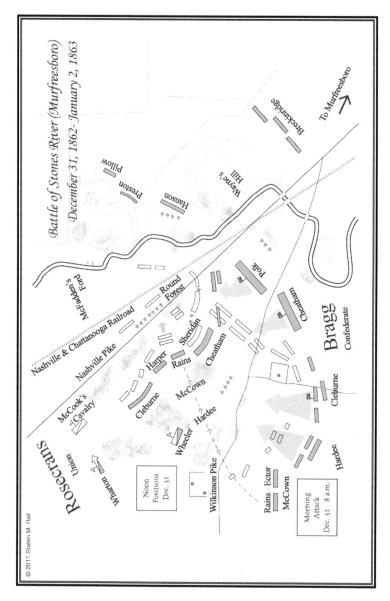

CHAPTER 2★

The two opposing armies fought the freeze that in a short time would affix the dead to the mud and grass. Rolling up in whatever coats or blankets they had, the comfort of a fire would be impossible for most of the frontline men, as their positions were exposed.

Without these rows of fires, Jon had no references of direction. The misty landscape erased his route from the regimental line and as he walked back through the terrain, he saw the same dark patches of trees or lumps of rock everywhere he turned. Soon he approached a narrow clearing, spotted with rocks and traces of battle debris. "Look for the fence or our wounded boys." he ordered himself, as a chronic shiver possessed his limbs.

Occupied now with his mission, Jon decided to count the paces out into the middle of the clearing to give him some measure of distance, but before he sounded off ten steps, a rock gave way under his shoe. While rebalancing himself, he looked down and discerned an ashen, dead face gaping up at him. He jumped at the sight, stark and sudden.

These spots in the dark field were not rocks, but numerous dead bodies. He listened for cries of any wounded men, but he heard only soft rain on his hat.

They were hard to identify at first, so he bent down, straining to see the uniforms. Surprisingly, doing this unnerved him. He had seen dead men before, but there were so many since morning, and now these. A strange fear came upon him in the isolated, dark place. Not a fear of death in battle, but of being suddenly grabbed by some demented soul, perhaps an enemy on the cusp of death, who knows not his last madness; and the fear of being strangled by a grip of cold flesh as the last, rancid breath leaves a dying face, bidding him to join the gore of the field. Shaking off this terror by talking aloud, he asked, "Is anyone alive?"

Waiting for a response, he held his breath. The words echoed over the dark bodies and faded into the nearby woods. Kneeling down for a closer look, he figured the body below him was a Confederate because he wore old shoes and no overcoat. The discovery of this gave him an idea, to find a dead Yankee and obtain his warmer wool overcoat. "Hell, half of the 11th are probably wearing the captured garb already," he whispered. "Damn if Martello wasn't right in his suggestion. I am a fool."

Weaving as best he could through the tangle of frozen limbs and weapons, Jon knelt occasionally to look for the sought-after Union winter coat, and in his hunger pains, feel for any full haversacks. With each search, he found a variety of ghastly wounds, broken limbs, and parts of men. Darkness fully took over the clearing and even under its pall, the faces and death poses were clear to his vision. He hurriedly frisked more corpses and moaned as the morbid task took him deeper into the open field and further into the morose result of battle.

Steady rain pelted a dead man's face and formed puddles in his dark, hollow eye sockets, the water running out like unending tears. Jon pulled a few hardtack crackers out of the riddled corpse's haversack. He quickly ate the food, soggy as it was. Grateful to find anything at all, he was nearly famished from a full day of running combat. He scanned the bodies for the overcoat as he walked, occasionally stepping on freezing pools of blood, which had become slushy in the grass. The reality of the dead soldiers began to prick at his mind.

They were mostly all Confederates with any Yankees being long since stripped of any useful supplies. With his teeth chattering, he knelt to mull over his situation amid the lonely place between armies, where land was taken and then abandoned like the casualties.

The rain collected on Jon's hat, trailed off the wide brim and fell onto his knee. A cold chill from the icy water shook him to his bones and sobered his thoughts about the field. A soldier never wants to be left in such desolation at the end of the fight. Jon fogged the air as he whispered in shaking, broken volume, "Kill me outright in a charge, or take me to die with my friends at the rear, but God no, don't leave me here to suffer the pain of my open wounds in the burning heat or slow cold."

Before he arose to leave, he picked up a haversack to replace his torn one. He gave the area one more glance. *My time among you dead is over.*

Standing, he mapped out a pathway through the bodies toward the trees and strode into the grove opposite to where he entered the open field. His fingers had stiffened in the cold and he groaned as he sat down on a high, round rock to take off his ripped haversack. His shoulders ached from his early morning pummeling.

The surroundings had not changed much, but he noticed the trees thinned out in the woods ahead. His eyes picked out faint trails and some open ground unencumbered by rocks or heavy bushes. Then, he noticed a welcome sensation. The steady rain was markedly interrupted in its fall to earth and afforded him a needed reprieve from its glacial affects. A musket shot cracked bright and close, followed by shouting. The voices fell off into echoes and faded out to silence.

Scanning the darkness, he saw no movement. *I must stay in the trees, move very little. Safe for now.* Jon stared into the field of dead men and worried if he would ever find his regiment. Most likely at dawn, the battle will resume, and he resided in the least satisfactory strategic position. Finding a focused stream of thought, he retraced his route and regiment's action from earlier in the day. A smile came, he sighed and shook his head. *So close,* he thought.

After the hand-to-hand fight at the snipers' rocky fort, Lieutenant Weston ordered the platoon to march the captured enemy troops back towards the nearest collection area indicated by an assigned guard detail near the enemy's captured camps. They did this hastily, as the brigade needed to reform for the fresh assault on a retreating enemy.

Their brigade commander, General Rains was riding with his staff to lead the renewed attack, when the sight of the quick prisoners surprised him and brought a proud posture to his tall, slender frame. Sitting high in the saddle, he was proud to congratulate the work of his home regiment in their first action of the day. He recognized Lieutenant Weston and held up his sword. "See the men of my beloved 11th!" shouted Rains, as he approached the company. "I will send them straight away to retake Nashville!"

The compliment brought a cheer from the platoon and from the staff officers present. Jon's face flushed with pride, and a wave of joy washed over the men. Sergeant Hillford, who together with Lieutenant Weston led the procession of prisoners past the general, laughed and said in a subdued tone, "We'll go anywhere you want, just give us the rations."

Lieutenant Weston elbowed his sergeant's arm. "Do not become insolent in our finest hour." he said.

Sergeant Hillford nodded in agreement even though his principal behind the joke was accurate; the inadequate Southern commissary could never carry the demands of an army in the field. Martello shouted to Jon, "Hurrah boy! We are such heroes! And Jon, you had better adorn yourself with one of those Yank overcoats."

Jon looked back at the line of blue prisoners. "Naw, I think to commandeer a prize in front of the general would be far beneath even *his* standards." The two men saluted the mounted commander.

General Rains rode alongside Weston's men for a time. Rains had joined the war effort under the banner of the 11th, led them as colonel and now directed the brigade during this large and momentous action. His dashing youth only enhanced the magnetism he carried into battle, representing the "new South" in a picture of handsome, uniformed perfection.

Upon the platoon's return to the 11th Tennessee, the whole brigade was ordered to shift east and join the sweeping assault on the crumbling Federal right flank, an attack that could be heard growing into a grand exchange. The regiment was placed at the far left position of the brigade's formation with the 39th N. Carolina, 9th and 3rd Georgia regiments in line to the right.

Marching over the fresh terrain, Jon admired the brigade's force and disciplined lines. The long, deep rows of troops conformed to the soft undulations of the land and they reminded him of a dragon, with its prickly spine of sharp bayonets, crowned with a mane of regimental flags. The long lines changed shape as the terrain forced the men around fences, tree breaks and swales.

Onward the monster marched into the trees, where its startled prey gathered to strike. Firing into the beast, the Yankee regiments steadily withdrew, leaving the ground under the trees littered with patches of writhing rebel soldiers. Jon saw that another

Confederate brigade had tracked to their left, McNair's Arkansas Regiments, extending the reach of the long snake-like lines.

The hair on his arms and neck bristled with the chill of anticipation as General Rains ordered his own brigade forward in the grand fashion of Caesar himself, slashing the wet air with his sword and shunning danger. All fears disappeared underneath the veil of numbers, and Jon was enthralled at his own audacity, charging head long into thick battle fire.

This day, the battle had come so quickly after waiting for months, maneuvering for days and deploying for hours. How rapid it all seemed to go by and how very short a time to conclude.

The Confederate lines surged forward around isolated Federal regiments, rocks and broken caissons, and then onto a wide, level plain. There, the gray wave struck a hard wall. Jon could hear the screeching cannon balls before they hit, and for a second, he thought he could have easily warned the men in line, but events moved too quickly for anyone to react.

The barrage hit the brigade in the center, staggered the lines and threw men like leaves in the wind. Jon and others were sprayed with dirt and warm grime, bone and blood. Their line stumbled on the crushed remains of those who had been standing strong only seconds ago. Thick, sulfuric smoke choked him while his ears rang with a piercing ping. The screams of the horribly wounded, and screams at the sight of the horribly wounded faded in with his hearing.

The rebel beast convulsed as several cannon blows opened new holes, but the overall strength of the monster was not easily tapped. Flags waved as the knightly General Rains rode out ahead of the lines and directed his faithful beast to rout the menacing cannons, stationed at the edge of the woods. "The Nashville Pike is just beyond those trees! Take the road home, boys!"

Across the field, the lone Union battery stood isolated and unsupported. Firing like mad men, the sacrificed Union gunners bought time for the other batteries to form behind them on the last desperate line near the Nashville Turnpike.

A headlong race started toward the guns. Jon ran with the wave, his heart pounding into a rhythm with the many footsteps of the brigade. He could see ahead, about 200 yards distant, men in blue arming the guns, some running to their wagons or forming lines, trying to fend off the inevitable swallowing of their command.

The precise order that had formed the neat snake-like Confederate lines broke in sections as individual units out-jogged the main line, their flags spreading out and away. To the Union gunners, this looked as if the tight gray lines had multiplied, giving birth to thousands of mad, yelling fiends. With doubled frenzy, they ripped their lanyards and the remaining four guns jolted with a horrendous blast.

The shotgun-like canister blew into the racing crowd, tearing down bodies like blades to daisies. The gray stampede reeled and faltered as Jon witnessed the frightful blow to his right, striking the brigade in its center. A 40-yard gap appeared in the lines, filed with swirling smoke, broken men and frantic action. Officers rallied the shaken ranks by yelling and darting around, waving their hats as they refilled the gaps with reserves.

Regaining their former pace, Rains' brigade dashed at the Union battery, which now with their ammo depleted, had become a harmless display of U.S. manufacture. In moments, the infantry captured the costly guns with ease, chased the cannoneers into the woods, and turned the guns towards the Union lines.

With every passing hour, the brilliant victory of the morning assault was proving to be only temporary. The shocked troops in blue had yielded over two miles of their right flank, and the Confederates reached a new Union line, which had been strengthened with fresh units. Rains' brigade ran into thousands of Federals clinging to a wooded rise west of the Nashville Pike. There under tall cedars, Jon Lyhton and his hometown boys traded volleys with men from Illinois and Ohio. The lines swayed back and forth with every counter attack until converging artillery fire forced the Southerners back into the trees for cover, or to be lost in the fog like Jon.

On this cold New Year's Eve, Jon sat on his rock dreaming of victories past and soon to be won. As he had done previously in his mind, he traced over the ground that the advancing Confederates had covered that day, but all the fields and woods looked the same, they were impossible to discern at night. He grew tired of thinking. Looking out to the dead, he sighed. Then a peculiar presence, slight at first, began to nag his eye.

It was only a shadow, something in the far left corner of his vision. Turning his head slowly, he focused on the dark clump, which blended into one of the tree trunks, low to the ground.

The shadow's smooth contour and familiar human shape exploded in Jon's mind. He saw the puff of frosty breath from the covered head, and his chest tightened. A man, crouching, waiting, how long ...what for? Within only a few seconds, Jon heard several warnings crowd his mind. One yelled louder than the rest...Ambush!

He reached for his musket across a long, silent space. His fingers grasped the cold barrel, but in his peripheral view, the shadow stirred, and then in a violent start, sprang at him. Jon could not wield the long rifle into level with the shadow, which was upon him in a blink. The pair's collision echoed into the woods and the frigid night broke with the sounds of cracking sticks, grunts, and rustling grass.

Jon felt a hand at his throat and then the other at his bayonet scabbard. Swift in his recoil, he punched the midsection of the attacker and at the same time, pried the fingers from his leather case. The sound of their desperate combat cascaded into the clearing, and alerted the dead that another would soon join them.

After grabbing at the man's arms, Jon realized his foe wore a large wool overcoat, the object of his nocturnal search, and tool for his survival. He doubled his swift blows to the head of the dark assailant. Feeling the man weaken, Jon pushed the enemy away with a kick, leapt to his feet and then pulled his bayonet.

With this action, the steel point smacked the large rock as he swung the blade free. The metallic ring froze the attacker. Jon held the long spike in both hands as he lunged at his enemy with all of his force.

The point caught the thick blue wool but found no flesh. Jon tripped forward, and the men went to the ground again. Wrestling on their knees, the Yankee caught hold of Jon's arm, and they both danced the bayonet back and forth in front of their chests.

The battle of leverage proved a tie, and with heavy grunts, they both shoved the bayonet into the hard earth. Jon quickly punched the unknown face and then went for the fixed bayonet, extracting it with both hands. Before he could use the weapon, the Yankee had bolted for Jon's musket, lying like an abandoned toy in the brush, loaded earlier for this very occasion.

His shadowed enemy took the Springfield and instantly spun to meet Jon's advance, now halted in silence. Jon could barely see the man's face, bearded and stained dark with gunpowder like his. There was nothing to read, no human expression, as the dark man pointed the muzzle directly at his heart and cocked the hammer.

Closing his eyes, Jon braced for the flash of flame and smoke that would end his battle, this war, and his life.

The gun's hammer clicked. The two men flinched, expecting a loud shot, but there was no shot.

Realizing his liberation, Jon grabbed the gun barrel and

pushed the rifle butt into the man's chest. The blow knocked the wind out of him and forced him backwards into a tree.

Tossing the gun aside, Jon re-gripped the steel bayonet with both hands and rushed the dazed victim. A feeble effort to thwart the blow failed. The steel point found the target and the assailant howled like a kicked dog. His hands grappled with anything within reach, which turned out to be Jon's throat. Jon gagged for breath when the man's death grip took hold. Realizing this, Jon forced his weight on the imbedded weapon. The man yelped and slumped forward.

Pulling away silently, Jon observed the dark, queer scene. His victim leaned against the tree, swayed like a drunken man and dropped hard to the ground.

Jon's knees gave out, and he dropped down in a flush of exhaustion. Sucking the cold air into his chest through a dry throat, he reached for his canteen and popped the cork. The unexpected sound of speaking halted the can at his lips. The dying man blurted out some odd speech in broken order. "You did it, I got to say. So cold now...."

Jon fought the urge to listen. He crawled to his rifle lying in the wet grass. Pulling the butt end around, he brushed the wet debris away, curious at how the gun had misfired, and then thankful that it had. Raising the hammer, Jon discovered that the percussion cap had fallen away. Obviously, with his cold hands, such a small thing was hard to feel. Therefore, the charge of powder proved useless; he would have never shot the attacker.

How bizarre, in this sick twist, that he spared his own life by making a lethal mistake. He would have laughed on any other occasion if he could have found the breath, but his chest cramped with every motion of his torso. Alive with adrenaline, his thoughts ran into themselves in an amoral mix of pride and pity. *What was the fool thinking, why the hell couldn't the man move along and leave well enough alone?*

Jon rolled over, sat up and looked at the body. Long before this campaign, he had heard of the friendly exchanges between enemies after a battle; a practice that was already commonplace, especially during searches for wounded comrades at night. The soldier's nick-name for a battlefield parasite, a "bummer", had jumped him outright, without a word.

The dying man emitted a low crying sound, and in time, wheezed, moaned and suffered out loud. This annoyed Jon, who never thought about the man actually taking any time to die. "I really skewered the poor devil," he whispered.

The sounds arrested his attention entirely; slow moans, vomitus gags in the throat. He listened in sad fascination to hear death silence them. Jon looked out into the audience of corpses, expectant of something, perhaps approval or justification. But there was nothing but blank, funereal applause from accusing stares.

"Please, die now. God have mercy on him and me, shall I hear this all night?" Jon said. He pulled his hat down over his numb ears, but the sounds were now in his mind forever. Jon wanted to run away and return later when the dying part was finished, but this was his deed, he would not leave nor forsake the coat.

Eventually all the noise from the man diminished, and the dark field returned to its former quiet state. Jon sat still, noticed the rain, and let out a long-held sigh. He watched the dead man for a while. Nothing. He crawled over to the lumpy shape, studied the soldier's accoutrements. The brogans on his feet felt like Yankee leather, soft and new.

He decided to strip the coat away swiftly from the body, but it was pinned to the corpse by the bayonet. He would have to get close and pull the weapon out, and undo some buttons. The bayonet was lodged deep in the man's chest under the breastbone almost in the center of the torso. Jon placed a foot on the rib cage and pulled the slim, wedge-shaped blade out in one effort, cleaning it on his old haversack. As quickly as he could roll the dead man over, he peeled off the overcoat, then adorned himself with his prize. The deed was done. Survival would be assured, at least from the cold, for now.

Jon collected his gun, and then slung his cartridge box and new haversack over his shoulders. He thought for a moment of replacing his older brogans with the dead man's new Yankee ones, but after measuring with his hand, they looked too small for his feet. He decided to move into the woods for cover from the weather and to avoid roving scouting parties. Keeping a steady stride, zigzagging through the trees and small clearings, he gained some distance from the bold killing.

Bold, for sure it was. Even though he'd been a soldier for almost a year and had witnessed short, fierce skirmishes, this was his first face-to-face kill, and it had to be dealt with quickly.

Peculiar thoughts arose in Jon's weary mind that the poor man had gone mad with the scenes and stench of battle. Happened all the time. *Sure, he'd probably lost his grip when a dear friend got killed and then upon seeing a lone rebel sitting defenselessly on a rock, he went insane with vengeance, wanting to right the situation in his anguished soul. Poor devil, now he joins his friend.*

Jon thought of things his father told him, tales of the Indian wars, and his feelings about killing. He said that a soldier's fight doesn't only pertain to the field of battle; it is a constant struggle between bravery and fear, guilt and justification, truth and denial. Only with the clear conscience of a justified war could one hope to corral such emotions. He recalled his father's credo; *Soldiering is the highest and damndest business.* You had to live with the things you did, even when done with the most valorous of intent. Jon knew he was absolutely no exception. He waited on that feeling of glory that had possessed him earlier, after the grand rout of the Yankees, but it never came.

* * *

CHAPTER 3 ★

Ducking low branches and skirting rocks, Jon moved further into the woods. His thoughts narrowed into simple memories. He recalled youthful days with his cousin, running and playing in woods like these years ago. The ringmaster of many adventures, Elias Ambersaile was out here somewhere in these cedars and stones, perhaps a mile distant, fighting or dying in the cold wilds. It had been last March when Jon saw the newly promoted second lieutenant from the 20th Tennessee at the railhead in Chattanooga. Jon was going out to the Cumberland Gap to join the 11th who had replaced the 20th.

When they met on the platform and traded polite words, they mused about seeing each other—how funny it was that relatives should meet, so far from home. Elias was, for the first time in years, cordial with his cousin. They shared their military news; we're going here and this or that general will be in charge, nothing to worry about but the gnats.

After that, Elias bragged that his wife, Sally, was expecting in September. The proud father-to-be found his stride and spoke at length about the child's future, hopefully in a new country away from the Northern schools, politics and immorality.

Jon listened, smiled and nodded his casual approval. He was again seeing Elias as a man's man, a success, an officer, comfortable.

A train whistle interrupted them. "See you some day, I guess." Elias patted Jon's arm. "You will love the mountains at the Cumberland Gap, much to learn out there."

At this memory, Jon shook his head. The thought of Elias with Sally had always needled him. Not because he had loved her, but that Elias had somehow beat the devil, and won again. Or actually beat old Trabel Letcher himself, who was pretty close to the devil in Jon's experience. It was Jon who was truly beaten by Sally's Uncle Letcher, until blood dripped. Adding to the misery of that memory was the fact that Elias had left him to the mercy of Letcher. That was a long time ago Jon thought, but in "cousin time," it felt like yesterday.

It was another classic instance where Elias never saw the punishments for the crimes he instigated. For all his aplomb and smarts, Elias loved a good adventure, at whoever's expense. Being cousins, the two boys grew up in the same family, in the same town. But since Letcher's hard lessons, Jon always carried a dislike for Elias, which grew more akin to an old-fashioned jealousy for a man, now an officer, who never seemed to get his just desserts.

Thoughts of this sort led Jon into his own passions, where the surprising touch of love had been felt in a mysterious valley near the Cumberland range. Bethanna was months in the past, like a warm summer breeze that had filled his soul with fresh purity, and now had become part of the bygone season as winter set in around him. He was losing her in his memory, if not totally by now. At least he could read her only letter, a sweet reminder, to keep her real, keep her close.

Jon loved words, and Bethanna's simple phrases lifted his heart like no poet ever did. It was something, anything, his only tie to another heart. Separation was the only thing the war allowed for him and the one he loved. The fate of their times did not permit them anything lasting, only something like a brief minute in their lives, which now proved to be more powerful than he had first concluded.

Elias said there would be much to learn at the Cumberland Gap, but the discovery of manhood, independence and his battle sense paled at the discovery of her. All of these sensations seemed to dissipate the farther he got from Bethanna. He did not understand that. Thoughts raced into fantasy then into dead ends, then to his family in Nashville. His father's voice was never too far away, motivating, criticizing, analyzing and reading those ever-favorite poems that he loved to this day. *Yes, that strange floating line from "Dream-Land", Out of Space—out of Time. Ah, yes Poe, you knew confusion well.*

The sense of smell is an acute thing to a roaming boy. Jon could smell dinner cooking nearly a mile from home, and then instantaneously appear in time for grace. An odor hit him like that there, walking in the woods, blindly going then suddenly a smell, getting stronger. It was smoke, but not from gunpowder. The odor woke him. His body, tired and bruised, obeyed the will of his battle-conditioned mind, *Campfire...Food cooking...Find it.*

He doubled his time, moving off and back onto the drifting odor trail several times and in the space of five minutes he saw a faint light, like a sunray, on a tree branch ahead. The light moved and jumped among the low-hanging cedars. Shadows formed as he closed in and surveyed the area from which the fire emanated. The actual flame was hidden in a low hollow, sunken in the earth. Sounds of mumbled conversation crept into Jon's ears, and he immediately stopped and ducked, trying to hear the low mutterings.

These men were smart, he thought, *building a fire below the plane of the ground, far into the woods. But who are these men?* he wondered.

Before he entertained any dreams of cuddling up near this fire and saving his numb extremities, he must answer the same old quandary: friend or foe? *Well, I can't kill everybody. I must take a chance and hope that these men, whoever they are, will be sick of the fight and lend a friend or enemy a place to sleep.*

Either way, Jon figured he was covered. *If they were Federals, then, I can be one, in this new attire. More than a few Southerners from Tennessee and Kentucky had joined the Northern effort, and his accent would prove it. And if they're Confederates, then that'll be a gift.*

Jon rose up and headed into the situation with caution. His heart began a nervous increase in speed, but his outward appearance remained calm. Casually, he slung his rifle onto his shoulder, showing no apparent threat to the unsuspecting men. It was a necessary gamble.

As he approached the group, he could see the tops of heads, about three, then two more bodies, lying on the ground. He edged the glowing hollow and at first, the flames hurt Jon's dark-suited eyes. Plainly, no one heard his footsteps, only yards away from them now. Jon stopped and stood in awe of the heat; even from this distance he could feel its healing touch. Then, he smelled the coffee. His mind made up, he called out. "Here, here, any place for a friend in need?"

The group of men swiveled their collective heads to find Jon stepping into the hollow through the smoke. They were startled but not frightened and nodded silent greetings. He noticed the three sitting were Confederates. One of them turned and said, "How do? Glad you didn't come in wanting to do some shooting, cause' we're at ease and all."

One of them, a smaller red-bearded man, let out a nervous laugh.

Jon un-shouldered his musket and leaned on it, feeling more relaxed. "Much obliged to just sit and warm up a while. I was separated from my regiment after our picket line was bombarded. I've been wandering for more than an hour, almost two."

The greeter stood and told of similar woes. He shook Jon's hand, and as he did, Jon noticed that he wore a Union overcoat caked with mud. "I'm Stokes, and this is Riles and Charlie."

Jon received their salutations with a friendly wave. "I'm Sergeant Jon Lyhton, 11ᵗʰ Tennessee." Pointing to the two sleeping men, Jon asked. "Who are they?"

Stokes jerked around, as if just noticing the two men. "Those be Union stragglers, who couldn't catch up to the race. We allowed 'em a haven for the night since they were unarmed, and carried plenty of bacon and real coffee."

Stokes passed Jon a tin of hot coffee, saying, "Well, sergeant, what a perfect thing is hot coffee, giving warmth where fire can't, and filling the body with hope."

Jon took the tin and smiled, "After a day like this, how right you are." His hands wrapped around the cup and the heat spread into his arms. Jon observed his new hosts. Stokes, tall and thin, had a broad smile and few teeth, but his large walrus mustache added a respectable touch to his worn face. Charlie was of slight build, maybe twenty years-old, kept a short red beard, and smiled too much. Maybe because he was glad to be alive, and warm, Jon thought.

Older than Charlie, Riles had a rough, narrow face accented with dark hair and sharp goatee. He was distracted, on edge, looking over and around Jon, not engaging him warmly like the other two. When he did speak, his hoarse voice had a spiteful edge, like a man unhappy about everything. "You're from the 11th Tennessee, eh? Heard your general got kilt."

Jon stiffened. "Wounded, I believe, but dead? God, I pray that's not true."

"Well, he's dead, what I heard. You didn't know that? Strange." Riles smarted.

Jon let the rumor hang. Many rumors traversed the battlefields—he doubted this one. Riles seemed to enjoy revealing the awful news to him. That was strange. "Very heavy fight today.

I've never seen it this hot," said Jon, attempting to divert the conversation.

The men talked about the resounding victory of the massive flank assault, the hard Federal resistance at the Nashville Turnpike, and the trouble on the far right, where General Polk's assault stalled near the small round forest, center of the Union lines.

Jon found out that the men were from the 4th Arkansas Regiment, McNair's brigade, now under Harper. A brief discussion ensued about the last position of the 11th Tennessee being to the right, or east, of Harpers Brigade.

Then Riles changed the topic. "Hey ya'll, where the heck is Bertram? He should've been back long ago."

"Who's this, a friend?" asked Jon, warming up to the company.

Riles looked into the trees and said, "Yeah, my kid brother, he's an adventurous sort; a little stupid, though. He took off to go scavenge up a rifle. You didn't see him running around out there, did ya?"

Jon paused, and was about to answer when Charlie broke in. "Yeah, ever since he found that overcoat, he'd been aching to get a new musket. That fellow's going to be a loaded-down mule train by the time he gets back here."

The other men laughed, knowing their friend well. Jon was thinking, *Overcoat?*

Stokes leaned over toward Jon, "Would you like some bacon? It was cooked a while ago, but we can warm it for you."

At the sight of cooked bacon, Jon did not hesitate. He took it and ate slowly, making the blessed meal last longer than a quick, few seconds.

Then Charlie spoke again, "In fact, I'd say that Bertram's overcoat was just like yours, Jon, with them sergeant's stripes and such. Ol' Bertram thought he could make us salute him by putt'n on a rank. Funny ol' Bert, eh?" Stokes and Charlie laughed a bit, but Riles leaned in and stared at Jon's coat with renewed interest.

"Yeah, Charlie," said Riles, pointing at Jon with his coffee cup. "That looks a great deal like Bert's coat." He leaned in closer to Jon, his eyes widening. "Even has the same Ohio State shield on the buttons."

Jon stared into the fire, mixing their comments and the night's events into a macabre impossibility.

"Hey, but wait ya'll," said Stokes, looking at Jon. "Bertram's coat didn't have them blood stains on it."

Jon jerked his chin down to see the front of the garment. Only slightly covered by the coat's top flaps, the blood stains surrounded a clean bayonet hole. Jon's face remained unmoved as he masked his shock over their sudden discovery. When the men leaned in to see the markings, Jon fumbled his cup and spilled the remaining coffee. "Damn, sorry, I'm a bit numb still."

"No, I guess them kind 'a stains wasn't there on Bert's coat," said Charlie.

Jon rolled out the words naturally, as he did when he told stories, and said, "Why this coat here was given to me by my friend after we had marched some prisoners to the rear lines. Let's see, that was, I guess about eight-thirty."

The lie sank in to each man's thoughts as Stokes refilled Jon's cup. Charlie and Riles started talking about Bertram. Jon tried to study the conversation, until Stokes began talking to him.

He asked about where Jon had fought and what he had seen after his separation from the 11th. Stokes was friendly, and the curiosity over the stained coat died to other distractions. Within fifteen minutes, they had all agreed to bed down. Dawn came early for the soldier, and during a fight, even earlier.

Lying down with his front facing the fire, Jon pulled the large shoulder flaps of the great coat over his head. During his short talk with Stokes, he had strained to hear what the others were saying, and he deciphered something about Bertram wanting to get into Murfreesboro before dawn. They had warned him that it was improbable to get away with a stunt like that, with the Army at alert during battle. Perhaps there was a chance of hitching up with the columns of wounded winding their way to the town; he could get to some supplies and decent food.

Jon thought about the fact that Bertram could have taken off for town and that he might have been the one who attacked him, needing the rifle to complete his supply hunt. This "Bertram" did not sound like a smart fellow. The evidence mounted: a lone boy looking for a rifle and a warm coat. Jon held high court under his coat flaps, presenting mental defensive arguments in vain. He killed Bertram, and he knew it.

This boy was his own countryman, a friendly one, too, corked with his bayonet and whose blood stained this exceptionally warm coat. The deed of killing for a coat was noxious enough; now made worse by the act of mistaken identity. The thought smoldered in his stomach.

These things piled up on Jon most of the night. The very spot by the fire was Bertram's, and these were his friends, whom he had just lied to. But, how could he not lie? The real story was an invitation to the realm of wild accusation and swift partisan justice. Jon anxiously laid there, in the spot he had taken, and the coat he had taken. Stewing inside, he hoped that he wouldn't be awakened by Riles impaling him for killing his brother. He could hear the smart-mouthed Riles saying, "Tit for tat, you murdurin' rat!"

As the freeze hardened over the fields during the night, the sniper fire abated along the mingled lines. Only those men hidden in the forest's glades and thickets could find the comfort of a fire and perhaps a few hours' sleep. Around the battlefield, officers quickly doused any open field fires, which gave away position.

Without the immediate threat of fierce combat, the troops had nothing to think of but the biting cold.

When dawn finally came, it was as gray as the day before and just as wet. Jon's three hosts prepared morning coffee and kicked the two Yankee stragglers awake, shooing them away and keeping their rations. "Happy New Year, see ya in a few hours," said Stokes, waving at the two wide-eyed northern boys jogging towards perhaps more Confederates.

Charlie approached Jon, sat down and asked, "So, I assume you never saw Bertram last night, eh?"

Jon looked away, into the woods. "I didn't meet your friend," he mumbled.

Charlie sighed with a wisp of disappointment. "Oh well, then. I gather by now he's taking a warm bath soma'where's. He's one to do that kind 'a thing."

"I'd say he's a fool for trying to leave a big dance in progress," said Jon, rubbing his eyes. "Officers don't like men to go missing."

"Bertram? He'd never desert, if that's what ya meant?"

Jon paused, and thought it didn't make a difference what he meant. "Look, I can't say what the boy did or what he's after. I don't know him like you!"

"Riles is his big brother. I'm his cousin. We take care of Bertram and make sure he stays safe as can be. However, when he runs off like this...."

"Safe? In a war, no one's safe, damn it!" said Jon, frustrated with the new knowledge. He stood abruptly, picked up his rifle and started cleaning the firing mechanism.

Due to his moral summons, Jon was drowsy and irritated, having slept intermittently. He did not want to hear any more details from a life that was no more. There was no sense in it. "I think I will go find my unit now, lest they list me as missing."

After noticing Jon and Charlie's debate, Riles and Stokes

quietly sipped fresh Yankee coffee and digested their observations. To them, Jon was a peculiar fellow. There was glibness in his demeanor that was, for the infantry volunteer, sometimes rather lacking. He exuded a hidden refinement found in officers, not ruffians like them. Riles thought Jon could be a fair-skin planter's son or university boy. With a good shave and trim, he could see it.

"Hey, Mr. Lights," he barked.

"Lyhton, it's Lyhton," said Jon stiffly.

"Yeah, good. You kind 'a being uppity with Charlie, ain't ya?" Riles' jabbed from across the ditch, his eyes piercing.

"Not particularly, no," said Jon, realizing Riles was in the same dour mood since last night. Same suspicious scowl on his hard face.

"Well, you're sure actin' like it. I think you're being rude, maybe on purpose. Now we've served you right kindly, given our coffee, bacon and a nice fire. Least you can do is be thankful and accommodate my friend with a little chin-music. Can ya do that?"

Stokes broke in. "Sure he can, Jon's scattered, damn tired. Now Riles, it's not any trouble. If he's gotta' find his regiment, no trick on us, just proud to help."

Jon ground his teeth, biting back any natural urge to respond as he should. Riles stared with a comfortable, vicious sneer. Actually, it was his horrid smile and Jon knew that look. He'd seen it plenty since joining the Army. Some of these hill folk, illiterate as they are, mostly vagrant, couldn't spell the word "fear," but they could read a personality like a book and this man was reading him closely. As with the blind, some senses make up for the lack of others.

"Begging your pardon, gents," said Jon, cool and concerned. "I was truly insensitive to your lost friend and your worry for him." He walked over to Stokes and Riles. "Especially you, his brother."

Riles cocked his head, frowned in mixed thought. Jon continued, "I was only amazed at your brother's audacity, not anything more. I apologize for my insult."

Jon offered his hand to Riles. He shook it quickly, loosely. He offered a handshake to Stokes, but he waved off. "'Tis nothing, please, please."

"Thank you for your kindness. I will spread the meritorious deeds of you Arkansas men." Jon gathered his accoutrements and shouldered his rifle. His only goal was getting away from Riles' accusing glare. Stepping up the slope, he reached the hollow's rim and waved. Charlie and Stokes waved back and cheerfully bid him good luck. Riles stood up and said nothing.

A wet chill made Jon's very bones ache. The night's rest, if any, only stiffened him more. If not for the trees, he would have been a wet mess. He strode hard, stretching and warming his cramped legs, thinking about how he had escaped serious interrogation over the overcoat. He noticed that Riles studied him with mean intent. *This damn coat, the blood stains, how foolish I was when I came bumbling into their camp. Riles acted as if he knew something. Perhaps that's just it. Acting. He was gaming me like he does everyone else, thinking how he could take something from me. Yes, he was sizing me up.*

Jon noticed sporadic pops of distant rifle fire and no cannon. Maybe the enemy had gone. Or the South had retreated. "Old Bragg would do that," he said, acknowledging the commanding general.

As he walked through the pale chill of dawn, dead bodies began to appear in the thin mist. Some clad in blue, most in tan, all dead and frozen. They were invisible to him in the dark last night as he strode toward the campfire, so willful was he of discovering safe haven. In their death poses, the bodies seemed to suffer still, as they lay twisted, bent and broken.

Then a new revelation hit him with a bullet-like suddenness. He had to find the body. *Bertram's body! If I identify the corpse as Union or Confederate, yes, that would solve it. I could free my conscience for good and damn what Riles has to say about it!*

Out of the woods, to Jon's back, came a call, growing in volume, a voice ringing out his name. Turning, he focused on the pair of soldiers jogging his way. A shudder forced him to halt. Riles and Charlie caught up to him.

The two were most certainly unwanted guests, but Jon knew that he'd have to placate them and give no clue of his apprehension. He could try to use his rank status, something he didn't do last night at the camp, though useless with Riles most likely, as with most any private that wasn't in D Company.

He greeted them with feigned brightness. "Hello again, gents, where's Stokes?"

"He's gone looking for Bertram up near the Yankees," said Charlie. "They're allowing litters to collect some wounded up yonder." He pointed to some indistinct location beyond the trees.

Riles offered a silent nod and looked around, suspicious as ever. The garrulous Charlie yapped incessantly about the fight yesterday and how the Yanks had probably run back to Nashville in the night. Jon paid little attention to Charlie, and wondered mostly about the reason Riles had decided to follow him. Charlie then fell on the subject of Bertram and then his girl, Ella. Jon didn't want to listen to more dribble about Bertram, but he felt drawn to it anyway. As he took in Charlie's description, he saw Ella as someone Bertram had loved madly, no doubt; green eyes and sandy blond curls no man could resist. Like anyone would at this point in the war.

Jon reacted to each of Charlie's narratives with a bit of inward sarcasm; however, it seemed that the boy could spin a delightful yarn and with style, too.

"Ya see, it was Bertram's uncle who recruited us, old Sergeant Mullibey, said we could join the company if we could catch his prize Plymouth Rock Rooster, 'cause if ya can chase down that speedster, you're in superb form for fighting. Now this is a key issue in Hampsted County; everyone wants to prove their stamina, and the yard is filled with folks waiting their turn. Of course, the jest of this is that it's not a genuine test; the Army doesn't care about catchin' a rooster, it's outright foolery and only the chosen of us locals know that Uncle Mullibey is treating everyone to a lavish bit of fun. There were a few older men that tried, but caught nothin' only dirt and laughs, still no rooster. Then, ole' Bert climbs real slow-like into the pen and starts cluckin' and kickin', as if he's telling this bird to sally off. But beat that, if Bertram doesn't up and catch that cock in ten seconds. Place goes stark mad, expecting him to be ranked a captain any minute!" Charlie saluted, animating the story.

He mellowed and blushed. "Ella was sure impressed, and she kissed him, in front of the whole town! Soon every young buck lines up for his turn, at the rooster or at the girl, I can't say." Charlie leaned on Jon's elbow. "Do ya know the real trick of it?"

"The rooster was his all along?" Jon said.

Charlie cackled at the revelation and patted Jon on the shoulder. "That's right. You're smarter than a fox!"

Jon found himself momentarily distracted by the anecdote. He guessed that any humor was a good thing; even Riles chuckled. So Jon, in a brief state of joviality, turned to Riles and asked, "How about you there, did you ever catch the rooster?"

Riles' smile flattened, eyes tightened, he literally spit out the words, "Everyone knows I can fight!"

They walked on a while in silence. Charlie looked at Riles and then stared at the ground, recalling the man's venal and bloody past. Riles loved the war. He seemed ready for it even as a youth, when in a school fight he pummeled four boys so badly that he crippled one in the leg. The others never looked the same afterwards with their scarred foreheads and cheeks.

Charlie had taken a beating himself for disturbing Riles and a young lady one evening down at the creek. He didn't mean to interrupt, and only wanted to go fishing with his friend. Riles had a different catch in mind and went skinny-dipping, until Charlie spooked the girl. Then Riles bloodied Charlie up. From that time on, he did everything Riles told him to.

Perhaps it was the exhausting night, or the dull ache in every part of his weary body, but Jon walked on with the two presumptive comrades and forgot about his mission to find the dead body. It came to him soon enough though, right when he saw a burial detail laying out bodies in the wide clearing of ground just ahead of them.

Stunned at his absent thoughts, Jon reared back in shock. He halted to rethink his new deportment. Riles and Charlie walked further, then stopped to look at the activity.

The opaque, gray mist deprived everything of its natural color, making the scene despairing and unreal. Ghost-like wanderers drifted in the fog and scoured the desolate carnage for missing friends or relatives. Other soldiers grouped the dead into sections for future burial, or whatever the frozen ground would allow.

How pitiful the corpses looked, as if they had been posed clamoring over each other in the confusion of death, with icy hands grasping for heaven. And set on their pale faces sad, astonished expressions, as if surprised that a bullet had found them.

Jon watched in morbid fascination as Riles and Charlie strode onward towards that horribly familiar, large rock where he acquired his blue coat. *This is not about to happen. How can I stop them? The sight of their impaled friend's frosty countenance will provide Riles all the evidence he needs. Proven by the coat hanging squarely on my hapless shoulders.*

"Hey, uh, I'm gonna take a squat, you go ahead," said Jon, reaching for his belt. Kneeling down, he rapidly checked his rifle's load. All set. He readied for what may come and whatever it was, he could only blame himself. Charlie may not fight, may not grasp what had happened, but Riles would surely avenge his brother. Jon would have quite a precarious tangle on his hands.

He crept around a tree, keeping Charlie and Riles in view. Unmoving in the underbrush, he hoped to hear their casual banter, in case he had to react to it. They shuffled to the edge of the woods near the rock and engaged in quiet conversation. *Hadn't they seen it yet?* Surely they were nearly on top of the corpse, hunched and frozen. Jon stretched his neck to find a decent view and waited, but there was no shout of discovery, or agonized cry of recognition. Could they not see their own friend and brother?

It could be that he had killed his true-blue enemy, and there be a dead Yank, scarcely noticed at their feet. The thought caressed Jon's heart with the faint warmth of hope. Hope that he had performed his duty to survive and that his instincts had prevailed even in the confused melee and black of night.

He watched the tall Riles and red-bearded Charlie, both sitting on the very rock that had witnessed the ferocious and unwarranted attack upon his defenseless person. They were as relaxed as two men on a fishing excursion. *There was the slightest possibility that with the victim's last living effort, he had crawled farther away, out of sight. No, how impossible.* He had listened as the pierced man died, heard the life gurgling out in his final dying utterance. They must be gazing upon a dead Yank! Riles and Charlie were much too passive, just sitting there and talking. Jon boldly stood, gritted his teeth and marched headlong toward the two meddlers.

* * *

Chapter 4★

Lieutenant Weston paced in long, thoughtful strides as his steps wore a groove in the soggy ground. Occasionally, he stopped to kick the frozen dirt ridges formed by hundreds of caisson wheels that had cut the road. His amber eyes shifted under the wide brim of his hat as he waited impatiently for the return of Captain Binns' courier from brigade headquarters. His request was sent over an hour ago and as he recalled, it was the third request for orders concerning resupply and preparations for the expected attack from the enemy. Asking brigade for anything was a long shot but worth the wait, for the regiment desperately needed ammunition.

Running over the surprised Federals the day before was a harrowing task, but repeated attacks on the tight artillery formations near the Nashville Turnpike dumbfounded Lieutenant Weston like no combat he had ever witnessed. Close range canister and rifle fire poured into their lines like sheets of hail, blasting men apart and scattering regiments. The brigade reformed in the woods but withered again in the open field. After three attempts, they left the ground covered with their wounded and dead, up to a quarter of their numbers.

Regarding the men from a distance, Lieutenant Weston witnessed the scenes of a regiment clawing its way back into working order. The soldiers dressed their nicks and scrapes as best they could, while others wrote letters, perhaps their last testaments to family. Huddled together in groups, they slept in defensive formations behind hasty works of fence rails, fallen timber and rock enclaves. Like Lieutenant Weston, they did not know what to expect this dreary, cold January 1st, in the new year of 1863.

A rider appeared out of the trees towards the south and the lieutenant reacted expectantly, but the messenger went elsewhere. He paused to watch the horse and rider fade into the gray mist, and then continued to pace slowly while he fogged the air with a long contemptuous breath. To him, the Army's advantages slipped away with every passing minute of precious dawn.

With no Federal counter attack imminent, nervously and with cautious quiet, some of the hungry troops found their messmates and began to prepare what rations they had left. The aroma of fried salt pork and bully soup began to waft through the lines. Lieutenant Weston smelled the soupy corn meal and hardtack mixture and his stomach growled. Expecting an advance from the Union lines, he had not eaten, choosing instead to prepare for an attack. When that didn't come, he waited for orders. When he received none, he sent requisitions. When none came, he waited to see if any of the regiment's 18 missing would show up this morning. So far, only one came out of the woods, Sergeant Hillford, who happily bounded into camp with two captured bags of coffee beans and sugar.

Somehow in harsh, wanton and famished times, the sergeant, without care of hazard and with little genius in his efforts, procured the most extinct culinary delicacies, as they were so rare to starved Army troops. This morning's round of coffee had fortified the sergeant's legend.

"Coffee, sir?" said Hillford, approaching with two cups.

The lieutenant stood in the mud with his hands on his hips, and lifted his gaze from his boots up to the square rugged face of Hillford, who held out a steaming tin cup in a large hand.

He took it, sipped the quaint, hot beverage of civility and remembered home for the first time that day. He reacted physically and then moaned at the gorgeous flavor. "Thank you, sergeant. May I inquire as to where... this time?" he asked.

"Absolutely lieutenant, you may. About three hundred yards to the west, an overturned Federal commissary wagon has plenty of bags for any brigand that could find it."

Lieutenant Weston nodded, sipped again and sighed. "Do you ever think of the fight raging around you? Or is your battle face shielding a more sinister desire to buzzard the field."

"I resent the word 'buzzard,'" Hillford said. "I'm only doing the thing out of the company's good interest, of course, sir."

Lieutenant Weston squinted at Hillford. "With unfailing earnest I believe. Perhaps 'buzzard' is too strong a word for all that is going on around here." He gestured to a line of dead Yankees up the road.

"Yessir. Plenty has gone on here." The older sergeant looked down, kicked at the stiff muddy ridges in the road. Hillford's face, lean and whiskered gray, held a relaxed expression most times. His long frame leaned to the right, even at attention. Although well accustomed to it, he complained of a childhood condition that made his back crook over. With his six feet, two-inch height, the abnormality lent a unique lumber to his stride and a familiar silhouette to his men.

Neither man continued the chatty course. They stood in the dawn chill and sipped in turns. There was a tremendous amount of intuition shared between them and often not a word passed, but only a gesture or glance communicated the appropriate sentiment. During heavy gunfire, these unsaid messages worked to save the men from confusion.

At present, the message from Lieutenant Weston told of underlying, pensive frustration. Anxious about the coming day's events, he had hardly slept, keeping vigil at the center of his line, his platoon. The coffee revived him enough to divert his senses and, for a few short minutes, warm his insides.

A soft drizzle began, barely noticed, then heavier. Soon a steady rain pelted the hat brims of the two comrades. The lieutenant sighed and turned to observe the men's reactions. Expectantly, they didn't seem to be phased by the shower. Though bothered, none of them would lament it orally, after yesterday's terrific fight.

"What's the count?" asked Sergeant Hillford.

"Eight killed outright. Not bad for as much ground as we took. Presently, there's sixty wounded that we've found. A good portion mortally, I'm sure. We're still discovering them out there." He said, gesturing north to east into the trees.

"Missing?"

"Eighteen, 'til you showed up. Hopefully, some of them will crawl back."

"None with such spoils, though," said the sergeant, raising his cup.

"*D'accord,*" said Weston, agreeing, with a gentle lift of his chin.

Lieutenant Weston defected from the genteel, knowing the sergeant's lack of French. He motioned to Sergeant Hillford, and the two sat down on a pair of small ammo crates near a soaked, smoking fire. His next question would be one that he had asked of scouts and random pickets coming in from the night. "So, any news of Jon?"

"He's missing, too, along with Lawsen and Dabney and Sheldon Daniel," said Sergeant Hillford.

Weston sighed. "Damn…he did so well, they all have done well."

"Yessir, all of 'em." Hillford said.

"Is it too much, sergeant? Too much to ask of the men?"

"No, sir. Not our men, sir, not the 11th."

"Colonel Gordon is doing well, though in much pain. More than twice this morning, he inquired about the men from his bed, and sent encouragements, checked on their needs. Overall a brilliant man, but I never thought so when I first met him. Our old Drill Master has become quite a leader. I am glad his capture last summer wasn't a permanent thing."

Sergeant Hillford nodded, reaching for his pipe and tobacco roll. "Ah, damned rain." He said, pushing the pleasure source back into his coat pocket. He yawned.

Weston rubbed his eyes. He realized that all of them needed sleep. It was a lot to ask of men who had never fought in such a large engagement before to keep up multiple attacks all day and endure such awful strains on the senses, then stay vigilant all a frozen night long. On this second day, they must find the will to hold up for more.

Sergeant Hillford showed no surprise at the lieutenant's humane notions towards his troops. Nor was he, or anyone in the entire company, at all put back by Lieutenant Weston's fuss over Jon's personal wellbeing. They all knew.

Jon Lyhton joined the regiment in March 1862 at the Cumberland Gap in east Tennessee along with several other late enlistees, having beaten the new Conscription Law by a month. The 11th Tennessee had just re-enlisted after serving out their original one-year term, an action that impressed the new arrivals. They saw that volunteering proved more patriotic than being forced by the government's hand. The new additions had plenty of catching up to do after leaving occupied Nashville.

First Sergeant Jeff Weston spent extra time with the new men at drill, teaching the School of the Soldier and School of the Company from the well-known book, *Hardee's Tactics*. Within a few days, Weston and Jon had found something in common, love of books and poetry. To Weston's joy, Jon possessed an education equal to most of the officers in the regiment, for his father, as former teacher, endeared his son to literature and did not easily consent to his enthusiasm for the Army.

Jon had explained it to Sergeant Weston, "I persisted. You see, I worked for my father's cattle business. He supplied beef to the Army, and Dad thought I was doing enough to help without actually fighting. He planned to pay a substitute, like some of the richer men have done. However, it wasn't long before I found the local Home Guards irresistible. This he tolerated with only minimal complaint."

He described how he snuck out every day for training, directed by the local judges and councilmen, not active-duty line officers. His chance came for real service during the takeover of Nashville by Union troops in January of 1862, without much of a fight from the Confederates. His Father Jack gave into Jon's zealous tenacity, agreeing that he could do nothing cooped up by the Yankees. Jon escaped Nashville with a late model Flintlock refit, an old cadet coat, and his favorite book of poetry.

Both Sergeant Weston and Jon read the English poets, quizzed each other on Shakespeare or Dickens and scavenged literary journals from the locals. They held extensive discussions on the New England writers vs. the fashionable Southern literati, how their morals differed, or their politics. More than once, the two were found staying up late debating with the officers over philosophical points of interest from religion to military history, and their role in it.

In late April, Jon began a company-wide campaign for the selection of Sergeant Weston for a second lieutenant's rank. With campaigning from Jon, Lawsen and Corporal Hillford, Weston was elected, took his exam, and commissioned in a group ceremony to the music of the brigade band and many wild exhorts from D Company. In a few days, Weston chose the reliable and resourceful Hillford for sergeant.

Another hour passed by and still no Jon Lyhton or his messmates, Lawson, Martello and Daniel. Lieutenant Weston, on his third cup of Yankee coffee, waited for the distant cannon and musket fire to goad the generals into a fight; hopefully, finishing the costly struggle at hand.

The rain abated, only to compose a hanging mist that solidified the cold into clothes, skin and the general spirit of the men. Adding to the dreariness, a large black tornado of encircling vultures formed to the northeast. The dotted funnel stole the attention of some curious onlookers, standing up from their campfires to view the natural oddity.

These black minions drawn against the pale-gray sky cast an unsettling omen. Some of the birds peeled away to feed on preselected targets, or perhaps, in a sick twist, become a meal themselves. The creatures served only as a reminder of recent deaths, and the many more to come.

A distinct bugle call echoed into the clearing and Lieutenant Weston stood slowly, rubbing his back. He had missed the rider trotting by on the other side of the adjacent grove. "Captain Binns' tent for a conference, I presume," he said.

Lieutenant Weston checked his pocket watch: 9:38. He marched the forty yards to the captain's tent—a small, square structure marked by a light-blue flag with a white "D." Greeting the other officers, he entered. Inside, there was enough room for a small cot, a travel trunk and desk, upon which a lantern lit the staff's faces as they looked over paperwork. Lieutenant Weston sighed with relief when he saw that the captain's tent was supplied with a ration of Sergeant Hillford's captured coffee.

Captain Binns, tall and hatless in a nondescript uniform, addressed his lieutenants and staff. "I regret to say that I have no immediate orders from Colonel Gordon or General McCown. For now, we remain where we are. You are allowed to search for wounded, but not beyond the present skirmish line, about two hundred yards to our front. As for our regrettable loss yesterday… well, we have all lost friends. Colonel Vance is a competent man. The brigade is in good hands." Captain Binns stared into his black coffee. He fingered his long mustache and nodded. "That is all for now, gentlemen. Dismissed."

Weston saluted and followed the flow of officers through the wet tent flaps. Some of the company's lieutenants were plainly missing; he noted only one first lieutenant, Jim Cabeson, the executive officer and three new second lieutenants, who just yesterday, were sergeants.

He walked slowly back to the regiment. *Not much to do yet, and a whole day to do it.* The men needed a rest, but they had to be ready for an attack. *They could face it, and do well again.* He remembered how Jon appeared yesterday; he did well, they were *all* obedient soldiers. In the thickest fighting, the platoon had taken the hardest Yankee blows. Some were dead, some wounded, heading back to town in an odd collection of wagons. The sight of the carts inspired an idea.

He walked back to D Company, nestled behind a row of blasted tree stumps. Scouting the personnel, he found his mark. "Private Cawley!"

The man stood and raced over. "Yessir." Cawley's eyebrows stood up, as they always did when Lieutenant Weston barked at him.

"Cawley, I need you to go find out some things for me." Weston liked Cawley but rarely trusted him with things of a complex nature. The simple-minded private had taken to Jon's patience and friendliness, which helped him learn new things with more ease than in school. He would be perfect for the mission.

Cawley stood and saluted, eager to serve.

Not much was known about Cawley. No one ever found out his first name. He had a brown beard with a spot of gray at the chin, a thin neck, and large Adam's apple. His eyes were unusually close together and he talked lightly. Slight of weight and thin legged, he proved surprisingly durable enough on campaign. Often, he talked about a girl waiting for him at home, but over the past months her name had changed several times, causing suspicion of his claim. Over time, the other men felt sorry for him.

Weston addressed the private. "Cawley, I need a man to go into town and take a listing of the company's wounded or dead. Find out anything you can on Jon. I'm sure you know he's a bit lost. You will be given the necessary paperwork to avoid being hauled back to the regiment or detained in any other way."

"Sir, I am honored to be chosen. To think I have made that sort of impression on…."

"Yes, private, that's good, but really, no one will harass you. Can I trust in your complete confidentiality?"

Lieutenant Weston thought he saw a tear in Cawley's eye as he received the signed pass. To Cawley, Jon was like his older brother, which puzzled the other men, because no one was exactly sure of Cawley's age, only that he was older than Jon. He could be 28 or 38 years old.

"The Wilkinson Pike is directly south; can't miss it. Leads right to town, understand?" As he watched Cawley jog for the main road, Weston shook his head. The errand might be for nothing. At least he will keep Cawley safe for a time.

* * *

CHAPTER 5★

Riles and Charlie sat upon the rock, a large outcropping almost three feet high, eight feet wide in some parts, the top smoothed over from centuries of exposure. The stones littered the surrounding land, especially down near the river. Charlie picked at a dead moss patch while Riles scanned the terrain and mumbled caustically.

Jon came bounding into their quiet scene with tense expectancy, his eyes darting left and right, head turning bird-like, searching the grass, his rifle ready in his hands. In the rustled grass, he found his old haversack, ripped and stained with the blood from the bayonet. He kicked it, then looked around for the body. It wasn't there.

He spun in several slow circular paths, nothing. His gaze fell upon a group of men arranging bodies for identification or burial. "They moved the damn thing!"

"What's that?" asked Charlie.

Jon whipped around, suddenly reminded of their presence. "Uh, the regiment, I mean the skirmish line."

Riles glared at Jon's face with sharp interest.

Jon turned away. He could not abide the man's eyes anymore and chose to walk a few paces into the clearing to think: *How can I find the truth? There must have been over a 100 corpses strewn everywhere. I cannot know the face. And now the body is gone. There will be no identification. If they've moved him already, he must be one of ours, so....*

Jon's body sagged as he leaned on his rifle. His clouded mind was now caught listless between two roads of doubt. On one side, a secure thought gleamed; there was no corpse to convict him. He could easily walk away. But that same absence would not acquit him of his certain crime.

Fostered by the emotional upheaval in his conscience, or the natural paranoia of a criminal, a repressed guilt kicked him at every thoughtful interval. He fought it.

Riles noticed Jon's agitation. He observed the silent, roundabout search Jon had conducted and it was obvious to him that the stranger had been disappointed. Riles was sure after thoughtful consideration, patient observance and plain common sense, the obvious conclusion came to the fore. Jon was a liar.

With the body nowhere near, Jon gazed at the dead men gathered like hardwood sticks, gray and stiff-limbed. *Could he be lying there, just yards away? What if they found him? Would that end this trial, or begin a new one?*

Taking a few steps toward the dead bodies, he needed only one pass, one look to know the truth. Then he screamed into his brain, *No, you fool! Stop. Do you want those two dummies to follow you over there? I have to break this up now. Find some way to get them moving back to their unit. How? I can't think.*

To Riles, Jon looked about as unsure as a teenaged groom at a shotgun wedding. His movements spoke of a man on the brink of a discovery that he could never predict. Discovery of what or maybe…who? Riles walked over to the torn haversack and picked it up.

A suspicious man like Riles never needed much to push him into drastic action, but with his new and confounded revelation, he found himself hesitant, not entirely sure of his own belief in such a conclusion. But again and again, the evidence sang.

His lean face wrinkled in a scowl, teeth gritted, exposed by his sneering lips. He clinched the frosty, bloodied canvas bag and a low moan grew from deep within his lungs, moving to the throat.

The sound was so unnatural that it froze Jon in his thoughts and slammed him into present terror. Jon turned to see the monster he had most feared upon him instantly. Riles' rough voice shook him.

"You, Jonny Lights…you're going to tell us what you know about Bert!" he shouted, waving the bloody haversack, shoving it into Jon's chest.

"I haven't any idea what you mean," Jon said, taking a step back.

"Oh, I'm sure you do. You scrounged that coat last night, and that ain't your blood, is it? Are you shot?"

"No, it was a dead Yankee, I say," Jon exclaimed.

"Shut yer trap!" In a swift leap, Riles shoved Jon to the ground. At this, Charlie jumped up from his seat at the rock. He bounded over to Riles, skipping around, excited. To Jon, he looked like a circus monkey following his master.

"Oh do tell, Jonny Lights!" Charlie said. He put his hands on his knees, rocked back and forth. "Don't be bashful there, Riles' gonna beat ya now!"

Jon reared back, thinking Charlie was madder than the unstable Riles, who began to kick at him. This sent Charlie into rapturous spasms. Jon deflected Riles' boot stabs with his open palms. "Are you absolutely crazy?" He eyed his musket.

The action of the three men on a quiet field did not go unnoticed. It caught the attention of nearby orderlies counting the dead and taking names, if possible. Riles saw the four-man team stare in his direction. He backed away from Jon and lowered his voice. "Charlie, go tell Stokes to find the major. He'll be more than willing to help me with this…mystery."

He pointed to Jon. "And you're comin' with me. We're going to have a look at them bodies." Riles pulled Jon by the arm. His grip wasn't kind. "Let's have a look over here for ole' Bert. Did you leave him out here, once you stole his coat? Did you kill 'em first?"

They started for the collection area and Jon's stomach twisted. Surely the dead Bertram would be splayed out in ghastly form, no doubt, for all of them to see his pale, sad face frozen with the look of pitiful anguish. All he could do was deny it. He felt a twinge of anger at Riles and unexpectedly, it gave him a slight jolt of nervous energy, perhaps enough to run or fight, but fighting would be seen as guilt, and it was too late to run.

Jon kept his distance from the battered dead. The freeze had delayed decomposition, but the odor of blood and intestinal ooze hovered over the area. After many hours exposed, there was no stopping the natural stasis. For men in the field, when possible, quick burial became a natural action, no matter what season.

Riles stepped up to the row of corpses, leaning left or right to gain an angle on the faces. He uttered a soft "Nope" over each body as if to emphasize the expected affirmative. After twenty dead men had been inspected, Riles grew impatient and rushed past the last dozen with outward agitation.

Seeing Riles fail to find the dead Bertram, Jon searched at a cautious distance, observing the few Yankees that lay separated. There were some wounds that could be bayonet stabs; however, they could be bullet holes as well. There was no way to distinguish between the two and Jon wasn't leaning in any closer. Combing over the dead at night was not as visually sickening as this daylight walk through a museum of gore, where men's heads were blasted apart, or their chest's opened by grapeshot rounds.

A distant spattering of musket fire stopped the activity around the line of dead men. Riles looked to the northwest towards Harper's position. The small arms fire turned rapid, then grew into evident skirmish fire, complete with the louder reports of answering Union pickets. Probing had begun and in a few minutes, the low moan of artillery joined in, perhaps multiple batteries testing their range, measuring the will of the enemy.

Jon thought of the 11th and knew he had to pull away from this mad man, return to the safety of his unit or perhaps more combat; the latter being more favorable than this hellish treatment. Within the safe presence of other men, he turned and marched aggressively through the stiff, dead grass. He heard Riles shout, "I'm not done with you, boy, hey you!"

Jon turned and shouted back, "I'm going to my company, so there's nothing more to do here." He continued on, carelessly expecting a shot in the back.

Riles, agitated that the Yankees ruined his mission, could not follow and subdue Jon, protected as he was by the eyes of others. Witnesses were detrimental to revenge. He decided to go see if Charlie had done what he told him to, he could deal with Jon later. "I'm on to you, Mr. Lights!"

Jon took direction from an orderly on the approximate location of the 11th Regiment, in line perhaps within 400 yards, maybe less. He followed the tree line in a wide arch and approached the active picket line retrieving fresh ammo from crates, precariously balanced on the back of a mule. Jon greeted them and discovered they were from his own brigade, men from the 29th North Carolina. They gladly showed him the way back to the main line.

He moved on through a thin cedar break, heavy with the smell of burned wood. In a sudden turn, he saw four Yankees lying in his path, blown apart by a shell that had found their hiding place and destroyed it. The nearby trees were shredded to pulp by a tremendous blast from a faraway gun. In a tree limb, some yards away, a man's arm hung from a branch by the grip of the hand. It looked to Jon, as if the arm was taken as the man climbed the tree. No cloth covered the arm. It was an appalling testimony to the human body's reflexes. He cleared the woods and saw another sad vignette; two wounded men near a burned out fire—one Confederate and a Yank propped up against trees, both quiet, drowsy. Jon collected their scattered equipment, opened a canteen and gave the Confederate a drink. The man swallowed, laid his head back. Jon approached the injured Yank and held the canteen for him, then stopped, fooled. The man was dead but his eyes had stayed open.

Jon shook his head at the poor sight and decided to take a minute to invigorate the fire the two enemies had shared during the night. He stirred the coals and used new cedar shards as kindling to fuel the larger sticks. It was all he could do to help. A voice in his head reminded him- *It was more than I did for Bertram.*

Jon took off his stolen overcoat and covered the severely wounded Confederate. "Here, this will do better for you than I can." Interrupting his kind act, the low rhythm of running horses arose from behind. Alarmed, he stood, turning to see where the riders might pass, but they abruptly pulled up. Three horsemen confronted him. The middle rider, a lieutenant, probably an adjutant, held a folded document.

Jon stood at attention, saluted.

"Soldier? We are looking for a sergeant from Rains' brigade, 11th Tennessee." The officer looked at a piece of paper. "Jon Lyhton… seen him?"

"Nope. I haven't seen anyone but d..d..dead folks…sir," The stutter was right on. "Just g..g..going to look for my c..c..company, sir. Why ya need that m..m..man, sir?"

"Eh… right sonny, he's wanted for theft and murder of an Arkansas man. And he is reported to be in this vicinity, an educated man, wearing a Yankee overcoat, Ohio Regiment. If you hear of, or see Jon Lyhton, you go tell your captain, got it?"

"Yessir." Jon saluted and stood at attention.

The lieutenant's eyes squinted and looked down at the wounded men. He shifted his horse, blocking Jon from the open field. "Sergeant Timms!"

One of the horsemen responded and dismounted. On his belt, he wore a pistol and what looked to be handcuffing irons. Pointing past Jon, the lieutenant said, "Take a look at that coat there. Maybe that is our man."

Jon moved aside as the sergeant inspected the kersey blue garb, and the brass buttons. He turned to the lieutenant. "Ohio, sir."

The lieutenant looked at Jon, then to the sergeant. "Well? Ask the man his name."

The sergeant hesitated. "Well sir, he's dead. I'll check for a name, sir." Digging through the clothes, the sergeant found only a few letters. He unfolded one and read. "Eh, looks like his name is George, sir."

"Drat." The lieutenant pulled his reigns, turned his horse. "It's never *that* easy, is it? We'll have to carry on then." Addressing Jon he said, "You must know we don't put up with bummers in this Army. We punish those who steal and then kill their comrades. Understand?"

"Yessir." Jon saluted. "I'll k..k..keep a lookout s..sir." Jon eyed the riders until they rounded the tree line.

How terribly swift their justice seemed to fall. Truly the spectacular trial had already begun last night around that fire as the court of gods, or Riles, saw to it that he was found out for his crime: one that he purposely hid. Perhaps he should go back and duel it out with Riles. No, he was still free, in a sense.

Jon knelt down, looked into the face of the man he covered. He had passed from the world without a sound. "No more hell for you now."

Although the oddness of keeping it crossed his mind, as did the need for it, he picked up the blue overcoat and rolled it up to fit through his equipment straps. Carrying it would be less trouble than wearing the conspicuous marker.

Jon walked on through a land pounded by soldier's shoes, heavy horses and wagon wheels; cut up by canon projectiles, strewn with corpses, clothes and accoutrements of every order size and purpose. Such were the many scenes that he witnessed on his way through the front lines, or what was now neutral ground. It had become a large waste area for everything in war; mostly lives.

Reaching the rocky fence line where he had fled the artillery barrage, he paused briefly to view the casualties. Two men lay broken and bent like rag dolls in the grass. He sensed that there would have been more dead, judging from the complete maelstrom that had fallen so rapidly upon them. The corpses he did not recognize; they were bruised, covered by mud and aged blood.

Jon checked for self-made wooden ID badges and found one. The man he knew; his name was Sheldon Daniel, who had recently returned to the regiment five weeks ago after recovering from a wound last August. Drained of its blood, bent and bruised, the body did not resemble his young athletic friend. It was a quick death. One that all men wanted, but only a few received. A low hurt gathered in Jon's chest, heavy and dark. "Oh Sheldon, I…I guess God has you now." He turned away, stuffed the badge into his pocket and searched the ground for more men. He saw no others as he walked the fence line. *I hope the company made it through, with most of us.*

Jon gazed at the battlefield. For the first time, since becoming a soldier, he saw himself as one of the things gone wrong in war. He had failed as a warrior. The rapturous image of the brigade's victory had been replaced with the sight and sound of a man being impaled by his own countryman, and cries of revenge from a grievous, enraged sibling.

There was his duty still to consider. He could not roam all day and ignore the fight that had yet to be finished. *Was there no grand attack planned for today?*- he asked himself. The Union Army seemed unable to maneuver, rolled up and ready for destruction. No, he could not be a part of that now. It was evident that the battle would not end with the heroic strains of a victorious Army shouting and singing its way home into Nashville as liberators, but conclude with his trial and possible execution. His thoughts crashed from one wall into another as his mind drew something like a sketchy newsprint picture of a hanging man. All the papers would feature it, even *Harper's Weekly* up North, with the caption, "Rebel Criminal Hanging."

He walked into a cedar grove and sat hard against one of the bullet-sliced trunks. Exhaustion overcame every thought as he tried to fend off a furious inner conflict. Never did he feel so far removed from the patriotic sentiment that prompted his enthusiastic and hard-won enlistment. It was not soldiering any longer. Certainly, this could not be the duty that he had so thoroughly trained for. The previous day's struggle had led not to victory, but to a crime, and a warrant. He had nowhere to escape. No regiment, no Army, nothing.

Right now, it may be better if I had been killed in the charge. Could he think that? It was easy: a battle-killed soldier is a brave one. A hung soldier is a disgrace.

He tried to talk himself up. *We are a good regiment; we have fought well, out in the Cumberland Gap and elsewhere. Lieutenant Weston knows, as does Colonel Gordon. God knows...Bethanna.* Then, out of a dusty place, an old innocence spoke. He flinched. *God help me.* But God had been a faraway being to him for a very long time. From the beginning, there was no one else in this inner war and now, that's all it was, just a fight for the inside. He longed and searched for, his true blue self.

* * *

CHAPTER 6 ★

RETREAT FROM LETCHER'S CREEK
1853

With the massive acquisition of land that had been added to the United States through the annexation of Texas in 1845 and the Mexican Cession in 1848, investors and capitalist adventurers traveled west down the Ohio and Tennessee Rivers to populate and harness the frontier's vast potential. Along with them, they brought the industrial mindset, factory goods and the bourgeoning railroad. With its speed and all-weather travel, the steam locomotive, like the river boat steamer before it, grew the economy rapidly and spawned the railheads linking the northern lines of Indiana and Illinois with the southern port cities of Mobile and Pensacola. One such rail line, snaking southeast out of Nashville, was the Nashville to Chattanooga, running through Murfreesboro, Wartrace, and Tullahoma.

But all of this didn't matter to the two boys bounding along its ties and running up and down the ballasted roadbed. Nor did they care about the nation's infighting over slavery, fostering resentment that was growing into genuine sectional strife. They only knew that today there would be an adventure of the highest order. One hundred paces back, they had jumped aboard an imaginary train car, carrying them to a distant battlefront only a few minutes away. The crisis was severe, the cause just and far above mere patriotism. They decided that today's nemesis would be Antonio Lopez de Santa Anna. The exiled leader had escaped his fortress prison and formed a new Army to invade Tennessee, targeting the capital, Nashville.

Each boy commanded a full regiment of the most heroic and experienced veterans, fully adorned in the dress blue and tall cadet-style caps of the American Army. As the train pulled into the station, crowds cheered, bands played and the two young generals addressed their battalions with the bravado reminiscent of the blustering politicians of the era.

"Soldiers of the Elite Guards, today we will march into history, and immortality."

"Hey, Jonny, that's pretty damn nifty!" said Elias. "How'd you come up with that?"

"Uh… I think from my daddy's copy of General Wellington's Battles," Jon said.

The sunlit day cooled with a soft autumn breeze, and a brilliant sky provided perfect visibility for artillery and massed charges. Both little commanders led their respective units out of the invisible town to meet the enemy in a surprise attack. Twelve year-old Elias Ambersaile led the right wing of the Army, and leading the left, his junior officer and cousin, ten year-old Jon B. Lyhton.

Since Elias was older, and armed with a real six-inch long buck knife, he instantly attained the rank of major general. Both had ample reserves of Cavalry Dragoons to assist in the final sweep of the field, their horses lined up to the flanks, eager to trample. With stick-swords in hand, they marched over a hill laden with tall grass and wild oats until they saw the perfect battleground. Framed on two sides by cedars and large oaks, lay a clear field of short grass, scattered rocks, and a broad slope beyond it. At the top of this slope stood the rocky fort where Santa Anna plotted the downfall of the United States.

"Look, Jonny! I knew it, there's the camp. All those heathens are preparing to move out against us!"

Jon saw troops materializing onto the earth, aligning their ranks to match the family's picture books. Company after company of soldiers, dressed in green and blue coats, and the characteristic crossed-belts on their chests, hoisted flags above their lines of rifles and cannons. "We mustn't wait," he said.

"On my signal, charge, and hit'em hard around on the left."

"Yes, sir."

"I'll meet ya in the middle, and farewell old friend… if I fall," said Elias.

"Yes sir, in the middle, farewell!"

Preceded by a loud vocal trumpet call, the shouts of "Charge!" echoed into the wide, empty clearing. The Mexicans were thoroughly surprised and fell by the dozen; many surrendered to the ranks closing up behind the young, brave commanders who, with steel resolve, had raced ahead of their lines. Jon fell wounded and soon recovered enough to pick up the fallen colors and carry them into the fray. "Follow me, blood or glory!"

Many of the retreating enemy had scurried up the hill, where they could make a last stand in the rock-fortified redoubt.

The U.S. Army rested for a while after the first stage of the battle. The boy-generals talked about going to the lake tomorrow, or perhaps visiting Mabel and Madge Perkins to pick cherries on their farm, if they felt like having girls around.

Very soon, the boys knew they would have to continue the fight at hand and take the hill. Reforming their lines and discovering multiple stick-pistols abandoned on the ground, the generals, panting and sweating like real warriors, took off for the summit, eager to prove their worth.

Jon halted and pointed ahead. "Look sir, it's the Matamoros Battalion!"

Elias nodded, not questioning Jon's knowledge of the historic unit. "Charge 'em!"

The battalion held the Americans at bay for about fifteen minutes as the generals led special detachments and stormed a few interesting rock outcroppings. The bastion fell with a great, final rush and at last, the troublesome Lord Santa Anna was beaten. By order of President Pierce, he was summarily shot for his trouble as the boys grossly wasted ammo on his corpse.

Falling down, winded and worn, the heroes surveyed the grand field from atop the hill. Embellishing their own view, the victory came at considerable cost as the horses and men lay strewn across the wide plain, caissons and limbers had been shattered into splinters, and smoke drifted overhead.

The horrid scene dissipated when Elias suggested a walk down to Letcher's Creek, about 200 yards distant, to put out the fire in their throats. This they did with immense joy as the cold creek's icy blast rebirthed their childhood energy.

A new adventure sparkled in Elias' eyes, and the Santa Anna Campaign soon turned into the ancient legend of King Arthur and the dragon-fighting knights of old. Elias dubbed himself Arthur, of course, and Jon became Lancelot. After a thorough search in the trees for the suitable swords and lances, the adventure took form. They began in earnest, saving maidens and jousting from tall, armored steeds. This time, they ignored the meadows and stayed with the course of the stream, leading them in and out of glades, tall reed breaks, and tapering ponds. Upon arriving at one of these ponds, the boys were jarred by the sight of a large turtle. The brute, over a foot in length, ate from a mulberry bush.

"Land sakes, Jonny, it's a dragon!"

Jon cocked his head, his long sandy-brown locks shading his eyes. "Looks like a giant tortoise to me, soft-shell, leaf-eater."

Elias pointed. "I'm telling ya, its' gonna be a dragon soon, look at the size of it. That thing will eat us all in a year or two!"

"How can you be so sure?"

"It's got scales, don't it?"

After several minutes of goading, Jon guessed that turtles, over much time, turned into dragons. And this one was well on the way to being a dandy.

Elias grabbed Jon's arm. "We gotta' kill it, Jonny!"

Jon showed hesitation; he wasn't enthused.

"Pshaw, Jon Lyhton, ain't you ever kilt anything before?"

Jon shuffled uneasily, kicking the dirt from his tanned brogans.

"Fish and flies is all, I think!" Elias said, laughing at his cousin.

He guffawed until his face turned red. Soon Jon's face turned red, too, but mostly out of ridicule.

Elias nudged him. "Jonny, how'r gonna get any power if you never kill nothing!"

"Power?" Jon answered, looking up through his long bangs.

"Sure, like the Indians, every time their warriors kill a deer or buffalo they gain a life force from the departing spirit, power!"

Jon knew a lot of things, but mostly about European heroes and early American colonials. "That true, Elias Ambersaile, ain't cuttin' a shine on me?"

"No shine, no lie!" Elias pointed to the tree tops. "Sure, that's why when Indians die their spirits occupy the things of nature, like trees and animals!"

Elias pulled out his buck skinner. "Alright now, put the beast on its back, and ramme'r home."

Jon grabbed the knife and reluctantly stepped towards the grazing turtle. "Well, how do I know I'm not killin' some old Indian chief?"

Elias laughed again. "Chiefs are eagles dummy. This is just a baby dragon!"

The "beast" glanced at Jon and stopped eating. On guard, the turtle pulled his outstretched neck into the shell, and only his nostrils appeared beyond the rim. His feet were still aground but not firmly set. Before Jon could study the beautiful shell, Elias ran by him and kicked it. The turtle slid sideways and then flipped over on its back. At this, the creature seemed to be in an all-out effort to regain his right position as his feet waved uselessly.

"There he is, Lancelot! Can't hurt ya now, kill it! Kill it!" yelled Elias.

Buried in all men, even boys, there waits the hunter's instinct: a natural inclination for the dominant species to possess or procure the other. Young Jon Lyhton had certainly never hunted anything. His father did not follow the rural methods of rearing a son in such parts as the Tennessee wilds. Although being a rather tidy and literate man from Baltimore, Jack Lyhton was well aware of the frontier customs concerning the hunt, but his life had been one of academia and the book. For him, knowledge was the ultimate quest.

He had seen the rougher side in his youth, well before refinement, with a four-year enlistment in the regular Army of the U.S., and experienced the shortest of combat in a skirmish with Indians. After such lofty adventures, his rough edges had softened with a long teaching career and marriage. Letters from his sister Katherine in Nashville coaxed him west. Now, he was a Tennessee businessman, a bona fide cattle agent and on the cusp of financial windfall, but still no hunter.

Jon gripped the elk-bone handle with both hands as a breath arose within him. In that breath, something possessed him. Perhaps it was a need to have the upper hand, or a curiosity about death. Or, as Elias alluded, some wandering ghost of an Indian brave drifting through the trees helped Jon to plunge the blade down into the exposed reptile. A shock of adrenaline blasted his chest with fear and energy, enough energy to repeat the deed even more forcibly than before. Elias was right; power had shot into him.

The creature writhed about, head twisting, eyes clamping shut. Red blood and bile dripped onto Jon's junior-size brogans. Six thrusts and six little holes didn't look like much damage, but the shell was permanently opened.

Elias jumped about, shouting wild exaltations and grand swear words. Then on a jealous impulse, he snatched the knife away from Jon's trembling hand and went for the head. Jon gaped at the graphic butchery born out in such merciless style as Elias cut at the turtle's neck.

A scream battered the two assassins' ears, and for a moment, they looked at the turtle with terrified awe. Sally Letcher screamed again and the boys turned to see the 11year-old strawberry-blonde aghast in utter terror at the mutilation of her beloved pet. Jon had never seen such a look of despondency as she dropped her basket, spilling a collection of freshly picked mushrooms and carrot tops.

Elias frowned upon seeing her intention. "Ain't a pet, I say!" he yelled.

"Sally, no, it's not a pet, it's a dragon." Jon claimed.

Elias giggled.

Sally Letcher stared at Jon, as if he were the biggest fool in Tennessee. She ran over and squatted down next to the bloody shell. Her shoulders began to quake, as her quiet sobs turned into mournful crying. She choked for breath while attempting a broken, emotional eulogy.

Jon's initial rush of glory melted away and pooled into an ever-deepening black guilt. He stepped towards the girl but before he could think of anything, Elias pulled hard at his shirt. "This is sour, Jonny, she's gonna tattle-tale for sure, let's make a run for it!"

As the boys raced away and into the grassy field, Jon thought he heard a man shouting after them. He did not turn around to see, or hesitate to listen to the angry man. He was in a full-fledged retreat.

* * *

For the rest of the day and most of the next, Jon lived with the knowledge of inevitable judgment. He knew that the man's voice was that of Trabel Letcher, Sally's uncle who owned the land and the self-named creek. Jon pictured the woeful scene Trabel must have witnessed as his niece cried out her broken heart. Her testimony most surely contained the names of the heartless perpetrators.

From a distance, Trabel Letcher cut a lean shape in profile, but up close he was quite a muscular fellow. He walked with a slight shoulder hunch; his arms seemed to come down to his knees, they were so long. Trabel's gray whiskers belied his age, and his dexterity. Blessed with speed, he could move his legs and feet like a titled pugilist. Having a straight nature with folks, he was to-the-point honest, rarely funny with children, and had no patience for anyone but his Sally. Not one to sit all day thinking about how to deal with his niece's feelings and those who hurt them, he moved on it rather quickly.

Hunting down two boys across a county of farms and horse ranches was easy for someone who kept a close eye on the mischievous local youths. And having a youth of his own, he knew the routes where he could find a wayward young person who could be enlisted into "fence mending" or some other rapidly learned trade in which he could employ the unsuspecting.

And so, finding a suitable spot on the outgoing spur of the Nashville & Chattanooga line, Trabel Letcher hid in a grove of persimmon trees and waited to confront the breakers of his niece's heart, who walked unknowingly towards him.

Jon, still in a pucker over the whole killing thing, decided that he would never again listen to Elias' brazen enticements. He wondered how his friend could stay above the high water because now, as usual, Elias had started his day like there was no yesterday, all new and open to his whim, and as they trotted along the shiny rails he began to taste the sour fruit of such a friendship, which was actually more like a forced enlistment.

Letcher let the boys walk by, lest they bolt at the first sighting of him. He followed close and gained on them quickly, then without a sound, snatched the two by their shirt scruffs and tossed them off of the elevated rail bed. Nothing broke their fall onto the ballast rock. The boys yelped and screeched as they rolled down. Letcher jumped after them swatting their heads with his open palm.

"Show me what you love, I'll kill it for you, bastards! Know what you done? Huh? That girl got the sweet heart o' Jesus and you like 'ta break it. Shitty little bastards!"

Elias tried to run but Letcher caught him with an outstretched leg, tripping him. "Where you off 'ta?" He said casually, as if asking the preacher.

He punched Elias in the head and the boy spun away, landing hard on the ground. Jon, seized with fear, scraped and bruised, cowered where he sat and knew that death was upon them; nothing else but death.

Letcher, satisfied that he could proceed, continued his rant. "Alright now, I know you're the ones that killed Sally's pet tortoise, no denials ever gonna change that. Now you need to learn a lesson 'bout killing for sport and killing for need, and deliberate cruelty, dammit! There's not much sport in staking a turtle and there isn't much need either, unless you gonna' eat it or use the other parts for useful trinkets. But since neither your daddies ever learnt' you them ways of making combs and shell guitars, I guess you were going to have a meal, eh?" He let the lesson settle. "Well, answer me!"

Jon wiped his forehead and saw a line of blood on his sleeve. Blood was serious. *This will not be a quick death.* He began to cry, low and gentle sobs. He glanced at Elias to answer the man's most logical question, why did they kill it? Elias looked back at Jon and then to Letcher. "We ain't' never seen no damn turtle," he said.

Letcher walked over and swung his leg to kick, but Elias jumped away. The older man tried again and Elias caught his boot and twisted it, sending Trabel reeling.

"God damn, you little bastard!" he shouted from the ground.

In a blink, Elias was up and ran into the grove like a mad boar determined to make his escape.

Little Jonny was alone with the raving mad uncle. A breeze fluttered the tree leaves and churned up the dust along the tracks. Letcher stood and searched the trees for any sign of Elias. He huffed, knowing the boy was well ahead of him. He made fast for the remaining criminal, Jon.

The man's large hand racked the side of Jon's head sending a lightning bolt though his eyes. He yelped aloud and uttered a muffled, begging cry.

"Now you're killers *and liars.* That's going backwards, boy! Didn't see any turtle, ha!"

Trabel paused, slapped his hands together saying, "But I did prepare for this." He ambled back up to the tracks and retrieved a burlap salt bag he had dropped in his first rush at the boys. His dirty hands worked at the knotted rope tied around the open end, and with a casual gait, walked back to the bruised killer. Jon had one guess as to what the bag held.

"Hope you're hungry, bastard!" Letcher said.

Jon thought he had a chance to run so he turned and bolted for the persimmon grove. It was easy an easy catch for Letcher,

63

the boy being so young. Jon landed hard. Letcher reached for his burlap sack again and upon opening it, the pungent odor of rotten meat overtook the whole area. Jon wished for death. He was sorry the very moment after he had seen Sally's pretty face so twisted in complete sorrow.

Letcher approached Jon and presented the rotting turtle carcass with its bottom removed, legs dangling. Dark and shiny, the smell of it gagged Jon as he gasped for a clean breath in the foul air. The rotten meat hovered ever closer to his face. He put up his hands to resist a forced feeding. One punch to the ribs from Letcher brought his hands down.

"By Lordy, you'll know hell now! Take your medicine, you damn scoundrel."

Letcher smeared the gore on Jon's face and mouth. An acrid rot laced his tongue and his stomach convulsed. He screamed full force in blind agony, spitting out as fast as he could any trace of the turtle rot. The taste overwhelmed his small palate and Jon vomited in repeated spasms. Letcher stood over him, satisfied. "You never go near my land again, will ye?"

"Never, sir, never go there." Jon sucked for breath with tears and black blood rot on his cheeks.

"What about your smarty mouth friend?"

Jon only nodded, too beat up and sick to push any kind of words out past his throat. Trabel Letcher wiped his hands on the sack as he backed away, then he stomped back up to the tracks. "Don't you ever hurt Sally again!" he yelled, before he turned and walked into the trees.

* * *

When Elias left Jon that day, he left their true friendship at the tracks, in the hot breeze, with a rotten turtle. As cousins, the boys were polite to each other throughout their advancing youth, that time when requirements of family decorum overruled animosities, even between adults. Family secrets, scandals, or feuds often started in youth and became the guideposts for social and fraternal behaviors. Playful adventures ended for the two cousins, but amid a social family, they were forced to share space.

They grew up relatively normal for their time; ignorant of where the Southern mindset was leading their political and economic futures. The North-South schism dominated their teen years, and during that time, all young Americans inherited two separate societies; two parts of one nation, that soon became frustratingly codependent and shoddily sewn together by weak compromises.

The scare of "Yankeedom" and its mass-industrial centers, complete with overcrowded slums, repulsed Southerners who espoused mild populations and relied on established systems of barter. They viewed their slower pace as healthy, productive, and a legacy to their ancestors.

Accusers in the North continued to charge the South with slowing progress, and restricting the black slave's human rights. In the nation's Congress, lines were drawn, old friends became enemies and moral duels took place, if not lethal ones. The North's determination to break the South's disinterest in growth resulted in zealous appeals for abolition and a radical change of the nation. And so it was taught that two countries existed inside the same borders.

Sally Letcher grew up into a lovely teen, polite and pretty, with bright eyes and womanly figure. Although he apologized for his crime, and his youthful ignorance, she shunned Jon Lyhton at every turn and never let him forget, when the chance should arise, what he had done to her. For his part, Elias replaced the turtle with one he caught for her. When that was coolly received, he gave her a kitten, which brought a favorable reaction: her forgiveness.

As the years passed, her pet collection grew under Elias' steady friendship and admiration. Even though a better behaved teen, Elias was never fully accepted as a legitimate suitor by Uncle Trabel. Then an amazing thing happened to turn his prospects; Trabel died while trying to clean a shotgun in the outhouse. Known for unusually long trips to the privy, and shooting foxes from his sitting position, it was hours before Sally thought to check on him. She discovered her uncle face down, pants down.

In the wake of this tragedy, Sally inherited a working farm, ten horses, more land than she knew about, and nine slaves. She was seventeen years old. Elias was hired to help run her businesse operations, which he excelled at. He also excelled at long walks with Sally, late night book readings and secret, but passionate, progress "meetings"; full of more kisses than calculations.

To Jon, it was the devil stealing the garden, and Eve. The bold cousin had won again, and even had the nerve to invite Jon to help him. Rejecting the offer, Jon stood fast on his own morals and was not going to be a worm and grovel for Sally's forgiveness, or work under his cousin's dominance. After so many years, removed from his childish deed, he had figured that he was never going to be guilty again. Plain truth, he was soured on the whole concept. Too many years could be wasted on such feelings. If it's one thing he learned from Trabel Letcher that day in '53, it was that the tender heart gets found out and trampled; ripped open and exposed like that poor turtle. One way to never hurt Sally again was, to never go near her.

After his horrific brush with Letcher, Jon gravitated towards his education, confident in his own ability to read and write the words of English authors and Southern poets. By age fourteen, his readings and recitations grew into family "play night." After Sunday dinner, all the local gentry were invited to the Lyhtons' ornate parlor in a new townhome in the city. Jack honored his son with only the gusto a proud father can deliver, "And now presenting that elephantine orator of boundless narrative, the protagonist of paraphrase…Jon B. Lyhton!"

It was Jon's time to shine, not only for a mere few minutes, but for an hour he mused on the day's news, recited sensitive poems, or a scene from a famous play. His sandy hair, gray-green eyes and slender frame garnered the right attention from the female guests as they giggled at his gestured portrayals. Jon laughed at his mistakes, which made others laugh, therefore killing any sense of nervousness. His father finished the evenings, and being somewhat a political man, talked openly of secession and the rights of self-determination, but often regretted that the votes were never to be found for such bold action.

After abolitionist John Brown raided the U.S. arsenal at Harper's Ferry, Virginia in 1858, Jon focused on more manly things. The seriousness of the times demanded adult-like attention to the future. The cattle business of his father took hold of him and he spent long summers at ranches where he witnessed brokered sales of livestock. He worked long days with ranch hands who had no need of fancy verses, written by some lace-collared English dandy. Jon learned to appreciate the poetry of messiness, the absolute rhyming foulness that the men and boys of the ranches uttered at each other; definitely not for the family parlor on Sunday "play nights."

Jon found his excitement equally in both worlds—the educated and the laborer. The world of the soldier was much like them, blended together. He thought about West Point, or the Western Military Academy, in Kentucky. But he knew that the soldierly life had its long separations, and without war the tedious life of drill made little sense to him. Cumberland University in Nashville was too small for his father's higher tastes, so the best choice for his son was to attend Transylvania University in Lexington Kentucky, the largest and best college in the west.

Jon's university plans came to a halt in the spring of 1861, when Confederate forces took Fort Sumter in Charleston harbor, South Carolina. All able bodied young men heard the call to arms as the new Southern nation would have to fight for her independence.

Entering adulthood, and national service, Jon remembered his childhood often; how he and Elias charged many battalions together, and created their share of mischief—especially that bloody day with Letcher. Although he had played soldier and pretended to shoot his friends and play dead himself, he carried a buried fear; in real life he never wanted to kill anything, ever again.

* * *

CHAPTER 7★

At the outset of the Southern war of the 1860's, a section of Virginia, the western half, seceded from the commonwealth and joined the Union under President Lincoln as West Virginia. To the map reader, it looks like God created a natural boundary between the two states by scraping the earth with his fingers, forming long rows of high rock stretching for hundreds of miles. This boundary, the Allegheny Mountains, stood as a reminder, if not the cause for the differences between the two regions.

From the Atlantic coasts of tidewater Virginia and into the hinterlands all the way to the Blue Ridge Mountains, the plantation system was the staple of economic and social development. Wide open, spacious fields grew tobacco and hemp, the cash crops that made Virginia valuable in Europe, well before the Declaration of Independence. Long rivers wound and curved through the state, affixing a ready-made transport system, reliable and permanent.

Separating the inhabitants during the early growth of the United States, the Allegheny Range protected western Virginia from the influence of the slave culture. The West Virginians grew up differently than their eastern brothers and sisters. As small farmers and traders, the people of higher elevations had no want of slaves or the political structure to support them. No mass production of cotton existed, or any other cash crop. The distinction in topography decided the fates of people, long before they picked up arms against each other.

The aforesaid rationale could explain the similar divisions in Tennessee at the outset of secession. East Tennessee was ruled by the western sibling of the Allegheny Mountains, the Cumberland range, separating the state's eastern third and changing the landscape, lifestyle and beliefs of the people. Their independent farming culture did not support large groups of slaves. The mountains prohibited large rail links to vital river cities. East Tennessee had been a sacred hunting ground to regional Indian tribes of the Choctaw, Shawnee Yuchi, and Cherokee. The hunting tradition continued with white settlers, as did their respect for the old ways and self-sustaining culture that the frontiersmen adapted from the Indians.

At the very western tip of Virginia, where the point meets the Kentucky/Tennessee borders, there is a break in the Cumberland range named, appropriately, the Cumberland Gap. To overlook this gap is to see the borders of three states—Virginia, Kentucky, and Tennessee. In the early days of the United States, a guide named Daniel Boone escorted settlers, surveyors and troops through this passage to inhabit and explore the fertile valleys of the Cumberland Mountains, therefore assuring access to the western territories.

From a tactical standpoint, the fame and importance of the Gap did not go unnoticed when the North/South War began in 1861. Knowing that control of the Gap meant control of the eastern Kentucky/Tennessee borders, local patrols from both sides probed and skirmished there from the very outset of the conflict. But control became illusory in this divided land.

Adding to the Confederate difficulties of a sound defense was the local population's split loyalties. In the east Tennessee hills north of Knoxville lived a brand of folks similar to those in West Virginia, very true to the farming and herding tradition, unlike the lowland planters in Nashville and Memphis. Scotch-Irish and German farmers, traders and merchants, maintained their simple livelihoods in the valleys and trails of this rough, but protective land. Emigrating from the Northern states, they moved west, looking for the ideal valleys, much like their old counties, only free and stable.

In 1861, most eastern counties continued to send legislators to the U.S. capital in Washington, despite the overall fervor for secession in the state. Passions became defined as people chose sides. When armed conflict proved real and present, partisan politics turned into anger and hence led to violence.

A twisted sense of justice took form against those on the frontier farms and villages who, in their eyes had only wanted to stay out of the fractious struggle. But to the radicals on both sides, that passive neutrality was the most villainous form of treason. It was met with harassment, which grew into terrorism, then quickly into shootings and lynchings. Both sides suffered; free-labor Unionists, then secessionist slave holders, and everyone in between who did not serve the two belligerents. Though the tales of atrocity unnerved the Southern government, their limited resources only allowed protection of vital routes and supply centers in the outland mountains.

Early in 1862, Confederate General Kirby Smith was assigned to protect the East Tennessee & Georgia Railroad, a vital artery running from Chattanooga through Knoxville, all the way eastward into Virginia, terminating in the Confederate capital, Richmond. With only six brigades to defend the expansive east Tennessee spur, General Smith kept a sharp eye on the vulnerable Cumberland Gap, knowing the Federals were bound to strike there.

The brigade of Colonel James E. Rains had fortified the position the previous winter and spring, supported by two batteries of artillery and the 3rd Tennessee Cavalry. From a high vantage point, their strategy was purely defensive as they spied Federal movements and performed their probing tactics in the rocky crags of the pass. Without maneuverable ground, a decisive blow for either side proved to be impossible. The mountain terrain slowed infantry and exposed units to the risk of being cut off in a dire time of need.

In May, Kirby Smith assigned fellow West Point graduate General Carter L. Stevenson and his three brigades to reinforce Colonel Rains with 5,000 men, and more artillery support. Stevenson was older, but Kirby Smith had been promoted to general a full year before Stevenson. Their West Point roots helped fashion trust, and the urgent needs of the new Southern country endeared them to duty. General Stevenson's goal was to form a unified division from the men available and create an independent command near the Kentucky border.

In June, Union General George Morgan had no plans for the Gap directly, for he moved his 7th Division to flank the strong fortress-like position and take the western passes into Tennessee. His fast-moving cavalry had discovered that the Southern defenders were concentrated in a narrow front behind the Gap. Cutting them off from Knoxville would open a gash in Smith's defense and expose the rail lines.

General Stevenson and Colonel Rains faced surmounting odds and maneuvered their separated units into a cohesive force. In doing so, the flanks had to be scouted, lest there be dangers, hidden in the vast ranges of dark forested hills and unknown valleys.

* * *

TENNESSEE/KENTUCKY BORDER
CUMBERLAND GAP JULY 1862

Sunrise broke the still dawn as a new day brightened the shadowed Cumberland Mountains and their foothills north of the Cumberland Gap. Fog floated above the valley floor and glistened in the morning rays like the whitest snow, laying blanket-like on the treetops. Up high on Cumberland Mountain, the wind ran its ancient currents over rocky peaks and deep crags, through timberlines and down into gorges where, like a reliable ferry, it lifted a pair of bald eagles over the heads of Lieutenant Weston and his Confederate scouts, resting in their defensive works. The tight ring of cannons and trenches, they called Fort Rains, after their commander.

Sgt. Hillford's pipe smoke whirled around his head as he watched the natural sequence of daybreak and the large birds of prey swoop around them, only to dive back down into the lower gorge. He leaned against a large boulder, relaxed, inches from a 200-foot fall. Looking out again into the Kentucky side of the Gap, his eyes squinted, discerning a distant dust trail in the clearing fog. The pipe stem disappeared under his large mustache for another puff. Turning his head, he observed Lieutenant Weston looking through his binoculars. "Do you have a sure look at them, sir?" He asked.

Lieutenant Weston lowered the glasses from his light brown eyes and shook his head. "No, they're shielded."

Sgt. Hillford looked back to the dust trail. "Only horses kick up that kinda' plume this early. The Yankees are screening their infantry I believe, most likely to outflank the Gap."

"Such as it is, we should look to our orders," said Weston. "Prepare to fall back."

The platoon stepped single file down the steep trail, past cliffs and huge faces of rock, on which soldiers had carved their names, as they desired to leave evidence of their stay. Reaching the saddle of the Cumberland Gap, the men marched on the original Wilderness Road, under no shade from the sun, as the slope was shorn of its trees; the wood taken to feed a large stone iron furnace located near a prominent mountain stream.

The men walked past the chimney-shaped structure, at this time being prepared by local workers and a detail of imported slaves. The Newlee Iron Furnace had been operating since 1819, putting out an average of three and a half tons a day at full capacity. On the streamside of the furnace the miller's wheel turned, working the large bellows that heated the fire pit. Repairman and soldiers worked together to renew production for the Confederate rail lines, or shipment down the Powell River to Chattanooga.

No one in Lieutenant Weston's platoon protested against this sort of duty despite the hard, steep climbs and long hours on watch at the garrison posts. The general vicinity, from the Gap south to the village of Tazewell, was a naturalist's dream, with high, remote vistas, plants of every sort, trout-filled streams and every variety of game running through the hills and valleys. At the Gap, the mountain was pocked with trenched redoubts, created by both sides as the occupation of the area switched hands earlier in the war. The scarring lent a warlike edge to the otherwise scenic vistas.

Lieutenant Weston halted the men near the mouth of a large cave, used as a hospital. Entering slowly while he let his eyes adjust, he saw Dr. Larkin at his camp desk, which was loaded with flickering candles. "Doctor, how are the sick boys - Any improvement?"

With a lift of his head, Dr. Larkin squinted past the candle glow, then smiled, his shaved face a novelty. "Ah, Jeff. Well, fever is a strange thing, seems the less we do the better. The worst is Sergeant Hollis; not much time left for him. But the others should pull through, as long as we don't move them."

Lieutenant Weston's shoulders fell.

The doctor reacted, pulled the long gray hair behind his ears. "Tell me they are not leaving this position here." Irritated, Larkin's stocky form shifted in his chair.

"Sorry, Doctor, but…"

"Ah, the generals will force us to drink heavily, won't they? How can we ever heal anyone, on the march?"

"That is a question you must answer, unfortunately, sooner than later." said Weston. Sympathetic, he grabbed the doctor's shoulder. "Be of good cheer, sir, for many have recovered since the winter." He looked into the dark cave and saw faintly lit shapes of men. With a slight whiff, the smell of vomit and urine made him dizzy, and he remembered why he was no doctor. After a polite farewell to the brave doctor, he quickly exited the cave into the bright daytime sun, sucked in the clean mountain air and cleared his nostrils.

Weston led the platoon through the small village below the apex of the pass. A few quaint houses remained from the early days, after the Revolutionary War. The men would point to the square-framed dwellings, bricked, trimmed with white and declare, "That's an old one." The troops greeted a few residents out working or walking, and soon discussions arose over the possibility of leaving the area.

Corporal Jon Lyhton jogged up to Lieutenant Weston. "We may have to leave the Gap and Fort Rains?"

"Yes, soon."

"Why? We have the advantage, don't we?" Jon asked.

Lieutenant Weston removed his hat and beat the dust from it. "We can't allow Morgan's whole division behind us, plus there's no way General Stevenson will leave Knoxville exposed. It is much more prudent in strategy and less costly in personnel for us to withdraw."

Jon lifted his musket to rest on the other shoulder. "In other words...?"

"In other words, someone told us to."

Jon nodded, not sure if that was even a valid reason. He thought on matters such as this, and tried to understand the tactical side of the war, like the why, when, and how of combat, victory and defeat. This came from his curious youth and hours of reading about Napoleon or the legions of Rome.

Though he was educated, Jon did not dive into the leadership opportunity. He held back his keen wit and intellect to avoid being pointed out for officer-ship, which he did not want, though Lieutenant Weston baited him towards a lieutenant's exam with visions of further promotion and the inevitable adoration of lovely belles.

Jon fended off the tempting arguments, although he was mildly persuaded to join the noncommissioned rank. This, he thought, was harmless, until Captain Binns promptly made him a corporal.

"We'll move you up to sergeant before Christmas, then you'll have to join the officer corps, Jonny." Weston exclaimed, as he passed the corporal's stripe to his flummoxed friend. Jon was flattered but wary of the responsibility, even though the captain liked how Jon quickly assessed things like the morale of the troops and their different talents for certain jobs. He could get the men to do things. In a volunteer force, making a group of men obey one man's orders took competent leaders, and Captain Binns needed leaders. Jon had a natural charm, persuading the men with no sense of rudeness. Still, he did not like being responsible for lives.

For Jon and the 11ᵗʰ, the war resembled a cat and mouse game. The Yanks probed the lines, and the Confederates did the same as they fired bullets into the forests and tested the other side's position, strength or patience.

In late 1861, the flamboyant General Felix Zollicoffer, a Nashville man, led the brigade into Kentucky and fought the enemy at Laurel Bridge and Rockcastle Hills, with mixed results. Jon had missed the two battles, presently having to settle for a contest of sharpshooters. By the time he arrived at the Gap, General Zollicoffer was dead, killed in a doomed Kentucky foray. Jon waited his turn to hit the Yanks, and thought it may be a long wait with the brigade retreating south.

For the platoon, the drama of the sectional conflict had by now possessed them fully and they whole-heartedly committed to the defense of their state. Louis Martello and Paul Lawsen were Jon's closest friends in the platoon, being from the same neighborhood and school. Cawley was an acquaintance from town, and now a loyal pal. He knew the other fellows like Stewart, Liddel and Dabney, who had been working mills and farms around the county. Most enlisted for the freedom and adventure. All of them, to some degree, laid down their morals during this time of war and dove into cards, gambling, stealing, cussing and drinking, eventually knowing those habits will die whenever the war ended. Like all volunteers, they figured that would come soon enough, and then they would go home and be good boys again.

Everyone was about the same age and shared a connection in family, church or friends that bonded the men, whether they wanted it or not, good or bad. Local men came into the regiment with local politics, rumors, suspicions, quarrels and downright nasty feuds. Keeping passions centered on the soldierly duty at hand was easy when there was talk of action, even a retreat.

"It's not a retreat!" Jon insisted. "Tactical withdrawal is the term."

Martello, Cawley and Lawsen listened to Jon's dictum as the four messmates sat around their evening fire. The cool mountain wind raised the flames under a small kettle, hanging precariously from a ramrod-crafted spider.

"Yeah well, same damn result, ain't it, *us* movin' away from *them?*" Lawsen said, staring into the red, jumping flames. He rubbed his beard, a patchy brown thing resembling an uneven, weedy lawn. He yawned, and then stretched his long six-foot frame so that his socks appeared from the other end of his blanket.

No one really wanted to go anywhere. The men had grown into their duty and the station was home. They had made a good camp here in the hillside burrow and knew the trails and heights better than most of the local foxes. Being assigned away from their home turf in west Tennessee had turned out to be a purely liberating experience. The mountains had toughened them up and given them immense confidence in their abilities as soldiers, scouts and overall defenders of the borderlands. They were young, at war, and for the last eight months had guarded the Gap and its environs successfully. Walking away without a struggle could tarnish their hard won reputation, and hurt morale.

Noted regiments from the middle Tennessee area had already been in the thick of things. The 20th Tennessee, for example, guarded the Gap the previous year and had fought at Shiloh in April. Jon and his comrades envied the "other" regiment from Nashville because they seemed to outpace the 11th. They kept a curious ear open for news of the 20th, especially Jon, because his cousin Elias Ambersaile was rumored to make the officer corps soon. It was strange that even with their falling out, the Army kept them close, in a way.

"Colonel Rains knows what's right," Jon proclaimed. "I think tactically, the movement is sound."

Lawsen rolled up in his blanket. "Yeah, sound. What sound? The sound of my ass running."

Laughter faded, and the men fell silent around the low fire. One by one they covered up and drifted into sleep.

A day later, the 11th was on the move and made their hasty withdrawal south through the small town of Tazewell, where they met with brigade command. Colonel Rains needed scouts and who better to trust than the Hermitage Guards, his beloved home unit from the 11th regiment.

He talked directly to Captain Binns, "Send Weston's platoon to the east, along the northern fork of the Clinch River, as far as possible without want of supply. Reconnoiter the right flank, extending as far as the northern Tennessee border. We must know if the enemy is moving to our covered right flank and what roads they may use. I will take the brigade southeast and concentrate with General Stevenson. We expect General Morgan's Yanks to try and push in behind us."

To his troops, Colonel Rains seemed always in the saddle, never making headquarters a permanent place. His youthful face and courtly goatee related him well to his men, as did his past life. In Nashville he grew up the son of a Methodist minister, worked in a saddle factory, and so impressed one of his fathers' friends that the man paid his way to Yale University.

Upon his return, he studied law, and under the supervision of Felix Zollicoffer, became associate editor of the *Daily Republican Banner* newspaper. Soon he moved into civic service as a Nashville City attorney. When war broke out, such experience lent weight to his commands and the air of brilliance to anyone who met him. He enlisted as a private in the Hermitage Guards, but his stellar reputation rapidly moved him up in rank. In May 1861, he was elected colonel of the newly formed 11th Tennessee, while his Guards took the D Company banner.

To Rains, Lieutenant Weston was a good friend from youth, working under him as a shipping manager at the newspaper. Both espoused the same political ideals, not leaning towards secession, but a long-term solution to slavery. When the war began, Kentucky divided its loyalties, but still remained in the Union. The vast northern Tennessee border was threatened and there seemed to be no other choice than to rally to the defense of their home state.

Colonel Rains addressed Weston personally from atop his horse, as the platoon looked on with quiet respect. "Jeff, take no more than two full days. I shall await your report, my friend. Make a good impression on the folks out there. Marching infantry through the hills can indeed bolster our image, but you'll be slow. Take to the heights as often as possible. I've detached a company of the 3rd Cavalry ahead of you; they will ride to the border. Meet up with them if you can." Rains' looked over his shoulder. "There is plenty of hospitality here in Tazewell, and I plan to continue good relations in these parts."

"I will stay wary in those hills. We are ready and eager to serve, sir," Weston said.

Colonel Rains pulled his sword. "I salute the Hermitage Guards once more!" He directed his horse backwards and the beast rose up and kicked his forelegs. This brought applause from the few companies standing nearby and the men shouted their appreciations.

Lieutenant Weston raised a cheer for the colonel. "Hail the Guards, hail the 11th and hail our Colonel Rains!" They repeated the cheer five times as the commander rode off, staff officers in tow trying to keep up.

* * *

CHAPTER 8★

Lieutenant Weston commenced his scouting mission the next day at 5 a.m. with no complaints from his men. His down-sized platoon marched out of their camp near Tazewell and after a few miles, started northeast up a valley road toward the small enclave of Sycamore. The heart of this small homesteaders' community was the quaint Missionary Baptist Church settled near a picturesque stream. The middle-aged minister offered them lemonade, and he seemed eager to talk to anyone. "Well, good to have some company, been weeks, please dip your feet in the stream, where ya' headed… Poor Valley? Sneedsville? This here church is 22 years old."

The platoon drank up the sweet lemonade and greeted a few women near outdoor tables. Lieutenant Weston listened to the reverend's mounting questions but declined him any solid information. He offered to pay the man for his kindness, but the reverend refused the money. Jon rambled up to Weston as the men fell into line. "A man over there says there was a freed slave colony up the next valley. Reckon that will you?"

Lieutenant Weston sighed. "Yes well, these folk have their slaves and freed men like everyone else. We know they have suffered for both. Let's keep to our business and out of theirs."

Taking the road again, they headed on to Howard's Quarters, a trading post a few miles away. As they walked through the beautiful land, Sycamore Creek sparkled down to their left and snaked through fields full of green grass, shade trees, fences and small cabins.

On their right flank, a tall ridgeline walled them into the narrow valley, curving gently with every turn of the stream. The good condition of the road afforded the men quick time in reaching Howard's Quarters. They were able to find out from the storekeepers that no troops of any kind had been seen there in weeks. About the border roads and their usage, no one knew anything. Even in the good weather, the locals traveled very little due to the loyalties of certain armed parties.

In view of the trading post, the platoon ate pre-prepared rations of dried corn cakes and local deer jerky, and then continued on. As they moved further into the hills, Lieutenant Weston observed the ridgeline to the right, knowing that from the top he would have a commanding view of the Clinch River's north fork, a perfect funnel for Union troops into Tennessee. He had to see the valley, at least for the general purpose of reconnaissance. Ignoring it may be a mistake.

The men hiked up one rise to the next until they reached the top of the ridge. Thick trees obscured the view and they had to march north to clear them. The effort awarded them a wide view of the river valley and the endless range of hills across its five-mile space. Beyond this they could see a long mountain stretching north and south in the haze. Sergeant Hillford looked at his map. "That's Clinch Mountain."

Weston chose to move north up the ridge for a few more miles, then retake the Sneedsville Road and make camp in the hills. In the morning, they could move out for Sneedsville, a town only a few miles from the Kentucky border, and then scout passable roads for the brigade to maneuver, knowing, too, the same roads could aid the enemy. "We must know every route east of Tazewell," he told Sergeant Hillford.

Not but a few hours later, Jon looked back at the men in line behind him; dusty soldiers with weather-worn faces and toughness in their eyes, a drilled-in toughness that drove the men's weary bodies through the hot summer afternoon and onto a narrow path, leading them up another hill. Jon found the new trail just off the Sneedsville Road and thought it would be a good idea to follow it.

Lieutenant Weston was intrigued to find a random path, to somewhere unknown. Indeed, farmers and traders had their means of getting around the numerous valleys, but mostly on the hard roads. "Maybe the trail is a shortcut through the ridges to the village of Mulberry Gap," he said, in more of a question than a fact. "Either way, it will keep us under cover for a time."

The hot, midday summer afternoon had heated everything, even the water. Jon uncorked his canteen and swallowed the warm gulp with a grimace. The patrol panted and groaned up the steep pathway, then greeted Jon as they passed him by on the crest of the hill. Some dropped to their knees and heaved for air or leaned against their rifles, heads bowed. Sergeant Hillford stepped up from the rear of the column, caught his breath and said, "I was just thinking of taking a rest."

"I know," Jon said, fanning himself with his hat. "We've been nonstop for three hours, I bet." He looked around, counted heads and turned to view what lay before him. He took an audible breath at the sight, one of pleasant surprise.

The rocky hills gave way to soft grassy slopes that framed a low, narrow valley. A road wound in and out of tree groves and then bridged a shimmering creek. In the hazy distance, just beyond a turn in the stream, lay farm fields tall with crops, sunflowers, and rows of new corn. Fences squared the properties, which from a distance, resembled a large patchwork quilt, covering the rolling land. At the heart of the valley stood a small cluster of dwellings centered on a crossroads, south of the stream. Beyond the village, the stream turned left or south, hugging a long wooded ridge that shielded the northwest side of the valley.

Lieutenant Weston joined Jon on the crest. "*Merci,* Corporal, *bon travail.*"

Jon nodded. "Sure…, *il n'y a pas du quoi.*"

Weston made Jon the first picket in line whenever he had a chance, knowing in good time, his friend may gain an appetite for leadership while he earned trust from the men. The lieutenant shaded his eyes and scanned the valley from the summit. It was surely a tranquil setting and quiet, but the condition of the small village couldn't be determined from such a distance. It would have to be inspected up close. Hopefully, he thought, there would be no radical Unionists awaiting them. Since Kirby Smith's brigades arrived, Stevenson's and Rains', the partisan violence had subsided, but not the sentiments of the pro-Northern residents.

The men rested and passed the news that they would be moving into the valley for investigation. Following the trail, the lieutenant's troops descended down the hill, through a thick woods and then onto a true roadbed. As they walked, the reality began to grow in them that this valley looked untouched and void of troop activity. Without fail, the presence of troops depleted any countryside of its useful crops and food storage.

The scenes of depredations were plainly familiar to the men, coming from a place where the armies had chopped down massive stands of trees and flattened every cornfield, turning quaint farms into fenceless, trampled fields north of Nashville, and even in the vicinity of the border near Cumberland Gap.

There it was splayed before them, undisturbed orchards, grassy lands unmarked by army camps or overused roads. Jon and Sergeant Hillford discussed a variety of reasons for this, among them being its distance from any main supply roads or rail line. "It's sure out of the way," Hillford noted.

The soldiers fell into a light mood, as they adapted to the inviting surroundings. Some of them whistled, while the more curious talked up the valley's prospects.

"Hey, Leonardo!" Lawsen called. "Hope you're up 'fer climbing trees. Looks like plenty of apples and pears."

Martello shook his head. "Don't climb trees no more, Paul, you know that!"

The other men laughed, knowing the story from youthful days when the two boys stole from Trabel Letcher's orchards. The sight of Martello hung up in a pear tree for a day lingered in everyone's thoughts.

Private Daniel spoke up, "We sure did eat good. Sorry you missed it, Leo."

Lieutenant Weston jogged up from the rear and voiced his quandary. "Is this Mulberry Gap?" Sneedsville?"

Sergeant Hillford stuffed a map into his coat. "Can't be, sir, we're at least eight miles from there."

* * *

On the eastern boundary of this peculiar village, near the valley road, a woman and two girls stood in stiffened anxiety as they stared at the gray and butternut-clad men marching steadily towards their fields. The mother stepped forward as if she could see better separated from the others. "I'm sure, zey are rebels," she said with a tight German accent.

"Will they hurt us? Should we…, " said the youngest, stopping herself and waiting for one of them to quell her doubts.

"Bethanna?" the mother said, turning to her oldest daughter. "Take Mirra to der house now, and stay in. I'll see what zhese men are doing here."

As Bethanna strained to see the advancing column, her mother turned again and repeated the order with sternness, this time in German, "*Gehen sie, schneller!*"

With a huff, she took her younger sister's hand, jogged through the fenced front yard and onto the shaded front porch. Stepping up to the door, she paused to look back at her mother standing stiff in the breeze, like a scarecrow guarding the turnips. Often, Hertha stood alone waiting, but today Bethanna sensed that something cold stood with her, born of recent agonies. The girls entered the house and in a silent rush, crossed the wood floor to one of the tall front windows. Mirra pulled back the end of a thick velvet curtain. "This will make mother crazy again." she said, squinting out of the bright aperture.

In a few minutes, the line of men crossed the small stone bridge on the edge of Hertha Gurtag's property. The woman calmly retreated to her gate in front of the house, turned and waited for the expected meeting like a cool duelist. Hertha was forty-eight but looked ten years older. Blond-gray hair hung in strands from a loose bun atop her small, round head. She wore a dark blue, dusty dress with a tan apron, and care-worn work boots. Her eyes were her most imposing feature— small, dark and hard to read. In lighter times, her lips formed an attractive smile, but in her present state of defense, her mouth flattened into a crumpled line.

The troops paused at the stream to fill canteens and wash the heat from their necks. Jon looked up and saw Sergeant Hillford marching down the path toward the woman standing rigid at her gate, his large shoulders tilting over, bouncing with every step. Hillford stopped to greet her. The woman listened to the sergeant with a frown on her face. Jon knew Hillford was telling her about the extending rear guard and their mission to find suitable routes east and possible forage for the regiment. As he talked, Sergeant Hillford motioned with his hands over to the main section of the village. She pointed to the hills and shook her head in a disagreeable manner.

Jon and Lieutenant Weston watched the exchange, trying to read the lady's intent. From where they stood, they clearly heard the woman's stern voice rise to shrill, broken peaks. After more conversation, Sergeant Hillford returned to Jon and the lieutenant. "She's obviously dealt with our kind before and I don't think she liked it," he said, taking off his hat and rubbing his brow.

Jon looked at him, puzzled. "I take it they have seen us Confeds quite enough, then?"

"Not recently, which is strange. She's worried we will bring a battle to the town and of course, steal everything."

Jon pointed to the unit of men, now sitting in the shade of a large oak. "Take a whole village's stores with fifteen men? We've not even one pack mule!"

"Where there's a platoon, there's soon to be a regiment and so on. That's what she's thinking," Hillford said.

Jon nodded in agreement, knowing the Army's desperate want of forage and fresh meat. "The lady's afraid were gonna steal 'em out, eh?" Jon said, rubbing his short whiskers. "I guess you didn't tell her we were about ten miles out of our camp, did you?"

Lieutenant Weston smiled and said, "No Jon, never let 'em know how detached you really are. If they think we can call a brigade down if we need it, good. Keeps them in a sweat, and gives us advantage in the eyes of the local partisans."

Lieutenant Weston gestured toward the village. "We need to find some friendly influence here, if any. Then we can survey the place. We'll do it quickly and friendly, so we do not panic them. Fall in!" he shouted.

The men groaned and left their small paradise by the shimmering stream, bellies and canteens full of fresh water. Lieutenant Weston led the men up the rise and under a clump of trees across from the Gurtag house. As Weston passed by Hertha, for a second, he thought he saw a mad gleam in her eyes—or perhaps it was the light. Wisely, he said nothing. The troops marched by in single file and tipped their hats or uttered greetings to the woman. She only nodded and sternly held her vigil with a dour look.

Private Stewart, as typical of most hungry soldiers, looked around the older woman and into her garden patch of fresh beans and cabbage, located on the side yard and extending to the back of the house. He stepped off to enter the gate, and Hertha bristled. *"Was tun Sie?"*

Jon, bringing up the end of the line, saw this and grabbed Stewart's arm. "Back off, Stew." Jon directed him out of the gate by pulling his equipment straps.

"Ready for some real food, ain't you, J.B.?" said Stewart.

"Absolutely, but let's not impose, that's all."

Stewart rejoined the line and looked back at Hertha. She stared at him.

Jon broke her concentration. "Sorry, Miss, just a hungry boy with big eyes."

Hertha nodded. "I vould keep zem away, if I were you, Corporal," she said.

Jon nodded, unsure what lay behind her statement or warning. He paused, relaxed his face, and pointed beyond her. "I like the flower garden, very pretty," he said, staring at the rows of color, the blooms bobbing and swaying in the light breeze. Hertha folded her hands together and cocked her head in puzzlement.

The floral waves transfixed Jon and for an instant, he was pleasantly unaware of dragging the rear of the formation. A movement of pale blue color caught his eye and he looked up to Hertha, then behind her. She reacted to Jon's new posture and turned to see what had changed his gaze.

Bethanna stood behind her mother, her face with a surprised

expression; first, that she had come out of the house, boldly disobeying her mother and second, that up close, the dusty soldier had such a smart look, with strong features in his chin and cheeks, but his eyes were soft and piercing her with deep interest.

In an instant, Jon absorbed her features of hazel-blue eyes accented with high cheekbones, pink from the sun. Framing her face were tangled streamers of blond hair, falling from under a floppy straw hat. Tilted to one side, it gave her a careless look. Jon noticed her mature figure; up close the girl was older than he had previously thought. The sight of her made him smile, and stare.

A breeze blew the flowers in small circles. Hertha moved back toward Bethanna, while somehow keeping a steady eye on Jon. "Go in now, girl. You have no place here," she said harshly.

Bethanna felt the heat rise in her head. At seventeen, she was not a child and to be continually treated like one grew into a discomfort that today, for some reason, continually gnawed her. She stepped forward. "Are you men from Bragg's Army?" she asked.

Jon, who had a worried grin on his face, removed his hat and said, "Uh, no Miss, from Stevenson's garrison at the Gap. Sure is nice to see a well-kept garden, though."

Bethanna looked at the flowers. "The garden is my summer joy." She turned back to Jon. The breeze lifted the loose strands of her hair onto her face, over her eyes, into her mouth. With a slow wave of her hand she brushed the locks away, embarrassed at the wind's random action. Hertha could take no more outright disrespect.

"I said get to de house now!" She yelled, her scowl turning grotesque. Reaching in a blink, she pulled at Bethanna's arm, twisting it in her special way and forcing a painful wince. Ordering Jon to leave at once, she pulled her daughter up the porch stairs with extraordinary speed. The front door slammed shut.

Jon stood alone in the breeze and stared at the dwelling. The house was solid brick, thinly white-washed. Black shutters framed each window, two in the front and two on each side. The roof was missing a few wood shingles, and the front porch trim needed painting.

Inside the house, the chided girl stepped quietly to the window, moved her curious sister out of the way to see the departing troops through the warped glass. From her father's descriptions of the Southern soldiers, Bethanna had envisioned a group of raving mad men, out to burn and steal. Quite the opposite. The young man she saw up close seemed agreeable and polite. She wondered if the whole Army wasn't going to show up by dark. Not all would be as polite as he was.

As they marched into the village, most of the men knew that the east Tennessee mountain folk were well known Unionists, and surprisingly, even the immigrants held fast to the Loyalists' ideal. This was heavy on Lieutenant Weston's mind as he gave precise orders to his men to sift through the village and find out who is willing to help them. "Look around, gauge their loyalties, and don't force your way into their property. Nice and friendly, got it?"

As the troops fanned out through the village, they found that the homes were simple farm dwellings, about twenty or more. Some were brown brick houses or half stone and wood structures, most with barns, well-sheds and smoke houses; typical homesteads of the mountains- -sturdy and weatherproofed. The main community covered about a quarter mile in total perimeter. Half of the houses centered on the crossroads area while some larger farms hugged the stream, which snaked southwest down the narrowing valley and fed Sycamore Creek, flowing to the Clinch River fork.

The men went out in groups of five and were met with a nervous cooperation from the inhabitants, who seemed to be mostly middle-aged men and women, some children and two old grandparents. The rugged troops communicated as best they could, took an accounting of all properties and tried not to beg for food. Most didn't have to as plenty was offered to them, and what an offer it was: fresh bread that didn't break their teeth like month-old hardtack. Soup, full of potatoes and large beans, replaced the typical water with a lump of salty pork. The feasting spread over the village, as each squad of men found a friendly meal among the cautious folk. Lieutenant Weston's orders were loosely obeyed, at best. The men sat and talked with the inhabitants on airy porches and grassy lawns about the latest news, civilian and military.

Lieutenant Weston took half the men downstream to inspect the scattered farms westward, while Sergeant Hillford, Cawley and Jon sought the leaders of the village. An older woman told them that the Reverend Grottmacher, who lives behind the meeting hall in the center of the crossed roads, was the acting mayor, or *Burgermeister*, as she had said it. Jon knew the word, from his studies of Europe and the Thirty Years War.

The Lutheran minister welcomed them into his humble abode, located at the rear of the meetinghouse, or church. He was a stalwart man of mid-40s, half bald with long sideburns and small friendly eyes. Much younger than he, his lovely wife was of agreeable fit and frame with red hair and a friendly smile. She had no fear, as she questioned the two soldiers with a charm very close to Southern. But she was obviously foreign. Jon had never heard the accent, almost British, but stronger.

"Will you clean us out again like last fall? We have worked so hard to recover. It's as if we work all winter for the quartermaster." She asked this to Jon while offering him and Cawley a slice of homemade pear cobbler. Jon shook his head in a "no" gesture, while he filled his parched mouth with cool fruit. Sergeant Hillford sipped the coffee he'd just been given, and said, "Likely not, Miss. We're traveling light and have no means available to drag off all the stores you possess."

The woman's relief brought a slight sigh.

Stepping in, the reverend opened up to them and gave the chronological tale of the small village called Taldorf. The founders were of German decent who migrated from Pennsylvania and Iowa. They established homesteads in 1844 and farmed the area, linking up with the traffic and trade along the trails of the Copper and Clinch mountain ranges. When the war started, the village elders were staunch Unionists and most of the local men went north to join Kentucky regiments, since that state's government had not been officially claimed for the Confederacy.

"A few of them died in Kentucky and here on their home soil," The reverend's wife said, her eyes dropping in sadness. She looked into Jon's eyes, "Where are you from?"

Jon said, "A long way off, Nashville," and thought of his mother and sisters for the first time that day.

The reverend walked Jon and Sergeant Hillford through his church sanctuary, simple but ornate with plain oak pulpit and pews. Four thin windows on each side, tinted with blue paint gave the room an evening hue, while a round window at the south end let in true light. The only decorative piece was a brass cross on the altar.

They exited onto the front steps and the reverend nodded, folded his large hands. "Of course, there are some who have joined the South, but to no good end." His wife joined him and he took her hand. "Still, we love our land, our state."

The three soldiers thanked the minister for the repast. "We will inform you of our plans regarding the platoon," Sergeant Hillford told him.

The couple waved to them from the meetinghouse doorway, which faced the clean crossroads at the center of Taldorf. The reverend's smile faded and his brow furrowed, fixed in deep thought.

His wife looked up to him. "You did well. Will they move on?"

The reverend crossed his arms. "Yes my Lorina, they will move on. But they will not go today. These men are foot soldiers, not cavalry. There are plenty more nearby. We must be careful."

Jon, Cawley and Hillford met up with privates Liddel and Stewart on their way to inspect the properties on the north side of the road. They met a farmer named Blatz in his house of stone and wood. The large man offered tobacco and cider. His wife spoke very little English, which baffled Cawley. "She talkin' bout us?" he asked Jon, confused.

"Yes, but she is saying very nice things, don't worry. They're apple growers. *Das apfel.*"

Jon tried his German, "*Guten tag Frau Blatz, wie geht's?*"

The woman smiled a little, "*Sehr gut, danke.*" She waved as the men walked on past her apple trees.

The five soldiers moved from house to house and found the same congenial, but highly guarded attitude. Every home appeared well kept and fully stocked with everything neat and orderly, and to their pleasure, very tasty. The winter and spring free of harassment had replenished the cupboards of the village. Food preserves were a rare gift to a community so close now to the front line.

"That will be the last one." Sergeant Hillford pointed to the Gurtag property. Jon winced at the familiar scene where the older woman scolded her teenage daughter. They walked up the gentle rise on a dusty road and turned toward the front yard gate.

CHAPTER 9★

Walking through the Gurtag yard, Jon looked at the flowers again, ones he hadn't noticed before—oleanders, poppies and mums. They reminded him of home, and Cassandra, his little sister, who picked flowers and decorated his bed with them in the mornings.

Then younger Eliza would jump into the bed and pop the flowers into the air, at the same time stepping on her brother.

Cassie, as Jon liked to call the oldest, laughed at the fun she instigated. She charmed the family with her winsome face and brown hair, entertained Jon with her backyard adventures. As a good sir knight, Jon did not mind rescuing her from tree castles. Turning twelve in October, she had probably grown an inch since he'd been gone, and he was missing it.

"Don't you sessech come and take *mein* stock avay again!" Hertha's loud announcement startled Jon out of his pleasant memories and froze his companions. She stood on her porch and at the hip, a double barreled shotgun swayed back and forth. Sgt. Hillford stepped forward and Hertha jerked the gun back toward him. He waved his hands saying, "Down with yer pipe now. We're not going to rob you of anything."

Hertha took one step back. "Then vhat do you come for?" she asked, squinting with hardened suspicion.

Jon's heart jumped at the sight of the shotgun. "Just looking around, ma'am." he said, interjecting himself. Under duress, he searched for the right words. "Eh...*kein schaden*." Mentally reviewing his language lessons, he remained calm and still.

Hertha glared at him in such a way that proved her earnest with the gun. "No harm, you say? You rebs were here last summer und took my Saul, you did."

Puzzled, the soldiers looked at each other, as the woman ranted on.

"You took him to fight Yankees! He died at Pea Ridge, never seeing a loving face, and never brought home to be mourned. No, you will never take from me again."

Jon soaked in her venom and figured she wasn't worth the effort. "Let's go, Sarge, leave this one for another time."

Sergeant Hillford scratched his beard, opened his mouth to speak, but was interrupted.

"She's hiding somethin', damn sure of that!" bellowed a voice from the yard. Hertha tensed and aimed towards the sound.

"Back off, Stewart!" Jon ordered, motioning with his hand. Stewart took a step forward, thickening the tension. "How come she's the only one who's threatened us?" he asked, pointing at the shotgun. Before Jon could think over the question, Stewart jumped onto the porch steps.

The bang lifted dust off of the porch rail and filled their faces with smoke. Jon fell to a knee, and looked over to see Stewart yelling and rolling into the yard. A scream faded from inside the house. The shotgun kick had knocked Hertha back and she attempted to cock the second barrel. Sergeant Hillford broke for the porch and covered the steps with one leap. Jon followed in short order and they struggled to free the weapon loose. The woman's grip seemed as strong as her cursing. Her cursing, rising in volume, was about as loud as the gun. Her face turned red as she weakened under the two soldiers' combined muscle. Fainting from the strain, Hertha released the gun and as she leaned on the brick, Jon reached out to support her fall. He saw the front door swing open.

"Enough! Stop, you're hurting her!" Bethanna yelled. She dropped down to her mother's side. "Let go!" She pulled at Jon's arm, scraping him away and cradling her mother. The girl's hair was down, presenting a wavy, golden-brown shawl around her shoulders as she glared at him with fearful but obstinate eyes.

Jon had seen that look, in a little girl's eyes, long ago. He froze.

"Hurt her?" Sergeant Hillford stepped forward, clutching the long double barrel. "She just blew away one of my men, missy!"

Hertha roused herself and tried to stand, Bethanna at her side, lifted her. Jon supported her at the elbow and wrist, moving slowly as the woman regained her senses. Bethanna looked at Jon's hands and looked away. Together, they helped the shaken mother into the house and put her gently on the couch. She was swaying, dizzy, but breathing normally. Her face changed back to a color of sunned pink. "*Ich hatte einen herzanfall.*" She said in a tired rasp.

"What did she say about her heart?" asked Jon.

"She said that she might have suffered a heart attack," said Bethanna. "Maybe she did; she looks cold. With what's happened, I am surprised she's saying anything." She felt her mother's forehead, and looked over at Jon. Maybe her father was right about the rebels.

Jon reacted to her searing gaze. "If you think I've sanctioned this mishap, you are patently wrong." he declared, for his own credible defense.

"You're telling me that man did nothing to warrant a shot? Four men with guns affronting our house?"

Jon did not appreciate the girl's accusatory tone. "We've been inspecting this whole village most of the day, and haven't fired a shot or harmed one soul. Violence is not my policy toward noncombatants."

Bethanna, nervous but determined not to show fear, stood to face him. Her breath arose in her breast as she placed her hands on her hips.

"Noncombatants? Let me say that we *are* fighting. Fighting fear and anguish, hunger and harassment!"

Jon starred into her eyes long enough to find his reflection. He blinked. "Hunger? Here? I've eaten more food today than I have in a week. Tell me about your starving compatriots. What hunger?"

Jon's educated tone gave her pause. She couldn't retort. Why should she? What did he know about her? He was just a dirty soldier with soft eyes.

She exhaled forcibly, and spun away toward the kitchen. As she passed Jon, her aroma washed over him and he smelled a scent of flowery perspiration. Inhaling it, Jon felt a small tremor in his chest.

Like a dinner bell, the shotgun blast had reverberated across the fields and brought out the scattered platoon. They jogged through yards and jumped fence rails to converge on the property where Stewart's body lay. In a few minutes, a group of quiet soldiers stared in shock at seeing one of them dead, from a gunshot. Illness had taken troops at the Gap last winter and men had fallen, breaking their legs or heads, but this death was a noncombat casualty from a local homesteader, something they had not dealt with. The buckshot had shredded his chest and neck; treatment was useless. He did not cry, or beg, only faded and died in the grass, near the bobbing flowers.

Jon walked to the kitchen and saw Bethanna wringing out a cloth over the water pail. She noticed him, and her eyes met his with stern defiance, then broke away back to her work. He chose not to push his case further with the headstrong girl. Exiting the house, he saw the crowd of dusty tan and gray soldiers gather near the body, and red blood pool. He noticed his ears were ringing from the shot, which had sent smoke in his face. The thought of near death made his heart pound.

Stewart proved that death was very close, and never expected. Jon shivered as he watched his comrades carry the limp body out to the road and cover it with a bedroll. Stewart's messmates and friends muttered over the tragedy, and found it shocking and demeaning. Jon wasn't sure how the platoon would react to a comrade being holed by a crazy German woman. Probably, most of them weren't surprised. Stewart could be a vulgar ignoramus and a hothead, but he was well liked and a dependable soldier.

The group at the road grew larger until ten men hovered over Stewart, all pacing around in the shade of two large trees, waiting for someone to do something. Three of them debated in turns, animated by the violence while the silent men waited. Jon eyed them from the porch.

"Damn Stewart. What do you think the boys will do?" Sergeant Hillford asked. He stood at the steps, dusting off his U.S. issue navy-blue pants, a remnant of his former service in that Army.

"We may have a storm brewing," Jon said, nodding in the direction of the agitated men near the road.

As expected, the group of soldiers began to file through the short gate. Private Dapelton, a jumpy, but knowledgeable man, led the formation as they gathered near the porch. "Sergeant, there must be some recompense for this deed, we believe," he said.

"Just what did you have in mind?" Hillford responded, crossing his arms.

"Well, me and the men here have been discussing that, and we would like to commandeer this abode, and kick these krauts outa' here. This killing is done by a traitorous folk. We have a right to retribution!"

The other men sounded off in agreement and one said, "run'em out!"

Another, "Eye for an eye!"

Soon a crescendo of ideas and insults arose in the yard, men raised their weapons, some stomped the earth, and some did nothing, gathering in the rear. Cawley was one of them, and Lawsen, too, taking fast sips from their canteens. Martello stood with the others, but said little.

Jon observed them. Most had no impulse towards action, but in a mob, the few rule the many, and some of these men had not seen Stewart's foolish mistake. If the troops ransack the house, the mission is over, then the trust that had been built as Jon and others ate from the villagers' cupboards will be gone. Their presence was supposed to encourage enlistment and friendliness while protecting Tennessee. They did not need a wasted effort.

From inside the house, Bethanna listened from behind her door as the men made their demands to the sergeant and the young corporal. She began to sweat, and grow hot with fear. She stopped her breathing to hear the exact words from the embittered men. They were not words of friendship. Her defiant stand against the corporal—a result of sheer panic—may have been a mistake. "Now I have done us in. Foolish, foolish," she mumbled.

Mirra sat with Hertha, still tired and dizzy on the couch. Both heard the noise outside and quietly waited, acutely aware of the immediate danger.

As Jon listened, his eyes darted while he studied the protesters. A complete vision of what could happen flashed into his mind. The men would storm the house, scatter everything and take what they wanted, then, moving out to the stockyard, kill and eat the chickens and the few cows roaming the fences for tall grass. Maybe things will burn—the house and barns; a black, smoky warning to the other villagers. After that, there was the question of the woman and her two girls. His friends were not rogues, but in a vengeful frenzy the daughters may garner awful attention. Jon thought of his two sisters. He raised his hands.

"Hold, you men, stop your noise!" He moved from behind the porch rail and stood above the steps.

The complaining men grew quiet, some expecting permission to do as they wished.

"I implore you as soldiers to think about your intentions here. We have eaten well today and have friends here now. Tell me how such revenge will reflect on our names, the 11th Tennessee Regiment and that of our good commander, General James Rains? Tell me what he will think when he knows of the deeds you plan here today. I need not tell you his opinion."

The men had heard Jon talk like this before, but not in direct reference to their character, and not with such unabashed authority over them. All listened as his point became clear.

"Please brothers, my hometown friends, do nothing as you wish, for we are on Tennessee soil, and these people, although Unionists, are Tennesseans. I want to say when I am old that I defended all of Tennessee and with this valiant regiment, did renew our forefather's declaration of the first Revolutionary War. We have an honor and a duty to the entire state, and if that means that we must risk ourselves in hostile lands, then I am proud to do so."

Jon's voice softened, forcing the men in the yard to gather closer. "God knows my final hour, and when I make my last charge into the Yankee guns, or die an old grandfather, I will know that I never touched a woman's hearth with foul intent and I fulfilled my duty honorably with complete faith, charity, and utmost bravery."

Behind the door, only three feet from Jon, Bethanna looked at her mother in disbelief. Hertha's eyes grew narrow as she listened to Jon's entreaty, hoping his words struck a sensible nerve in those rebel idiots, but at the same time, she doubted they had the smarts to understand him. She motioned for Bethanna to come away from the door. This she did, and sat with her mother and sister, holding their hands.

Jon paused. The men squinted, some smiled while others scratched themselves in various places. Jon hopped off the porch and picked up his rifle, then walked up to Dapelton. "Go ahead if you must, I can't stop all of you. But here approaches the lieutenant yonder, so make up your mind, my friend, before he discovers your plot."

Jon looked on while Lieutenant Weston suddenly halted on the road and uncovered Stewart's body. He was followed soon by one of the villagers, Mr. Blatz the apple merchant, who jumped at the sight of a dead man. Both men inspected Stewart's white corpse as they whispered unheard opinions. Lieutenant Weston shook his head, disgusted. He dropped the blanket over Stewart's face and stomped through the Gurtag gate. "What are you men doing loitering here? Move out and find camp near the stream, over there." He pointed east, near where they had entered the valley.

The group broke up and filed through the gate. Sergeant Hillford berated them as they lined up on the road. "It's a shame Jonny had to make a speech like that. You'll tighten up, by God!" Hillford's eyes drilled them. "You break order, you break the unit!"

The platoon stiffened, gathered themselves in rank. No cheery banter arose among them, like when they entered the valley. Hillford heard Lieutenant Weston call him. He started for the gate, and then abruptly turned to address the quiet formation. "You men…at ease, but not too much!"

Lieutenant Weston addressed Jon and Hillford together. "Did you not hear my orders clearly? Now what kind of panic will the villagers be in? Lord only knows! We can't lose our soldiers to civilians."

"The fool disobeyed Jon outright, sir," Hillford explained. "With his impulsive nature and all, he just rushed the woman on her porch."

"We conducted ourselves in the same manner at every house, why should we risk an incident here?" said Jon, glancing at Stewart's covered body.

"I depend on you two to keep the order and discipline of the platoon when I am unavailable. Out here on detachment is when I need that reassurance the most. Now I'm dubious of it. Jon, you physically make your orders known, both of you if need be, and don't drop your station for a moment. Understood?"

Mr. Blatz approached, nervously rubbing his large belly. "I am sure that the Reverend Grottmacher will perform a proper burial for the killed man." Weston agreed, "Yes, I think a little dignity will help the men. See to it."

At twilight, with a glowing western sky, Stewart was buried with honor in the graveyard behind the meeting hall. Reverend Grottmacher put on his long black frock coat and performed the quaint but rushed ceremony in some form closest to the Baptist tradition, with a German accent.

Jon stood behind the reverend as the weight of responsibility, like two massive hands on his shoulders, pressed down with the strength of an army. Additionally, a sense of failure sank into his soul when they shoveled the dirt into Stewart's grave, now a hump of earth, with a wooden marker. Still, he did not think this death had been his fault entirely.

The men set up camp near the stream, down the grassy slope from the edge of the Gurtag property. Some pitched tents while others noted the fair weather and set their bedrolls around fresh fires. Most of them didn't need to fix evening rations. They were full enough.

Looking at the stars overhead, Jon thought of the crazy German woman and her daughter. The young girl had quite a tangle to deal with that day. He thought of her face, her strong words, and his curt reaction to them, which was more like an impulsive need to defend his character, even though he could have dismissed her, wrecked her home and her life. With a flicker of warmth in his heart, he found their tussle quite stimulating. Did he offend her? Probably. Even with the events of the day flashing in his mind, Jon fell asleep to the sound of the rushing creek.

Bethanna stood in the dark. The soldiers' campfires blinked like small candles against the dark mass of trees that surrounded them. She leaned on the fence at the far end of the property and scanned the distance, the dark void between her and the troops, thankful that there was such space between them. She, too, had seen in her mind the picture of destruction that the soldiers could bring to their home. Such treatment was common in the remote areas during the war, and so far her village had been shrewd enough to avoid the pillaging. Last fall, before Kirby Smith's brigades had arrived in the Cumberland range, the Unionists held the torch and rooted out Southern sympathizers, slaveholders, and secessionists. Now, with the Confederate Army in Knoxville guarding the railroads and passes, they asserted their reach when they could, and protected loyal citizens.

Near the border in Taldorf, the villagers were caught between two sides with relatives serving both armies. However, there was never one doubt as to the first and most important priority— the village. Bethanna knew all these things as the reverend had informed her from time to time.

When the Confederate platoon gathered in her mother's front yard, Bethanna expected the door to break down and a violent raid to ensue. To what degree she knew not, but as the corporal quieted the men, he quieted her nerves also. His voice had a tone of power without the need of harsh disrespect. She thought of his hands and how easily she had pushed them away from her mother. He surrendered that power to her. Why?

She had seen the small burial ceremony down the rise from her fence, the Reverend Grottmacher in his long, black coat, his wife holding a flickering lantern so he could read his bible. She felt sorry for the soldiers who had come into their valley of peace, only to find death; something the villagers expected the soldiers would bring. A good night's sleep may calm things down, help the men think about the corporal's words. Surely, the men will move on and avoid civilians after this bitter lesson, she hoped.

The calm of the night reassured her. The stars were out, the crickets sang and the owls hooted, and down the gentle rise from her fence, the Confederates slept around their fires. The half-moon hung low over the east ridge and peeked through trees to look at her, like God's hidden eye, blinking. A song came from her lips, talking first, then a tune.

"Guter mond, du gehst so stille,
an den abendwolken hin…"

Kindly moon, you roam so gently,
through the evening clouds.
Your friendly light is refreshing,
after the heat of the day.
Mild and friendly you look down
from the blue tent of heaven
and our songs surge upward
to the Lord of the Universe.

She was not sure how old the folk song was, only that her father learned it when he was very young. "Sing to God, and he will sing back to you," her father Vogal would say. She sang her thanks to God for lasting the day with soldiers present. The quiet night filled her ears, and she walked back to the house through the blue corn, lit by the half moon.

* * *

The early morning birds woke Jon before the sun graced the ridgeline to the east. He shuffled down to the running stream, knelt and hit his face with a shocking cold splash. A shiny streak in the water flashed by, and then another. Trout were running in the lazy current. He jumped up and ran back to his haversack, pulled out his sewing kit and cut a length of sock thread to about three feet. Searching for any kind of hooking agent, he came upon an old broken, leather necklace. Yes, perfect. The clasp had a hook shape, sizable enough for bait.

Looking in the grass under the dark shade of an oak, he found several brown grasshoppers and collected them in his hat. Within ten minutes, he'd thrown two small speckled trout onto the bank and started fishing for a third. "Biting like mad weasels." He pulled at a bite, and the fish swam away. "Damn that slicker." Then he enjoyed another bite and a catch.

The excitement helped to wake him and he reveled in the fun of the work. One man, Hobston, observed Jon's progress from his blanket and rubbed his eyes. Seeing the fish writhing on the bank, he shot upright and walked over to inspect. Without a word he went into the stream with his hat, scooping up plenty of water, but no fish. Jon chuckled as Hobston tried his best persuasion. "Come on now you filets, time for breakfast."

Jon chuckled at the futility and coaxed Hobston into taking over the line for him. "I think six is enough for me," said Jon. All the soldiers awoke to join in the morning sport. An assortment of fishing methods amused the men, from spearing with crude sticks, or netting with coats and hats. Jon laughed at Lawsen's and Martello's attempt to corral the trout into a large pack. Boys they were, still. Within the hour, everyone had a bite of fresh fish for breakfast.

The sunlight beamed bright over the trees and the familiar wind began its journey south into the valley. As Jon cleaned his mess kit, he got an idea. It was a risky thing, but out in the hills there were no hometown mothers to judge him, only a German woman and her daughters. He picked up his remaining three fish and headed for the road.

At fifteen years old, Mirra Gurtag was a small, quiet girl who had few friends in the village. There were no teens around to share the loves and frights of becoming a woman. Her older sister had been her only portal to adulthood and together they blossomed as well as they could with no admirers in their foreseeable future. Mirra's features favored her father—freckles, a strong nose, green eyes and strawberry blond hair. Like her sister and mother, she had shapely lips, high cheek bones, and slight frame.

Bethanna brushed Mirra's hair with soft strokes, humming a tune. She had dressed early for the dawn chores, wearing a tan front-laced dress with a dark blue bodice tied snug at her waist. Her hair was tied in a blue scarf, which trailed down her curvy back. Her mood was light, considering the event involving her mother yesterday.

But Hertha had recovered and awoke at sunrise feeling a strong moral reward for actually killing a "traitorous rebel." She sat in bed reading her Lutheran prayer book, falling in and out of a morning snooze.

Bethanna looked in on her mother and smiled, glad for a restful night, made possible by the stalwart corporal, whose name she had not overheard.

Hertha awoke and lifted her book to read again. Only recently, and with encouragement from Reverend Grottmacher, the church prayers became a morning habit. After her oldest child, Saul, had been killed, she refused to accept the fate of her boy and lashed out at governments, men, and all martial representations, especially God. Though the family was churched well, Bethanna saw her mother's grief turn into morose depression, a low state that even the prayer book could not readily fix.

Bethanna thought she heard a knock on the front door. She walked into the hall, then another knock, light and respectful. She looked in her mother's doorway. Hertha read and heard nothing. Again she looked back at the front door. She approached it, thinking she should check the visitor from the window. She went for the heavy brass handle and pulled it open. There stood Jon, holding up a line of fish. He hardly looked like the dusty soldier from yesterday. He wore no uniform coat or hat. A pair of blue suspenders added a civil touch over his cotton shirt, striped with a faded plaid. "Good morning, miss, I'd like to present..."

"What is this?" Bethanna interrupted.

Jon soaked in her piercing eyes and said, "Please accept this as a token of friendliness. Eh, from... the soldiers of Tennessee, of course."

"Is this a peace offering?" she asked, looking around for the other soldiers.

"Uh, actually I was thinking of a trade,"

"Oh? And what for?"

"I would love some real coffee, if you have it, with sugar, too."

"But I could catch my own fish," she said.

Her converse logic amused him. "Yes, I bet you could, but

you don't have to." Jon held the shiny batch aloft. "See, fresh."

Bethanna liked his smile. She turned to look inside. "Mother is resting, so I will check. You had better wait out here." After partly closing the door, she spun inside and hesitated, putting her hand to her head. She checked for sounds of her mother, who was audibly fumbling through her wardrobe cabinet.

She rushed to the kitchen and in a minute, returned to the door with a small measure of coffee beans and sugar wrapped in a tied rag. "I don't think it's good if my mother sees you here now. Take this." She handed him the coffee and took his fish.

Jon's eyes widened and he immediately put the bag to his nose and smelled it. "Oh, that's divine, miss!" he blurted aloud.

"Shush up, she'll hear you," she said, looking over her shoulder into the house.

Jon nodded and whispered, "Oh yeah, what's your name?"

"What? Oh, Bethanna… Gurtag."

"I'm Jon Lyhton," he whispered. "Or…J.B., whichever."

Bethanna held back a smile and then said softly, "It would be rude if I did not thank you for helping my mother yesterday, and preventing your comrades from raiding the house out of reprisal."

Jon nodded, recalling the incident. "You're quite welcome. It would be detrimental to have such things happen behind our own lines," he said, thinking the statement was rather sterile.

"Oh, and please know I am sorry for the loss of your comrade. I thought about it later, it was a terrible accident. My mother, well, she…"

Jon put his hand up. "Your kind sentiments are accepted. And welcome, after yesterday's loss."

Mirra whistled as she walked behind her sister at the door. She moved on to the kitchen. Bethanna pushed the door, eager to end the risky encounter. "I must go, goodbye, Jon." Her apprehension was evident to Jon, who tried to hide his own.

"Thank you for the trade," he said. Walking through the yard, he admired the garden once more.

Jon shut the loosely slung gate behind him and as he walked to camp, he realized that the blonde girl had a hint of the German accent in her voice. He didn't notice it the day before. It intrigued him.

"*Vas es das?*" Hertha asked, looking into the serving bowl. "Fish?"

"Yes, Mama, a gift from the soldier who helped you inside yesterday," said Bethanna, in a bright way, trying to suggest how nice it was of him.

Hertha frowned and buttered her filets. She examined her oldest daughter. "You...have seen zem today?" she asked, squinting as if the question pained her to ask it.

Bethanna served Mirra her bread and applesauce, then a few bites of fish. "Yes, he came to the door, wanting to..."

"Why do I not know this?" Hertha asked. "These men...be warned, girl!" she said, pointing her fork at Bethanna. "They are stealers." She stabbed at her fish and after sufficiently teasing it, ate a little.

Mirra looked at Bethanna and managed to contain her comment on the matter, but not her amusement at her mother.

To Mirra, the soldiers were a welcome distraction that would likely be temporary. She was growing quite curious of them, but she couldn't show it. She already knew what her mother thought. The shooting had convinced Mirra that her mother was crazy.

Bethanna looked at Hertha. She remembered that with the death of her brother, Saul, her parents had lost the gleam of pride that comes from having a son to grow the family. They lost him to a war they wanted no part in. Now the war was upon them. No longer were they spectators waiting for the show to end soon. The pain of Saul's loss drove Vogal into service for the Union as a drafting artist and engineer. His neutrality over with, he would vindicate the loss of his son through Northern victory.

But Hertha had no such outlet for her suffering. Her work on the crops and orchards kept her focused, now and then. The two sisters noticed more enmity in their mother as they grew more independent, and her temper sometimes showed in violent outbursts and constant nagging. Bethanna saw a woman who was once pretty, now given into bitterness, and the fear of losing her husband to the vile rebels.

"Today, I am to help Frau Blatz," said Bethanna, to ease the moment.

"Must you? Why not help me?" Hertha said, frowning.

"We need the apples, Mama. You should rest after yesterday, remember?"

Hertha's slow smile cracked her cheeks into more wrinkles. "Yes, child, I remember."

Mirra could not help giggling at her mother's deviant tone. Hertha giggled, too, appreciating her daughter's attentions.

Bethanna served her mother coffee, and then sat to eat Jon's catch. The young corporal had a bright mind, and a friendly way. She began to think of how she could meet him again.

* * *

VILLAGE OF TALDORF

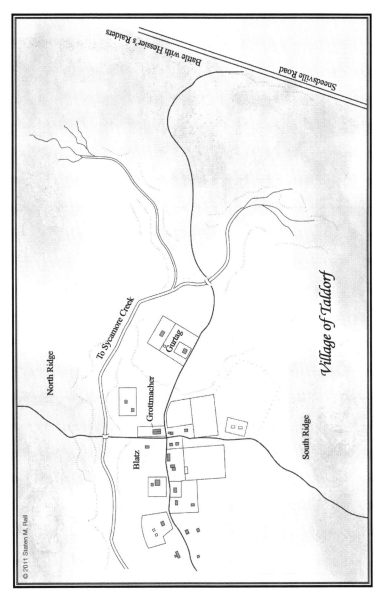

CHAPTER 10★

The east-west road through Taldorf had been hardened with stone in recent years, especially in the village where the people liked to walk on a solid base. In contrast, as the road wound between the wooded hills to the east, high grass, wild aster, and goldenrod almost completely concealed the path. The tall trees there hid the turns and dips over long intervals. Its junction with the north-south Sneedsville Road held no more importance than a walking path into the hills.

The Reverend Grottmacher described this fully to Lieutenant Weston as they sat on the steps of the meetinghouse, drinking cider from the Blatz orchards. "That's why you have remained free from depredation for so long. And what of the road here that crosses to the south, in the center of your village?" Weston asked the reverend.

Grottmacher motioned to the road. "That is our main wagon road, the easiest way out. It will take you to a farm, and then back to Howard's Quarters. There, the road appears as only a dirt side path, another hidden door, if you like. We've seen no travel on that road in some time, so you see, when you walked into our little valley… yes, we were quite surprised."

"And where does the road lead north, over the ridge there?"

"It is part of the old road to Mulberry Gap. It disappears into the shrubs long before you see Powell's Valley beyond. You have to be a few miles off the main road to find it."

"How enchanting! Truly a secret little town." Lieutenant Weston smiled at the sentiment. Thinking about his options with the roads, he rubbed his fashionable goatee. "I believe we will scout up the Sneedsville Road, then to Jonesville. Of course, we'll stay one more night, down near the stream. We have a rendezvous in a day or two, but I think one more night here and three more meals, will do the men good."

"Make sure to post guard, the blue troops have found us before. Take caution."

"That, I will certainly do." Reverend Grottmacher's suggestion made sense, presumably because he told the truth. Union troops in the hills concerned the lieutenant and he didn't waste any time debating that point of interest.

Weston's pocket watch read 8:25, time enough to start for Jonesville, easy, with a march of three miles each hour. Walking back to camp, it was plain to him that the reverend's advice came from personal experience. Lookouts were needed on the ridges north and south, overlooking the valley and beyond. From a tactical point, the temptation to scout northward around Jonesville, over the Virginia border, was too much for the lieutenant to resist. Surely, avoiding the area without proper reconnaissance fell short of his mission. He had seen no sign of the cavalry detachment Colonel Rains mentioned and figured he might meet up with them at the border.

Lieutenant Weston assigned Jon for lookout duty and pointed out the lofty ridge northwest of them as a good vantage point. "Take Cawley with you; I am marching the platoon to the border."

Jon did not question the decision, although he'd rather join the scouting team and see the sights in Virginia. To Cawley, the boring duty meant adventure, and he talked incessantly while he and Jon geared up and quickly headed for Taldorf. They passed the Gurtag property and took a wide berth from the gate, though

Jon's gaze lingered on the window to find Mirra peeking through the curtains. He waved and she waved back.

At the meetinghouse, the reverend's wife offered Jon and Cawley fluffy biscuits and a small pull of deer jerky from the cornucopia in their cellar. They thanked her profusely and she blushed as the two soldiers bowed, doffed their hats, and dedicated themselves to her service.

She pointed down the road and said, "There are very nice apples at the farm across the creek."

The encumbered lookouts walked along the fence line behind the meetinghouse, its white boards guarding the small cemetery. With more eagerness than manners, they crammed two biscuits each. Cawley spoke up with his mouth half full, "Hey, J.B. Is everyone here a kraut masher?"

"The proper title is German," Jon said, chewing.

"Ok… all of them are German?"

"Most, I suspect. I think it's quite appealing."

Cawley scratched his head. "Say, ain't that the funny language you and the lieutenant like to speak?"

Jon chuckled. "No, we're practicing French, not German."

"All sounds the same to me, just jabber-jawin', like two niggras don't know what they sayin'."

"You should work on your proper English if you wish to judge another tongue, my garrulous friend. And some blacks speak rather fine in Nashville. My father's man Marshall is well read, and Mr. Taney, the porter at the train station is an eloquent poet. He doesn't write a line of it down though. I guess he can't write, just speaks it."

"Pass the jerky," Cawley said.

Jon's mood had lightened somewhat since the disaster of Stewart's death. The fact that Lieutenant Weston had passed him over for the scouting mission was probably meant to be a lesson in trust and leadership. He was willing to learn such things, but he refused to carry the blame for Stewart's death solely, for it was not he who had disobeyed. Lieutenant Weston often said, "When you do stupid, you die stupid." Well now, Jon guessed that was really true.

They walked out of the village towards a lovely grove, and beyond, the north ridge loomed like a protective hedge. Jon noticed movement under the nearby trees. A familiar form stood under the shade of an apple tree. He knew it was Bethanna. Wearing her tan dress with blue apron, and holding a basket of yellowish-green apples, she looked like a very natural part of the land. Her hair was tied up in a blue cloth, with loose strands catching the sun like golden jewelry. The scene could have easily been cut from a European artist's masterpiece.

Even the stone and wood barn nearby held the same old country charm, as did the stone bridge across the creek ahead of them. A woman standing near the barn loaded a barrel with fruit from a hand pail.

"Stay here, Cawley, I'll see if I can obtain a few." He left the road and walked to them as Cawley hung back, eating his last biscuit.

Jon greeted the older woman, Frau Blatz. "*Guten morgen,*" he said, to her surprise.

She recognized Jon from the day before and answered with a smile and cautious wave. He approached Bethanna, caught her eyes and she smiled. Relieved at her positive reaction, he admired her smile, a memorable one. "Enjoy those trout, Miss Gurtag?" he asked.

"Yes, and thank you, sir. But honestly, I don't believe my mother was impressed."

"Why? Is she such a talent with the hook and line?"

"No, certainly not. I meant, not impressed with who caught them."

"Truly, it wasn't her I was aiming to impress."

Bethanna looked away, presumably to Frau Blatz. Jon wasn't sure if he had made her blush or not; her face was red and sweaty from work, her sleeves rolled up to her elbows. He noticed that she appeared shorter than she did yesterday when they had stood almost eye-to-eye in Hertha's house. He looked down and saw her bare feet in the grass.

Frau Blatz approached and she asked Bethanna, "Who *es… Wie heisst er?*"

In German, Bethanna introduced Jon Lyhton as a "good rebel" and told Frau Blatz about his friendly peace offering that morning. They talked a little more. Jon thought he heard something about apples and jars in the quick discourse.

"She will let you take some of these now." Bethanna handed Jon four apples and he called Cawley over to receive his, which he did and softly muttered his thanks.

"*Danke* means 'thank you'," Jon said into Cawley's ear.

Bravely, and with a gapped smile, he said, "Dunky, dunky." The two ladies could not keep from laughing. Cawley laughed too, and a bit longer than the others.

"He is a cute one, yes?" Bethanna watched Cawley take to the road again.

Jon nodded, "I guess, like a puppy he is… dumb, but loyal."

Still amused, Bethanna said, "Oh no, not too dumb I hope."

Her joy pleased Jon, as did her openness to humor. "What counts is - he's a smart soldier."

"Where are you going, Jon?" she asked.

He liked the way she said his name, strong on the "N." "We'll be up on the north ridge to keep a lookout. I'll be up there the rest of the day."

Frau Blatz walked to her barn, unpinned the doors and requested that Bethanna help her gather the apples. Inside, the many barrels were to be filled and stored, then later transported by wagons and sold in Sycamore, maybe as far as Tazewell. Bethanna stood to make 50 cents a barrel for her labor.

"Sorry, I must go now, before the midday heat rises," she said.

"All in a morning's work, Miss Gurtag," Jon said, rubbing an apple on his sleeve.

As she reached the barn door, Bethanna looked over her shoulder at Jon, who, with his happy partner crossed the stone bridge, and headed towards the wooded trail.

* * *

From the top of the ridge, Jon could hardly see the village of Taldorf below him, only glimpses of the shimmering creek remained through tall oaks and fat spruce trees. To the east, he made out the Gurtag fences and the road. From the north side, the view opened up nicely with more woods and ridges. Down below, and on the ridge adjacent, hundreds of tree stumps proved the villager's dedication to keep their veiled existence. Although a field of stumps could be suspicious, collecting their wood from other areas worked for many years, preserving their valley trees. But how fruitless it seemed now, with the armies using the area as a chessboard.

One thing Jon had noticed about the war in northeast Tennessee; the more people wanted to avoid it, the faster it came upon them. Quickly, like a flood or fire, it used up the vitality of the land. If the Union didn't seize it, then the Confederates will drink it dry just as readily. Or even worse than that, the partisan rangers, whose loyalties roamed with their saddles and to whom everyone was the enemy, will terrorize without warning or reason. Tennessee was broken up by region. Nashville, the heart of the state, had been an early victim in the year, its vital railway veins and industry choked off by the Union Army. "Occupation" was word that Tennesseans had to learn before any other Southern state.

From the summit, Jon tossed his spent apple core down the hill and it hit a large scrub oak. The noise flushed a flock of wild grouse. Cawley laughed and went running down the trail to flush more birds. "Hey, Jonny!" he yelled. "I'm gonna' scout down here anyway."

"You do that private. Good thinking!" said Jon, sitting on a large, granite outcropping and taking off his coat. Jon liked rocks and here in the east, the variety was staggering: sandstone scattered about, marble in the valley floors, granite, shale and above all, coal. Back home in the plateau areas, there was mostly gray species and clay. East of Walden's ridge and into the mountainous regions, there was black "Chattanooga marble." Jon studied the surfaces around his post and found several interesting shades of color.

Three times, Cawley came up the slope, reporting on a new fantastic discovery he'd made. "J.B, I seen a wild cat" and "Hey, I think there's a creek down there." He passed his time wisely, Jon thought.

It was not long until Jon clearly heard the sound of footsteps on the trail they had taken up the ridge. Jon ducked and looked over the boulder down towards the path. He saw Bethanna pop out of the trees and look around. She carried a small tin pail.

Jon stood, surprised and pleased it was she. He lifted his unloaded musket, aiming into the air. "Halt! Who goes there?" he shouted.

Bethanna quickly looked up to the sound of Jon's voice and smiled, trying to catch enough breath to answer him, being half-winded from the steep hike. "Just me," she managed to say. Usually, she found walking the hills not as difficult, but today she had hurried her efforts. Jon saw this, and let her rest a bit.

"Or, perhaps I'm a spy," she said, hesitating in her steps toward him.

"Huh? A spy? Just as well I'd like the company," he said, as he closely eyed her. The blue bodice or apron she had worn earlier was gone, and the blue scarf on her head, too. Then he observed that she had tied it around her waist for a nice accent. As for her long hair, it was rolled up into a neat bun in back. Her bosom rose and fell with her breathing as she stood sweating in the sun.

"But I hear tell the lady spy is the most dangerous," Jon said.

Bethanna squinted as she looked at him, his coat off, shirt loosely buttoned and sleeves rolled up, all revealing his tanned chest, forearms and hands. His humor invited her to play. "Then... you will have to watch me," she replied. Comfortable with the rebel scout, she walked over and sat next to him on the rock.

Jon watched her, investigating closer than he had earlier, awkwardly staring. "Oh, excuse my manners. Some water?" He reached for his canteen.

"Thank you. Wait, I have something better for you." Bethanna reached for her pail. "I have a gift, the most wonderful cider from Frau Blatz." Her pail contained two jars full and a brick of cured ham with pumpernickel loaves.

"My, my, more food, I'll never have it this good again." Jon popped the seal on the glass jar. "Smells delightful." He took a long drink of the cinnamon-sweet, apple cider.

"Hey, J.B.!" Cawley yelled from below. "Who ya yapping with?" He marched up the hill out of a thin tree line.

"Miss Bethanna. She's got a gift for us." Jon showed Cawley the cider jar and the happy private danced a reel before gently handling the glass, tenderly unlatching the top and sipping, fingers spread like a dandy gentleman. Bethanna smiled while the two soldiers enjoyed half of their allotments. It pleased her to repay Jon's kind deed with the fish.

Jon noticed Bethanna's enjoyment. He was enjoying her and the surprise of her. Unlike the powdered belles in Nashville, with their white gloves, petticoats and social clubs, she was real from the moment he first saw her, standing near the garden under her floppy hat, asking him a logical question. She was truly an opposite, with her sunned-pink cheeks and simple farm looks, very natural and radiant, at the same time.

Jon missed the former seclusion they had a few minutes before.

"Private Cawley?" he said. "Think you could reconnoiter the slope down to that stream, in our front here?"

Cawley paused with a swallow in his mouth and pointed to his cider.

Jon raised his glass. "You can take it with you."

Cawley swallowed hard. "Ya know I just might fill our canteens, if you want?"

"That's the spirit, soldier. In fact, take yourself a nice nap down there near the water, an after-dinner repose, if you please. That's a direct order!" Jon commanded, patting him on the back. He made sure Cawley took his portion of the ham and knew that his private would be asleep in no time.

"Yessir, boss!" Cawley said. He turned and marched down the slope with renewed agility.

"I am afraid that I have sent Cawley away with the water I was going to give you."

Bethanna reached for Jon's cider jar. "We will have to share this." Jon held it out for her and she sipped it while holding it steady.

"Does your mother have any idea where you are now?" Jon asked, the shotgun still vivid in his mind's sight.

She shook her head. "Frau Blatz wanted to make a nice gesture to you rebel scouts." She drank again.

Bethanna knew how the villagers had to placate troops from either Army. In her own way, she was doing her duty to help, and now, perhaps too much. She still remembered the way Jon had looked at her yesterday, near her garden. And at the door this morning, he had an intimate, searching gaze. Had she made a certain impression? She did not mean to gain his attention.

"Why did you send him away?" she asked, after wiping her mouth on her sleeve.

Jon chuckled, and said, "I asked you the first question."

"I don't care what mother knows," she said, surprising herself.

"No, I'm sure you don't. Not after yesterday. Is she always so strong in her admonishments?"

"She is."

"Why?"

"Well," Bethanna paused, then said, "She is going mad, I believe."

Jon laughed, but Bethanna didn't. Noticing her lack of humor, and quite serious stare, he sobered. There was flatness in her awkward statement, a plain truth. He looked into the brown cider. "Well, I'm sorry for making light of it; obviously it's hurtful to you," he said. "Truly, is that what you think?"

"It is true, you saw it yourself, and she could have shot you as easily as the other man. How funny is that?" Bethanna said, placing her hands on her hips.

"And, your gist...?" Jon said.

Bethanna shrugged, raised an eyebrow. "Then, I would be up here alone."

"Oh, right. Didn't think of that." Jon smiled—again, her logic charmed him. "You have a funny way of pitting the past against the future of your present outcome," he said.

"What?" Jon's grammatical joke confused her.

"Look, I'm glad I lived so you wouldn't have to be alone up here," he said.

"That's what I said. Can you not discover this without debate?"

"I believe I have made the discovery." Jon dipped his head, looked at her through his hair.

Bethanna reached for the glass again, her fingers brushing Jon's hand as she took a healthy sip. They looked at each other, eyes resting easily. She liked the way Jon's gray-green eyes matched the foliage around them. "Why did you send Cawley away?" she asked, the apple cider shinny on her lips.

A cloud blocked the sun for a time, and while Bethanna waited on her answer, the pair cooled off and shared occasional glances. The wind blew surprisingly calm for midday atop the ridge, which caused the heat to settle. They both hadn't really noticed until the moment when the clouds moved away and the sun broke out again over the wild land.

* * *

CHAPTER 11 ★

The Sneedsville Road appeared reliable enough, although rutty and worn in those places where it sank into the earth from years of use; its rocky base eroded by flooding. Lieutenant Weston noted that a heavy supply train of Army wagons would be delayed in certain areas unless the pioneers prepared the way in advance of the column. For his small platoon, the road was quite a relief from the overland maneuvers of the last day, and with ease they reached Sneedsville at 11a.m.

Lieutenant Weston avoided an inspection of the town, for he wanted to march as far north as the morning would allow, and have plenty of daylight for their return. They crossed the Virginia border at Mulberry Gap and proceeded north, up Powell's Valley Road.

Jonesville required a seven-mile hike from the border. The men took to the march in a serious way as they refrained from idle banter and paid close attention to their surroundings. The ground leveled out with only a few undulations topped by grassy fields and thick groves. Fingers of the river cut through the fields and irrigated the land from deep ravines, sheathed in thick under growth and old trees.

Lieutenant Weston ordered his men down into one of the ravines to rest in the deep shade and refill empty canteens before they moved any closer to Jonesville. Sgt. Hillford lit his pipe, stood on the high bank and kept an eye on the road. Private Liddel tried to play his harmonica, blowing a few notes before Lieutenant Weston's stern gaze put an end to any music. The tunes were most welcome at camp though, and Liddel tossed out the favorites from Steven Foster's folkies to the latest sentimental ballads the troops so loved.

Lawsen helped himself to Martello's Federal-style backpack and pulled out the dried fruit chips he received in Taldorf. The other men saw no need to carry the large, black leather square on their backs, but since one of them could tolerate it, they didn't hesitate to make Martello their personal pack mule. Carrying everything from flour, hardtack, ammunition and secret whisky rations, the sack was perfect for out-marches like this one. Martello received a few bites more for his labor and perhaps a few more minutes rest. The Italian-blooded twenty year-old took off the pack and shuffled up the opposite bank from the others.

As Martello relaxed and lay down to view the sky, he noticed that the trees thinned out across from him and he could see a low hill topped with maples and pine. The town lay a mile or two beyond there, as Sergeant Hillford had said. He looked at the two leaders on the other side of the wide ravine and wondered why the platoon was this far out from the brigade. The unit's isolation worried Martello, chiefly the lack of support, which was a full day's march away.

Something unusual about the sky caught Martello's gaze. A thin dark cloud had appeared, tapering south with the wind, then a thicker trace, billowing up behind the tree-topped hill. "Black smoke?" he mumbled.

Before he could stand and shout alarm, Lieutenant Weston and Sgt. Hillford scampered down into the ravine. They had seen it too, and within seconds, Weston had a plan. "Sergeant, take three men with you, stay in the woods to your right. That hill there beyond should afford you a capital view of the action. Come back as quickly as you can."

Sgt. Hillford took Lawsen, Hochkis and Dapelton out of the ravine and into the woods, almost a 150-yard run. The others bantered about, asking more questions than could have logically been answered by any man at one time. Liddel pulled a double plug and chewed nervously, forgot to spit, and let the juice run down his chin, which made the others nauseous.

Lieutenant Weston found it hard to think with all of the chatter, but soon gained the presence of mind to quiet the men. They waited impatiently for the group to return with news that they hoped was the least threatening kind: a barn fire, old cornrows alight, a massive hog toasting, anything of non-importance.

Seventeen anxious minutes later, the scouts bounded out of the trees and ran across the field. They jumped into the ravine and Lieutenant Weston's inquiry was buried amid the men's hurried and crowded questions. He quieted the din with an uplifted arm.

Sergeant Hillford reported, "It's not Jonesville, sir, we're about three miles from the town, but a large plantation is burning. The stables are on fire, horses being run out and stolen. We met one of the slaves hiding his family in the trees, and he said the men who did this ain't Union regulars, but a partisan raid by a band called the Black Feathers, or Ravens, probably out of Kentucky. Most ornery sons'a bitches, I recon, by the racket. What they're doing in Virginia I can't say, unless they're clearing the way for someone."

"Main body?" Lieutenant Weston guessed.

"Could be." Hillford shrugged. "The slave also said that the raiders hit Jonesville earlier this morning. Most likely they're out to deprive the region of anything useful. I don't see a large column. It could be a reprisal raid, a blow for a blow. Out here, who knows what's going on?"

Lieutenant Weston nodded, "Yes well, I think we'll stay out of their scuffle. And I'd like to see our friends in the 3rd Cavalry about now. Their company must have reached Sneedsville and circled around to the east, leaving us vulnerable in the front - unwittingly, of course."

The troops took to the road with a jog, and after two miles, rested under the cover of trees. Lieutenant Weston realized his vulnerabilities and posted a forward point man and a rear guard to hike sixty yards behind the small unit to eliminate total surprise. Private Liddel protested the duty.

"All the way back there?" he said, pointing towards the rear. "No one's even gonna be able to hear me yellen'. I'll be bushwhacked nice and quiet-like."

Lieutenant Weston bristled. "Look, Nathan, give me your mess." Liddel gave him his small tin plate fold out. "Take your bayonet and beat it as hard as you can, then we'll hear you." Liddel happily agreed as he beat the signal loudly into the lieutenant's ear.

"Wait, boy! Wait until you see someone. Understand?"

In a quiet hurry, the platoon marched into the late afternoon, up into the higher lands and back towards the secure valley.

* * *

Cawley approached the pond that looked so small from the top of the hill, and uncorked the canteens. The work required no rush, so he knelt down lazily and plopped a canteen into the cool mountain water. Taking a look at the new terrain, he noticed the creek had been dammed to create the pond. "Thanks, brother beaver!" he remarked. He filled Jon's canteen and started his own, and then he saw a familiar thing in an odd place. It looked like a boot stuck in the mud, down on the waterline not seven feet from him. Surely, upon closer examination, a horseman's boot no less. "Cavalryman!" he exclaimed.

It was a strange thing to find so far from the village. He searched the local shrubs to see if there was a match for it, careful to poke for snakes with his rifle. He didn't find anything near. "Damn, that would be a fool's chance." he mumbled. "Two long boots fer free." The boot was damaged anyway, with its sole broken.

The novelty occupied him for some time while he ate his new ration of cured ham and fresh cider under the shade of an elm. He thought about casing the area for other treasures perhaps more useful or valuable, but the yawns crept up on him and his body called for sleep. The mystery would have to wait an hour or two. Besides, he was under direct orders.

* * *

In the shade, Bethanna's skin cooled and regained its natural tones, while the renewed breeze dried the perspiration on her head and arms. She watched Jon finish his ham as he leaned his back against a large oak, his legs crossed and cozy. To her, it was funny how the joy of food turned the soldiers into relaxed, normal young men.

Jon didn't say much while he ate, he wanted to listen. Bethanna sat across from him and spoke of her family, its history and how the three Gurtag siblings had traveled on a ship to America in 1843, leaving family behind in the old country of Bavaria. Her uncle Hinchel, the oldest, had moved from Pittsburg to Knoxville in 1845, taking his wife and two young sons. Her father, Vogal, had done the same a few years later, but stayed in Taldorf after overseeing the laying of improved roads and upgrading many of the houses. Finding the village welcome and peaceful, he built a house for his growing family. "I was born soon after the house was finished," she added.

"There is Aunt Mirrasane, papa's little sister, who learned English in Baltimore, and journeyed west to work for Uncle Hinchel at his inn. She did not stay a year in Knoxville before she married a horse rancher from Tullahoma, Tennessee, who was only in town to sell his dead brother's livery stables. They have two children now. My father says I have grown up to look like her, but sadly, the last time I saw her was before the war, when the family traveled down to Knoxville for a reunion. It was a tense celebration due to politics and the expected hostilities. Also, Hinchel's two sons chose the Confederate side, enlisting last spring. I'll never understand why they did that. One of them, Carl, married last year, but I had not heard news of either one being in a battle. Carl I have not seen in two years. I know he was a responsible young man, always supporting his parents in any way. He went to the veterinarian school in Louisville for a time."

Bethanna smiled in fond memory. "Stephan, the older brother, is so much trouble, an adventurer, leaving and coming home again. He is so handsome and caring, and always worrying his parents."

"Sounds like half the boys in the regiment," Jon said.

Bethanna laughed. "Yes, just like them. I remember he used to play with Mirra and me, push us in the swing and run us tired. Then he would leave suddenly and I would be sad."

"Didn't you have other friends here in the village?" Jon asked.

"Yes, but Stephan was a hero to us, and I loved showing him off to the older girls. He shared stories about a large world—his world—outside the valley, and promised me one day I would see it."

"It's a large world, even in this state. Where have you traveled, how far?" Jon asked.

"Only those towns where the family lives, of course, and east to Rogersville, where there are rails for transport. I have gone with my father on his surveying errands, but not since the fighting started."

"Do you ever want to go to Germany, *Fraulein Gurtag*?" Jon thickened his accent.

She reeled a bit at the notion. "I don't know, I've never thought on it seriously.

I know it is beautiful, but there is no chance of it, at present. It is strange that you know some German. You have very good pronunciation."

"Thanks, I learned from reading language books. My father was a teacher for some time, and from that, he created quite a library; German books aplenty. Say, you have enough relatives in Germany to stay a while, I would guess."

"Surely, but my father left it for good reason, no telling what it is like now, better, perhaps worse," she said.

"Well, that's all right, cause there's nothing like the great United... well, Confederate States of America!" Jon shouted.

Bethanna laughed. Her brightness touched a space in Jon's soul, a spot starving for the feminine warmth. *Oh, if the platoon could stay here all summer*, he thought. Jon tried again with her mother. "Why is your mother the way she is, so rough, and what was it that happened to your brother?"

Bethanna's face changed. It seemed a sour subject, but she was clearly going to speak on it. "Well, my mother makes it sound very cruel, like Saul was taken away and forced to fight for the South, but it is not like that. He wanted to join the Army, like father had done in his youth. He ran off with other men from the county, joined the fighting in Kentucky, and died there in a great battle. We never will now what his fate was, or what side he fought for, there are no records anywhere. Father has been looking because there are Kentucky units for both sides."

Jon's eyes expressed a sympathetic stare. "I am so terribly sorry. Such a loss is truly the worst kind. Forgive my intrusion."

Bethanna shook her head. "No, forgive my mother; she suffers a pain of losing a son. She is very strange lately, as you have seen. No more sad talk, please?" she asked.

Jon nodded, sure that Bethanna suffered no less. "No more sad talk, my lady."

"Jon?"

"Yes."

"Why did you send Mr. Cawley away?"

That question again. He knew the answer, but should she know? Jon looked out over the land below, then at the dark clouds over the northern range. He investigated their nature and direction. "It's only the safer thing to do, have us spread out like this. Two men can see more this way, that's all," he said.

Bethanna rolled her eyes and her head sank a bit. Her arms rested on her knees as she sat, and her hands came up to support her face. Her eyes met Jon's.

"If I am to stay here, please be honest with me," she said.

Jon took the last of the cider, a grainy but sweet taste. He gulped, wiped his lips and nodded. "Very well, I won't pretend that I'm not being selfish with you. There, that's honest."

Bethanna tried to tame her joy at his statement, but she could not hide the warmth in her eyes. "I appreciate that." A little smile graced her lips for a few seconds. She searched Jon's eyes, tested his feelings and found pleasure in his gaze, but did not linger too long there.

Jon regretted his attempt at misdirection, and knew it had come from being in the company of teasing soldiers. He had told her the truth she wanted to hear. How refreshing, he thought. Jon looked at his bedroll and got an idea he hoped not too daring. He beaconed with his hand. "Come sit with me."

He untied the wool double-weave and spread it for their backs to rest against. Bethanna got up and waited, unsure, then with a growing trust, sat next to him, leaning against the strong oak, glad to have a soft place to rest. Her mother would burn her alive if she saw this, but she quickly spurned the thought.

Jon dragged his coat over and pulled out a book. "I'd like to read when there is a quiet time like this. Do you like poetry?"

"Yes, but sometimes I cannot make sense of it, and I don't read such things around mother. The sentimental words she does not abide well."

"Too bad, it's about the only sentiment that I can abide."

Jon fingered the pages of the eel skin-bound copy of *Great English Poets; Selected Works,* and looked for the right mood, emotive but dramatic, nothing too flowery. "Ah, the reliable Tennyson," he said, flipping the pages to a familiar title.

"Let me take you away to a time long ago with a rapturous tale of a beautiful lady in the days of the chivalrous knights...The Lady of Shalott."

Jon's voice wrapped around the words with the rhythm and timbre of a well-practiced reader, illuminating the story as if he had seen it himself.

Bethanna closed her eyes as the scenes formed in her head. She passed through the bright environs of Camelot, where a lonely maiden is kept mysteriously away from the world on the river isle of Shalott. The images overcame her and she became more engrossed with every passing rhyme.

"That's part one," Jon said. "There are three more, still interested?"

"She's a fairy?" Bethanna asked.

"No, but the people are not sure. They hear her song, so the reapers have dubbed her The Fairy Lady of Shalott. Get it?"

"Yes, continue. You read very well, Jon," Bethanna replied. She turned sideways and leaned her head against the tree to look at him while he read. His sandy hair hung low over his forehead in a heavy shock, which accentuated his strait nose. She watched his lips as he continued the story. Again, she closed her eyes to imagine.

It wasn't too difficult, after a few verses, for Bethanna to pity the maiden who lived to weave a colorful cloth, cursed forever only to gaze at the outside world through a mirror that hung before her.

As the scenes of life around great Camelot passed her by, she was neither a participant nor a true witness, for she could see only a reflection of its true charm.

Thus for Bethanna, as she lived in the secure valley, walled in from the world, she has truly been "embowered" herself. Now as a young woman, she yearned for more than a passing glimpse. With her father gone, the family weave was unraveling quickly and she could not prevent it, or her mother's role in its separation.

The tale turned when Sir Lancelot rode along the way to Camelot and the princely description of this shining knight overruled her connective thoughts. From line to line, the image grew of a handsome rider, bedecked in the glowing armor of olden times, bright with the sun's reflections. She instantly thought of Jon in this role and his form did not easily occupy the grander. She laughed softly.

"What?" Jon said, halting his recount. "What's funny? Lancelot isn't funny!"

"I know." Bethanna quieted. "I'm sorry, could you please read that part again?"

She hid a yawn from him, a drowsy one, not one from boredom. She was relaxed in a way that lately had become rare, because of her unpredictable mother.

Jon resumed his narrative at the beginning of part three. By the time he had started part four, Bethanna's head gently touched his shoulder. She was sleeping.

Jon stole a look at her. He noticed in her hair, strands of red and brown mixed in with the blonde. Only this close could he see it. He continued anyway, assured that somewhere in there, she was listening.

The day passed into dreams and soon Jon himself fell victim of the still surroundings as his head came to rest near hers. A cool breeze enriched the lazy day, supplanting the heat that had created the weariness in the pair.

* * *

Down the Sneedsville road, a few miles from where the dreamers lay under their oak, 17 horsemen cleared a hemlock grove just north of Lieutenant Weston's small file of troops, marching their way over a short rise. Animated by the fresh plantation raid, the brown-hat riders did not mind hunting a detached patrol in open country, and thanks to secret local informants, the rebels had been easily tracked. The leader, dark-bearded, tall in the saddle, pulled a brass tube from a leather case. He snapped it open and inside its little circular frame, silhouetted perfectly against the sky, he saw a lone figure. He had to sweep his view back again, because it looked as though the man was playing a harmonica.

"Confederate infantry isolated, too," the leader said.

A younger man chimed in, staying his eager blood bay stallion. "Captain Hessier, can we get 'em?"

"Soon, boy. Let's see where they lead us." The captain cased his telescopic tube and in seconds, the riders headed slowly for the tree line, out of sight from the trailing guard. They halted a short time to load pistols and shotguns, or sharpen long Bowie knives and hatchets. A whiskey bottle was passed between them, a prize taken from the saloon in Jonesville. In a routine they were long used to, more stolen items, saddles, guns, and boots were dropped in a pile for them to retrieve later.

The unit sported the dark brown western-style hat with a wide brim, and in the hatband, each man tucked a black feather from a raven's wing, a brazen badge of pride and signal to their enemies. Another trademark—a pair of nervous hounds whimpered and jumped, eager to lead the horses on a chase.

A darkening shadow passed over the valley as gray and purple storm clouds formed in soldier-like rows, their charge announced by the drums and bugles of distant thunder. Nature prepared the setting and the men would act out their roles in the history of the day.

* * *

A sharp thunderclap boomed across the sky and Jon jerked into consciousness. His startled movements awoke Bethanna. They gawked in silence at the low clouds hanging just above them. The wind blew heavy with moisture. "You'd better start home now! You may beat the worst of it!" Jon arose and helped Bethanna to her feet.

A rifle shot rang out below them, echoing off the low sky. Both of them looked at each other and paused, then instantly, they ran to view the darkened plain below and saw a puff of smoke being carried in the wind, like a runaway balloon.

Cawley stood on the far side of the pond, in the open, waving his hat in frantic circles.

"Something is wrong. What is he shooting at? You two can't stay out here!" Bethanna said as she grabbed Jon's arm.

They both hesitated while the thunder rolled in a long, deep roar. "Go please, the sooner the better. Cawley is signaling me; I have to answer his alarm," Jon said.

Bethanna's frightened eyes searched Jon's; they showed no fear, only concern.

Such a day has to end like this? she thought, giving his arm an endearing squeeze.

Jon collected his rifle, hat and coat, and bolted down the hill.

A heavy, cold raindrop hit Bethanna's face, and she removed her scarf from her waist and tied it over her head. She noticed Jon's maroon bedroll and when she picked it up his poetry book fell

134

to the ground. She quickly retrieved it and rolled the book up in the blanket. She jogged for the path, stopped, and could not help turning to look at Jon on his way down the slope.

When he reached Cawley, the private talked so fast that Jon had to pull rank just to get a discernible word. "Yes sir, J.B, this is it… see, I was sleeping, then, I awoke, and well, before that I found this here boot." He pointed to it lying in the grass. "But, I thought nothin' of it, so I slept. When I woke up, I wanted the other boot, cause' there's always two. I looked across the pond and, oh God, what I found. Come on." They both ran towards the tree line near the creek.

The sight of the dead bodies sent Jon back a step. He yelled, "Jesus, damn!" His stomach wrenched at the malodorous whiff on the wind. It was not as strong as it could have been for these men had been dead a good long time, three of them, dried out and well decayed. Jon regained his stamina and studied the corpses with Cawley.

Gray coats, yellow piping on the collar and sleeves, they were Confederate cavalrymen sure enough, laid out in a row. There were no weapons or boots. A thin covering of leafy dirt proved too weak to conceal them for any long period of time.

Jon thought aloud, "Looks like there was no real attempt to bury them. Someone didn't care to take the time. I wonder what they're doing out here, abandoned?"

Cawley grew animated. "Ain't fair, they bein'out in the open! Damn, looks like everything that could, had a bite of 'em. Is this what it comes to?" Releasing nervous energy, he stamped the ground with his heels, ignorant of the tears that flowed down his cheeks.

The rain increased and pelted the worm-holed coats and wetted the hair, giving the corpses a slick, dark hue. On one of their collars, Jon noticed the rank, one bar denoting a second lieutenant. He lay on his side and his decayed fingers clinched a small book with brown, weathered pages. Jon knelt and fought the stiff fingers until the book slipped out. It was a New Testament. He thumbed the pages, allowing the rotten edges to release in the wind. In the flyleaf, he read words written in a female hand,

> *To my darling Carl Fitz,*
> *My dear husband, may the words of our Lord give you peace*
> *in this time of war.*
> *Your loving and faithful bride, Darlene*

"She may never know she is a widow. Cawley, we have to see if they have any name tags or identifying effects." He closed the bible and his voice became reverential. "This is not what should become of our men."

With sticks poking and lifting, they combed over the corpses as best they could, audibly repulsed at their task. "This is stinky work, J.B." Cawley said, holding his nose.

"Yes, I know. Seems the more we disturb them, the worse they smell."

They found only one tin-stamp plate and the testament for naming two of the dead; the other would remain unknown. Jon looked over the officer again and saw a disturbing mark, a small bullet hole in the back of the corpse's head near the ear. It was either, a great pistol shot from distance, or an easy one, execution-style. Ignoring the foulness, he inspected the others. Both had been shot in the head at close range, easy to see by black powder burns in the hair. Jon reared back and stood, shaken by the evidence.

"We have no diggin' tools, J.B.!" Cawley yelled, competing with the thunder.

"We'll have to come back! Bring the reverend, do it properly!" Jon shouted.

They turned to leave, heads bowed against the rain, now a steady wind spray. They walked a few yards and the sudden form of Bethanna stopped them both. She stood shocked, a hand over her mouth, she had seen the bodies.

* * *

Chapter 12 ★

Along the Sneedsville Road, Lieutenant Weston's Confederates had almost reached the hidden path back to Taldorf. A hundred yards before the trail, the hard road sank into the earth and a high embankment stood to their right, covered in shrub and rock.

Lieutenant Weston ordered Martello to collect Liddel, walking behind them. "The rain is getting heavy and it's not good to have a man where you can't see him," he had said.

Martello jogged only a few paces when shots rang out, echoing off the hills. Lieutenant Weston and his men jerked around to see Liddel drop like a sack. Martello wasn't sure who had fallen. He stared while the horsemen galloped over the body and began to fire at him and the stunned group. Few of the muskets were loaded and men scrambled for their ammo.

Lieutenant Weston pulled his cap and ball Colt and aimed patiently. The nearest rider unsheathed a sword and made for Martello, who turned and ran for cover into the sunken part of the road. Weston fired, hitting the man's horse. The beast faltered and turned out of the action, for the moment.

Captain Hessier had followed the rebels for an hour or so and wanted to attack the small column clear of the hills, but the storm forced his hand. To the joy of his men, he reluctantly ordered, "Hell, better get 'em while we can still see 'em."

Seven riders had been ordered to take the road while Captain Hessier led the other half through a wooded trace parallel to it. His team came thundering across a clearing from the east of Weston's position. Lawsen saw them and shouted a warning. The lieutenant fired in that direction with no discernible result. Two muskets fired from the road, one horseman fell away from Captain Hessier's line, now spreading out to envelop the platoon.

Hochkis and Dapelton began loading at the first sounds of gunfire and sounded off that they were ready. Weston shouted, "Make for the rocks up the slope and find enough cover to fight from. We'll cover you!"

The gray troops scrambled up the hillside and the three loaded guns boomed from the sunken area. Dapelton fired up the road, sending a man sliding off his horse to the ground.

Hochkis aimed at the group coming out of the trees, and was shocked to see two dogs leading the formation. He wasted only a second on the oddity and fired, missing high.

Lieutenant Weston took a shot in both directions and saw nothing beyond the gun smoke. He hurried up the slope with the other two, while the raiders' pistols opened up on them.

The horsemen reached the sunken road and fired up the hill at the fleeing Confederates. Two privates went down, Hochkis and Daniel, both wounded and crawling. Daniel cried out, "I'm shot, I'm shot!"

Captain Hessier ordered his men to dismount, their advantage on horseback eliminated by the terrain. Horse holders removed the animals to the trees beyond the grassy field. This necessity reduced Hessier's force by five men. Moving into the sunken road, he observed that it worked well as a natural trench and as the blue troopers took cover, they shot intermittently at the rebs who now occupied the higher ground. Thunder blended with gunfire, as both sounds echoed off the hill and out into the plain. The rain came stronger, blowing into faces and across gun sights. The platoon from D Company, 11th Tennessee regiment, struggled to load and fire their weapons, on a craggy hill, under a pounding rain.

* * *

Forced by the harder rainfall, Jon, Bethanna, and Private Cawley ran up the slope and found the trail down into the Taldorf Valley. The heavier woods shielded them somewhat from the slashing effects of the sheeting rain. Trees swayed in the gusts, forcing long branches to reach out and snag the two soldiers and the girl running down the narrow way. They reached the north road, crossed the stone bridge to the Blatz orchards where Bethanna led them to the brick and wood barn. She knocked a wooden pin from the door and they entered an organized room stacked with barrels and baskets, along with tools and wheelbarrows. The three caught their breaths, shivered in wet clothes and remained quiet.

Bethanna looked at Jon's silhouette at the doorway as the rain fell in torrents only a few feet from his body. Without a doubt, she would tell him what she knew; he and Cawley both deserved it. Upon seeing the dead bodies, she had discovered a horrid truth and to share that truth meant to hurt the village. She began to cry in a quiet way, as if she wanted to hide it, but could not.

Jon heard the faint expressions of sadness and turned to see Bethanna wiping her face. He gave a look to Cawley, who shrugged his shoulders.

"I'm sorry you saw the dead men, but you seemed determined to. Why?" Jon asked.

Bethanna forced back her sobs and took in a breath. "Because I saw them when they were alive, here in the village."

Both soldiers stared at her, knowing she would continue.

She breathed steadily and calmed her voice. "The three gray coats rode in one night and took supplies from Herr Dansell's store. Then a day later, they were captured on the southern road by the partisan rangers. They tied the prisoners behind one of their mules, and dragged them through the village. This I did see, from the small loft here, hidden as I was by Frau Blatz. They took away the gray coat men with tall boots, but to prison, I thought. We heard no shots. I am not sure, but it is thought that they were given up by someone in the village." At this last statement, her voice broke, shaken as she was by the decayed bodies.

The two men said nothing as Jon thought about Bethanna's story, the village, the raiders and their prisoners. He pictured the vivid pistol holes in the corpses' heads and the dark woods around them, hiding such vicious actions. There had been plenty of time for a villager to report the platoon as well.

"When did this happen?" Jon asked.

"Late May, I believe," she said.

"We have to go tell the lieutenant," Cawley said quietly.

"Yeah, they should be getting back soon." Jon hesitated to speak further. Questions came to his mind that he did not want to force on her now. He trusted what she said was the truth, but it was an old truth and they had come upon it very late.

"Please stay," Bethanna said, drying her eyes.

Jon walked to her. "You are safe here on the Frau's land," he said. "But we have to warn our comrades. The village may become dangerous for us, too." Jon touched her head gently, letting his fingers brush the soft skin of her cheek. He turned away and signaled Cawley with a nod.

The two soldiers left her alone in the dark room, under the pressing storm. She had heard the suspicion in Jon's tone and it hurt. He may never trust her as he did on the ridge, where they had slept against the tree. Why did she not take his hand, hold it, and tell him to hide with her? She looked down and saw that Jon had forgotten his bedroll. She picked it up and held it close, felt the book inside, then realized that she had not heard the ending to Tennyson's poem.

* * *

It is known, on a clear day especially when the wind is calm, gunfire can be heard from local hunting, echoing down the stream, off the hills, or even carried on the breezes. Or, in contrast, the sound of guns can easily be redirected by hard valley winds and thick walls of trees. Jon and Cawley heard no gunfire from the Sneedsville Road when they arrived at their camp near the stream.

They found Rossberger, who was supposed to be guarding the southern road, but the storm forced him into his tent for a nap. Earlier that morning, he had a villager, Herr Dansell, shave his face at his small trading post, and Jon and Cawley barely knew him. They crammed into the tiny shelter, which leaked at the seams. "Hey, Rossy, you look real nice," Cawley beamed.

Rossberger touched his chin. "Thank ya. Had to clean it off; too many critters in it."

Before Jon could tell him of the dead cavalrymen, a head popped into their gathering through the tent flaps. It was Lawsen, dripping wet and gasping for air. "Yank raiders! We need every man we got, shooting's started!"

The three nearly pulled the tent down as they tried to exit in a bunch. Jogging for the road, they crossed the eastern stone bridge and entered the dark, dripping forest. The half-mile soggy trail led to a grassy rise where they first spotted the village. Lawsen led them off the path and down through a deep pinch between the hills. As they cleared the hollow, gunfire reverberated overhead, echoing amid the pelting rain. With an all-out effort, the three soldiers climbed a steep, slippery hill, crested a high smooth summit and landed under a thick oak. Sheltered for the moment, they caught their breaths and primed their weapons.

White smoke floated over Jon from down the hill as shots rang out with stark, jolting volume. Jon heard a peculiar cracking sound nearby and looked around to see a large chunk of bark exploding off a nearby tree. Bullets were flying, overshot and random. The three soldiers spread out and began their rush down the slope, zig-zagging around trees, shrubs and rocks.

Through the rain, Jon saw little of the action as he tripped repeatedly over natural obstacles, keeping himself low. Squatting down near a tree, he spotted the platoon's order of deployment, which was nothing orderly.

Recognizing the sharp report of Lieutenant Weston's pistol, Jon was able to glimpse his location near a line of large mossy stones. The platoon was spread out, firing whenever they found a target. Sergeant Hillford shouted orders on the far left and the enemy fired his way.

Jon imagined there to be more Yanks, judging from the noise. As he saw them pop up and fire, then disappear behind the white smoke, he counted nine. Wanting to help his friends with a clear line of fire, he darted down the slope and crouched behind a thin pine. This would not do. At the next lull in the shooting, he jumped down to the lieutenant's rock line.

Martello was a few feet over from them and shouted his welcome. "Reinforcements at last, has the regiment arrived with you?" he asked.

Jon caught his breath and answered. "In spirit, my friend!"

Lieutenant Weston could only hope. He had lost three men already, one presumed killed, laying in the muddy road. The two wounded men had crawled to safety evidenced by their woeful cries of pain. One Yank had been felled by the first volley from his men, but he lost track of how many they may have shot after that. Keeping score in the loose mayhem of combat struck him as foolish. He stopped the useless analysis and began to shoot.

Jon lifted the small, hinged sight of his Austrian-made Lorenz .54 caliber and aimed down the blued barrel through the driving rain. He could see the brown hats clumped together under the grassy ledge, their rifle and pistol muzzles hovered as they anticipated a clear shot. More hats popped up from the right and he aimed for those, held his breath, and pulled the trigger.

The blast infused him with energy, as had other shots, but this fight was not the distant and timid skirmishes he encountered earlier at the Gap. This was face to face, or as much face as the participants would allow to be exposed, almost like a duel.

Martello's older musketoon flintlock refit boomed out its opinion of the situation as did Rossberger's 1851 Mississippi rifle, the prettiest gun in the outfit. From the top of the hill, Lawsen fired his over-under double barrel shot gun. His scatter-shot ammo was limited, so he had to pick targets at great discrimination. The variety of weaponry used by the platoon had always humored Jon. Now, it was strange to hear them fire in sequence. The clear uniformity of the raiders' weapons impressed him. He cursed quietly under his soggy hat, "Damn it." *Even these louses have better arms and ammo.*

Bullets slapped the stones guarding Jon and his platoon. The raiders used their pistols waterproofed with grease, throwing many shots in a short amount of time. For the Confederates, the rain hampered their reloads, having to expose dry paper cartridges. Jon dropped one, the load made useless in a few seconds. He shoved himself into the rock for cover, his hat folding down to one side. The rain poured into his collar from his hat brim, but did not bother him much compared to the careening bullets cutting the wet air around him like many sabers swooshing by.

For some reason, he thought of a random quote from Lieutenant Weston. "There is a feeling that accompanies this danger, this personal intrusion by another to seek your death with a shot of lead. A feeling of smallness."

Acute was the feeling when this moment of truth reached Jon Lyhton. It wasn't so much as fear, but sadness at the lack of control over his very existence. He figured he and the enemy can call it even now and being that they both had been given a fair chance at arms, should depart this brave and marked place of battle. But, alas, the enemy stayed, firing more rounds up the slope with no new successes at dislodging the Confederates. Jon became more angry than afraid, which relieved him.

Captain Hessier looked up and down the natural trench and saw the location of the sunken road becoming more perilous as the fight continued. The rebels easily pinned the riders down from their high rocky fort, and quickly reacted to any flanking movement faster than he could carry it out.

His men sloshed through four inches of running water and tried to fire accurately in the drenching rain, their pistols almost run out. One of his men lay dead, shot through the brain when he stood to squeeze off a round. Three men were on the ground in agony from their head and neck wounds, their blood carried down the road by the rushing water. Captain Hessier cursed the enemy rain as he switched his pistol's empty cylinder out for a full one.

Jon heaved his rifle over the rock and searched the trench. He saw a man darting about, shouting as he held a pistol, he could almost hear him and see the words, "Lay low and wait for a good turn." He measured the distance to the road at forty yards or more, but it may as well have been one hundred with the water blur in his sights. Jon shot at him, and did not take time to hover his head out in the open to see the result. A lightning bolt shrieked down above the battle and blasted the hillside with a blinding flash. The affect was disquieting and the gunfire stopped for a moment. This happened more often as the heart of the storm passed over the embattled troops.

Lawsen had observed the fight from the low branches of a short, fat scrub oak and saw three Yanks scamper into the field to their rear. He had a perfect pigeon's eye view of them and dropped his sights on one of the men and fired. The gun smoke hung in front of him, concealing the sure hit from his vision. He held his breath in anticipation. The raider was down and crawling for his life.

To the Bluecoats covering the retreat from the road, Lawsen's gun smoke hung like a still target, high and white. Two raiders fired into it, as did Captain Hessier with his pistol.

Lieutenant Weston ducked at the volley then looked down to see the Yanks running to their horses, held by troopers near the trees. More raiders carried their wounded comrades out of the sunken road, and with that action, the fight was done.

More shots boomed from the rocky hillside and Lieutenant Weston shouted, "Cease firing! Cease firing! Save your rounds!"

The platoon watched quietly as the blue troopers mounted up and rode off into the grove from which they came. Their hounds barked out a final curse at the victorious rebs, and turned to follow. No one moved until Lieutenant Weston stood and ordered them up the hill into the cover of the larger trees. "Get our wounded first," he emphasized.

Jon reached a group of men helping Private Sheldon Daniel. A bullet had shattered his wooden drum canteen and sent the splintered pieces into him. Luckily, the round had been stopped, but his wound promised to be complicated and for a long time, painful.

Hochkis was shot though the upper side, near the armpit, the pistol ball breaking a high rib. He could walk, but could not lie down to ease pressure, or his bleeding increased.

Lawsen awoke after being knocked out of his tree. Wood splinters had cut his neck and his hat was shot in two places. He laughed as he put his fingers through the holes. Lieutenant Weston greeted him with a terse comment. "You're lucky, tree climber."

Some men wanted to retrieve Liddel. Weston said no, then after a moment's thought, he noticed the rain had lightened. "The raiders may come back with greater numbers and by then it would be too late to get him. I'll do it," he said, gesturing to himself. "I'm the one who assigned him the post."

No one argued the point. Lieutenant Weston chose Martello to help him and they jogged down the wet road towards the body. When they reached him, Liddel lay face down with his bayonet in his right hand, and under him, blood ran in washed-out rivulets. The tin mess plate lay in the road, crushed by a heavy hoof. Lieutenant Weston picked up the boy's harmonica and put it in his coat. He knelt and touched the muddy head of hair. "Damn my mind," he mumbled. Martello recited a Catholic prayer before they lifted him up and carried him back to the hillside bastion.

The troops on the hill watched the sad procession in quiet, fixed thought. The stark vision of the two men carrying the limp boy through the drizzle caught them emotionally and stifled the rising joy of victory. Today, they suffered real casualties, one dead, one of *them*. They had carried him half way up the hill when Jon left the trees to help them. He lifted one of the dead legs, a weight with no tension, equal to a side of beef, but dressed in a boy's body, a friend's face. When they laid him down, bloody and wet, the men gathered around saying nothing.

Without shyness, Martello prayed again over the body, an example to the others that they should not ignore the chance to eulogize.

Lieutenant Weston cradled the boy's head in his arm as he sat with him under the low, dripping branches. With patience, he wiped the dirt from Liddel's face and mouth and took the time to comb his wet hair back into attractive shape. "I'm sorry I left you back there, you were brave to do it, brave, my boy," he said.

At this, some of the men wept or turned away. Jon gaped in shock as tears marked his powder-black cheeks with lines.

Cawley cried, as expected, because the men knew he cried at everything; happy, sad, didn't matter. Poor Liddel never had a chance to defend himself. Jon swore that he, nor anyone else, would be put in that situation on his orders.

The rain abated within half an hour and the men began to move about the area to take account of the action. Two of the enemy had been killed and lay on the road. Jon and Cawley dragged them to the adjacent field, knowing that their friends would be back for them soon enough, or perhaps not, due to the horsemen's roving nature. The two friends shared a look as they stood over the dead Bluecoats. Both recalled the three dead, rotted cavalrymen near the pond.

At a slow and careful pace, the platoon carried their casualties down the winding trail, through the muddy and pitted puddles back to Taldorf.

* * *

CHAPTER 13★

The creek ran with unfettered speed due to the previous hard rain. Fresh and cool, the racing water eased such chores as cleaning crockery and rinsing laundry. Bethanna dipped her laundered dress into the current and watched the soapy fabric clear. She did the same to the other garments in her straw hamper, one of them, Jon's bedroll she picked up yesterday. The mites were a soldier's closest friends, and she used plenty of salt and boiling water to wash them out.

The platoon did not return from their patrols yesterday, and she noticed that the thin smoke was not present above the soldier's camp this clear morning. Bethanna grew anxious about their sudden absence. Most of the night, she had thought about the dead men, abandoned near the pond, and the cruelty that befell them. She may need Jon's help to tell the reverend about them, but the poetry reader was nowhere to be seen.

Her morning chores—milking, fetching water and eggs for making dough—seemed to distract her from yesterday's trauma. The birds sang their welcome song to the sun and Bethanna whistled along with them to lighten her spirits.

Returning to the house, Bethanna settled on her kitchen work while Mirra did her school lessons at the dinner table, though her eyes often strayed out the window. Bethanna told her to switch chairs, to avoid the distractions of the lovely day.

Mirra did so with a complaint, "You are depressing me."

"Now, Mirra," Bethanna said, spinning around to face her. "What is the only thing you must be doing today?"

Mirra sighed and tapped her thick pencil on the mahogany table as she thought. "Lessons," she said, rolling her eyes. Irritated, she observed her older sister.

Bethanna looked different today, with a secret in her eyes.

"What is it that you are worried about?" Mirra asked.

"What?" Bethanna said, guarded.

"You are off somewhere else, is it your soldier friend?"

Bethanna stared out the open window toward the village. "Never talk of that here," she said with an unusual sternness.

Mirra frowned. "Now you sound like Mother."

Bethanna's mouth opened in surprise. She sat down hard next to Mirra. "What do you want? That mother should hear us talk of it? Think sister, what she will do."

Mirra didn't have to think or even say. Hertha will make them both suffer equally. She continued on her scholarly track, still concerned about her sister's mood.

As she continued to cut vegetables, Bethanna imagined her future there in Hertha's house and saw it clearly for the first time. Without father, the war and fear of raids will hurry the decay of her mother's mind, and the girls will stay trapped in her descending melancholia. "If only Papa was here," she mumbled. Looking over to the front door, she eyed her father's thick, Black-Forest walking stick. Familiar reminders of him lay everywhere: drinking steins, pipe cleaners, books and his favorite rocking chair, boot scratches on the coffee table, and his drafting tools in the upper room. She loved those things, because he held them, used them, and often told stories about their use or history.

She was truly his girl. Vogal had reared her to be smart, gracious and attuned to the provisions of the land. He molded her for a world that was fading, the old world of small villages and a trader's economy, where a good name can buy things, and where people learned to serve others in kindness. He wanted her to be a lovely person, with an intimate knowledge of people, a small town girl at heart, but with an American spirit.

In America he knew that the future was change, and change came fast, not like in the old county. Seeing how Europe failed its people with dynastic rule, revolving religious wars and famines, the unending promise of the United States became the utmost for his daughters. Vogal enriched their hearts with the free will and independent vigor of his new adopted country, which he loved now beyond all dreams. The U. S. was a land of dreams, where the sky never ended and nothing could hold back the people's potential. It should be free, for his girls, and all who lived there. Witnessing the war's toll, he took a commission in the Engineers and served in the U.S. Army to make the dream so. These were his thoughts to Bethanna, and Mirra, when she would listen.

Near two o' clock in the afternoon, Bethanna left Mirra reading in the front sitting room and checked on her mother. Hertha slept, snoring peacefully. She climbed the steps to the upper room, her only private place to think, read, or cry when she had to escape the others.

Reserved for Vogal's drawing space, the room contained a drafting table, good leather chair, and a light-framed wooden camp bed from his service in the Prussian military. On the floor were crates of German and French books, prints and drawing supplies, in which Bethanna had found an interest. Brightening the gray walls, old etched prints of the German countryside hung in a crooked row around the room. Above his desk hung an ink drawing of Vogal and his sergeants in casual pose, dated 1835.

She began her typical summer routine and removed her dress so she could stay cool and not sweat in her undergarments. The room did not vent well due to the small window and in the hidden place, she enjoyed the freeness of being partly clothed. With a quick kneel to the floor and reach under the bed, she produced Jon's book of English poets and sat back on the pillows. She opened it and read the inscription written in a fine hand on the flyleaf.

To Jonathan Braddock Lyhton, on your 16th birthday 1857
From your Father and Mother

She ran her finger over his full name and spoke it aloud. The sound brought a smile. In the table of contents, she found unfamiliar names like Shaw, Burns, Byron, Wordsworth, Tennyson, Keats, and a special revision including Chatterton. Searching for the Lady of Shallot, she began to read, eager for the ending. The phrasing did not come easily like Jon's reading. She took her time and reread some parts just to grow used to the flow.

The ending did not go well like she had envisioned. The fair maiden had defied the curse and turned away from the mirror to view the grand Sir Lancelot, only to die on her boat as she drifted down the river to reach Camelot. Strange, she thought. Perhaps Jon would know the meaning of her death. Beautiful nonetheless, she chose another, shorter poem called, "Ode to a Nightingale," by John Keats.

It made no sense to her with its jagged stanzas and heavy language. She read two more poems and paused in reflection at some of the strange words, perhaps old words she did not know. Some lines were plainly sensual, with talk of lovers and kisses. *Was it right to be reading of these things?*

She wondered what Jon loved about the poetry; the beauty of the language, surely, or maybe the romance. It was interesting that he chose to read these words to her, deep with meaning and passion. His soothing and melodic tone definitely opened her heart, but to what, she was not sure. With these warm and exciting thoughts, she rubbed her bare feet together, looking for another inviting title.

Soon a thought came to her about the young couples in the village, before the war, how they played at romance and chased each other into dark places to kiss. Bethanna thought it was silly at the time. She was fourteen years old back then and her body was growing faster than her knowledge. Vogal had walked her around the farms when she was young and told her of the mating ducks, geese, cows, and how all of them continued. The system was pure, methodical and effective for procreation. Sex was thus for animals.

Still, she wondered at the foolishness of the older teenagers and even followed the couples to find their secret hiding places, where the great mystery would be revealed. It only confused her more when she saw them in the moonlight down near the creek, where the rushing water dimmed their laughter and moans, as they lay close, touching each other.

The young lovers were married at the outset of war and they left the valley, escaping battles, or to choose a side and fight. With no young men to court her, Bethanna did not experience this kind of illicit behavior, nor did Mirra have to witness people like this. Their mother never discussed it.

In fact, the only mention that related to her womanhood or sex occurred after Hertha had done laundry one day. "I see, your bleeding is here." she said. "Then you are no longer a child and I will not tolerate childishness." That was all from her mother.

Bethanna realized how little she knew of these relationships, men and women. Could Jon be romancing her? It seemed so, but he was not plain about it. Why did she run up the ridge to be with him? Because she wanted to. She wanted to be close to him, she did not know why, only that she wanted to. Maybe she was misjudging his intentions and overindulging hers, which if true, would be quite embarrassing.

She imagined if she would let him touch her, like the lovers would do. The thought was shocking; she felt it wrong to think in that way. The whole thing gave her a headache. She lifted the book and eased back into the words, reading the more sensible poems about friends and seasons of the year.

* * *

When the sun went down in the valley, the shadows came early and darkened the lowest lands of the hilly region. Toward the east, the ridge top glowed orange with the last trace of the setting sun and the dark blue sky began to show stars through red-feathered clouds. Bethanna left her house by the back door.

She had decided to mail her father a letter to be put into the postbox that evening for weekly pickup Saturday morning. In it she drew attention to her mother's behavior, the shooting of the rebel Private Stewart and how the corporal had prevented sure retribution. She asked him to come home, perhaps to move the family to Knoxville, away from the barren security of the valley, to be not so hidden.

Out in the backyard, she walked to the fence and checked the lower fields near the stream once more for Jon's troops. The place was dark and empty. She shook her head, fearful that some unknown fate had befallen them or in a more hopeful thought, they could have marched back to Knoxville. Either way, they were never to be seen again.

By the time she arrived at the meetinghouse, the night fell upon her. A group of men standing in the light of the open door parted for her to enter the building and they offered gentle, cordial greetings. After dropping her letter in the box and exiting the doorway, she overheard talk of soldiers, then about the Confederates. She walked very slow along the fence line just out of the light's reach and strained to listen. The men always gathered there to talk of the latest news while they smoked their tobacco away from the nagging wives. There must be some news of interest, she figured, if they are here tonight.

"One of them is dead," someone said.

Bethanna stopped cold. She looked back and saw the minister step into the conversation from his doorway.

"Yes that's true. Before they left, the lieutenant told me a dozen Kentucky raiders came down on them yesterday afternoon on the valley road, when the big storm commenced," he said.

"Strange that we heard no shooting," one man said.

"The war has come to us at last. Soon we will have to fight," exclaimed another.

Questions arose from the group about the Confederate platoon; where are they? And, what will they do now?

Reverend Grottmacher rubbed his hands together, like he did during his sermons. "The soldiers have moved away from here to keep the village clear of trouble. The lieutenant appreciates the kindness we have shown his men, even after the shooting of one of them."

"That's what is troubling," said Mr. Dansell. "We are kind and then we have to be involved." No one commented on the remark. Robert Dansell stood six feet, four inches and was not a man to be frightened. The villagers knew him as the best hunter, staying out for days while tracking one deer. "We have no choice. Armed soldiers must be treated with friendliness," he said.

The group nodded. They stood drinking from clay steins or packing their pipes with the hearty tobacco from nearby Virginia. Dansell carried cigars from his trading post, the best from the eastern states. Smoke swirled in the light, washing them in a glowing fog.

The large Mr. Blatz puffed on an ivory-trimmed pipe stem and spoke. "Yes, but if we are not kind, there is still trouble. Whoever comes into the village must be treated well, it is the only way." He crammed his hand into the pocket of his canvas farmer's coat. "Soon the rebels will be pushed farther south and we can enjoy the peace of the Union again. Until then, there can be no talk of bounties; the lines are too close now."

The others nodded with varied degrees of approval. Grottmacher stepped off the front stoop and looked around. He saw Bethanna standing in the dark. He turned back to the men. "Gentlemen, we must not talk of that."

Bethanna looked at them from the darkness and felt the heat rise in her head. Jon was correct that the village might not be safe. Herr Blatz's cold statement made her heart pound. Clearly, there had been a bounty passed among them for turning in the three cavalrymen, and that act had caused discord.

"Father Grottmacher, can I have a word?" she said, walking into the light of the open door. The others stopped their banter immediately. They stared at the girl from under the dark shadows of hat brims. The reverend pulled away from the hazy light as he received strained looks from Blatz and Dansell. Bethanna guided him over to the fence, away from the door.

"Are the gray troops in danger?" she asked quietly.

"No, not at the moment." he said.

"There is one of them, I must find out if he was killed or not," she said.

"I cannot say where they are; it was never mentioned where they are hiding. Why should it trouble you so?"

"Because I have seen the dead men on the other side of the ridge, the same Southern horse soldiers that were taken through our village, turned over for bounty, and killed!"

The reverend's voice darkened, "No. Quiet, girl. Watch what you say." He stepped towards her and his shadow blocked the light from the doorway.

Bethanna stepped back. "Yes, I have seen the bodies, and two of the visiting soldiers have seen. I told them only what I saw from the barn when the men were taken away, but there is danger here for them too, is there not? I cannot let this happen to him, or any of them."

The reverend glanced at the group surrounded in smoke and light at his meetinghouse door. He wondered what they would think if they knew that the prisoners were never exchanged as the brown-hat partisans had promised. Or did they know? He looked at Bethanna and had no intention of telling her any details of the prisoners, the horrific truth of one of them, his betrayal at the hands of a family member.

The hard fact had been known for some time that the founding villagers were staunch Unionists and because of Captain Hessier's border tactics, there was no room for Southern loyalty in the valley. In the past and recently, signals had been left on the Sneedsville Road to inform the brown hat raiders that a traitor is in the village, better yet a gray coat.

Hessier's money was good, private, and always given, even though the fate of these "prisoners" was unknown and never questioned. Over time, the captain demanded more from them, but paid less, on the premise that he had spared the valley from rape. Hessier's regression had caused a rift among the village elders and as their judge and mayor, the reverend preached quiet neutrality. When Lieutenant Weston's foot soldiers came, the divided elders waited for the opposing side to act, but no one did. Now, it was only a matter of time.

The reverend knew all this but could not explain it to the child before him, or now a young woman with a child-like trust.

Because of that, he pitied the girl.

Grottmacher sighed, rubbed his hands together. "I can only say that the soldiers have left a wounded man here and guards for him. They are in my cellar if you want to see them. Please child, be very careful about this."

Bethanna glared at him, "Are they to be turned over and killed also?"

"I…" Grottmacher shook his head.

In a quick turn, Bethanna headed into the darkness.

Returning to the group near his doorway with a heavy shame on his chest, Grottmacher knew that Bethanna's heart would be broken and he could do nothing to protect her from it. She was no longer the gangly girl fishing and farming with her father or roaming the streams and hills. Now she was a curious young woman with a spiritual mind, vivid dreams, and at present, Grottmacher found her to be the only glimmer of virtue and discipline in the whole valley. But just then, before running off in the dark, her eyes tore him apart. She had lost some innocence in the last day, and the reverend mourned quietly, for the mistakes of the past, and the pain that would come.

With a sharp turn, Bethanna changed direction and found the side path around the meetinghouse. In the dark cemetery, she nearly stumbled over the pale stones, turned blue in the moonlight. The body markers appeared out of the dark as she walked and the sight chilled her flesh. She found the entrance in the rear of the meetinghouse; the steps to the cellar were hidden in shadow, ending in the dark square door. She descended the bricks carefully and began to tremble. For a second, she recalled Mary Magdalene running into Christ's tomb, questioning what she would find, and who.

Her breathing and heartbeat filled her ears like the rush of wind. She mumbled to herself to quiet the noise in her head. "I must ask them about Jon."

The door latch snapped under her thumb and it creaked as she pushed it open. Immediately, she noticed a small candle burning on a nearby shelf. Her eyes adjusted to the glow as shadows danced to the flame's command.

Moving into the room, Bethanna gazed wide-eyed into the dusty shelves full of preserves and stacks of crates. Then she saw them in the dark corner: two small beds, each with a body on it. Her heart leapt into high speed. Doubting her nerve, she obtained the candle to help her see the features more clearly. Moving respectfully over to the beds, she extended the small flame in front of her and then near the face of the man closest. *Are these the dead ones?* Aware of her trembling hand, she held her breath. It was he... "God, no!" she cried.

The body jolted, Bethanna yelped and flung the candle into the unknown. The room went pitch back.

"What the devil?" said the now-alive corpse.

Bethanna, realizing her folly, covered her embarrassment. "Who are you to scare the sin out of me!" she cried, catching her breath.

Jon knew the accent. "What? Bethanna, is that you?" he said, standing upright, the darkness hiding his excited smile.

"Yes, it's me!" She blurted.

Jon smelled her and the dark room warmed at her presence.

"I believe you scared me, coming' up on a sleeper like that." He waited for a response.

"I came to see if you were still here,"

"Why, what's wrong?" he said, shuffling a step in her direction.

"Because I wasn't sure if you were... there was talk of a soldier dying."

"That was Liddel. One of our youngest men, it's a hard thing..." Jon paused, cleared his throat. "He was a good man. But, did you come here thinking I was dead?"

"I came here hoping you weren't. What happened?"

"Kentucky border jumpers hit our patrol very close to the east pass. The men responded to the surprise remarkably well. I arrived later, because I was with you."

"I kept you from your duties, your friends?"

"I mean to say, I was on guard, and you happened to be there. You have not harmed me or my duties."

"Who is that with you?" she asked.

"Private Sheldon Daniel. He's out cold with the reverend's opium. Has a bad secondary wound."

Bethanna shuffled in the dark. "Where did I drop the candle? I feel the need to see who I'm talking to."

"I don't have to see," Jon said. "I know perfectly well what you look like."

"Have you memorized me in so short a time?" she asked.

"Your face has been in my mind, yes."

Bethanna's heart quickened again and she didn't know what to say. Then she remembered. "I have your book of poems and your blanket. They are safely kept under my bed. Well, my father's bed, upstairs. I picked them up after you ran to Mr. Cawley, but forgot to give them to you when we reached the barn."

"Thank you, that was nice," he said. "You have been kind to me, Bethanna."

"Please forgive me for keeping the three cavalrymen from you. I could have told you, but it was not a horrible thing until I saw them dead."

"You don't have to explain, but perhaps the other people should."

"No, Jon they will only lie. I heard them talking about you, and the fighting. It is all very frightening to me and even Herr Blatz is talking of a bounty. I am not surprised that there was a secret amongst the people here. You were right, it is very dangerous. That's why I had to find you."

Her panicked tone concerned Jon. "I see your trust is shaken," he said. "Tell me, whom do you trust among the people here?"

"Now? Reverend Grottmacher and his wife only."

"Then give them this." Jon reached in the darkness for his coat and took a moment to search the pockets. "Come closer, I'll give it to you."

Bethanna stepped over to him. Her breathing his only guide, he reached out and caught her at the waist. She jumped. "I'm sorry, just trying to find your hand."

"Here's my hand," she said, grasping his arm. "What is it?"

"It's the bible I found on the dead lieutenant. And here's a name plate belonging to one of the victims."

Bethanna grasped the two souvenirs of death and put them into her canvass bag. "When the reverend sees this, everything will change for him as it did for me, when I saw those bodies. Nothing seems right in this place now."

"Was it ever right?" Jon asked.

The words faded into the darkness, unanswered.

"I must be home soon. I take great risk being here with you now, forgive me," she said.

"Understood. I'll lead you out of here." Jon reached for her.

Their hands touched timidly at first, then firm together, both of them sweaty.

Bethanna lost a breath as she held his hand, feeling a strange nervous excitement, close to fear. As they shuffled across the floor, their pairing reminded her of a dance. It had been a long time since she danced, and Jon would be a nice partner. Their bodies fit perfectly with his arm around her, hands so gentle.

Reaching the slash of moonlight near the steps, they looked at each other, clear and blue. "The time is coming when I will have to go," Jon said, gently lifting Bethanna's hand to his chest, feeling her fingers giving in to his. He pulled her hand up to his lips and kissed it.

Bethanna, surprised at her own surrender, looked away. His lips were softer than expected; the thin beard tickled her skin. A shiver went up her spine and she trembled, knowing what would happen if she looked at him. Then, in some sort of rebellion to everything in her life, she did.

Jon's gaze met hers and he brushed away a wild lock of hair from her cheek. He touched her quivering chin with his thumb, wiping away a shiny bead of sweat.

Bethanna closed her eyes, preparing for, or bracing against the unknown. In a matter of seconds, a point of light flashed upon her face.

Lawsen's lantern flooded the room in a swift ray. "Hey! Who's that?" he said. Jon was about to answer when Bethanna, startled and flushed, moved past Lawsen through the door and disappeared into the night.

"Paul, what the hell are you doing here…now?" Jon said, exasperated.

"Sarge is coming back in the morning to move Daniel to the farm south of here. Says he needs an operation very soon. The lieutenant has sent for Doctor Larkin." Lawsen dug through the shelves for another candle. "Why's this place so dark? Or should I mention it?" He chuckled and elbowed Jon. "Practicing strategic maneuvers?"

Jon ignored his friend's teasing and stepped up into the yard. The moon had come up fully, and in its light he saw a lone figure moving through the tall grass, up the rise to the Gurtag house.

* * *

CHAPTER 14★

Captain Hessier's attack of the rebel column near Taldorf and the news of his raids had all but killed traffic along the Sneedsville Road, usually a steady route for border tradesmen. The road had been macadamized in the mid '50s, a method by which crushed limestone was used to bed the roadway and then tamped down by hand into a hard surface suitable for faster wagon travel. It provided a solid, less shaky route for merchants, when the area was free of violence.

In the quiet before dawn, two horsemen rode at a fast gallop down the macadam way as their horses' clattering hooves kicked up fine white dust and startled the roadside deer. Pushing the animals for speed, the riders hoped to beat the first light of day and, and if lucky, spot the rebels still thought to be camped in the vicinity.

At a particular place in the road and in natural tandem, the riders sowed their mounts, then reined in. Both men eyed the same stand of pine trees to their right, which held no vast difference to any other growth along the road, only that this spot carried a purpose worthy of their full attention.

With a grunt that marked many days in the saddle, one of them, a heavy and bearded man, dismounted his horse and left the stallion to wait without tether in the middle of the road. The beast, a shiny black, stood unusually still with its head up and ears erect. After a short stretch to crack his back, the rider walked to the tree line and stared at a tartan rag, lined with the Scottish green and red, tied to a tree branch. He had not seen anything hung there in a few months. He jogged over and pulled it down, waved it in circles for his partner to see clearly. "Look, go tell the captain, hurry!" His comrade pulled hard on the reins and spun his horse northward, back the same direction they had come.

The trooper watched his partner's trail of dust arise like smoke over the road and with a yawn, stretched again before remounting his stallion. Tucking the tartan cloth inside his coat, the signal did not surprise him, as he noticed the terrain.

The ground there was very familiar, with its sunken road and high craggy hill. It proved to be a hazardous place to fight the rebel infantry at close range.

In a short time, atop the eastern hills near Taldorf, along the same path Lieutenant Weston's platoon entered the valley, the rider observed the distant village in the golden mists of dawn. He pulled his binoculars, or those he had recently made his, and scanned the outer dwellings, mostly farms and groves, under which moved a few small dots of people tending early chores.

Once again, he dismounted and rested his glasses on a low branch to quiet the scene for his weary eyes. Behind him, his horse licked at small dew puddles on the ground, dropped there by the nightly fog. The horse's lapping made the trooper chuckle and he lowered his glasses. "Don't worry, there's a lovely stream down there for us."

He lifted the wide rim of his dark-brown hat and continued his observations, though he stopped often to clear the glass of moisture with a wipe from his black leather gauntlet. The kindness to his horse and a promise of comfort did not reflect his inner mood, which now held more anger at the victorious rebels and resentment over being chosen to scout them. The boring duty only added to the bitterness of Hessier's defeat two days ago, a wasted affair that gained his men nothing.

Like most men without work, and adrift in his state's bloody neutrality, he wanted in on the action or the thrill of pursuit, perhaps some treasure of war, and to defend the border from those who are traitors in his eyes. He and his partisan company had punished many local secessionists, who harbored Kentucky's Confederate enlistees, men who chose the Southern side and traveled to enroll in Tennessee's forces, daring to form Kentucky regiments. If such men were not caught, then the raiders punished their families with rape and death.

He had no feelings for his killed comrades, or the murdered civilians, nor did he care about sweeping the land free of slaves. Out in the undeveloped free range, Captain Hessier's methods agreed with his own version of the war, his own rules, and whatever the duty required. Hessier planned short aggressive campaigns and never fought without having the advantage until two days ago, in a trap-like sunken road during a miserable rainstorm.

Stepping carefully down the path through the trees, the horse carried his master onto an open field toward the stream and there under a stand of maples, the scout found all the evidence he needed of the rebels' presence; the area revealed recent fire pits, fish bones and the disrupted earth of camped soldiers and their latrines.

The scout dismounted and kicked at the spent fire holes. "Bout' a day old," he said to his horse. He saw no hoof tracks, no evidence of wheel or wagon. "No supplies, eh? Their brigades must be near, less than a day's march." He eyed his horse as it took to the running stream with a snort. "That's right, Jeddy boy, suck it up quick. We'll see what some of these villagers say, when they see me again."

The last time they saw him was the end of May, when he had been party to the quick execution of three traitorous rebels.

* * *

Early August in the valley meant hot days, but in the cool morning breezes, Bethanna's flowers celebrated her presence as they danced and swayed under her gentle efforts to weed and water. Since the Confederate soldiers had come, she had ignored her gardening, an important part of her daily routine. The work brought a measure of distraction from her mother, who lately remained in a foul state because of the soldiers.

She left the worms alone to purify the earth and the snails she put under the porch where they could live comfortably in the dark. Even now, attending her favorite chore, Jon was on her mind. This is where she first saw him, looking in at the garden with an interest very out of place with his war-like bearing. In retrospect, it was a good thing that Private Lawsen had interfered with Jon's kiss. Logically, she could not oblige every handsome soldier's whim on a foolish impulse, even if he liked her. Hertha might end her life if she knew of her cavorting with a "Rebel" soldier in a dark place, with his arm around her.

In more focused introspection, she knew exactly what she was doing when she closed her eyes to invite a full kiss. Though it did not happen, still, Jon's touch on her hands felt very nice, as did his soft kiss on her fingers and before long, the scene lived again in her memory; his touch, his gaze. And to her surprise, the daydream went further than the reality, when she imagined if they were not interrupted.

"Ah, enough." She could barely concentrate on her tasks and as she washed her hands at the water pump, she realized that in the confusion of the night's events—the elders' secrets and Jon's caresses—Reverend Grottmacher never received the dead lieutenant's bible. But today, she would make sure of it.

Her mind raced as she walked briskly into the village to complete the morning rounds. From Dansell's General Trader, she picked up coffee, tea, and salt. Down at Frau Blatz's orchard stand, she traded fresh eggs for lemons and apples, great for her mother's pies and sauces.

She acquired the north road and decided it would be nice to have some quiet time on the stone bridge, a place where she went often to view the water and think over life.

Jon thought he saw her, and after a few moments, he was sure. He gazed at her from the graveyard fence, where he drank a cup of Grottmacher's fine coffee. Bethanna stood out from the green land in her dark blue denim long dress and to Jon, there was nothing in nature so fine. She looked very much a part of the valley, like it had been hers for ages.

It was plain to him that because of their dealings with the Kentucky raiders, the elders of Taldorf betrayed not only those three cavalry boys, but also the other villagers. They did not deserve the enjoyment of the beautiful valley, nor its bounty, or her. Bethanna represented freedom amid this enclosed space, this trap and because she was a child of them, perhaps they would not let her be free. Jon hoped one day she could be.

He saw her lean over the stone ledge and gaze into the running creek. Jon could tell she had something the other villagers did not, for sure something her mother lacked, and that was peace. Even in the middle of her family trials, with soldiers roaming the land and the war's relentless weight, Bethanna's steadiness weathered it all. Someone like that was rare, and in his heart, very desirable.

Lawsen's snores echoed from the cellar and Jon chuckled. He moved toward the dark doorway but hesitated halfway and he figured it would not hurt to allow Lawsen another hour of sleep. They had moved Private Daniel hours before dawn in secret, thanks to the reverend's cart and team, and the veil of darkness. Lieutenant Weston ordered Jon and Lawsen to resume their station at the meetinghouse for rear guard, mainly because of the dead cavalrymen they found on the other side of the north ridge. That horrific story did not please Lieutenant Weston, who forwarded a detailed message about the atrocities to regimental command. He did not want to expose the platoon to more hidden surprises at the very close of his mission, so he camped a mile down the southern road from Taldorf, near the abandoned farm.

This, the third day in the valley, Jon reflected on the events he had experienced among the immigrant Germans and first above everything, Bethanna was the most intriguing. The platoon would depart soon, perhaps in mere hours. He took his place by the fence and looked at the girl, who stood alone framed by green trees and a large ridge. In the distance, he could make out her hair, riding on the wind.

Bethanna's hair blew around her head and she retied the locks up in her blue scarf. Bright dots from the sun-sparkled stream danced on her face as she leaned over the stone guard to observe the smooth rocks under water, the long grasses and the occasional fish. She remembered the fish Jon B. Lyhton had given her, such a nice gesture, after she had given him her most stern send off in the defense of her mother. Jon was not typical as a soldier, out to raid like her father had warned. His face did not meet the picture of a mean person, a man out to hurt defenseless women in their homes. There was a soft authority in his eyes and his voice pleased her with reading she had never heard, in the poet's English.

Most impressively, Jon possessed a gentleman's quality much like her father, the only real model she had for such comparisons. It was a short time she spent with him on the ridge yesterday and she could tell he was probably someone who would be a great friend. To fall asleep with him on a hilltop was a lovely trespass. She smiled at her wavy reflection, on the face of the moving water.

"Miss Gurtag?"

Bethanna turned and saw Jon. He stood with his arms crossed, hat tilted back, and no soldier things on him.

"Mr. Lyhton. Good day." She dipped her head.

"Not thinking of jumping, are you?" Jon leaned forward on his toes.

Bethanna thought over the statement, played the humor. "Oh no, sir. Too much to do today."

Jon sighed. "Thank God, because I would be very distraught over any action that may come to harm you. And it is such a lovely day, too."

Bethanna laughed, more because she had been just thinking of him. "Have you been watching me, the spy?"

"Ah, the spy… yes." Jon stepped closer. "I have been watching, but in a protective capacity only, I assure you."

"I see. Then I am so grateful for such… protection."

They shared a warm smile as Jon walked over and leaned on the stone rail next to her. Quietly for a time, they watched the action of the stream with its ripples and dips flowing easy and peaceful. Two points of interest occupied their minds—the dead bodies that Cawley found and Jon's eventual departure—but neither one raised the subjects.

"I cannot say when I have felt more at ease than with you" Jon said.

Bethanna looked at him, his gaze on the stream. To her surprise, she felt nervous, but not in a confused way like before, when Lawsen had interrupted them. "I am glad that you feel this," she said.

He turned to her and rested on his elbow. Her eyes held more fascination than the stream, more movement and much more beauty. Jon studied her flush skin, her full eyebrows, strong nose, all framed by the graceful lines of her face. Her lips parted into a smile, revealing a slight overbite. In the morning sun, she was the most perfect thing. Such a moment, and a person, inspired poems.

And of poetry, what did he really know? This fair maiden deserved pages of it. Could he even write about his lovely dame of the valley with the right words? Bethanna was very different in that it mattered more *what* people said, than *how* they said it. "*La belle dame sans merci.*" Jon said, in a wistful sigh.

Bethanna put a hand to her ear. "Pardon?"

"Oh, did I say something?" Jon tapped his fingers on the stone.

"Yes, something French, I think."

"You are correct. Oh, just a reference to another poem, nothing really."

Jon looked at the sky, then the hill, and finally to her.

Bethanna thought he was being very cute with his smart grin. Finding a serious tone, she said, "Oh, you are full of smart things, aren't you?"

"Ah, that is true." Jon, put a hand to his chin and looked into the water. He frowned and turned back to her. "Hey, is that an insult?"

Bethanna laughed. "I got you. Your face was, so very serious." She poked Jon with her finger.

Jon repressed his urge to giggle, but what came out sounded like choking. He laughed.

Bethanna laughed at his laughing. She had forced it and to do so made her heart soften, warm up and burn a little. She could not take the smile from her face, nor did she want to hide it from him as he enjoyed it. She noticed Jon's eyes searching her face, perhaps exploring new places to remember, to memorize, as he said before in the cellar. She regretted the time she did not study him, avoiding his gaze, his eyes so gray and green, always tracing her movements. Why had she not done the same?

"I am glad you were not hurt in the battle," she said.

For the first time, and with much meaning, she touched Jon's hand, resting on the stone.

Surprised, he gave it to her, with only a slight hesitation at first. The caress of skin flushed them both. Fingers moved over palms, the lightness of hers and the strength of his. They were young beautiful hands, dusty, now caring. Quietness surrounded them, a welcome end to discussion, to flirting, and to shyness.

Her peace entered him, and his brave chiseled hand held her safety, and above all, her trust.

The fast pace of her heart within such stillness amazed Bethanna. She knew little of what controlled the impulse to hold, and touch, or if it could be controlled. Together, their hands seemed to know what to do. In the same moment, they were searching for, and finding, their own answers. Bravely, she raised her eyes as all these thoughts ran their course.

Jon found her gaze to be different now; she was no longer looking at a total stranger but searching him deeply. In her eyes, he saw blue, silver and gold, and green, and all the colors of the valley reflected in her deep wells of emotion.

That quiet emotion flickered in an instant with a dark reflection. Bethanna shuddered as she looked over Jon's shoulder. She gripped Jon's hand. "My God, a rider is coming."

The sounds of hoof beats arose over the soft din of the stream. Jon jerked around and saw the brown hat raider trotting up on a large black stallion, wet with lather. The rider's wide bearded face showed nothing but callous regard as he glared at them. He had no weapon pulled, although there were plenty of choices strapped to the man and his saddle bags; Bowie knives, pistols, and two sabers of various lengths hung openly for all to see.

Bethanna freed Jon's hand and she backed away a step. The rider approached the bridge quickly and inspected Jon with a casual sneer. The man and horse blocked the bridge so that they cut off the road into the village.

The trooper nodded at Jon. "Seen any rebels this'a way, boy?"

Jon took off his hat and scratched his head, "*Wir haben nicht rebels!*" He tossed his hands up, shrugged.

Bethanna stared at Jon, his instant change into a Deutsche farm boy was total, and beyond surprise.

The rider frowned. "English boy! Where are they?"

"Why do you ask us here?" Jon responded, in a decent accent.

"You must find zhe elders."

The raider reached into his dusty blue coat and pulled the tartan rag. "Don't waste my time, boy, or Captain Hessier's. He won't be happy today if there's nothing here."

Bethanna put her hand to her mouth, but could not suppress her audible shock.

The raider turned his eyes to the young lady. He moved his horse closer to her and then frowning, put his hand to one of the long pistols to intimidate Jon. Swaying its head, the large horse passed and forced him out of the way.

Jon raised a hand and smiled. "*Gutten tag.*" He sauntered off the bridge and onto the gravel, where he waited.

The raider turned to Bethanna and his leather saddle creaked when he leaned forward. "Well, little pretty miss, is he correct, concerning the traitors?"

Bethanna rattled off in German, explained her chores and how nothing had happened all morning, much less the sighting of said rebels and their traitorous faces.

The countenance of the blue rider changed remarkably, as if in deep thought, distracted, and then a mischievous grin parted his beard. "Hey, boy, run along now and leave us. Tell the elders Hessier is coming to do business."

Jon smiled, but inside he began to heat up. "When is he coming?"

"You heard me, now git." The rider waved his hand at Jon, like he would a fly. "Leave me with her, you stupid kraut." Confident in his rebuke and sure of his new-found hunger, he dismounted and backed Bethanna against the stone guard to gain an intimate view. His eyes widened, eager and wanton, when presented with such a rare treat as she. The man reached for his new prize but missed the fast girl, who out-stepped him off the north end of the bridge, where tall grass and bushes grew near the stream.

Bethanna looked at Jon, who to her shock, was trying to pet the raider's horse. Confused, she backtracked as far as she could, but the man was on her. She could not scream, cry or breathe a word. Her silence scared her, almost more than the attacker. Where was the heat in her head; the rising energy of anger, anything to make her fight? Before she could blink, the rough man stripped her head of the blue head tie and it fell to earth. Her fallen hair set ablaze the man's eyes and he doubled his efforts with a furry, feeling anything, grabbing denim and thwarting her swinging hands with his wood-hard arms.

"Make it easy girl, then I will!"

With a swift kick under her legs, the raider downed her to the ground. At this, she cried out in fear for the first time. Working his belt loose, his pants dropped exposing his yellowed long johns, and his obvious excitement.

A loud bang clapped Bethanna's ears and she flinched at the noise. The raider shuddered, took a step and fell over in the grass.

A few moments before, Jon figured very quickly that the soldier must have been tired from his long ride. Although his body did not show it, his mind and actions did, as he casually abandoned his weapons. Jon had calmly walked to the horse and when Bethanna saw him, she led the man over to a stand of bushes fronting the far side of the creek. Jon went for the gear quickly and searched the ample assemblage of pistols. He made an effective choice, a very large handgun from one of the dangling holsters, no doubt prizes of numerous raids.

His search agitated the horse and it turned to meet him. It was not the first time Jon stared down a horse. On the cow ranches with the trail men, Jon learned how to ride, how to shoe and how to read the health of a horse, and when needed, he helped to break them. Undoubtedly he had a nasty one in front of him, but the animal was clearly ridden out that morning and ready for a long rest. Jon quickly took the hanging reigns under the chin, avoiding a bite. He pulled the animal to him as it pushed forward with aggression. Using the animal's momentum, he turned the horse's head and wheeled the animal past him. He had little time to waste.

The pistol, a Savage 44 Caliber, had a longer barrel than most, and Jon studied it as he walked the bridge, the raider constantly in his sight. There was a small ring inside the trigger guard—pull it and the cylinder turned, the hammer cocked. Jon knew the design, but never held one before now. No doubt, he thought, that this gun had fired at him on that rainy hillside, not many hours ago. He armed the pistol and found it carried two rounds.

With the weight of the gun, Jon thought he could knock the man out with a precise blow, but he had little time to figure out where to strike. In all of his prolific reading, anatomy was not a subject he visited often. As soon as Bethanna hit the ground, he had the clear shot he needed.

After the weapon fired, Jon and Bethanna stared at the dying man, his large body made useless. As if carried on a gust of wind, the shot's last echoes rolled up the ridge into the thick trees and in moments, the trickle of the creek overtook their ears.

"Damn that was loud," Jon said. "Everyone's' gonna hear that."

Bethanna sat up. She looked at the shot man, his blood, open eyes, and his gasping mouth. He said something and she jumped. Jon reached for her and helped her to her feet. Together they looked at the man's wound; a bullet hole bled just below the left shoulder blade. He attempted to crawl, grasping at clumps of grass but instead imitated a baby unable to make way. He stopped moving.

Bethanna put her hand to her mouth. "Jesus almighty, is he...?"

"Yes. I had no choice."

Jon took her by the arm, noticed she was trembling, and walked her away from the scene. "I'll hide the horse. You must go home, to safety."

"Safety?" she said in a whisper.

"Yes, I think I just ended our guard duty here."

His statement carried finality, the end of him in the valley, a man who will march away down a long road and is lost into war. Bethanna stepped to him and stood close. They both breathed heavily, eyed the dead man, the shock of his death very fresh, and in no way subsiding. She began to accept that Jon could not stay any longer, for the danger had taken a new direction. "Jon, you have taken a grave chance because of me."

"You are worth the chance." Jon took her hand, and pulled it gently.

Bethanna let herself be guided into his arm. She grasped him, holding his warm, muscled torso. A tear fell slowly down her cheek, but in her anxious state, she didn't notice.

Jon looked up and heard footsteps. "Oh good, here comes Lawsen. We need to do something."

When Jon fired the pistol, a few things happened. Lawsen jumped at the shot while pulling up his pants and unbalanced, he fell onto the hard cellar floor. After sufficient cursing, he ran to the door, grabbed his rifle and stepped up into the yard. He saw Bethanna at the stone bridge and near her a loaded black horse wandered the creek. "That's a military horse." Lawsen scanned the area and cautiously jogged over to meet her.

The shot echoed over the Gurtag house and Hertha, having just come in from her garden, froze a knife over her long beans.

"How much of this must I endure?" she mumbled. She angrily tossed the knife down and walked to the front door. Mirra was out in the yard, playing with her favorite barn cat.

With her head very still, Hertha's eyes scanned the surroundings. "Mirra, did you hear zhat?"

"Yes, Mama." Mirra stood. "It came from there." She pointed to the north ridge.

Hertha nodded, assured. "Right. I'm glad you heard it, too. I do not want to hear things that never happen."

Mirra shrugged, bemused at her mother's oddness. She noticed the cat running for the dark space under the porch and she chased it. "Hoffen? Where are you going? Come here, you." She crouched down and saw the gray pet cowering under the stairs.

"Forget it, Mirra." Hertha frowned. "Somezing has spooked him. Me, perhaps."

To her chagrin, another noise interrupted Hertha's morning. The sound was many horses approaching from the east, making for the bridge on the outskirts of her property. Mirra saw them and ran past her mother for the door. Hertha stood still, alone. Captain Hessier's raiders had arrived.

Lawsen tied the large black horse under the apple trees on the hidden side of the Blatz barn. As for the dead raider, Jon had dragged him into the thicker shrubs, close to the creek. Dropping the man's arms, he easily identified the uniform as that of the Kentucky partisans; a short, blue shell jacket, black gloves on his belt, and the telling dark brown hat with the black raven's feather. With thoughts of the dead Private Liddel in his head, he tossed the hat and the pistol into the stream. Bethanna picked up her basket on the bridge and the three of them walked back to the graveyard. They noticed a few villagers had stepped from their abodes and wandered in the roads to discuss the shot heard only minutes before.

By habit, Bethanna glanced at her house up the slight rise and saw a commotion under the copse of trees near the road. Quickly, she improved her view by standing on a fence rail. Horsemen gathered on the road near the entrance of her mother's gate.

"Bethanna?" Jon called, wondering what caught her attention.

"Jon, they… they are here!" she cried.

"Who?"

Jon and Lawsen jogged over to share the view, which proved to be a line of mounted brown hats forming under the shade of trees, many with weapons in hand. Jon heard shouts of command from the leader atop a white and gray horse and in seconds, six troopers broke off for the village at a fast gallop.

The three heard a voice behind them. "Please, into the cellar, now!"

Reverend Grottmacher stood at the open door to his cellar. The two Confederates went in first and thanked the minister. Bethanna looked at him, as she went in last. "Is it safe here?"

The reverend began to close the door after Bethanna entered. "Just stay quiet," he said.

Jon and Lawsen tried to find a place for two men to hide amongst the maze of shelves and boxes. Bethanna scrambled, not sure what to do, still in a daze from attempted rape and witnessing a violent and very loud death. In no time, horse hooves pounded the road past the meetinghouse and the vibration rattled jars on a nearby shelf. Lawsen exhaled in relief when the horses continued on down the road. "Damn, there's too many of them to ambush, I recon."

The two soldiers quizzed each other on several plans of escape and Bethanna, eager to know what was occurring outside, looked around the room for a window. Spotting a few slivers of light on the beds in the corner, she ran over to the wall and saw a hinged glass, painted blue. She forced it and the old frame reluctantly creaked open. From ground level, she could see all the way to the main road and up the gentle rise to her mother's gate. To her terror, the horsemen lingered there, dismounted, and casually took over the yard.

"Why are they at my house?" she wondered.

Lawsen shuddered, "Oh shit, J.B! That's the old fool that shot Stewart!"

To Bethanna's senses, it looked like Hertha had made the deal with this Captain Hessier fellow, mentioned earlier by the raider dead in the bushes, but still, her mother could not make her way, without a long absence, over the eastern pass to tie a signal flag. An assistant, perhaps? She had never seen that tartan cloth in her house.

Jon pointed to the door. "Bethanna, you cannot be caught with us. If you leave, this will be easier on you."

"I can't go home *now*, can I?" she blurted, slamming the window.

"What can your mother tell them?"

"Nothing, she doesn't know you ever returned here."

"Why are they at your door, then, missy?" Lawsen said, aggravated.

Bethanna stared at the two men, her face flushed red. "She does not know!"

"Come here." Jon led her to the door. "Don't panic. We'll find a safe place. Go to your mother later and see what the men are telling her, then go to the reverend."

"Jon?"

"Bethanna, I trust you." He took her hands in his, smiled briefly. There was fear in her eyes, but fear for him and caring for him. It was very clear, with all that had occurred this day; he would never see her again. "I will miss you very much." He leaned in and kissed her quivering lips.

Bethanna ran up the stairs and out into the sunlight. She took the lower field near the stream and planned to enter the back gate of their property when the raiders dispersed. Stomping through the tall grass, she realized her precious time with Jon was over. The panic racing through her had nearly stolen the sensation of his kiss, given at such an unexpected moment. It seemed foolish that she was not ready. Her first kiss—not the sort of kiss she imagined— but altogether perfect. She had no time to smile over it.

Vividly, she saw the troopers hiking down the road with their horses in tow and in the lead, Hertha, as if she personally led the detail into some unseen battle. "Oh Lord, no." She halted in the tall grass.

What is she doing? she wondered. *How could she know about Jon and Lawsen hiding in the minister's cellar?* Bethanna thought that if there were some news that was near impossible to find, her mother could be the one to do it. She could not go home now.

She walked, then jogged, and without delay made the road rather quickly. With her nerves already tested by the unsavory soldier earlier, she braced for the unexpected and for the unexplained. The group of soldiers approached her.

Hertha spied her daughter and scowled. She halted, stood stiffly in front of Captain Hessier and his men, stopping the formation to their obvious dislike.

"Who is this?" the Captain said, his dark eyebrows rising.

"My unruly daughter, it is. Come girl, you can see the rebs with us!" Hertha yelled, pushing her along with them.

Bethanna shivered at the coldness in her mother's voice, a tone that proved Hertha had found out everything, somehow. She tried to think of anything to thwart Jon's discovery, but nothing came clear. A feeling of helplessness overwhelmed her in front of so many odds, the soldiers, and her mother's relentless rebel-hating mania. With her spirit breaking, she did something that she hadn't done in a long time. She prayed to God in her mind, without words from a prayer book, only her words.

Jon stared from the basement window in a despondent disbelief. "I'll never be a prisoner and die in a Yankee hole." He said looking back at Lawsen, who was loading his rifle.

"That meddlin' Hun ain't gonna serve me up!" Lawsen proclaimed, as he replaced his ramrod.

Jon shut the window tight. He turned and the sight of Bethanna's groceries gave him a new alarm. On the floor above him, he heard chairs moving and voices.

With every step, Bethanna's breath grew short, as did her ideas. She could not tell her mother anything that would raise suspicion, but she had to do something. Her hands became clinched fists as the heat arose inside her. The group approached the meetinghouse, she prayed, please *keep walking.*

With a shrill cry, "Over dis vay!" Hertha turned into the yard and then towards the side path leading to the rear of the building.

Bethanna stopped and allowed the raiders to pass her, all of them armed, unclean, and cold. She could not find her usual rebellious strength that had buffeted her against Hertha's growing dementia. She leaned against the fence and held herself steady, thinking of the cruel timing of the last two days, Jon and his friendliness, his affection. She looked up to see the blue soldiers gathered in the graveyard, and her mother pointing down, surely they would break down the door and take Jon to the hidden side of the ridge and shoot him dead. She began to hate her mother for taking him away forever. The emotional waves crashed inside her.

"No, please, just leave them be!" she yelled, running down the path.

Captain Hessier reared back in surprise and then looked at Hertha, puzzled.

"She is fond of zem, such a crazy girl." Hertha shook her head, rolled her eyes.

The captain gestured to the ground. "Well, she can look after them all she likes now. As long as they're dead there's no harm," he said. His men laughed and began to file out of the yard.

"Is there one day that will pass when you do not embarrass me?" Hertha asked, frowning at Bethanna. She grunted and turned to follow the soldiers.

Bethanna looked around dazed, and then realized what her mother had shown the captain. She fell to her knees at the graves for Liddel and Stewart. The two rebels... "Lord, you are merciful." she said, as tears of relief fell on the fresh dug dirt.

The horsemen hiked back towards the Gurtag house, disappointed that they had not found any living Confederates. The captain had accommodated the old woman's bravado and zeal for the Union by allowing her to lead them on the fruitless walk. He began to question the *frau* more closely as Mirra listened from upstairs, hidden safely.

Hessier lit a cigar, tossed the spent match and told Hertha to sit on her couch. "I have not heard from Corporal Estlen, my advance scout. Have you seen him? I must stay here and reconnoiter with my troops," he said, pacing the *frau*'s parlor, grinding in a day's worth of mud into the rugs. "Will anyone in this krauty place help me today? Well?"

Bethanna, filled with hope again, crept into the reverend's cellar. She called for Jon. There was no answer. She looked through the boxes and old pantries repeating his name softly. They both had gone, but for now, safe. It was after a while of reorientation that she retrieved her basket of groceries. She searched the basket for the bible and ID badge Jon had given her and they were still there. She had a mission to give these items to the reverend, but not before she had a look at them.

Sitting on the doorway steps, she pulled out the aged book. Its gold trim had weathered away on the front cover but not on the back, where the sun could not reach it. She thumbed through the pages, silently reading a few of the psalms. Curious, she turned to the front cover and opened it. She read the personal inscription in a female hand and it saddened her. The name "Carl Fritz" stood out. Her breathing stopped dead as she turned another page. In sharp, black ink, was her cousin's signature, "1st Lieutenant Carl F. Gurtag."

The shock held her motionless. The scene of rotted corpses crowded her mind, their inhuman blackness and impersonal, unburied remains were the horror of all wartime families. How tragic for the new bride, Darlene, so young, pretty and surely ignorant of her husband's death. The breath leapt from her in fits. Tears flowed from her eyes and they reddened as she wiped them. She remembered her cousin; light curly hair, blue eyes like hers and a loud laugh. They were close before the war even though he was older. He would have turned 23 in November, the same month as her birthday.

Jon would not have caught the name at a glance, she knew. *He did not realize what he was giving me. Now he is gone.* She cried for her cousin, for Jon, and at the treachery of her village.

* * *

CHAPTER 15 ★

Captain Hessier grew impatient as he paced Hertha's parlor. He could not stand Germans with their unrefined living and Protestant ways, to him the lowest scourge of Europe besides the Balkan states. His French Catholic roots held no regard for Tennessee slaveholders or ignorant mountain folk either, people very much like the cousins who chose the Southern side and cut him off from inherited land on the Holston River, 45 miles away from Knoxville. If he had to rape all of east Tennessee for recompense, then so be it.

Reliving the German woman's tales of woe and sufferings under the rebels had worn his patience thin. Hessier tried fishing for the biggest fish with the correct bait and he felt a pull on the line. "So you, as the wife of a renowned officer, keep a loyal eye out for these rebels? I have heard of Major Gurtag. Are you as steadfast, and willing to uphold the cause?" After setting the hook into Hertha's ego, she could not resist the swelling temptation to prove her allegiance. "I shot zhat rebel bastard!" she shouted.

Captain Hessier disliked one detail in her story; the fact that the village had been used as a base of operations for Confederate infantry. Furthermore, he grew agitated upon hearing about a pistol shot fired earlier that morning in the land of shotguns and flintlock muskets. Orders went out for the troopers to assemble the adult villagers at the crossroads and to find out what occurred with the rebels while they were here. He ordered two riders to fetch more troops from their camp near Mulberry Gap. The captain was anxious to do more fishing.

The people of Taldorf knew by looking that the troops amongst them this fine, late summer day were not regular Union cavalry. They were well known in these parts as older militia units turned partisan rangers. Once the prime force when the war had started, they had drifted into second-level duties and began to find their true calling in that business known as raiding and foraging. They were not leashed under any centralized authority, instead, being Captain Hessier's independent command, ranging from 300 to 600 men, depending on the season. Cut off and solo from the main Union forces, they had developed into a vicious weapon for border politics, policing, and reprisal. Their manners reflected this as they tore into the village with little supervision or respect.

Soon smoke arose over the outlying farms as the hay bales burned, a delightful pastime of the raiders. Anything they judged useful to new conscripts—shotguns, ammo, powder, digging tools, and hatchets were gladly broken, stolen or turned into a potential bonfire. Standard for their mode of operations, this destruction of valuables motivated the inhabitants to divulge all they knew about their former visitors. And today it worked without fail.

With some time to cool down and gather her strength of will, Bethanna ascended the steps from the reverend's cellar. She turned the corner near the northern road and stopped short, then jumped back behind the meetinghouse to hide. She saw the raiders depositing people in small clusters on the road. Separately, they were questioned and bullied by the captain's officers, who were no more than decorated fear mongers. They kicked at the older folk and threatened them with drawn swords. It was evident that some were drunk as they cursed and laughed at the scared villagers.

At the back stoop of the meetinghouse, she knocked on the door and waited for the reverend to come. He appeared, sweaty and nervous. "What now child? Come in here," he said. He led her through the living quarters into the sanctuary.

"There is something you must see." She handed him the bible.

As he inspected it, she directed his attention to the inscription and name, to which his reaction revealed plenty. "Go away with this, I don't want anything that the Yanks can use against me. It is tragic, yes, but we cannot bury him until there is quiet here."

"You knew, didn't you!" she yelled, her voice echoing off the wood pews and walls.

"I only knew of his capture, nothing of his fate," he said.

"Who turned him over to the raiders?"

"You will never know, none of us will." The lie was not fair, but easy to utter in front of the ignorant girl.

Grottmacher calmed himself, mainly to calm her. "Go home, child, and see to your own, for this will be a long day for us all. Please, go now."

Bethanna walked the trails near the stream and trees to avoid the roaming troopers. Her heart drummed out the rhythm of danger, a throbbing anxiety that crushed her head from the inside with one astounding thought; her mother had shown Captain Hessier the dead rebels, so… what would keep her from giving up a live one? Or three? The idea nearly made her swoon with illness and in the midst of that woe, another fact fell upon her like a cold bucket of water. The village that birthed her, taught her, and in whose image she had been made, at this very moment had become evil to her and she was about to witness its punishment.

When she reached the path to her mother's gate she turned and saw smoke rising from the farms and homes to the west, along the creek as it turned south. Closer to home, raiders entered the meetinghouse while the reverend and his wife looked on, cowered and pitiful. The final fear had come. It did not matter how many prisoners they could deliver to Hessier, the village could not deal its way out of danger. Their deception was over.

It was then, in a quiet breath, the life she had known ended, and with the village smoke, floated away like a burnt offering to God, spent and finished. She did not cry but inhaled deeply, knowing she must ready herself for the coming storm. Aware of this, her spirit became armored, alive for war, and awake to the womanly instinct to crave, to possess and fight for herself, her home, wherever it would be. God could only know the outcome.

Upon entering the house, Hertha attacked her. Bethanna had seen a dark flash and could not react in time as the fisted blows sent her reeling into the wall. After multiple strikes she became aware that Hertha was not going to stop any time soon so she punched back blindly. She did not know how to hit, only that she had found the will to.

Hertha, stunned at her daughter's wild punches, paused for a few seconds as her mind dealt quickly with this new resistance. The girl's eyes stared with a hot spite she had never seen until now. It meant disrespect. Hertha scowled until her face became a leather mask of hate. She then went for Vogal's heavy cane behind the door.

Gripping the hardwood, Hertha yelled, "You bring shame to me and your fahzer!"

Faced with such a weapon and clear injury, Bethanna used her youthful speed and raced up to her father's room. She bolted the door.

Hertha yelled as she banged the small door with the cane. "I vill not have a rebel whore in my house! You vill obey me child! *Schande, schande!*"

Her mother's German repetition of *shame* went on, as did the beating on the door. Bethanna covered her ears. Her mother's voice penetrated, pricked her heart, and could not be accepted anymore. Bethanna screamed to suppress it. Like the maddest woman alive, she would scream herself insane to the end of the day, if need be, and somehow win. The door shook under a barrage of loud bangs. If her mother beat it down, then she would have to fight; there was nothing else to do. She quieted and looked around for a makeshift weapon but before she could pick one out from the clutter, the noise ceased. She heard Hertha's shoes descend the steps and then silence.

Mirra cried under her bed, never hearing such rancorous noise in her life, and certainly not from her meek sister. Maybe love had made her crazy, and she had misbehaved with her soldier friend, only to gain her mother's wrath. Mirra had brought in her yard cat Hoffen, and held the shaking creature to her chest. God help her if she was discovered with it. Out in the parlor, she heard her mother complaining in German, crying also. In a few moments, the door slammed.

Hearing the front door shut hard, Bethanna's senses returned and she checked her door to find it had held strong. She noticed, too, her face stung and throbbed with sharp pains at her nose and mouth, and she wiped the area with her dress sleeve. A streak of blood stained the cloth. Tears flooded her eyes as she fought for breath. Part of her, the little girl, wanted to fall to the floor and weep, but she wouldn't let it.

She reached under the bed for Jon's poetry book and held it close to her heart. The old camp bed creaked as she sat down against the rustic headboard, brought her knees up and leaned against the pillows. In the quiet, hot room she heard a voice, her own voice, perhaps for the first time praying outside the church, "Lord, take us from this valley of sin. It must end, all of the pain, must end. Dear Jesus, son of God, hear my plea."

Rocking gently on the bed, she meditated and thought with a new reason, a new mind. Without panic or long deliberation, a plan came so clearly that she reacted verbally, "Ah ha," she said softly, when it occurred to her just what to do.

* * *

A curious dog—one of Hessier's blood hounds—sniffed out the very thing that dogs cannot resist: a dead creature. After the dog's discovery of his scout's shot body, Captain Hessier spent a leisurely day in Taldorf like the rebels had. If the Confederates could, by God, why couldn't his troopers? He wanted to leave his stamp on the territory before Colonel Rain's brigade swept up and cut off the whole area, and with new motivation—a dead scout— that stamp would be lasting. News from his local informants told that the Confederates were collecting their scattered units, and the chance for the raiders to feed on the rich valley would be gone soon.

Not wanting to leave anything to the reinforced enemy, the captain's men burned the crop storage barns and in a nasty gesture, invaded fruit cellars and axed the jars where they sat on the shelves. In a kind spirit of paternal admonishment, Captain Hessier did not allow killing. He needed the Germans to farm for him and regrow something for the fall harvest. In one unfortunate incident that the captain could not control, Mr. Blatz had no explanation for the dead scout's horse found tied to his trees and eventually he was shot as he tried to stop the spoiling of his apple stores. He lived, but there was general fear of instant death to anyone who resisted. To keep the farmers from sharing their bounty, the raiders shot a third of all livestock and cut away what meat they wanted from the carcasses, to which the ever-droning flies gathered. Wild hogs and vultures fed openly on the dead animals laying in fields, yards, and the village roads.

Although Hertha annoyed him, Captain Hessier restrained his men from her property and instead, nailed a note to the Gurtag doorpost which declared the house a loyal Union dwelling and the home of Major Gurtag of the Engineers. "This is mostly for my men; they will forget in a few weeks," said the captain. He had made other examples like this in the territory, but this one may pay off in the future, as the major knew high-up Army brass.

Wisely, Hertha offered the captain two cows from her meager stock, a donation to the Union cause. He tied them to his personal supply mules, already loaded with booty from his latest campaign in Jonesville.

He was tempted to nail a note to the reverend's door, but without Union service, Grottmacher was forced to deliver the one desirable thing he possessed, his younger wife. Hessier wanted the pretty twenty six year-old redhead at first glance and he wasted no time. Lorina said no words in protest as Hessier told the reverend to, "depart to the Gurtag house until dark!" This he would do, but not before a visit to his cellar, where alone, he attempted to blur his brain on hidden drink. He never drank to excess, especially when there was a need of clear thinking amid rebel troops and the raider's unexpected visits, but now, a new endurance was needed. As he sipped whiskey amid fallen apricots, pears and candied preserves, he sucked up the pain, gulped a bitter repast, and listened as his wife sacrificed for his very life, just above the floorboards. Even in her state of odious service, Grottmacher could not leave her.

In midafternoon, he sobered enough to sweep up broken glass and bad fruit, but before leaving the cellar, he smelled food cooking upstairs. He presumed that the captain planned to stay with his wife all day, have a meal with his officers, and then…She was young and strong, and would recover from the torture with his love and care, if she were not too ashamed to remain with him.

Lorina had come from strong stock overseas, reared in Nova Scotia. Her fire and will burned deep, and he knew only death could extinguish them. Their five years of marriage had been more like missionary work, than a passionate union and to encourage himself, he nurtured the idea of their future together, perhaps children and a home elsewhere. At the Gurtag gate, he turned to see his house, God's house. He wondered which dweller had left it first.

Grottmacher saw Hertha sitting on her front porch, rocking slightly, and at her feet, the hard wood cane. She responded, and stood. "Vhat can I do for you, sir?"

"With no safe place to go, I was instructed to come here and wait. Why do you look as though you have lost all? You have not been abused, have you?"

"You have no idea," she said.

In a short time, and with the reverend's help for a truce, Bethanna came down from the upper room and paused at the landing. She had been napping and was groggy. Grottmacher saw her bruised face, messy hair and said nothing, but evidently, a battle had started between the mother and daughter, a fight that for once he thought, the daughter would not concede. He studied the girl and detected the same stout will that he witnessed last night, before her foray into his cellar. Strange, he thought, was her fascination over the rebel visitors, altogether a valid reason to conduct a truce in the house and ready them for evacuation.

The reverend stood in their parlor as the two women sat in opposite chairs, indifferent, like two in-laws who hardly knew the intent of the other in some long-raging feud. Not bothering with family issues, he decided to explain the immediate facts. "Taldorf will soon be ruined. Most of the animals have been stolen or killed. Many homes are damaged and folks left with little means to keep themselves safe. I believe I must take all those who are willing to leave and…."

"Do not say it, sir." Hertha interrupted. "I refuse to go. They will not touch me here." The sudden wry smile on her face was genuine, though misplaced, and in some rare comfort she relaxed and leaned back in her chair. "I have my husband's name, his records. We will stay."

In recent months, the reverend had noticed a depression of Hertha's mind, her speech and mood, and that's what made her lightness now even more disturbing. How this depression worked, he did not know, only that it had caused harm to Bethanna. "Must I remind you, Frau Gurtag, about the treatment of young girls in the hands of lewd and desperate troopers?"

Bethanna touched her face, winced, and shared a look with Grottmacher. His eyes, in a blink, offered sympathy, but could not linger in consolation because, as she knew, he always worked like a wise shepherd to keep the goats and cows on even ground and never to favor one over the other. In him, her trust had been shaken, but his plan met hers exactly—to leave. Obviously, the reverend noticed her mother's oddness, but was not willing to openly acknowledge it; a wise strategy if he wanted calm in the house.

Bethanna recalled the near-rape by the trooper that morning. "Yes, Mother, what about the raiders and their horrid appetites, how will you defend us?"

"They cannot enter. We have a warrant on the door post," she said. "I vill not leave your fahzer's house to ze rebels, your friends."

"But, Mother, you must remember, it was a rebel corporal that saved us from pillage. And who now destroys the valley? The Bluecoats from the north."

Hertha chewed the thought like rough bacon. Although the statement was true, and the soldier had performed admirably, she figured the rebels had owed her such treatment, but that did not make it right for her daughter to owe them back. As Bethanna's sympathies came to mind, Hertha gave little thought to her daughter's wisdom and presumptive care. She glared at Bethanna. "We should all be loyal to our clan, our town. I vill stay here and wait on Vogal, until the end."

The reverend stayed for the remainder of the day, while the raiders searched the heart of the village. Before he left for home, he met Bethanna near the well shed as she fetched water for soup. "Listen, I am planning to leave at dawn. The Dansells are gathering supplies in a secret place, where we have hidden oxen and carts at the ready. Meet us on the south ridge before the full sun and we will carry you to Knoxville."

"The soldiers will not harm us?" Bethanna asked.

"No. They will let us go. If your mother chooses to remain here, do not stay with her and do not listen to her. Understand?"

That night in their bedroom, the sisters mulled over the reverend's offer. Mirra thought leaving the only wise choice. To stay meant to trust Hertha's judgment and thin protection. "She always thinks that Father's shotgun will save us? Look at what she has done with it. She is dingbats I say."

"I know, she is not being a mother anymore," Bethanna said. "We must leave with Reverend Grottmacher tomorrow, and hope that she is angry enough to follow us. I will leave a note saying that we are safe with Uncle Hinchel in Knoxville."

It was their last night in the valley, for how long neither knew. They locked the bedroom door and crawled into their double bed, fully dressed, as they expected a sure interruption during the night, be it Hertha's wrath, or the dark captain's men, they were ready to jump out the window. Not for some years had Mirra needed serious comfort from her big sister, but as Bethanna held her close and hummed the old folksong about the moon, Mirra rested in the embrace. As she closed her eyes to sleep, the thought of going to the city made her smile.

Early the next morning, before the sun touched the hills, Bethanna stood on the south ridge road and looked out over the smoke-laden fields of her valley. Most of the central village burned as the meetinghouse collapsed in a cracking tangle of wasted timber. The wind blew hard, renewing dead fires and spreading embers over the fields. Flames stood out in the shadowed plain like jumping demons set loose to play on earth. It looked as though to her the Revelation of the Bible, the prophecy as it pertained to the end destruction, had come upon them with its hellish curses and fiery lakes. This definition she quickly accepted and it helped to dampen her emotions, as everything she had ever loved died in fire. It was not God's wrath she decided, but Satan's reward for sinners.

The wind struck Bethanna's face, filling her lungs with the smell of charred crops and dead animals. She knew it as the smell of war and all of its uncertainty, which like this dark cloud of smoke, shrouded her future in doubt. Whatever that future, she will face it with God's help. Already, her responsibility for Mirra brought new focus to her role of protector. As for Hertha, her wellbeing amid the ruined fields of the valley would be up to the Lord. Bethanna's eyes stung and watered as she viewed her mother's house for the last time through the smoke.

She turned and raised herself onto the reverend's ox cart. Next to her, Mirra held Hoffen in her lap. The small cat chased the oxen's flicking tails with his wide eyes. All was ready, but there remained one last thing to do. "Now you must take this, and tell his parents the truth." She handed her dead cousin's small bible to Reverend Grottmacher.

"Yes, I will take it now," he said.

Ahead of her on the road, several more carts stood ready to make the long drive to Knoxville, where her aunt and uncle will care for her and Mirra.

Pulled by oxen and mules, a line of rustic farmers' wagons turned down a small winding road and left behind the shadow of the valley.

* * *

To Major Vogal Gurtag,
2nd Kentucky Engineers Army of the Cumberland, Dept. 3

Dear Father,

I miss you very much and pray that you are well. This is the second letter I send you in a few days. I am sorry not to write good news at this time. The valley has been raided and much destroyed. Captain Hessier's Kentucky troopers have returned with many horses and fought with a Confederate patrol. Mother talked with them and I am afraid she thought they were friends. However, they have done nothing friendly.

There have been bargains made for the exchange of rebel prisoners by our village folk. This I found from seeing. I know other things, Father, and cannot say in a letter. Our house is untouched, but only because of your service record and your reputation in the country here. During the raid of Taldorf, I feared for Mirra and myself. We have escaped with Reverend Grottmacher and he will take us to Uncle Hinchel's Inn. This letter comes to you from Howard's Quarters way-station on the road to Sycamore. As for Mother, you know her dark moods, and she has refused to go with us. She says that she will wait for you, even though you are not expected back soon. Please, if you can, come home and see to mother. Bring her up north, where she will be away from the combat.

It disturbs me that I left our house, but the Northern troopers have hurt people and destroyed food preserves. I am very sorry to leave Mother there, but I am thinking for myself and Mirra. Please be safe, and come as soon as you can. We love you, Papa, God hold you, Bethanna.

* * *

Battle of Tazewell

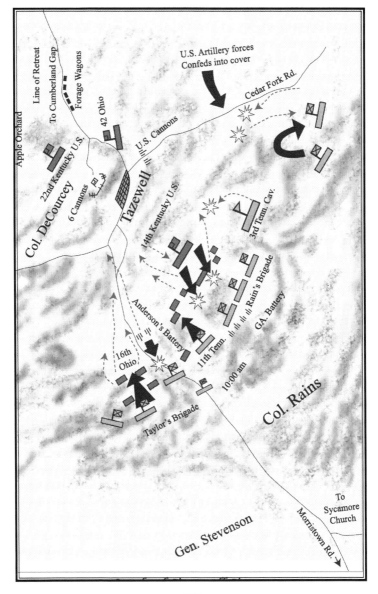

Line of Retreat

To Cumberland Gap

Forage Wagons

42 Ohio

U.S. Artillery forces Confeds into cover

Cedar Fork Rd.

Apple Orchard

22nd Kentucky U.S.

Col. DeCourcey

6 Cannons

Tazewell

U.S. Cannons

U.S. Cannons

14th Kentucky U.S.

3rd Tenn. Cav.

Rain's Brigade

G.A. Battery

Anderson's Battery

16th Ohio

11th Tenn.

10:00 am

Col. Rains

Taylor's Brigade

Gen. Stevenson

To Sycamore Church

Morristown Rd.

CHAPTER 16★

On the evening of August 4, six horsemen rode through the narrow and darkened valley of Little Sycamore, a hamlet five miles east of the town of Tazewell. In a hollow to their left, Sycamore Creek trickled black and shiny through the valley floor like a watery snake creeping south into the Clinch River. The horsemen stopped in front of a rustic cabin, 100 yards from the small, boxy Missionary Baptist Church.

Confederate General Carter L. Stevenson ascended the cabin steps while behind him in the yard, his staff waited on their mounts. At the cabin door, Colonel Rains greeted the general, a man who was sixteen years his elder, and a graduate of West Point. "Sir, I am honored and a bit worried. I expected you at dusk."

Stevenson took off his wide brim hat. "Yes, pardon my late arrival. I spent an hour trying to find Captain Yeizer in this pitch-blackness. It shouldn't have been difficult. His Georgia gunners sing well into the night." He walked into the modest HQ, a primitive home built long ago when Indians roamed freely. Black drapes covered the few windows and many candles burned in makeshift stands, inkwells, bottles, and a pie plate. "I must see to your accommodations, Colonel. It looks as though you have just held Catholic mass in here," Stevenson said.

Rains chucked as his boyish eyes twinkled in the glow. "I have been writing orders with my adjutant, Henry."

Ringed by candles in a corner of the room, a young lieutenant sorted through papers on the flat top of a travel chest. His makeshift camp desk proved great for writing, but having no matching chair, its low posture hurt his back. He winced as he stood and saluted. "General." He reached for his uniform coat.

"At ease, Henry. Please take notes, if you will be so kind," Stevenson said, while he inspected a nearby chair. His tired frame took the seat with caution and when it proved steady, he thumped his boots on the floor. Relaxing, he brushed his thinning hair with his fingers. "I need to inform you on the latest developments concerning the Yankee brigade and their advancements on the town of Tazewell. Without delay, I must show you my plan to deal with them."

Rains sat opposite Stevenson and offered him a cup of coffee. Stevenson waved off. "No thanks, upset stomach." He pulled a folded paper from his coat and spread it out over his leg.

Colonel Rains filled his and Henry's cups with the dark brew. "Sir, has Colonel DeCourcy retreated from Tazewell?"

"No, worse, I am afraid. He has occupied the town and allowed his men to commit outrages against the citizenry." Stevenson rubbed his head, as if it hurt. "It is strange, but typical; the enemy assaults the very people who have surrendered to him without complaint and yet whom he calls his *Unionist ally*. He has attempted to forage every corner of Claiborne County and if unchecked, his advance will encourage General Morgan to increase such actions in east Tennessee. And sink his teeth into the rail link."

"I see. Can we meet DeCourcy and tell him how rude he is?" Rains asked.

"Yes, Colonel, we will. Here is the lay of things, as we stand now." Stevenson showed Rains his local map. "Colonel Taylor's men ran into the Yankee column near the Clinch River and put a scare into them here, about six miles from town. DeCourcy took his forage wagons and retreated back to Tazewell. Fortunately, yesterday evening in a wooded area east of the town our pickets obtained a dozen cowbells and under the disguise of a herd, they were able to approach the Union lines to reconnoiter. A small skirmish ensued, but we were able to determine that he commands a brigade, including two Kentucky regiments, volunteers from the divided state, no doubt a result of fresh recruiting there."

The General loosened his collar, and continued. "His artillery is mounted in a small redoubt of earthworks above the town, on this hill here. And most of his troops are camped behind the guns, near this large groove of apple trees. Colonel DeCourcy relies on his cannons to cover any approach though the valley in his front, but this evening, his most inexperienced pickets guarded the hills east of town and their deportment was somewhat foolhardy and relaxed. If he dares to repeat this again, we will have a clear go at them."

Colonel Rains, now very interested, pulled up a chair closer to Stevenson. "Looks like the Federals have no idea of our strength. Sir, can our guns reach that hill?"

"As you know, I put into action your Eufaula Alabama battery and deployed their mountain howitzers northeast, on the Cedar Fork lane. After dueling with DeCourcy's fort above the town intermittently, we discovered that the Union guns can easily cover the valley road, but lack the range to strike the hills on the opposite side."

General Stevenson pointed out the contours on the map. "These tall hills are the key, as they afford great cover for an assault. My plan calls for Taylor's brigade to sweep up the Morristown Road, take the small gap in the range of hills, and remain centered on the road towards the town."

Stevenson found a position on the map and pointed. "Colonel Rains, your brigade will fall in on Taylor's right and scale the heights to the east, do you see? Advance your troops through the valley and push back the Union reinforcements that arrive there, if any. However, do not lose contact with Taylor's right. Is that clear to you?"

"Absolutely, General." Colonel Rains nodded. He noticed his aide, Henry, writing every word. The young adjutant gulped his coffee and rubbed his back.

Stevenson continued, "The 3rd Tennessee cavalry will cover your northern flank and assail those units of the enemy who attempt an escape up the valley. My determined time for a fully coordinated attack is the morning of the sixth, or as soon as Colonel Taylor's whole brigade is assembled. There may be an issue with the recent morning fog. In the dawn mist, uniforms of both sides turn a pale gray. This could cause problems. Take every caution, Colonel."

"Sir, it's a sound plan," Rains replied, tracing the map with his finger. "We will be ready, and my old 11th will hinge the line with Colonel Taylor's brigade, here on this ridge."

* * *

AUGUST 6, 1862

On the ridge that shields the north side of Tazewell, a tall, well-dressed Union commander walked briskly out of his tent followed by his aides. Trailing behind them was a sweaty courier who had just ridden fifteen miles from Cumberland Gap.

"It's too bloody late for that now!" Colonel DeCourcy yelled, responding to General Morgan's messenger in a refined British accent. "What kind of timing is this, Corporal? The general may have to wait for his wagons, as you can plainly hear; we have been attacked!" DeCourcy spun away from Morgan's courier and approached his staff, who readied several horses for their ride into the battle zone.

The messenger slapped his thigh with the dusty gauntlets he carried, an outburst in symbolic defense of General Morgan and against the ruination of his anticipated return to the Gap for a large lunch, now nullified by Confederate attack. From what he had gathered, in Colonel DeCourcy's exchanges with his aides, his advanced regiment, the 16th Ohio, had been completely surprised on the range of hills, two miles across the expansive valley.

The colonel mounted his white charger and took on an air of command that the corporal could not contend with. DeCourcy was a soldier since his early teens, trained in the British tradition, and had worked his way up honestly in the American regimental system. Today, his experience and polish would be tested, and he jumped at the chance.

"Sir, should I wait? Or ride back to the General?" The courier asked, standing under DeCourcy's high gaze.

"Forget it, I have already sent a message out telling General Morgan that there is a large force coming down on our positions east, south, and who knows where else. I will resist the enemy for now." In a flurry of clear speech, DeCourcy tossed orders to the waiting riders. "Tell Captain Foster to advance Lieutenant Anderson's two guns. If you can, find Major Kershner, tell him to pull the 16th back behind Anderson." In flash of dust, the colonel and his aides dashed off to observe what was surely to be a disorganized front line.

As the exasperated courier approached the Union gun emplacements, dug out in an angular semi-circle on the crown of the hill, he saw for the first time an overall view of what DeCourcy had seen through the clearing fog. In the hazy distance stood a range of hills across the valley and on two of them, clouds of battle smoke drifted and peeled away in the high breeze. For an instant, he beheld the tiny red flags of the Confederates as they glided out from under the tree line.

* * *

In the valley south of town, Lieutenant Anderson, a young officer of the Wisconsin Artillery, unlimbered his two guns astride the Morristown Road, in open view of the enemy. His drivers started the limber teams, as if to pull them fast to the rear. "No, keep them nearby, we may need them very soon!" He turned to his men and yelled, "Load the canister rounds for close range!"

The gunners looked at each other, only for a second, eager to try the *hellfire* on massed troops. The shotgun-like rounds devastated infantry formations effectively at 200 yards, more preferably, closer than that. The teams went into action, eight men per gun, each man with a distinct position. Loading, charging, priming, fuse cutting, and sponging occurred with a drilled-in professionalism, marked by cool hands and clean work.

Anderson aimed both guns towards the gap to their front, where the Morristown Road entered the valley. He wanted to hit the enemy ranks much closer, so he sighted on dead reckoning, where the road curved 125 yards away. "When the enemy makes the curve, we will let them have it!" he shouted.

A company of infantry came up behind the lieutenant's position for support. "Been told to hold the road sir at all hazards," their captain announced.

Lieutenant Anderson nodded with approval before shouting at his gunners, "Fire!" The canister rounds flashed from the battery and streaked towards a rebel company testing the road's safety beyond the curve. Fogging the gunners' view, sulfuric smoke floated momentarily in a pair of white circles.

"Plenty of hazards here, sir!" Anderson shouted, as he pointed down the road with his gold-handled sword.

As the infantry company took positions to the left and right, their captain searched through the bank of smoke and saw the rebel casualties being pulled out of the roadway. "They have been staggered!" he shouted to Anderson.

In an instant, more gray troops converged astride the lane and formed in mass for a charge. The infantry captain looked back at Lieutenant Anderson and received a nod, assuring him that the battery had seen the rebel threat.

Looking up the long slope to his right, Anderson saw more rebel rifles firing in echelon by battalion. Scattered units of the 16th Ohio, unable to form enough numbers to counter the swarming rebels, broke in disorganized groups towards the valley floor and the cover of dense woods.

On the slope to the left, the same scenario took shape as a Confederate regiment cleared the trees and traded fire with the Major Kernsher's detached companies. In a matter of minutes, the battery would be swallowed up whole. Anderson shouted, "Load!"

Like unexpected hail, bullets struck the caissons only a few yards to the rear. A horse went down in harness and was killed instantly. Seconds after, two attendants fell wounded at their posts. From their high vantage point, the Confederates rained easy shots onto the exposed battery from every frontal position. Another man fell as he attempted to bring up ammo and soon the teamsters were brought up to assist the gunners in their isolated, targeted space. The buzzing of insect-like bullets forced the cannoneers to bob and duck in wasted gestures while they worked to load the tin canister rounds into the gun barrels.

"This is it, gentlemen!" yelled Lieutenant Anderson. While sighting the road down the smooth cannon barrel, he noticed a pull at his coat. A messenger handed him a folded paper.

Lieutenant Anderson,

I send to your relief Colonel Cochran and the 14th Kentucky,

taking position to your rear and left. They will cover your flank.
Can you hold? What is the condition on the right? Col. DeCourcy.

For Anderson's battery, the condition on the right had ceased to be, and he wasn't about to pencil off a dispatch to describe it. In contrast, on his left, and in that rare moment when paper orders made good on promises, 300 yards behind Anderson's cannons the 14th Kentucky Infantry rushed into hasty lines and took position on a knoll. In their front on the long ridge, scattered remnants of the 16th Ohio retreated down the slopes, most of them without rifles. The sight of their comrades' disorganized retreat did not encourage them. But their leader tried nonetheless.

That leader, Colonel Cochran, steered his horse between companies and gave orders for the deployment of his reserves. At an interval, he observed two more Confederate regiments cresting the long ridge to his left, which extended the enemy flank further north. "How many sons 'a bitches are there?" he exclaimed to his adjutant.

The lieutenant glared at the enclosing enemy, his wide, young eyes took in the danger as the Confederates fired down the ridge. Although he was not a veteran of combat like his commander, he was more afraid of disgrace than death, and he did not flinch in the presence of danger. "This is a good place to hold them, sir!" he yelled. Colonel Cochran nodded, knowing they could never *hold them.*

* * *

Lieutenant Weston sent Colonel Rains a gift of twenty-five prisoners from the 16th Ohio regiment, with his compliments. The 11th Tennessee fared well during the opening moments of the attack when they swept easily up the ridgeline adjacent to Morristown Road without resistance, thanks to the piles of stacked arms left there by the Yankee pickets. Now, the skirmish pace quickened as they pushed westward over the top of the tall hill and met the Federal holdouts, who still possessed weapons. To their right, and in perfect line, the brigade topped the ridge to the north, crowned by trees and tall grass.

Two hundred yards down the slope, Jon could plainly see the Bluecoats scurrying into tree breaks, and the ground behind them littered with their canteens, rifles, and knapsacks. On the valley road, a two-gun Union battery fought for its life as the cannoneers scurried about the caissons. Only a few minutes ago, he witnessed one of Colonel Taylor's companies take the canister rounds like hissing lightning bolts as the scatter-shot knocked men over in groups and slowed their advance in the narrow roadway.

Jon loaded his musket, aimed down the slope and fired at the Union battery, partially obscured by trees. The fact that the gunners were still there amazed him. He wondered if he could work as they did, calmly, perfectly, under the open rain of bullets.

The company moved toward a fence line and Captain Binns halted the men. A sudden cry arose from the gap, its pitch easily heard above the rifles. Jon looked to his left, down the long slope, and he saw a massed formation of Confederates charging up the tree-lined road straight into the sights of the battery. Four flags waved at the head of the screaming column. A lone man was out front leading the living train, whether he was an officer or not, no one could see. Jon felt his heart explode with pride and he jumped up on the highest fence post to lift himself above the other men. With all he could muster, he gave a loud, shrieking cheer.

The yell caught every one's attention and shunning danger to see the charge themselves, they stepped up on the rails like Corporal Lyhton. Around him, the men in D Company were electrified into the event and the whole fence line joined in with their yelling comrades, careening up the road.

Two massive reports shook the area and echoed through the gap. The lead elements of the rebel charge were swept away in a cloud of red mist, and the onrushing column stumbled forward over dead and maimed comrades, now a shredded heap sprawled across the road.

Jon gasped at the mass killing as the men fell silent around him, with mouths open in utter shock. None of them had never seen such a sight, or heard the horrific screams of wounded and dying men. One flag waved in a weak circle over the scattered fragments of humanity crushed by the point blank iron spray. A flag bearer had survived long enough to encourage his stunned comrades with his last honor. The torn banner stood upright for a few seconds and then finally fell onto the bleeding heap of flesh.

* * *

Colonel DeCourcy lowered his binoculars, still trained on the smoke-filled lane between the hills. "By God in heaven, that's how it's done!" Snapping his reigns, the colonel turned his horse and found his courier. "Tell Foster I want every gun in support of Anderson and the 14th. And he must cover the 16th's retreat!" The dusty courier jumped into his saddle and beat the horse's rump with his broad, blue hat.

Closer to the action now, Colonel DeCourcy scanned the wide valley in front of the town with his binoculars and saw where broken cover and undulating terrain could slow the rebels in their advance, during which he could rain fire on them from a superior height. By then, he knew that the rebels would be spent from their constant advance. What he didn't realize was that his men were well on their way to exhaustion.

Lieutenant Anderson had no time to admire his work. The heroic stand of the Wisconsin gunners would only be a high note in a tragic requiem if his guns were overrun by the rebel tide. The gunners collected their wounded, while the teamsters backed up their horses and latched the guns.

"Yes, exactly. Gentlemen, we should go," Anderson said cheerfully. He jumped on his horse and doffed his cap to the onrushing rebels, less than fifty yards away.

Smacked and chopped with lead bullets, the battery ripped up the road like two runaway train cars and within minutes, their former position became crowded with Confederates from Alabama, Georgia, and Tennessee. These troops happened to land on the southern flank of the 14th Kentucky, holding fast to the woods at the base of the ridge, unsupported.

* * *

Jon took this time to reload, and in the attempt, found heavy resistance in the barrel as he hammered the bullet with his ramrod. "Damn this fouling!" he yelled. His heightened nerves peaked as wayward bullets splintered low branches over his head and the wood chips fell about him. To his left, a squad of men in C Company halted, lifted their rifles in one steady motion and on a lieutenant's command fired a perfect volley. Gaining his attention to his right, Lawsen and Rossberger waved gleefully as they regaled their iconic friend. "I swear to high Canaan Jonnie, you got the men goin', sure as hell!" yelled Lawsen.

"What do you mean?" Jon shouted back, as he replaced his ramrod.

"Back there." Rossberger pointed up the hill to their previous position. "That humdinger of a rebel yell, that's what he means. Standing up in sniper fire, that's what he means, hell, I thought you were gonna lead the second assault on them guns!"

Jon did not react proudly, only nodded, perplexed. He didn't notice any *sniper fire*. The bravery of others enthralled him for a moment. Perhaps some spirit floating about in the high energy of battle, where the senses are more receptive to foolhardy impulses, moved him up on that fence rail. It was nothing compared to charging cannons. "Yeah, well, sometimes ya need to yell!"

Cawley, who stood behind Jon in the second rank, shouted. "Yell? When do we start yellin'?"

Jon accepted his friend's adoration and prepared to move out on Sergeant Hillford's signal. Behind them, he heard Captain Binns ordering a contingent of the company forward. To his right, extended across the ridge, a large portion of the brigade's formations rose and fell on the lumpy terrain as the lines disappeared into swales and tree stands. The attack progressed in full order.

Lieutenant Weston eyed the alignment of his men. "Keep ranks, prepare your weapons!"

Throughout the morning advance, men who needed better weapons had the opportunity to get them. New U.S. issue .58 Caliber Springfield rifles lay in the open like crops ready for harvest, or like earlier, stacked in threes, complete with cartridge boxes and with luck, bayonets. The dependable Northern weapons were well known to the Confederate forces that had experienced an inequity in arms at the outset of the war. To their officers' horror, a third of the men in the 11th used their outdated hunting flintlocks from the 1830s. Some had been modified to fit the newer percussion cap firing system, but were still non-rifled weapons.

Jon heard Lawsen laugh and joke as he talked up his new rifle with Rossberger, though he saved his shotgun, strapped to his back. Strange place to laugh, Jon thought, but the men dealt with combat in different ways. He could not laugh, nor could he turn quiet and angry like Martello and Hobston. Still, his animated display on the fence surprised him. Amid the guns and bloodied men, he could not resist the excitement, the panic, a sensation beyond fear that made him march, fire, and want to kill. Surely, it was the regiment that pulled him into the enemy, like the will of a large animal with many parts, weapons and brains, born in training and enticed to fight.

Sergeant Hillford was the instinct of that animal, as he paced the rear of the double line. His job was to catch any man who ran away and kick him back into place, but today the need for such discipline did not arise. The company moved with the regiment in renewed order down the slope through scattered pines and oaks.

As they marched out of the trees, sporadic sniper fire took a few men at their knees. They rolled forward, yelling like they'd been swatted with cow prods. Jon felt a shockwave between his calves. In seconds, he realized it was a wild bullet. Thankfully, the regiment halted, and an order sounded from the rear, "Fire by rank, squad, ready. Front rank, aim!"

In his view, from side to side, 200 muskets came up and made steady. Down the barrel, about sixty yards away, Jon saw a group of Federals scatter from a tree cluster ahead and run for a fence line located behind them. Shooting someone in the back did not appeal to most men, but in the heat of this large fight, Jon did not worship the gods of fairness. With vivid clarity, he had seen the great carnage of his fellows in the road and upon their deaths he was turned into a tool for their vengeance.

Colonel Gordon had given the orders to aim, and before he fired, Jon's heart leapt at the sound of the young colonel's voice. "Volunteers, fire!"

The hillside exploded and through the hanging white smoke, yells arose from the trees ahead. Jon prepared to reload for close combat. The heavy Austrian rifle had performed poorly and a pain in his armpit gave notice of the gun's nickname, well earned. "The mule" had a hard kick and after many shots, Jon's shoulder throbbed as he worked to reload. He recalled Lawsen's lighter Springfield.

"Rear rank, ready, aim!"

Stepping up and placing their rifles between the men in the first rank, the second line paused. "Fire!"

More smoke and flame covered the hillside. The men pulled in their rifles and within seconds, the first rank was ready to fire again.

Colonel Gordon darted into view on his chestnut stallion and with Major Thedford, second in command, rode to the stand of trees. With his binoculars, Gordon scanned the base of the ridge in front and apparently found a target. He turned back to his men. "Fix bayonets! Prepare to advance!"

Like an angered beast taking a breath, exposing its claws, the regiment made ready to pounce upon their enemy. Ahead, the ground leveled out to a fence that ran along the edge of a grassy field dotted by a grove of cherry trees and there, Gordon had seen blue columns of the 14th Kentucky. "To the fence, charge!"

The whole regiment stormed down the hill, through the copse of trees and found that the enemy had moved away again. The wounded Yanks were left alone except for a few random acts of canteen-sharing. The color guard climbed over the rails first and waited on the companies to re-form. As the troops maneuvered the fence line, staff officers kicked a gap into it for Colonel Gordon's horse to trot though. Gordon's voice rang out, "First rank, fire at will to cover our advance!"

As men took their places, they began a skirmish fire, meant to belay the effects of snipers. As this was done, a fuller volley boomed from the field and the 11th absorbed it. Troops fell out wounded and a few, never to move again. The regimental lines thickened and the unit stood solid again.

On his horse, Colonel Gordon moved in behind the color guard and shouted, "Advance, at the quick step, ho!"

The men stepped off into the field, which rose gradually up to the cherry grove and as they neared it, they could see three companies of the 14th Kentucky kneeling under cover of low branches.

Coming into full view, the 11th stretched beyond both flanks of the Kentuckians, a sure mismatch in firepower. Gordon halted the men, gave the order to aim, and when the guns went up, the Kentuckians wavered. Before the 11th's rifles blazed the field, the Bluecoats withered and ran, leaving in their wake an empty space of trees, grass and a few kicking wounded. For a second, before the smoke cleared, Jon thought the 11th had killed every one of them.

Along the ridge base, broken volleys rang out further north as the 42nd Georgia gained the valley floor and engaged pockets of resistance sniping from hedges and woods. Every passing minute, the battle moved steadily into the heart of the valley.

Colonel Gordon sent out F Company as skirmishers, to probe the enemy, if they remained to fight. The Yankees' green troops angered him, as they chose to inflict casualties, then run, without facing him honorably. Perhaps wise tactics for men unused to trading blow for blow, face to face. He called Major Thedford and the two men advanced to reconnoiter with the skirmishers.

Jon noticed Lawsen laughing as he held up a red hand. His nose dripped blood like a leaky pump. He didn't seem to mind the crimson trickle as he checked himself for more wounds. Jon and Martello helped Private Hale Daniel, who was grazed in both legs. His brother, Sheldon, had been wounded a week ago near Taldorf.

"Darn it, that's both of us," Hale moaned, embarrassed. They walked him to the fence line, where Jon was shocked to see Dr. Larkin scrambling down the hill towards them.

"Doc? What the hell are you doing this far forward?"

"J.B. Lyhton, I'm walking my dog, what do you think I'm doing!"

Jon shook his head, confused. "Okay, but…"

The doctor wore his black hat and tan coat, a familiar sign to the men that help was on the way, want it or not. Donning his spectacles, he went to work with his assistant to quickly stop the serious cases from bleeding to death before they had a chance at treatment.

Jon stepped over to care for Lawsen, whose humor had changed in mere seconds. He was visibly shaken and upset.

"Paul?"

Lawsen pointed to a body. Rossberger lay flat, not moving, his face a purple mask. "Jonnie, I never saw it." Lawsen's previous euphoria evaporated.

"Damnation." Jon walked over to Rossberger and knelt. It took no real inspection to know the man was dead. The bullet had hit his temple, bashing it like a hammer blow. Jon picked up Rossberger's hat and covered the swollen face. Knowing the time for proper prayers would come later, when Reverend Pitts would commemorate their dead, Jon paused briefly in reverence.

* * *

From a wooded rise in the Tazewell valley, Colonel DeCourcy observed the retreat of the 16th Ohio and the near flanking of the 14th Kentucky. The men spread out across the tree-clumped valley, which forced the Confederates to spread out, also in their pursuit. Near the Morristown Road, the units tangled and blended into each other, causing many Federals to be trapped and captured. He could not order Foster's battery, posted on the hill above town, into action until he was sure that his harassed units in front had cleared out of the way.

Evidently, because of the larger Confederate presence, he knew this was not a fight he could win with a bold, properly placed counter stroke. He received reports from the front that there were more Confederate regiments on the ridge not yet engaged and that his men had been outnumbered at every position. The only option remained to escape without heavy loss and allow his artillery to open on the exposed rebels, to bloody them for a change. He sent out orders to fulfill his new plans.

* * *

Captain Binns and Lieutenant Weston assessed D Company's situation. They had lost a man and three had been wounded bad enough to be carried to safer positions, but overall they had pulled through without heavy loss. Proud and energized, Captain Binns paced the area as he flicked the grass with the tip of his sword. "Not bad for a bunch of Nashville boys, I'd say not bad at all." He noticed Lawsen standing over the slain Rossberger and he tapped the mourner's leg with his sword. "Please, sonny, forget the dead for now, we have more to do."

Lawsen recalled Rossberger's dead face, a sight photographed in his memory, then he looked hard at Captain Binns and when the captain saw him, he reared back. Like some painted savage, tear tracks had cut long lines through the powder stains on Lawsen's face and in a gross accent, the blood from his nose streaked his chin and neck. He stepped up to speak and his eyes widened. "Then I'll forget you when you die."

The captain blinked at him, and walked away.

Lieutenant Colonel Gordon placed his horse behind the 11th's colors once again. His sword rang as he pulled it out into the dusty air. "Prepare to move out!"

Within a few minutes, the men marched quickly as their mounted leader took them forward through the cherry grove and into a field laced with small cedars and shrubs. From there, the lines marched up a gentle rise, thick with wild barley. Looking over the land from his saddle, Gordon noticed the flags of the 42nd Georgia moving forward to his right, 100 yards ahead, where it had reached a second fence line oblique to their front, and was spreading out along its width.

"Fall in with the Georgians, men!" he yelled, directing them with his sword to their place in line.

Before the 11th Tennessee reached the fence, the nasty sound of falling shells hailed their worst fears. Thick chunks of sod erupted from the earth in front of them as fragments of stone and grit flew into their faces. Exposed, the regiment scattered in sections as the flanks ran for cover amid the windbreaks adjacent to the field. The middle ranks held onto the fence and dared not move forward or back.

Colonel Gordon spun his horse while surveying the confusion. Through the smoky field, he saw the color guard huddled together in a dark pile near the fence, as they waved the 11th's flags. Through the dust and smoke, he rode toward them, eager to rally the men to the regimental banners.

Lieutenant Weston's men dove and planted themselves on the earth like human grass. Lawsen shouted to Jon, "Hey, J.B.! Now we're duckin' like cowards, after such a nice march!"

"I can't see a thing...what did you say?" Jon looked for troop formations and saw only rising dust. He looked back to Lieutenant Weston, who had crawled over to Captain Binns, motionless in the grass. If the captain were dead, it would not shock him.

The shelling stopped and Jon popped his head up to listen for orders. His ears rang in a continual high note and he could not distinguish anything certain, as all men seemed to be shouting. In moments, the incoming shells fell again; their deadly vibrations shook the earth under the men's chests.

Jon decided right there that he hated artillery, the damn whizzing, screaming whine of incoming. There was no fighting in it. A good infantryman had no chance in hell against the monstrosity. He yelled aloud against the noise, "Shut up! Shut up!" This was not a gentlemanly thing to do to any one, not even your enemies.

Overhead, random shots exploded prematurely, their fuses blessedly mistimed. Shards of iron rained down on the men in the form of hot metal chunks.

To Lawsen's disappointment, Captain Binns lifted his head from the barley and scanned the area like a half-hidden turtle.

Binns spotted Lawsen, who madly chuckled through his black and bloodied face. He shouted to the private, "Where's the Colonel?"

Lawsen shrugged, disinterested, and pointed to the sky.

Binns frowned. "Damned fool!" He lifted himself up on a knee, and spotted Major Thedford. Verbal orders had failed in the noise, and the major pulled at men's coats to gain their attention to fall back with all speed. So went the orders over the field.

"Take cover in the trees!" yelled Captain Binns, pushing himself up and slapping Lieutenant Weston on the leg.

The bombardment of the 11th stopped, and after a short lull, the Union guns began to scatter the Georgia and South Carolina regiments, who had chased away the 14th Kentucky with a very short-lived skirmish.

To avoid useless casualties from artillery and with no solid Yankee regiments left to fight, General Stevenson ordered the brigades under Rains and Taylor to reclaim their positions on the ridges. As the day wore on, the Union cannons occasionally fired into shady trees or low swales, in attempts to kill hidden rebels, who in separate packs, continued to chase lost Yanks up the valley. Units of both sides mixed among the trees and hollows in the valley floor, and for some of them, it would be a long day before they found their way back to camp.

One of those men turned out to be the missing Lieutenant Colonel Gordon of the 11th Tennessee. When the bombardment started, his staff had seen him ride to the colors and then disappear in the dust and smoke, never to be seen again. Major Thedford sent out men from H Company to find Gordon. Encountering the enemy in a close fight, they succeeded in capturing 42 union men, but had no luck collecting their commander.

Later in the day, Captain Yeizer of the Georgia battery unlimbered two of his guns on a knoll east of town and tossed departing salvos into the Union lines. A genuine duel took shape as Confederate and Federal gunners targeted each other across the embattled space, and at every turn in the contest, their accuracy was measured with shouts and groans at the hits or misses.

Soon, at Colonel Decourcy's urging, all six Union guns were trained on Yeizer's two, and within minutes, the rebel guns stopped. The Georgia battery suffered one damaged cannon and five wounded gunners in the scrap, forcing Captain Yeizer to withdraw for the safety of the guns and crew, as the artillery in the Southern war effort was very difficult to replace.

* * *

CHAPTER 17 ★

FROM THE DIVISION HEADQUARTERS OF;

GEN. CARTER STEVENSON, C.S.A.
To the Honorable *Colonel De Courcy,*

Colonel, under my courier's flag of truce, I call for a halt to hostile fire. I understand that you have in your possession officers of this division, one being Lt. Col. George Gordon of the 11th Tennessee Regiment.

I humbly request an exchange. We have in our possession over seventy-five (75) men of the 16th Ohio Regiment. Also, there are many of our unattended wounded who lay exposed in the heat. I submit that any Union man found in this capacity will be delivered to your lines post haste. In addition, my men have retrieved the remains of Captain Edgars of the 16th Ohio, killed at the outset of hostilities this morning.

I demand nothing in return for him, and he will be moved to the town when suitable transport, fitting an officer, can be found. I also humbly ask for the assistance of a surgeon, since our ablest doctor has been wounded and one of his assistants killed.

I expect a reply, and remind you that my forces stand ready in any event.

Respects,

General C. Stevenson

* * *

Dusk settled in the Tazewell valley, now a quiet place where men searched for wounded, missing, and dead friends. Upon approval of the flag of truce, Lieutenant Weston, Lawsen and Jon went to fetch Rossberger's body, as it still lay in the spot where it fell.

"I done let him down, Jonnie." Lawsen's true feelings poured out as they collected the man's personal items. They retrieved a comb, a religious tract, sewing kit, pipe, folding spoon with knife, and letters from home. Weston picked up Rossberger's 1841 Mississippi rifle and slung it over his shoulder.

Lawsen whined, "His mama's gonna be upset with me."

"Paul, please. He was a soldier, he fought well and is at peace now," said Jon, unsure about the sentiment, but very convincing with his tone.

"Yes, well, he never had a chance to say goodbye. Never had a last word to us, just taken." Lawsen cried for the simplest reason of tradition. The death was bearable, but if possible, a dying man must have last words for his kin to know the condition of his soul. For posterity, this was a remnant of the person and an example of the family's successful rearing. "We had a responsibility," he lamented.

Lieutenant Weston's shadowy form stood over them and spoke behind his lantern. "We will relate his merits to his family. Don't worry, Paul. They will hear his voice again through us. But you must understand, we are lucky just to be able to carry him off, for in war, things may not always work out as properly as we wish."

Lawsen grabbed Jon's wrist. "Jonnie, swear, if I ever get it, and can still utter a word, be there for me. You swear? Someone must be there."

"I swear, I swear. I will see to it with every effort," Jon said, grasping his friend's shoulder. They shook hands over Rossberger's body and when picking him up, grunted at the dead weight, a stiffened, awkward, and uneven load.

"Let's take him down to the road, where the walking is much easier," Lieutenant Weston suggested.

For his family to read his deeds and last words through letters would be much better than seeing the boy's dented and cracked head, and as they carried the body, Lieutenant Weston wondered how to relay the facts about what the relatives may expect, if they come to disinter Rossberger for burial at home. He'd have to make the letter somewhat truthful and tolerable at the same time. As far as his legacy, Rossberger's last words to the enemy, minutes before the charge, were not heavenly. Jon could make up something nice for his mother.

For the troops still hanging on to life through terrible wounds, comfort was given them in the form of a small church and its patron volunteers. The Little Sycamore Missionary Baptist Church accepted the overflow with grace, if not wonder. Well over two hundred wounded men littered their yard, many arriving on the backs of their friends, who continued to step out of the dark woods and trails late into the evening.

The women of the church ripped bandages from tablecloths and transformed their worship pews into treatment tables. Picnic areas turned into triage zones, where men's blood leaked into the holy grounds, now a sacred place of earthly sacrifice. Inside, under hanging brass lights, a borrowed Federal surgeon amputated limbs, or extracted deep bullets while Dr. Larkin, who lay in the corner dosed with morphine, suffered from head wounds received during the earlier bombardment, an unfortunate result of his brave efforts to reach wounded on the battlefield and speed up triage.

After transporting Rossberger's body to a clearing south of camp, Jon and Lawsen sat near the soft trickle of Sycamore Creek and washed away a day of dust and black powder. In low conversation, they reminisced about when they had seen the same church on the platoon's scouting mission more than a week ago. Realizing the irony, they both appreciated the church and its friendly folk.

"Hey J.B., reckon if a man was to be buried after battle, this might be the perfect place?"

"I believe that, yes. You have a peaceful valley, small creek, folks singing hymns every Sunday forever. Yes, it's perfect."

"J.B. That was a hell'uva fight today. I think this war may get worse the longer it goes. Poor Rossy."

"Right now, it seems so. I think each side's waiting for the other to give in. After today, I guess the Federals know we're determined as they are."

"Hey J.B., we should bring Rossy over here and see if he can be buried in that little cemetery on the knoll. Do you see it across the road?"

Jon nodded and recalled how they did the same for Stewart in the Taldorf cemetery. A pleasant warm rush filled him when Bethanna came into his mind. How ironic, too, that her village stood only miles away from this spot on a stream that fed this very creek. He imagined, at this moment, she was standing at her back gate in the dark and looking at the moon, perhaps remembering him fondly. Or not.

His abrupt disappearance from the reverend's cellar may have relieved her fears and caused panic at the same time. In complete distress, Jon and Lawsen had heard the raiders' boots stomp the side path outside the meetinghouse, as they stood ready with their muskets, behind the cellar door. A clatter above them produced the reverend's head, through a trap panel. He lowered a hand to them and they stepped up on a barrel to enter the kitchen. When the grave yard was clear, they ran out the back door to a grove opposite Dansell's store shed. Eluding the busy raiders, they headed for the stream, which led to the platoon's camp, a mile down the valley.

Recently, thoughts of his valley maiden had been easily swept aside, as the anticipation of battle and death took precedent over everything. Now, in the aftershock, his memories of Bethanna seemed an unfair pleasure among the suffering wounded scattered on the church's property.

That night, the 11th made their camp in a grassy hollow near the large ridge. The air was very pleasant and tents were few. D Company settled in and as usual, Jon and Lieutenant Weston talked at the fire.

Jon poured captured Northern tea from Sergeant Hillford's small pot into the lieutenant's cup, then into his. The few men around the campfire snored into the night, hard asleep from the longest day they have ever lived.

The two friends chewed a rare meal of Yankee rations, left to them on the victorious field. The canned pickled herring was especially novel and hard to open, but worth the pains. Jon chuckled as he passed the tin to Weston. "The man who lost these must be sore. He probably got them for his birthday."

Weston grinned. "Yes. They taste very fresh. Indeed, we gained valuable supplies today."

Jon thought about the large number of troops he had seen. "I'd hate to see what it was like at Shiloh. That was thousands of fighting men. I doubt the generals can handle three divisions on the field. How do they see?"

"Shiloh, Tazewell, or back at the hills of Taldorf. It doesn't matter, Jon. Everything we can do for the country, the Army, right down to our little platoon, is all that matters. You need to see the whole effort, without being distracted by doubts."

Jon took a sip of the tea. "I don't doubt the reasons for fighting, nor do I doubt the regiment and its competence."

"Perhaps you doubt yourself?" said Weston.

"What?" said Jon, his back straightening. "The hell you say. I've never doubted my will to fight. You can't either, Jeff."

"I know, true. But what of your will to lead?" he asked.

Jon sat still and shook his head at his friend's old tact. It was a friendly push.

Weston smiled, sipped, and patiently waited. "*Repondez, s'il vous plait.*"

Jon said nothing, even when baited with French.

"Jon, you have the brains and the courage to lead them, but you lack confidence in your decisions. I can see that, if anything," said Weston.

"I do pretty well deciding for myself thank you," Jon shot back. "You forget, these men know me, I grew up with them. I've never bossed anyone around. If facts be known, I've been the fetch-n-carry for them since I was twelve. Yeah, I can see it now - little Jonnie wants us to charge some guns - Pshaw, they'll say!"

"Jon, that's true in every regiment. But, when *you* talk, they listen."

"Perhaps they do, but I know my place."

"Ah, but that's what's great about the Army, you know. Promotion is based on merit and the men's trust." Weston fingered his goatee and his eyes lit up. "They do listen to you, more than you think. Yes, I heard about your little speech to the men in front of that German woman's house when Stewart was shot. Yes, quite impressive. Sergeant Hillford remembered much of it."

"He did?" Jon said, surprised. "Well, I had to intervene or our advantage would have been compromised."

Weston nodded and studied Jon, whose face had revealed deep longing. "That is true. And there were young women in the house?"

Jon picked up leaves and tossed them into the fire. "I could not see harm coming to them. Neither could you."

"Yes, you are correct." Weston smiled. "You gave attention to one of them?"

"What?" Jon crossed his arms. "Lawsen talks like a jealous maid."

"Yes, he does. But was he lying? Did she gain a little of your affections?"

"I think more than a little, she…," Jon stopped himself.

For Weston, the admission was enough to expose true feelings. Jon, if anything, was a gentleman, and his heart was indeed alight for the girl.

Weston's voice lightened. "She was a plain girl, but merry on the eyes, not dressed at all like a lady should be. You did well to protect her and the house."

Jon remained silent. Weston ceased his banter and knew that Jon would figure things out, about leading the men and all. As for the girl, unfortunately for Jon, she would stay in the past. "Think it over, Jon. A promotion awaits you at the proper time. I'm going to sleep. *Bon nuit.*"

Jon watched his friend hike over to an area shared by the lieutenants. He respected Jeff Weston as a leader and a good one at that. He wondered if the men could ever see *him* that way or really, if he ever could. At least he did not shrink in the face of the enemy. One thing he noted about his time in battle was that his senses seemed to expand during combat. While on that high ridge, he could see everything clearly—the distant Yankee cannoneers, Colonel Rains' flashing sword, bullets, shells and the retreat of DeCourcy's forces. Engulfed in the smoke and din of battle, his mind was calm, although his heart beat wildly. Battle had a fever to it like nothing else, and the dangerous lure of victory.

In such confusion, anything could happen and did. In a few days, Lawsen regained his old humor and shared the stunning news that his nose had been broken by the same round that killed Rossberger. He told the story one night near the camp fire.

"As we advanced in line, in view of the sheltered enemy, I heard the bullet strike Rossy and in a blink, a fragment from it smacked my nose. I fell back, as a man punched in the face, but not altogether taken down by it. I collected my senses and marched on a bit dazed, and mad enough to overlook poor Rossy who had fallen behind me. It's a sad and strange thing to be associated with another's death in that way."

The story spread and besides a scar, Lawsen gained respect and the best thing a soldier could have—the aura of protection.

* * *

To the delight of all Confederate forces in the area, Colonel DeCourcy retreated northward into Kentucky. Though his mission succeeded in supplying General Morgan's division, his hold on Tazewell and the Wilderness Road were broken. Organized, the Confederates took advantage.

To the Honorable *Colonel Rains*

From: *General Carter Stevenson*
Aug. 16, 1862

Colonel,

 It is my pleasure to inform you that Lt. Colonel Gordon has been returned to our lines unharmed, with horse. General Morgan paroled him this morning. I know you will be pleased to have this gallant and valuable officer in the ranks again, considering he is from your "Hermitage Guards" and esteemed 11th Regmt.

I congratulate you again for the brigade's performance during the action at Tazewell and as we lament the fallen, we know that their names are forever enshrined in the temples of victory.

General Smith will arrive soon to inspect the division for future operations. He presents a plan to invade Kentucky with General Bragg. Together, their forces will inflict a final blow for that state's liberation.

I know that we will be involved in some capacity with Gen. Smith's movement to secure the Cumberland Gap, once more. I believe our affair at Tazewell has done this very thing, well in advance of the general's plans.

May God keep you.

Many respects,

General C. Stevenson

* * *

CHAPTER 18 ★

KNOXVILLE, TENNESSEE OCTOBER 1862

After the fight at Tazewell in August, Bethanna checked the short casualty list for what the press called a "sharp skirmish." Involving almost 9,000 men, it did not look like a small affair to her. The 11ᵗʰ Tennessee was listed as a participant and she feared for Jon's wellbeing, and for the docile Private Cawley, whom she could not imagine fighting anyone.

Now, two months later, Bethanna's stomach tightened as she read the local newspaper with reluctant enthusiasm. "Rains' brigade, Rains' brigade," she said in a low murmur, glad to remember anything about Jon's command structure. No words within the splotchy print identified such a unit and like many concerned people in Knoxville, she fearfully read the posted casualty lists from the Confederate's latest effort, the battle of Perryville, Kentucky.

The lead stories explained that General Braxton Bragg, joined by Kirby Smith's force, had won at Perryville, although the talk in town and in Hinchel's Inn, told that Bragg's Confederates had narrowly escaped a disaster. Weakened from the long march back to Tennessee and succumbing to disease, his Army fell off by the hundreds.

From the reporters who gathered for morning coffee at the inn, she learned that Rains' brigade in General Stevenson's division, under General Kirby Smith's command, had marched to join Bragg's grand campaign into Kentucky. The list of generals confused her and to keep up, she had to listen closely to the reporters, whose talk was not always encouraging.

As Mirra poured more coffee for the reporters, she tossed a glance to Bethanna standing quiet and forlorn, reading the papers near the large front windows. Mirra wondered if her sister was ill, which would make sense of the strange moods she displayed lately.

With a messed napkin under his crumb-filled beard, one of the older newspaper men sitting at the round table in the corner read his latest draft to his contemporaries. His voice rang out over the room. "Bragg's overall strategy was to win over the loyalists in Kentucky. He believed the mere presence of such a large Confederate Army would throw the state over to the Southern side and completely isolate Union forces in Tennessee. Bragg guessed wrong."

His cohorts chuckled as they tapped their spoons in coffee cups, or onto the hard table in fraternal applause.

"Ah, there's more," continued the reporter, "Bragg mishandled the affair at its zenith. While he had successfully marched into the heart of the state, he did not create the necessary fervor for enlistment. Instead, he chose a more congenial path by attempting to reinstall the Confederate government that had evacuated during the Union occupation. The ousted lieutenant governor was more than willing to try and in a short ceremony at the capital of Frankfurt, Bragg attempted to secure the salvation of the state with a hurried inauguration." The reporter paused and sipped his coffee. His friends begged for more.

"Yes, where was I? Ah yes. At the time of this political coronation, his Army was retreating toward Perryville. A celebratory artillery barrage by the converging Army of the Ohio forced Bragg's retirement from the political scene in Kentucky.

The new governor ruled for half a day before he, too, retired from politics. The poorly fought battle at Perryville and the ensuing retreat capped the Army's Kentucky Tour."

More spoon applause approved his version of the news.

Bethanna smiled at the stupendous nature of the general commanding the armies in Tennessee or perhaps she found humor in the way the reporters told of it, as they swam in pots of coffee. But in her heart, she feared for Jon's safety even more. Garnering any additional information she could from the papers, she stood in the light of an open window. She took a deep breath and noted the people in the street as they gazed at storm clouds. Eager to start the day with a proper breakfast, new customers headed for the inn door.

On average, folks arrived for breakfast at 6:30 in the morning, a late hour compared to her mother's schedule. Bethanna loved the inn and the old country trimmings: the blue and white Dutch tile furnace, Black Forest clocks, hunters' horns, and Uncle Hinchel's pride, the large copper beer vat in the window. There were some new things, too; Verna's ice cream maker and flavored candies from Pennsylvania arranged in neat pots on clean new counters.

Even with comfortable surroundings, Bethanna did not open up to her relatives completely. She kept Jon to herself. Their understanding and patience had already been strained enough from the behavior of Hertha toward her children. Furthermore, the peace of the inn need not be shattered with the story of their son Carl and his death, beyond the ridge, under the very chins of his relatives in Taldorf.

* * *

When Bethanna and Mirra arrived in Knoxville worn and weary, Uncle Hinchel and Aunt Verna knelt to thank God for their safe passage through a perilous land. Reverend Grottmacher was pleased with the faithfulness of Bethanna's relatives and after he blessed them with prayers, they in turn welcomed the reverend and his wife into their Christian community.

Hinchel and his family were members of the small Evangelical Free Church, which had been introduced by migrants from the Iowa and Illinois plains. In its original form, the ministry began as a German language church, its pastors traveling a circuit and preaching a Methodist doctrine. As families grew, the new generations of German-Americans spoke English, and worshiped with new songs. In such an atmosphere, Hinchel and Verna stayed true to their traditions with a mix of old-world purity and new Southern gospel zeal. They were not shy about praying for peace and victory, or for some stranger prostrate on their parlor floor.

Bethanna had not witnessed this kind of activity from laymen before. Only the Reverend Grottmacher or the deacons usually prayed aloud in earnest. Her father had blessed the meals at home and when he left, Hertha took over for a short time, until she passed the job to Bethanna. But here within her uncle's home, there seemed to be strength in their asking and true expectations of their pleas. Their faith in the Lord was remarkable and touching. Interested, Bethanna sat quietly during their weekly prayer meetings and soaked up the believers' love and community spirit. She looked forward to the Wednesday nights, complete with a dinner and sharing time. It was during one of these meetings that Bethanna saw her vision.

The mood that night was intense with sorrow. Parents, still in shock and with nowhere else to turn, had shared the dreaded news of wounded or killed sons. Openly, sympathetic tears flowed for their loss while earnest prayers and confessions where raised to the Almighty. Moved to emotion, Bethanna prayed for them and in this moment, she found strength to give her own petitions.

She sat in her usual place, on the stairs behind her Aunt

Verna's large chair, and thought about her situation. She had left her mother alone in the valley. She had ignored her father's order asking her to go home. The letter had been posted from occupied Nashville and arrived at the inn a week ago. Confused about her father's tone, she hid it from her uncle and had felt guilty ever since. Maybe her father did not believe the things in her letter, or was not sure about her true intentions. Whatever the reason, it had caused conflict between them and in fact, created doubt in her conscience, which contrarily under God's direction, had seen her safely to the inn. On the steps with her face in her hands, she cried. In a small voice, she uttered, "Oh Lord, where do I go?"

Nowhere. She could do nothing but stay with her family. Surely, there had to be reasons for her removal from Taldorf. Having time to reflect lately, she suspected a guiding hand was present in her travails, as well as in her passions for Jon. When her thoughts turned to the young man who had set her heart ablaze with a pure and wonderful feeling, a blasting light flashed into her face, and she went limp.

She saw Jon walking on railroad tracks with a little boy at his side. The boy held a canvass sack soaked in blood and as they departed the tracks, he gave the sack to Jon, who tossed it up to his shoulder. Jon reached down and from a pile of rubble, picked up a Confederate battle flag, torn and bloody. Confused, Jon looked at the boy for direction. Without hesitation, the boy pointed into the air and Jon raised the flag proudly. When he did, the banner burst into flames and Jon waved it franticly to extinguish the fire. His face lit up with uncontained rage as the effort failed. To his shock, the action summoned thousands of soldiers to his side, armed and eager to fight.

The ear-shattering rebel yell arose from the swarming Army as Jon ran forward, leading a grand charge into a hail of fire and death. Smoke engulfed the mass of soldiers and the little boy sat smiling as he waved goodbye to his burden; then blackness. Bethanna came to, as the low light of the room regained prominence in her eyes. Shaken by the sight of her beloved in such chaos, she could not hide her distress and in a few days, she told Hinchel and Verna about the horrid vision, its detail, sounds, and fearful end. Wisely, Bethanna shared the vision only with them and guessed Mirra would think her crazy as Hertha.

Hinchel and Verna did not overreact. Perhaps she had seen it, they thought, or had made it up so she could feel a part of things. But they did agree that her emotion over this soldier in the vision was real. As usual, when spiritual matters are beyond them, they prayed for their niece's heart and mind, and that God may reveal meaning from this vision, or provide relief from the emotions it caused.

* * *

Mirra walked over to Bethanna at the large window and took the newspaper from her sister's hands. "Customers first," she said. She gave the papers to a man who had just sat for coffee. He smiled at the polite service and the pretty, young hostess. The midmorning crowd gathered outside on the steps, as they ditched their cigar stubs in the street. In moments, the oak coat rack next to the door was covered with wool coats, rubber slickers, and hats. A small fire flickered in the stone hearth and the smell of hickory smoke blended with the scent of fresh-cooked breakfast. Four tables filled and the patrons called for coffee.

Mirra put in two orders of hotcakes and bacon before she noticed Bethanna still in thought near the window. She approached her sister, "Hey, day dreamer. Please help me. Here's the fresh coffee." She put the kettle on a nearby table.

"Sorry." Bethanna smiled, embarrassed. Through the open pane, a cool autumn breeze tossed her hair about. While she tucked the loose strands under her bonnet, she thought of the windy valley and her dancing flower garden. She missed the morning ritual of its care, the peaceful stream, her private walks, and her father's upper room. Those things were gone now; hurled away by the stupidity of those whom she had most trusted to guard them. *What was it like at home now? What was Mother doing today? Surely she would have the sense to come to Uncle Hinchel's, or perhaps not.* The rain began to fall and cold drops blew in on the wind. She closed the window.

Though Knoxville felt the strain of war, overall, the area still operated with rail lines and a fairly good food trade. Prices rose steadily, giving an ominous warning that the town is not immune to the South's shortages. Breakfast at the inn was still a manageable 20 cents, but with a cup of coffee and sugar, it could swell to a $1.12. Using a rag to grip it, Bethanna took the hot kettle. She made her rounds, filling the colored clay cups of anyone who asked. Early risers gladly paid for good coffee.

For Hinchel, it was a blessing to gain the help of his two nieces. The customers liked the girls and their German family charm. Breakfast brought the largest crowd while lunchtime waned. Dinner was served only to the inn customers and if the girls worked all day, they earned $2.00 or more in tips. Although distracted, Bethanna did not mind the work.

Mirra loved it. Taking to city life, she appeared more "Southern" than Bethanna, and she engaged in lively conversations more readily. She was glad to be rid of farm chores and animal dung, in a place where the old world hung like fog. Now, after working and living in the town, the thought of being cloistered away in that valley for the rest of her life made her cringe. She had found a new life and a new esteem in the town, and especially in school, where she learned among peers her own age for the first time. Already popular with the guests and customers of Hinchel's

Inn, Mirra, even more than her sister, had made enough friends to dare to venture out among the other blocks of the town.

Bethanna did not share her sister's eagerness to know everyone, but Mirra's new-found freeness impressed her and in some way encouraged her to be the same. The customers gave Bethanna enough discourse to keep her head swimming with new information. It always came from the reporters. She had learned more about the war in the last few weeks than she ever heard in Taldorf. Names like Lee, Stonewall Jackson, and McClellan or Forrest gave the war a broader scope and flair. Today, another event would send the reporters scurrying for news.

"Bragg's leading elements are arriving!" a pageboy shouted from the wide front doors. The group of four newsmen at a round table in the corner perked up and proceeded to eat like animals. They managed another pot of coffee between them before they collected their hats and ran out the doors to the street.

Bethanna gathered the dishes from the messy table with shaking hands. Mirra noticed her sister's concern at the sudden news. She walked over to help, patted Bethanna's arm and whispered, "Be calm, there will be a lot of time until the troops settle in to camp. Then, you can find him."

"Am I that apparent?" Bethanna mumbled. She shook her head. "So sorry."

For the moment, Bethanna felt like the younger, as Mirra soothed her nerves with a reassuring phrase, and she was right. Troops may be pouring in for days, and who knows where they will end up. Then the questions started. *Was Jon even alive? Was he in a bloody ambulance bouncing mercilessly down some mountain road?* She could only work to keep herself busy and, of course, pray.

* * *

Within days, the news spread about General Bragg's campaign and how the Army was officially wrecked on the retreat from Perryville. Over 15,000 men—one third of the whole—had been stricken by disease on the long, 400-mile march from Harrodsburg, Kentucky. Horses, cannon, shoes, coats and blankets had been lost, not to mention the effectiveness of the remaining troops, numbering just under 27,000.

They had marched for weeks over a dry, parched land, only to return in the cold and pouring rain while being harassed by pursuing cavalry. Muddy roads had slowed the long lines of men. A story was told that a lower Kentucky farmer, who observed the stragglers lying out on the side of a country road, declared he could walk on them all the way to the Tennessee border without touching the ground. True or not, the reporters printed the tale.

Rumors spread that some of the troops, when they had crossed into Tennessee, took off for home, never to march with Bragg ever again. This would be the beginning of a chronic problem for the general the rest of his active career—desertions.

As the Army gathered in safe territory, General Bragg saw to refit his troops through the vital chain of the railroad. Knoxville linked up with Chattanooga via the Tennessee & Georgia Railroad, along with a short spur of the Memphis & Charleston. Careworn and fragile, the efficiency had suffered, but the main line was being patched for Bragg's use. Cavalry from John Hunt Morgan's and Joe Wheeler's brigades secured the depots along the way. By the 27th of October, the whistle of an inbound engine could be heard north of town.

* * *

Bethanna had not seen a train in years and the sight of one impressed her. Though dull and grimy from overuse, the large engine sounded powerful and fit. Carrying the number "36", the black-and-red Baldwin was one of four trains that ran weekly from Chattanooga and as it slowed to a halt, the open valves blasted their familiar hiss of steam. Bethanna flinched, surprised and unaware of the typical locomotive sounds. In her new blue wool overcoat and hood, a gift from her aunt's church group, she stood covered and comfortable, waiting on Verna who was sending a wire message to a couple in Chattanooga about their house and property. From the inn, they had walked the six blocks to the northern side of town and the outing, even in overcast weather, gave them a nice time to talk and enliven their feet from hours of standing over tables.

The previous day, Uncle Hinchel had taken the wagon to search for his son Stephan, somewhere amongst the cavalry's maze of camps posted miles from town. Hinchel's absence from the inn made it difficult for Bethanna to run off and find Jon's regiment. She could not pull away from her duties and it frustrated her openly. She grew impatient with the delays and today, waiting at the station in the cold rain, she thought of something drastic.

When Verna finished with the telegraph service, she walked out to meet Bethanna, but the girl was not where she had left her. Verna, at forty-three years old, stood in good fitness, and could work through her morning errands without a rest; however, she was not about to undertake an extensive search for the teenager. She waited to see if the lost girl would come back, but it was not to be. Bethanna had ditched her.

Jogging onto the wooden side walk near a cobbler's shop, Bethanna darted for the alley between the streets. Stepping out the other side, into a new block, she headed north again, towards the camps of the Army.

She didn't know where to go, only that the smoke of a hundred campfires had filled the sky north of town. Reaching a smaller depot, she then headed across the road over the tracks and latched onto a group of people lugging baskets and jugs. "Pardon, would you know where the Army is staying?" she asked.

A gentleman turned and laughed. "You are on the very road towards them, my dear!" he said. Bethanna fell in with the ladies of the group. One of them she had seen in a prayer meeting and she stayed close to her. Listening attentively to the lady explain their son's illness, she found that scurvy, dysentery, and typhoid where just some of the maladies inflicting great discomfort to Bragg's ranks. The cold weather worsened their sufferings with exposure. The woman's son had contracted pneumonia in the dreary, rainy march back to Knoxville and was near death several times. Bethanna was horrified at the graphic description and not at all encouraged by such news of widespread suffering, rampant among thousands.

After marching some time themselves, the group of family and friends entered the camp. Soldiers sprouted up everywhere and soon the tents and stacked arms became regular. One thing that became prominent to Bethanna was the smell. The pungent odors of vomit and waste overtook the air, causing her to gag. Reaching for her blue scarf, she quickly laid it across her nose and mouth. She wondered how the other ladies could stand it, while they smiled affectionately at the quiet men.

They walked by a corral of horses and the animals' haggard appearance jarred her. They were so emaciated that their weak skin stretched over protruding bones and their eyes sagged, half open. Near the gate lock was a sign painted in a sloppy hand saying, "Jerky Platoon." She felt the first pull at her stomach.

In a few steps, she saw a red hospital flag waving over a tall, elongated tent and on it was sewn the white "H," for hospital. This was the treatment district. Plenty had to be done to prepare those who had not yet been diagnosed. The Army had filled Knoxville's public buildings with the wounded soldiers and here the most serious cases passed through the camp surgeon's tent for dressing or even amputation. Wounds that had festered for days on the march were now too far gone for any nominal treatment. Drastic measures were taken and heard by everyone nearby.

This is not where Bethanna wanted to be. She had to find Jon's unit, but she thought, *If my search brings me back here, then so be it, Lord.* She veered away from the group of visitors and let them enter the hospital area. Walking swiftly, she went another direction down a wide lane where tents stood on both sides and near them, men lay or stood, staring at her. Bethanna dared not look, but after a few paces, she could not ignore them.

White faces with dark, gray eyes peered out of the tents as she walked by. Flies swarmed the area, ripe with nesting grounds. Those who could shout at her did, craving any help to make their suffering easier as they cried for help, water, or God. Whisky was most mentioned or morphine, which happened to be a rarity at the moment.

Those who could walk approached, catching her by the arm, begging help for themselves or their friends. Frightened, she quickened her pace and began to push away from them. An unexpected panic arose in her as she sensed the very angels of death around her and the stricken men.

A stout man wearing a bloody white apron halted her. "You must gather yourself," he said. He tipped up his wide-brim black hat to gain her attention.

She looked into his eyes, calm and caring. His wavy gray hair hung behind his ears. "Please don't worry the men, they will respond to any politeness from a woman. But please, be careful not to incite fear in them. They have enough of that already." His voice fell to a whisper and he leaned towards her, "This is a quarantined section, so I suggest you make your way, dear."

She nodded silently, fully understanding. There was an odor of liquor on his breath. The man moved on and entered a treatment tent. She wondered how someone could be drinking during the practice of medical care or meticulous surgery.

Bethanna looked back down the lane, into the faces of men with hollow eyes. They did not look so threatening now, very lanky and pale, most of them shoeless in the cold, shuffling back to their beds in obvious humiliation. Bethanna shook her head at her own folly, realizing that these men were proud fighters and had no scrap of dignity in their present state. A familiar droning noise settled into her ears. The coughing of hundreds of men filtered throughout the tents. She suddenly felt a jolt in her throat and moved quickly over to a stand of trees and became sick. The smell had finally turned her stomach.

On the other side of the trees, a group of men lay wrapped in their blankets. She decided to go over and ask them where the 11th might be encamped. After wiping her face, she approached the resting troops. She was halfway through her salutations when the look and smell of death raped her. All of them were dead and stiffly posed in final pain, with eyes open, matted wild hair caked with dirt and blood, and their dried mouths swollen, open to flies.

Bethanna's face whitened with horror as she shut her eyes against the revulsion and like a sudden slap, the scene jarred her emotions, so carefully controlled until now. Her breathing stuttered and turned into sobs, each one laced with a word "No, no, no...God!" She ran from the area and covered her face with her scarf. Tears blurred the path ahead and she stopped to wipe them. In her fluster, she tried to breath and only inhaled the stench of rot, which gagged her. She had to vomit again and as she braced for the event, she understood why the doctor in the bloody coat had been drinking.

After her second stomach trauma, she walked clear of the ward and as she left, a fear chilled her. Jon was surely one of these walking corpses or perhaps a real one by now. Her kind friend was dying alone without someone whispering love to him, or a prayer. That had to be the most fearful thought for the lonely soldier. "Dear Lord!" she prayed. "Please, pity him."

* * *

Dr. Larkin completed his rounds for the brigade surgeon and walked to his lodging in the large tent city after a long 10-hour shift. His head ached from overuse, stress, and the wound he had suffered in Tazewell—a glancing ball fragment to the head—the first and last time he ever tried to *pretreat* the wounded. He had adopted French theories that lives could be saved by medics present on the battle field, where they could stop bleed-outs with immediate treatment. After his wounding, the theory had been shelved by Colonel Rains.

Larkin entered his tent and greeted his assistant, who lay ill on his cot, and wrapped in blankets. "Well Joshua, I've had it. These civilians must remain out of our way, just for a few days, by Lord."

"Yes, Doctor," said the assistant, as he lifted his head. "Save for the carriers of food stuffs."

"Yes, of course. I just saw a girl, lost in the sick ward, and she had no damned mind of where she was or what she was doing. She had no food either. Nor drink. Ah, that's what I came in for." The doctor was no drunk, but the brandy mellowed his racing mind and produced long sleep. "Joshua, if Colonel Rains calls, I am off duty and delirious with fatigue. I am out." Dr. Larkin took a swig from his bottle and let the heat go down. "Ahh...been a very long month, my boy, very long indeed."

Camped just north of Knoxville, among the rolling fields, the men of the 11th Tennessee nursed their wounded feet and battered pride. To their fortune, the regiment was not used in the failed

Kentucky Campaign, at least in battle. Even so, during the forced march back to Tennessee, many men had worn their shoes through or lost them altogether, exposing their feet to the harsh earth. As for their weapons and equipment, only half the regiment—nearly 300 men –qualified as soldiers.

Captain Binns counted twelve missing from his company of sixty-five men. He presumed some had deserted and some went missing along the roadside, their fates never known. Sixteen more had walking fever and three rode in the ambulances on the long march home. So far in the war, the regimental casualties came more from illness than combat.

Being starved, dehydrated, exposed to the elements of foul weather and never having fired a shot, Jon Lyhton was not in a good way himself. He lay resting in a tent for five days before he could walk without careening into the ground. His acute dizziness was caused by lack of food and the flu.

Others in the company came through the ordeal in relatively good shape. Sergeant Hillford seemed not to be affected by the grueling conditions. He spent most of his time now taking care of the sick. Lawsen and Martello were ill but recovering quickly. Dapleton remained in fair health and Lieutenant Weston, though suffering from a badly twisted ankle, managed to hobble back with his platoon. Private Dabney had the runs for a week and was on the cusp of death with dysentery, but with plenty of rest and fresh water, he rallied and spent the next week over-eating, only to be constipated later.

The men found some comfort in being in camp again and away from the Kentucky front, but there were rumors flying that soon they would be shipped out to Chattanooga. No one seemed to question it. The troops were ready for a change but not for more marching. Fortunately for them, Bragg did do something right by marching his troops to the nearest rail depot at Knoxville, where supplies would soon be arriving.

* * *

CHAPTER 19 ★

It was near dark when Bethanna arrived home and naturally, Aunt Verna was frantic with motherly worry. Uncle Hinchel showed little concern over the older girl until he heard where she had spent the day. The Army's camp was the last place they expected her to be, and with parental care, they explained the dangers she faced walking among disheartened soldiers. "Anger, resentment, and outright desperation prevail over there. What will keep you from the advances of desperate men?" Hinchel shouted.

"No one will protect you. The dangers are endless, my dear," Verna added.

After a sufficient amount of reasons why not to do such a thing, Hinchel rested, and then asked her why she had run off on such a venture.

Bethanna hesitated. Before, she did not want to tell them anything of Jon, but the strain of the day bore down on her and she began to crack. She walked to the large dining table, sat down and invited Hinchel and Verna to take their respective seats.

"There is a man there," she said, taking a breath and sighing, "whom I need to see."

Verna mellowed. "Why didn't you say? There are other ways to seek someone out."

Hinchel huffed at the notion. "A man?" He lit a Black Forest pipe and slid his large wicker-seat chair closer to the table's edge.

His elbow thumped on the oak plank as he leaned in. "Do you love him?" he asked.

The question surprised her. Bethanna nodded. "I am most certain I do."

"Let me guess. Is this the same soldier from your vision, the man with the burning flag?" Hinchel asked.

"Yes, it is him."

Hinchel's eyes rested on Bethanna with a hint of sympathy, knowing that she would not give her affections lightly, to anyone. His brother Vogal had always kept him aware of the girl's growing character. Therefore, she must have a genuine reason for such rash action and perhaps, he thought now, a more serious one. She needed pushing.

"I can see now why you left the village," he said. Verna looked at him with puzzlement. He ignored her. "Your father would not hear of such a thing, you and a rebel. You had to leave…for this man?"

Bethanna did not like the implication in Hinchel's statement. She did not leave only for him. "I left the valley to escape danger. But yes, I have affections for him. He saved me from the sure abuses of the Kentucky raiders who came to search the village. These were the same men who my mother favored."

Hinchel's body creaked the chair with an uneasy shift. "This war has divided us. Vogal has gone north to help build bridges. I have one son missing, Carl. You know how it is to live with a missing family member, yes? His brother Stephan stands guard four miles away at the cavalry horse stalls. You have chosen to leave your mother, and now this man in the rebel Army divides further. Now truly, you may want to rethink your choice." Relighting his pipe, Hinchel waited for her to explain.

Bethanna discovered an awkward sensation. Attempting to convey her emotions about a man she had known briefly, even to her, sounded odd. But what she felt for him, she could not readily explain.

Verna noticed Bethanna's resistance and tried to move her along. "What of your soldier friend? Did you find him?"

Bethanna shook her head. "No one knew where his unit was located. There was no order there and I was lost, separated from those who guided me to the camps. I got very ill near the medical area. I saw dead men out in the open, like animals. It was horrid. I walked and walked, but only to find the same sick and hurt men. It is a vast Army. I've never seen such numbers in my life."

"That's hardly a large force," Hinchel said. "That's not all of them. Most are still out there." He pointed to the window. "They are searching for food or a place to hide, or the way home."

Hinchel found it unbelievable that Bethanna would leave the village for a man. His mind kept going back to Hertha and her household. "I heard of the raid. Herr Dansell told me his brother's grains are gone in Taldorf, taken for the raiders' horses. Their windows are broken and house sacked. I understand why you left that, but now you leave for this soldier?"

"Or stay there with Mother?" said Bethanna, her face calm, eyes strong.

Mirra spoke up from the kitchen doorway. "We left our home because Mother was going crazy!"

"Hush you, go away!" Hinchel yelled, waving his pipe at the girl.

"No! She stays," Bethanna said. "She was there, she has seen."

Mirra came into the room and sat next to her sister at the large oak table. Bethanna pulled her in with a gentle hug. Hinchel signaled for Mirra to continue. "And...?"

"Mother killed a rebel from the company that foraged there. They never threatened us. She risked everyone's safety with her stupidity. Since Saul died, she has become obstinate and angry, even beating... " Mirra halted the detail.

"I see," said Hinchel, not wholly convinced. He tapped his pipe on the tabletop.

Bethanna felt the heat rise in her. She had no patience for Hinchel's slow but gentle interrogations. "You go ask the Reverend Grottmacher. He has seen everything—the friendly Confederates, the cruelty of the raiders. He knows the real truth about Carl and what was done to him!"

Both Hinchel and Verna stiffened and looked at each other.

Mirra's eyes widened and she didn't want to be in the room anymore.

"What do you mean, young lady?" Verna asked.

Bethanna stood. "Tell the reverend I sent you and he will describe our loyal little village!"

Hinchel eyed Bethanna through a puff of smoke and then spread his hands on the table, as if to stand. "What do you speak of, girl, what about Carl?"

Verna crossed herself in a silent prayer while Mirra left the room.

"I will go with you. It is time you heard the story of my loyal mother and how it is to be her child." She ignored her aunt and uncle's quizzical faces, and before the questions started, she hurried them along to the entryway and put on her coat and hood. "Let us go now, before it is too dark." Bethanna grew mad at herself for breaking the news so suddenly, but there seemed no good time to reveal it. Now they will hear the long, untold truth.

Reverend Grottmacher greeted them at the door of his wife's cousins, the MacGibons. "Hello my friends, would you like some super?" he asked.

"No, Reverend," said Bethanna. "This is my Uncle Hinchel and Aunt Verna, Carl's parents."

The reverend braced against the door jam. "Oh? God bless you and welcome," he said, allowing the group into the house.

Bethanna stepped away to excuse herself, knowing the scene to come. Grottmacher stopped her near the door. "No, please stay," he asked. "I think I may need you."

The four sat together in a small parlor with a crackling fireplace. The reverend paused to collect his thoughts, and nerves. "God, give us strength." He pulled the small, worn New Testament from a table drawer and passed it over to Hinchel. "You must see this, and know."

Hinchel reached slowly and grasped the book. Verna recognized it and drew a breath.

"What is this?" Hinchel asked. His frown grew, lowering the corners of his large mustache. He looked at Verna, then opened the book, reading the inscription. "Where did you get this?"

The reverend looked at Bethanna.

"From Carl's hand. From his body! He...is dead, *Tante*." Bethanna used the German word for aunt out of respect and affection, but her voice cracked, forbidding clear speech. "I saw him dead, it is true. I am so sorry, *Tante*."

"Dead...?" Hinchel fingered the pages. "Where? He was reported missing months ago near the Cumberland Gap. Now he is dead? How can you know, girl, if it was..."

"I was with that soldier we talked of before, a corporal. He found the bodies of the three horse soldiers across the north ridge and pulled the book from the hand of..."

Verna began to weep. She touched Hinchel's arm, then the worn Testament, and withdrew her trembling hand. Hinchel starred at the two messengers. "Can there be a way that this is not my son?"

The reverend shook his head. "I doubt this bible, with a wife's writing, would be casually passed along, or lent out, but the chance exists, nevertheless."

Hinchel moaned, his eyes closing. "Carl would never give away such a thing."

"I assure you," Grottmacher said, "we did bury the young man in the church yard and his two comrades." He glanced at Bethanna; she ignored the lie.

"Uncle, *Tante*, there is other news that hurts the family. In our village, someone gave up Carl and his comrades to the Kentucky raiders, men who, well..."

Grottmacher filled in the rest, "Troops not under direct U.S. military authority. They enforce the border areas with little respect for property and values."

"Yes, that's right," Bethanna paused, tucking a lock of loose hair behind her ear.

Hinchel thumped the bible on his knee. "Who gave up my son?" he asked.

Bethanna felt a knot in her throat, but swallowed the urge to cry. Her jaw quivered and she found enough bravery to push past her emotions. "Hertha, my mother, your brother's wife."

For the confused parents sitting helpless on the couch, the horrid meaning of the statement lingered in their minds. They could see their son being marched out of the village, where he sought shelter with his aunt, only to be turned over and gunned down. The stunning reality destroyed their simple perceptions of the war.

The reverend broke their trance and explained the power of the guns, the fear of reprisal and the sure loss of all harvests. "Hertha was the chief rebel-hater among us. How could she not be, after they impressed her son, Saul, to fight for the South. The way he was enlisted, under duress, when the Southern patrols were more prevalent in our area a year ago, it was too much for her. When the infantry showed up in July this year, they were friendly and disciplined, but she hated still."

Hinchel broke in, "My son was betrayed?"

"Yes." Grottmacher paused as Verna stood and walked over to an artist's impression of a youthful Scottish highlander holding a saber. Her weeping overtook the room and Bethanna arose and held her. "Please *Tante*, he is resting with the Lord, you know this more than anyone."

Hinchel wiped his eyes. He stared at his boots. "I thank you, Pastor, for giving him proper burial."

Grottmacher nodded. There was relief in the confession, but not all of the truth. Indeed, he had failed as pastor to the villagers, but as their shepherd under the threat of wolves, he chose which sheep to protect and which to sacrifice. Even so, his care for them never stopped and from genuine compassion, he wanted to give Hinchel and Verna, especially Bethanna, some sort of reassurance, maybe a hint that his pastoral care had not faltered.

He stood at his open door as they departed. "You have my deepest sympathies, and know that the Lord shepherds those who suffer in his name. It is in the valley where we are tried the most."

Bethanna did not appreciate the symbolism. She waited until her relatives reached the dark street and glared at Grottmacher. "We know perfectly well about trials in the valley, do we not?"

* * *

Hinchel took to the bottle for three straight nights, sitting there in his large chair staring at the fire trying to find reasons. Until the early hours of morning, he moaned and napped out his sadness. Business continued normally, as he quietly operated his inn during the darkest days he had seen in a long while. He found no answers in that state of mind and most importantly, no peace either. Afterwards, he regretted his drinking deeply, repented to his wife, and offered apologies to the girls. They understood the episode, and were thankful it had not lasted any longer.

Verna had reacted differently to her son's gruesome end. She was not going to fill the busy inn with her grief. Instead, she chose to weep or pray at the church and accepted the belief that if God wanted her son with him in glory, then she will not complain against it. Nonetheless, the pain of Hertha's action would linger.

After three months of mystery for his parents, the knowledge of Carl's fate did come as a relief, but the discovery of family betrayal brought added concerns and strain. The family pressed onward, keeping ahead of them the standard of God with morning prayers, and Wednesday Bible night. The added presence of Bethanna and Mirra eased the pain somewhat, as the girls' warmth and charm filled the breakfast shifts with repeat customers and full, talkative tables. This cheered Hinchel to some extent, but the circumstances of his son's death haunted him, and upon deeper thought, perplexed him. He told himself that Hertha could not do such a thing, unless forced. Deeper mysteries evolved with every new question he pondered.

Although congenial in her work, Verna noticed Bethanna's quiet mood at night. The wise aunt knew love when she saw it and with a simple idea, she coaxed her niece into positive action. If she wanted to contact Jon, a letter was the best way, and knowing the brigade, regiment, and company helped tremendously. "The regiment will know him as soon as they read his name. There will be no trouble," she had told her niece.

Sitting at Verna's desk, she worried over how to write him, what words to use, how he may perceive her. She could not state her points in eloquence as Jon did. Then again, she knew that Jon saw her as a person, in her home, daily in the village, so she pushed away the worry.

That night she kept the letter close to her body as she slept. Having no perfume, nothing that Jon would know, except her natural scent, she wanted the paper to smell like her for a long while. The sensual gesture felt a bit silly, but romance made people do strange things. When she awoke, she folded the letter into an envelope, a rare luxury at the time when most letters were mailed folded and sealed.

She walked down to the post office and laid her precious words on the largest heap—the military stack. She was partially satisfied that she had done all she could do, for Hinchel would not allow her into camp. There was no way of knowing if this "Jon," was still alive, he had told her. They would find out soon through the regiment, Hinchel and Verna assured her.

* * *

CHAPTER 20 ★

On the 28th of October, the sound of train whistles leaked into the inn and rumors filled the breakfast tables that the Army was moving to Chattanooga. Troops had already entrained for the first trip out of town. Again, Bethanna's hopes were crushed. She would not know if her letter had made it into Jon's hands unless he wrote her back, and even that could take weeks. In a quiet and heavy mood, she served breakfast to four officers sitting in the corner and was, for a second, tempted to ask them of the regiment.

Before she could, Hinchel approached with plates of bacon and rye bread. The soldiers grabbed the goods and were too busy chewing to talk. *Why interrupt them?* she thought. Then she heard something that astonished her.

"So, gentlemen," Hinchel said. "What do you know of Colonel Rains' brigade?"

Bethanna nearly poured coffee on the table at the sound of her uncle's question. She re-aimed over a cup to fill it and stared at her uncle.

He gave her a wink.

One man spoke up, "Should be on their way to Chattanooga and by week's end, so will we." He stuffed a warm biscuit into his mouth, ending the statement. Hinchel shrugged at Bethanna and he moved on to clean the larger family table.

Bethanna leaned in and tapped one of the officers on the arm. "Yes, miss?" he said.

"How long will they be in Chattanooga?" she asked.

The officer paused, blessed as he was by the girl's loveliness. "Uh, seven, maybe ten days for resupply, depending where they are assigned."

"Thank you, sir. God bless you." Bethanna smiled and with that, gained the interest of the whole table. Then at once, all four of them began to vie for her attention with tidbits of information. She giggled, charming the men even more.

* * *

The business had to be done. Carl's young widow, Darlene, had avoided them long enough and Verna became worried. "You do not shun your family in times like these. She is alone and depressed over Carl's death. We must go help her."

In the damp weather, Bethanna rode with her aunt in the family's fancy rockaway carriage. Almost four years old, the dark brown gloss had not worn away, due to proper storage. Hinchel had a more rustic buckboard for hauling and delivery, but Verna wanted to make a good impression for Darlene; only the best for her family.

Darlene lived on the property given to her and Carl by her parents, who were now in Chattanooga running their furniture business. The house and land were perfect for a new couple and any future children. The lot was outside of town on the western Kingston road.

They rode out over the rolling hills, through muddy patches from the recent rains. Bethanna gazed at the desolate land. The trees reached for the sky with gray, skeletal branches, yawing in the racing winds. There was little promise in the future for most farmers here. It would be a rough winter because of the Army's stay before and after the Kentucky campaign.

Verna pulled the reigns and the carriage veered off onto a rutted path, cut from the ground over years of use. The remains of a disassembled fence, probably used for firewood, guided them to the property gate. The two women dismounted the carriage and walked under a low covered porch. Verna knocked on the heavy door.

A dark-haired young lady, slim, well groomed in a black satin mourning dress opened the door. "Hello, Verna." She looked at Bethanna. "Hello there, please come in."

Entering the dwelling, Bethanna looked around. The place was a simple homestead with a great room, a half kitchen and bedrooms to the left and right. The cooking quarters were in a separate shed to the rear of the house, but the smell of a recent potato dinner remained. Quaint carpets and colored wall hangings helped to liven up the whitewashed wood paneling and stonework fireplace.

Darlene was polite but cautious and visibly suspicious. She eyed her guests as if they were little children, bound to break something. "Verna, who is this?"

"This is Bethanna, Carl's cousin, Vogal's oldest daughter."

"It's a pleasure to meet you," Darlene said. Her manners and accent were perfectly Southern and to Bethanna, very refined and feminine.

Bethanna smiled as much as she thought she should. "Nice to meet you, also."

Not wanting to waste time, Aunt Verna explained that the family should pull together over the winter. "There is plenty of space at the inn for you," she pleaded. "We have gathered a large winter surplus and still have connections with Chattanooga suppliers, so business in doing well. You are welcome as a member of the family, my dear."

"I am where I need to be," she said. She looked at Bethanna and fixed her hair, embarrassed for her looks at this unexpected visit. "There is a time when I might come to you, but this is still my family's land. Should I abandon it?"

Verna tried to explain the dangers of being isolated and alone. Darlene caught her meaning. "I can manage for now."

"How can you?" Verna asked. "We are responsible for you. You're our daughter, still." Verna walked over and embraced Darlene, whose face made no noticeable change. Bethanna thought her reaction to Verna was very odd.

Verna stepped back from her. "Look now, you've lost weight. Please reconsider."

At twenty-one years old, Darlene was still pretty, though she had been worn from worry over Carl for the last three months. Her deep-green eyes were like jewels, set in a smooth and very clean face. Her cupid-bow lips defined her prominent chin and her strongest feature, her hair, was as dark as the raven's coat. When at home, she often wore it down and pulled back from her face.

For the effort to bring her to the inn, Darlene was appreciative but adamant about staying. "There are things I must settle and think through; my marriage was cut short." Her set emerald eyes left Verna no room for further parley and she turned away satisfied. She noticed Bethanna taking in the mantle display and walked to her. "All that is left of him." Darlene said, commenting on the items there.

Verna and Bethanna said a prayer with the widow and left the house. At the carriage, Verna looked back to see Darlene gazing at them from the window. "I guess we shall try next week, then. Hinchel won't be satisfied with this."

On the road back to town, the women said little about their failed mission.

On Darlene's mantle, Bethanna had seen the gray-toned tintype photograph of her cousin Carl, standing strong in his uniform and saber. Surrounded by dead wedding roses, the gilt-framed image had pierced her heart and she spoke up.

"She is not yet over his death and still thinks he will come home." Bethanna shivered, remembering the decayed body of her cousin and his two fellow soldiers, so close to Taldorf.

"We will come for her, when she will be low on food and money." Verna sounded confident, but not happy for her prediction. "It is hard to see her suffer, alone."

* * *

The second week of November saw the Army disperse even more, when the healthy troops transferred to Chattanooga. The wounded from the Perryville campaign had been spread all over north Georgia and the lower Cumberland Valley, wherever the rails could carry them. The colonel of surgeons used Hinchel's Inn as a headquarters where they could find food and rest at any hour. Continually, doctors came and went as they attended councils on everything from amputations to intestinal wounds. Most churches and residents housed patients of all varieties and for those townsfolk missing a family member, caring for the patients gave them an opportunity to cheer the homesick and lonely during the coming Thanksgiving season.

Again, and in the holiday spirit, Aunt Verna wanted Darlene home, but she did not think the grieving widow would come on her invitation. She had suggested that Hinchel go and retrieve her, as a father should. He waited, and thought Darlene would come soon, on account of money.

"Where is her money coming from?" Hinchel questioned from his chair. "How can she make it another week?" He thumped his head on the wall as he leaned back too far. "Damn." Moving the chair to the table, he went for his pipe to think. "She acts strange for a person in need."

Bethanna sat at the end of the table while she prepared the weekend menu in a notebook. She listened to the two concerned in-laws and understood their love for the beleaguered widow, but to her, it was evident that something oppressed Darlene, more than grief. She had three months to get used to the idea of her husband being dead and in that time, there had been little change. Evidently, a spiritual dilemma existed and at this notion, Bethanna's heart warmed for the dark widow. "I will go, *Tante!*"

Hinchel's match hovered over his pipe bowl as he looked through the flame like a sorcerer, reading the future. "You will go? Let us think about that."

Verna clapped her hands at the genius of her niece and blatant evidence of her mature intuitions. "Hinchel, this is perfect. Bethanna, you need a break from work and the hospital atmosphere of the town. Go in the evening around four o'clock, so that the darkness will force Darlene to take you in. Then you can stay for a few days and become her friend."

Hinchel nodded, surprised he did not think of the idea himself. "Of course. This I can approve of."

Verna snapped her towel at Hinchel.

"What?" he said, rearing back from the near miss.

"It will happen whether you approve or not." Verna stuffed her towel in her apron and hugged Bethanna.

As she packed her baskets and clothes bag, Bethanna thought of the trip as her first mission of mercy. God was testing her bravery, her faith and for this honor, she was thankful and nervous, also. The family prayed for her that afternoon and even Mirra asked the Lord for blessings and protection, her voice quiet and nervous. Bethanna hugged her, elated.

Hinchel prepared the newly winterized covered buckboard and in it placed fresh supplies, but only enough for her stay. "I hope that necessity will bring Darlene home. Stay to your instructions, there is rain coming. Want to try another day?"

"No, it must be now. I know this," Bethanna said, putting on her leather rain hat.

Driving through town, she enjoyed the team of horses while directing and singing to them, mostly to keep her cheerfulness on the late evening journey. In ten minutes, she headed west on the Kingston road and with a sudden wind, the rain fell.

The road had seen little upkeep after the Army had overused it. Wicked gusts beat the canvass and the wheels slid in the mud. The test had started and the slow pace worried Bethanna for a time as darkness settled over her. Enduring the rain and road for two miles, she looked for the turn onto the property. Fortunately, there was a faint light from the house that guided her down through the drive.

Near the end of the rutted lane, she pulled the team to a dead stop and in a lighting flash, saw two horses tied to the rail in front of the house. She inspected the scene and after a few minutes, felt uneasy not knowing what could be happening inside. Bethanna walked through the open gate while eyeing the house. Her heart raced with nervous energy as she crept closer to the tied horses. The animals carried the trappings of the cavalry—military saddles, ammo satchels and yellow-trimmed saddle blankets with the letters "C.S.A." Troopers had come.

No sound could be heard but the wind rushing through the trees and the rain on the roof. The smell of beefy food drifted around the house. Thinking someone was there, she quickly checked the kitchen behind the house. It was dark. Obviously, something cooked over the fireplace as the house chimney smoked above her. It wasn't long before her stomach growled.

Bethanna worried about Darlene. Then she worried about herself. What would she do then if these men were assaulting the pretty widow? She had no trusty shotgun like Hertha. She sneaked up to the window, took off her hat, and peered inside.

Through the hazy glass she saw a large man sitting at the table drinking from a bottle, and eating from a bowl. His beard was long and dark, like the hair that covered his shirt collar, and a pistol belt hung on the chair next to him. Some movement forced her to look harder to the right, near the light of the fire. Darlene was standing with the other man, who was fumbling with her clothes.

Bethanna gasped as Darlene's dress fell to the floor. The man pulled her close and began to kiss her. He was shirtless and groping at her with his hands, his bare back towards the window. Then he pulled her into the bedroom, leaving the door wide open. The man at the table was indifferent to all of this and kept eating, like someone having a pleasant meal at the inn.

Bethanna stepped away from the window. *How can she resist them?* she thought. *They will surely harm her with....* Her head grew warm as she imagined the terrifying crime. In a panic, she ran around the house and saw a flicker of light from the bedroom window. Perhaps she could scare the man away by making noise. "But then what?" she said, tossing her arms out.

Inside, a double candle stand lit the small room and clearly illuminated the actions of the couple. Darlene was being stripped out of her chemise and the man seemed to go about it slowly. Bethanna had expected him to be attacking her, but now the action seemed to relate a different tone. To her, it was strange to watch this slow rape, or whatever it was.

Darlene lay naked on the bed, her head very near the window. Her skin glowed in the soft yellow light, beautiful like the old German oil paintings from Vogal's art books. The man kissed

Darlene's legs and she giggled. Perhaps Darlene had to play along for the man. Bethanna leaned in and watched, transfixed.

She was able to get a good look at the cavalryman. His hair was light, of medium length, perhaps a dark blonde, and his face was trimmed in a thin beard at the jawline. He stood and took off his pants. Bethanna, fearing immorality, closed her eyes to the sight of him, but in a few seconds, curiosity won out and she looked as the man's uncovered muscular form moved onto the bed. He sat with his back partially to the window, his face clearly lit, and smiling, his hand sliding onto Darlene's legs, and between them. She moaned and reached for him, pulling him onto her. After a short pause, the two began to writhe and move in rhythm. This was lovemaking, and Bethanna's head sank onto the windowsill in disappointment.

She thought that this woman had been lovesick over Carl, but actually she had found someone, perhaps soon after her new husband had been reported missing. Who knows how these things happen. Bethanna, confused by the discovery, lingered at the spotty window and it was a while before she realized the rain had almost soaked her through. She ran to the shelter of the porch and then sprinted back to the wagon. She waited there, hidden under the canvass and wrapped in blankets, as the images of the two bodies played in her dazed mind. It did not look like sin—the actions pleased them greatly. They must be in passionate love, she figured. All of this would explain Darlene's guarded mood, but not her depression.

It was more than an hour later, she thought, when the door to the house opened and the soldiers came out. Mounting up, the men soon rode away, their horses splashing down the lane. Bethanna threw off her coverings. She was quite warm now, as the heat from her body warmed the wool cape but she couldn't stay outside all night. She would have to get in the house and try to understand this lonely woman. Besides, she had been sent for a purpose, and could not give up now.

Expecting one of the troopers, Darlene flung the door wide open and there was no hiding her embarrassment when she saw Bethanna. Wrapped in a flannel sheet that covered her body but exposed her legs, the stunned mistress hesitated. Her dark hair was tangled and wild on her bare shoulders. She raised her face to speak, but had no harsh words for the new visitor. Maybe because it *was* this girl, she did not slam the door but instead, walked away from it, inviting Bethanna in from the cold. "Shut the door, thank you."

Darlene pointed to the stewpot hanging out from the fireplace on a hinged bar. "Go ahead and warm yourself." Bethanna walked over and glanced at the iron pot, then back to Darlene who sat on the floor near the fireplace. The two said nothing for a long while. Bethanna noticed dishes on the hearth and fixed two plates of the stew. Darlene took her plate, avoiding eye contact with her unexpected guest.

The taste was adequate, but to Bethanna the stew was joyfully warming, and that relaxed her. She did not know where to start with this stranger—the woman who wrote the passionate lines into her cousin's bible. A woeful creature that had been a faceless victim for so long, now sat before her, naked in a blanket and as passive as a hungry child. She wasn't quiet for long.

"So, Beth, now you have me at your advantage," Darlene said.

Bethanna hesitated at her half-name, thought it nice. "How?"

Darlene smacked her lips over the spoon. "You saw those men. What do you think, girl from the mountains?"

"I don't think anything," Bethanna said, defensively. The two finished their stew in silence, occasionally stealing glances at each other. Without a word, Darlene left the room. She returned soon, dressed in a wool robe, and appeared more proper with her hair tied up.

They sat opposite each other on the long sofa, the nicest piece of furniture in a room full of old wood things, chairs, and benches. Darlene hugged a pillow and laid her head against the tall, arched back. "Why are you here? It is strange they would send you alone."

"They want you back with them at the inn," Bethanna said.

"Plain truth?" Darlene asked, staring into Bethanna's crystal-like, blue eyes.

"Yes."

Darlene gazed across the room at nothing, "If they knew what I've done, they would throw me from the highest trestle." Her eyes blazed red in the reflective firelight.

Bethanna frowned. "How can they kill you for being in love?"

Darlene smiled and then she laughed.

Bethanna did not laugh. "There is nothing wrong with that. After what you have been through, it is a fine thing to love again. I do not look at you as being Carl's forever."

Darlene studied Bethanna and the girl's naïveté fascinated her. "You see me as someone in love?" Darlene smiled, briefly. "Why would you think that?"

"You and him..." she almost revealed herself.

"Me and who... what?" Darlene lifted her head.

Bethanna searched for tact. "Is one of those men your new man?" she asked uneasily, afraid of describing the images through the wet windowpane.

Darlene sat stunned, starring at her knees. She covered them. Perhaps Bethanna did have her at advantage, more than she knew. The funny thing was the blonde girl with the accent had no idea of it. The girl's innocence touched Darlene. For the first time in months, she trusted, and saw a possible way out of her wretchedness. How could she tell this unknown person what she must? She choked back tears.

"Darlene?" Bethanna, reached for the widow's hand.

* * *

The wind blew cold all night, in long wailing gusts. Inside the house, Bethanna held Darlene as she slept. It had been a night of tears for the young, beautiful widow, and now Bethanna cried.

Earlier, Darlene had broken down completely, revealing that she had been made a prostitute to survive. In July, after Carl had been missing some time, she had taken up with a soldier, a former beau whom she had trusted before the war, but she did not reveal his name.

She loved him and thought that he would take her in. But as time passed, this was not so. Soon he began to abuse her affections and he directed her, using her promiscuity against her, to lay with his comrades for a price that would be split between them. She had fallen into the trap, set so cleverly by her lover, that she avoided the family and the town as much as she could, out of fear that he would expose her.

During the fall months, she had laid herself down many times and the turns grew more frequent every passing week. Sinking deeper into shame, she could not find the resolve to pull herself from the trap. If anyone found out, the news would tarnish Carl's memory and cancel any rights to her in-laws' support.

Darlene wept as Bethanna held her. The secrets had soiled her soul and there was no stopping her tears. Bethanna assured her that confessing would renew her before God and she prayed for her forgiveness as the widow shook in her arms.

Bethanna put her to bed, wrapped her in warm blankets and opened up her own life. She told Darlene about Jon and how they met when her mother had shot one of the rebels, and about his protection of her. "He is a romantic poetry reader," she added.

With a bright smile, she described the characters in Jon's platoon: the smart lieutenant, Lawsen's loyalty, and Cawley's cute humor. "It is very difficult to contact him with Bragg's Army spread out and on the move. I am like most sweethearts, I guess."

Darlene, touched by Bethanna's notions of first love, felt sympathy with her new friend. "How wonderful that first feeling is, when you know that someone loves you, as much as you love them. It is the strongest, my dear, the first love always will be special." Her expression wilted, as if the experience were something distant and unreal. "Rarely is it the only one. But for you, it can be."

Darlene's statement on first love explained it well; someone who loves you the same way. Did Jon love her as she loved him, with longing and a hurt inside over the other's absence? This was one reason why she must find him and her profound vision of him in battle, was another reason. The answers to both these questions, together, may bring immense joy and sorrow. The risk was great, but she had to trust her resolve, like she did when leaving the valley.

Bethanna kept the vision to herself and they continued to talk of the future and how they both could help each other find it. With a small suggestion, Darlene formed a plan, then Bethanna added to it. They promised to stick together and Darlene said that she could come to the inn, since she had a new friend there who understood her.

Now, Bethanna lay in the early hours of a long night, crying in small sobs. Her thoughts had drifted from Jon to Mirra, her father, then to her mother; she had surely left her to the wilds of war. Visions of dark torture and fire assailed her. The village burned and her beautiful valley turned to smoke, closing off her family and Jon, covering his sweet memory. "Dear Lord, please care for them all, what mistakes I have made, make them right."

She began to count the weeks away from the valley, the days in Knoxville and then she realized what day it was. November 6th, her birthday. She turned 18 years old.

She wiped her face and held fast to a snoring woman, who had suffered more than most. Eventually the wind calmed and moved away. Bethanna fell asleep to the patter of rain.

* * *

The hard wind and rain moved north into the Cumberland range, raced over the Clinch River valley, and followed a forgotten road into the dark and lifeless valley of Taldorf. On a rise east of the burned-out crossroads, a battered wooden gate rocked back and forth, untouched for days at the Gurtag's overgrown property.

Inside the dark house, a small candle flickered to its last glow, then blackness. A cry of the most frail, desperate creature could be heard in the back bedroom, bemoaning the failing light. All around, the house moaned with her as the wind assailed its angles. Hertha waited for the ending.

She held her shotgun, aiming it at every sound. In her bed, she sat wrapped in blankets, listening wide-eyed to the terrors that, within moments, would surely bust into her house. Many nights now she had waited in the cold darkness for the horrors of war to attack her.

Weeks before, she had dared them, boasting of her recent renown as a rebel captor and killer. Soon the empty valley began to ring with shotgun blasts, as the haunted woman threw pellets into phantom raiders and moving shadows.

Without her even knowing it, the ammo had outlasted her food. Soon she was out of both. Then the terrors had come again. On the wind, she heard faint sounds of voices carrying across the field and down into her cellar. Horses neighed, and bounded up and down the road past her gate. She ran to her room and barred the door.

There bravely, she was able to hold out for days, until the last candle burned out. Weakened and delirious, she cried for the wind to stop its torturous voices. "I vill die before I let you in!" she groaned. Falling to a heap in her blankets, she waited for death on the cold, drafty floor.

The sounds began again with talking voices outside the window, then a cry of some sort and the banging down of the front door. Hertha screamed as footfalls neared her room. She saw her bedroom door slam open in halves and a large figure with a sword bounded inside. Somewhere in the clamor she heard the voice of her husband. Vogal was there at last. He choked on his first words as a lantern revealed his wife, shriveled and worn, clinging to a rusty shotgun. "Wha...Why didn't you go with them, why my dear?" he cried.

Vogal had received the letter from Bethanna and she alarmed him with her talk of raiders and rebel patrols in the area. Bethanna's tone, especially at the end of the letter, showed confidence and decisive action. That was good. The girls were safe, thank God, but the state of his wife was a troubling mystery. The mail had taken only a short time to reach him, but Vogal had to wait much longer to get back home.

He had requested leave after the arrival of Bethanna's letter in August and was allowed to go, only to be interrupted by Bragg's invasion of Kentucky. The Confederate troops had destroyed many bridges and depots that needed his corps' attention. Finally after a month, the area was clear. Starting from Cumberland Gap with a cavalry escort, he rode a few miles into enemy territory and then took his chances, with only a corporal to aid him. The north county roads were familiar near the border, as he was involved with their design and upkeep.

Vogal put Hertha on the bed and gave her water from his canteen. She drank quickly, sobbing as she grasped his strong hands. He thought of where he could keep his wife and if she could ever recover and be the bright woman he loved. As he looked at her pitiful form he knew his family was broken, perhaps lost forever.

* * *

CHAPTER 21 ★

Acknowledging the failed campaign in Kentucky, the Southern government's focus in the western department shifted to middle Tennessee and the Union Army massing there. The military strategists in Richmond became bent on holding Tennessee, not only to retake the vital rail links and factories of Nashville, but to entice new recruits to join a soon-to-be victorious General Bragg.

In November, a Union General by the name of William S. Rosecrans had taken charge in occupied Nashville. Previously successful in West Virginia, and as a combat commander under Grant in west Tennessee, Rosecrans charged into his new job with confidence and in a few short weeks, reconditioned the Army of the Cumberland, beefed up the supply lines, and trained fresh troops. His presumed target was a supply base on the Nashville-Chattanooga Railroad called Murfreesboro.

Needing a check on Rosecrans, the Southern government moved General Breckinridge and his division into the small town, which stood only two miles from a branch of the Cumberland, named Stones River.

And so the news spread around Knoxville and into Hinchel's Inn that hopefully, Bragg's Army of the Tennessee in Chattanooga, with tons of supplies, will stave off this new invasion and end the war in Tennessee for good.

Hinchel huffed behind his countertop, saying that, "the Federals will keep sending them and our boys will keep fighting them, until one side runs out of boys." He was serious, though some customers had chuckled at the remark.

Hinchel was in a sense talking about his own sons. The war was personal for him now, and after interviewing Reverend Grottmacher privately, he was not convinced that the good pastor knew the whole truth about Hertha's involvement. In no way did he doubt Bethanna's viewing of Carl's body, but she had no direct evidence against her mother either. The tale of betrayal was too horrible, and strangely incomplete. Instead of liquor to dull the pain, he drank the word of God as he attempted to fill his mind with forgiving verses and wise proverbs. But more often, Hinchel avoided direct conversation with Bethanna, unless it was about her job. Partly, it was for her benefit. He did not want to chastise out of rash anger and hurt the girl.

For some time after Carl's death was revealed, Bethanna felt that her relatives looked on her with doubtful eyes. *It was Hertha they were judging*, she thought, *not me*. Presently, there were divisions within the small family of the inn that cut Bethanna in ways she had never felt before. Soon there would be another.

Verna kissed Mirra goodbye as she left for school. The fifteen year old strode with confidence in her new gray over-cape, passing a group of soldiers at the door. They touched their caps, showing respect to a lady. Mirra smiled and dipped her head, then giggled as she met her friends for the walk to school. She seemed unhurt by the family fractures that had uprooted her from Taldorf and she adjusted well to life and work around the inn. Hinchel and Verna were glad to be her parents in trust and they could see that Mirra benefited from their solid guidance. She had grown up in a short time. This meant that Bethanna could see to other things.

One of those things began to obsess her thoughts as she served the noon patrons—the plan that she and Darlene had dreamed up while talking in bed. They decided to leave Knoxville together.

It was understood that in their present situations, neither could achieve their ultimate happiness or destiny. Darlene must go to Chattanooga to stay with her parents and in time, restore herself into a proper relationship and marriage, devoid of her lover.

Bethanna's aim was a bit simpler. She would take the trip to Chattanooga to find Jon. No telling what would happen if and when she found him, but she was drawn to the effort by her vision's clear warnings and a growing faith in God's will. There was something she must do for him even if it was unknown at the time. *This, the Lord will reveal.*

She knew the train out of town would cost money and she had saved enough tips in the last months to complete her end of the deal. Darlene's father would provide a room to live in above his wheelwright and furniture shop, near the riverside of town. They had not decided *when* to go. Of course, when the time came, it would all be explained to Hinchel and Verna in a very clever way.

Thinking this over, Bethanna served lunch to two reporters in the corner. "Where are your friends, gentlemen?" she asked, setting down their steaks.

"Chattanooga, where *we* should be," said one man, with a cigar in his hand. His partner chuckled as he picked up a hearty glass of Hinchel's pilsner. "There's nothing here to write about, except the damn cold!"

Bethanna smiled and rolled her eyes at the two smelly journalists, big city men from Richmond, used to travel and fast living, and it was obvious they had just arrived from a night's frolic. Carousing all hours of the night offered them cheap excitement when the combat died down. The taverns and bars did great business and floated above the economic low tides of the times.

She quickly made her coffee rounds and took a small break to roll up the clean silver. Standing near the serving window, she looked into the kitchen from time to time. Darlene was there, taking Mirra's job, running meals out and dishes in. It was a slow day so there wasn't too much to do. Then she heard uncle Hinchel shout, his voice unmistakable. He greeted a young soldier at the door with more cheer than usual.

Bethanna stopped what she was doing. Uncle Hinchel led the man over to her and he proudly said, "Bethanna, this is your cousin Stephan. My oldest son!"

The young man gasped. "You are little Bethanna?" He smiled brightly and immediately hugged her, firm and close.

Bethanna tried to smile politely, but a sudden shock held her speechless. This was the man who had made love to Darlene, as she had witnessed through the wet windowpane. She could not believe her eyes.

Stephan held Bethanna at arm's length. "Look how pretty you are now!" He smiled and fawned, saying those things that cousins should say. Stephan was 25 years old, six feet tall, blonde and square at the shoulders. His boyish smile belied an experienced, crafty, extremely shrewd man. This dichotomy of looks and cunning he used to full advantage when needed.

In his youth, he gained a poor man's education as a roaming free spirit, working the rail lines and riverboats in Chattanooga and Nashville. He had worked in a library, at a printing press, and even cut tunnels for the railroad. When the war came, it was just another opportunity, ripe for his talents. Rank, stature, even heroic fame could take him farther than he ever dreamed possible. His only problem? Women.

They had played him in the past, broken his heart as a youth, stolen friends and money. After much time, he had learned what to say to them, how to manipulate them, and satisfy them. He could not settle on one, nor could he suit them with truthfulness. The weak ones were his favorites, like Darlene. She was genteel and polite, raised to please others before herself. He did not always use her like he did now. In the past, he did love her.

She was a seventeen year old, visiting at the inn, when he first saw her in the summer of 1858. Her father made recent trips through the area to deliver goods and open a second wheel shop. He soon brought his family to the smaller town and they stayed at the inn while their shop was built.

Naturally, Stephan courted Darlene, as did his younger brother, Carl. She gave her affections to both, thinking that either would be a good choice. She leaned toward Stephan and his strength of will. Carl was sweet and caring, but he did not excite her passions. A true gentleman, he could not bring himself to hint at anything improper.

But Stephan didn't care; he kissed her one night as she was going to bed. His approach in the dark room threw her into a rapturous panic and after the encounter she was hooked by his furtive touch and stolen kisses, always unexpected, thrilling and in very bad taste.

Stephan sat at the round table, sipping coffee and talking over his recent action in the area. He asked his father about the condition of Bragg's wounded troops and the overall status of the town. As Hinchel responded in detail, Stephan could only think of the pretty cousin he had just met. His eyes wandered like his thoughts and never rested.

Stephan knew women well. Using his imagination, he could almost see beneath their clothes, how their bodies would look, naked and waiting. Looking at his cousin this way was a new thrill, something that had surprised him. She wore a maroon velvet dress with a brown apron. The neckline of her dress was open to the collarbone, hair up in a neat capped bun. Her simplicity and quiet demure was attractive, even alluring.

As Bethanna walked around the room, Stephan's eyes raided her form, taking glances and measuring with his mind the gentle movement of her hips, the arch of her lower back and her smooth neck. Her face was most surprising to him, so different from the awkward thirteen year- old from his youth. She had a strong chin and shapely lips, but her eyes were the most interesting. A pure and clear sky-blue, they had a determined, strong, but private resonance. Stephan searched for a weakness. He would have to get closer to discover it.

Bethanna felt the heat rise in her again when Uncle Hinchel asked for biscuits. Her brow began to sweat and she could feel Stephan's gaze as sure as if he were using his hands like a blind man to look at her. She became keenly aware of his stares and in a wasted effort she loosened her apron over the tight dress to detract from her shape. Since arriving at the inn, she had gained weight from eating more heartily and living without Hertha's added stress. Bethanna's figure filled out within weeks and her clothes revealed a woman's full form.

After her coffee rounds, she wheeled into the kitchen to tell Darlene about Stephan. Then she stopped. She had to remember Darlene knew nothing of what she saw at the window. Instead, she veered into the walk-in pantry. A nervous heat oppressed her, then a shortness of breath. For a moment, she thought she might faint dead away.

Thoughts came at her like flying arrows; how Stephan had been her favorite cousin, as a girl she bragged on his good looks and great stories from his travels. When he visited Taldorf, always unannounced, she fell into joyous crushes and fawning behavior, and how not? Stephan was the ideal young man—hardworking, strong and independent, but often so lost.

Now, this idol had lain with his dead brother's wife, a scene that Bethanna still could not believe, though she had viewed it through a rainy window. Such foulness caused tears at her eyes. She rested her head on a shelf loaded with pickled hogs' feet. Somehow she must face him, and find courage to do it. She could not easily run up to her father's drafting room and hide from the day. She exited the pantry and grabbed a fresh basket of biscuits for her cousin.

"Bethanna has been a large help to us, Stephan!" Hinchel bragged.

The trooper smiled, as she leaned over and placed the basket on the table. "I hope we can help her, too," Stephan said. He picked up a biscuit and buttered it, looking into Bethanna's face. She was sweating and nervous. That was good, for it meant that he affected her already. By the stunned greeting she had given him when they met, there was no doubting it. He thought Bethanna would be a delicious little side item on his sexual menu, if he was smart and patient. That's how he succeeded with them.

Hinchel leaned in, "So, my son, what is the status of your new company?"

Stephan chewed and talked. "Father, Colonel Parker's company has been attached to a new Confederate battalion, finally. I'm proud to be a part of the regular Army now. Colonel Parker is very clear and precise with his training."

"Great, no more wondering what to do and roaming around like police."

"Right. Now we can join larger forces."

Hinchel nodded. He supported his son's new career, but not the Southern government. The fact that both sons had joined the Confederate service did not shock him. They were Southern raised and had no great love for the overreaching Federals in Washington, or sympathy for the blacks, like their Northern cousins in Pennsylvania and Iowa.

Carl was more patriotic, while Stephan had other motivations. It pleased Hinchel greatly to see Stephan so honored and with some sort of future, as far as reputation was concerned. People could look at him as a man with purpose, brave, and always moving forward.

In the past, the two found conversation difficult, due to Hinchel's constant but weak discipline. Now they had much to talk about and he did not want to lose this newfound camaraderie with his only surviving son.

"Colonel Parker was a junior officer under John B. Hood in Texas, back when he fought Indians! Can you believe that?" Stephan sat back, his chin smeared in butter.

Hinchel asked seriously, "He has a scalp, I presume?"

Stephan laughed, and said, "Yes! It's quite handsome. In a matter of weeks, we will be consolidated further with new units. We will make a grand regiment and be shifted west, towards Chattanooga. Colonel Parker likes me. I know he will make a lieutenant soon."

"So, an officer, eh? You will be transferred anytime?" Hinchel beamed proudly. "To the main Army, then?"

"Yes, under Wheeler and Forest. Where the true test awaits me."

* * *

That evening, Bethanna and Darlene shared a mirror while brushing each other's hair. In their room, with the door shut, they could plot and dream and share those intimate things that only another girl can understand. Darlene opened a treasure trove of family secrets and her own.

As she explained it to Bethanna, it turned out that the best son had died. When the shooting started in 1861, Darlene was desperate to hold Stephan's love in the uncertain times as the roving lover looked beyond for adventure. So she offered herself to him one night to secure his promise of devotion. Stephan took advantage of her and after several sexual encounters, she became with child.

But the young adventurer had other plans; he ran away to the recruiter and left for the war. His foolishness angered Carl, who as an honorable man, cared for the mother-to-be and tried to help an abandoned girl in a scandalous situation. The pair already shared a mutual affection and soon married, maintaining Darlene's reputation.

The marriage of his brother and his lover made his parents happy and did not affect Stephan at all in a negative way. He had figured that good Carl was just saving her for him. He would take hold of her later on, after the short war with the foolish Yankees was won and he was a hero. Only, it was not short like the politicians predicted.

After many months, thousands had been killed and wounded horribly out on the bloody fields of battle as the war brought campaigns into central Tennessee and Mississippi. Under an established government and a flag, Carl stood up to take the oath and was commissioned a lieutenant after a company election. Darlene was proud, pregnant, and ignorant of her impending doom. Inside her tender body, forces were unleashed to expunge the small life growing inside her, for it was imperfect, and did not meet the human standard for survival.

The miscarriage had thrust a damning sword through her heart and she secretly mourned for the loss of her true love's seed. With the disappearance of the faithful Carl, and many weeks alone, she waited like a battered daisy, ready to be picked. And so she was, as the older brother began to display her for the clink of the coin.

Bethanna sat motionless as Darlene explained it all. The facts were too fantastic to take root in her young, virgin mind. These most distorted scenes of sexual lust and greed could never be believed, but she had heard it all, from the woman who had lived it.

Darlene had seen her lover, Stephan, sitting at the round table with his father, rollicking in laughter. She knew that he would never leave her alone. "And honestly," she said, casting her gaze from the mirror. "Even now, I cannot resist him. Who else will have me? Everyone in this town knows about me, I'm sure."

Bethanna listened with burning ears as Darlene admitted that the only way was to run and hide. "Time and distance will put out the fire he has started, at least dim it a little. Then I could be free." Her small, curvy lips smiled weakly.

"Or his death in the war?" Bethanna added.

"I could not take that. Not now. Maybe, after I have been away from him a long time."

Bethanna thought carefully. "So, you would stay with him, if he did not use you for money?"

Darlene sat on her bed and lowered her face, surrounded in waves of dark hair. "Yes."

Bethanna stood up and walked over to look at herself in the mirror. She put on her nightcap and looked at Darlene. "Tell me something. What does it feel like?"

"Well, it feels horrible to know that I cannot have a true love who…"

"No." Bethanna interrupted. "What does…lying with a man feel like?" The low-lit room hid her blush.

"Oh, well." Darlene raised her head, gathered her hair, and smoothed it as she talked. "I guess you would not know. How nice. Um…let's see." She looked over at the younger girl, tried to read her intent. "Well, you must understand that when you really

274

love a man, being undressed with him is not as embarrassing as it seems."

Bethanna turned around. "Really? And?"

"Yes. You get used to it, I should say. There is a warming up before the moment you join together, kissing, touching—at least there should be."

Bethanna reviewed the scene of Stephan and Darlene together. "Right, then what?"

"The feeling of him inside is very thrilling, like the deepest tickle, and the motion you share increases the pleasure, like a good rubdown feels, only a thousand times better."

Both of them giggled for a time. Bethanna frowned. "What about pain?"

"Perhaps the first time. But with a man who loves and understands, it passes very quickly." Darlene watched Bethanna's eyes seeking those imagined feelings. "Please, Beth, when the time comes, you will be ready. Wait till you marry the man who touches your heart, not just your body. Someone who values both equally."

With a single candle burning, the two young women sat on the bed and dreamed over their promising futures, which to their humor, involved men. Bethanna's aim, as far as Darlene knew, was to find her true love and do what true lovers do when they find each other.

Darlene planned a new integration into society, complete with a well-to-do older businessman. Who he turned out to be was of no concern, because all she wanted was to escape into a world where Stephan would have no access. They had decided to leave in five days, on the 16th of November, but something, or someone, put a rush on their plans.

He had visited the last three days and assisted the family in the winter preparations for the inn. Stephan helped his father in the livery to add stalls for the patrons' mounts and more importantly, to collect a wagonload of logs into the backyard to cut for firewood. Their stacking created large pyramids of neat splits.

The women worked to gather as much cloth and blankets as they could afford, and they reorganized the tub room behind the kitchen area. Stephan, with charm, even helped the girls arrange their room to better accommodate Darlene and her things. As long as the young man stayed busy, it seemed he was no trouble.

After four days of work and preparations, the women insisted on an evening of baths. The girls had to use the water in turns and Mirra was first. Darlene took a while to wash her hair and stole most of the heat out of the water. Bethanna waited patiently as Verna poured in a fresh, steaming bucket. "Now, there you are, good and hot again."

Verna closed the door and Bethanna turned down the lantern light to a soft flicker. The small paneled room felt warm and private enough so she quickly removed her wool robe and linen chemise. Walking over to a dressing mirror she looked at her nude self in the light and stark shade. She loosened her hair from a gathered bun and pulled it out to full length. Longer now, the blonde had darkened a bit with the colder season, but in the yellowed light it glowed in the mirror as she moved it around in different styles.

She cocked her head, looking at her figure. She guessed it was satisfactory. Her body was full enough in the right places, though she wondered if too full in others. She poked her hips and measured her waist with her hands. Eyeing her form in the mirror, the scene from Darlene's window came to mind, its stark sexuality.

She compared herself to the dark beauty and was not too disappointed. Darlene did not seem too embarrassed in front of Stephan. She became naked very easily. Bethanna imagined if she could ever be so brazen, what it would be like, a man's touch on her skin, in her body. Darlene's description lacked anatomic and emotional details. Those would remain a mystery until experienced, hopefully before she turned thirty.

She thought of Jon and what he would see. Letting her arms drop to her sides and around her back, she stared, thinking of him and his imaginary reaction to what was in the mirror. A slight smile crossed her lips. In the glass appeared a woman, attractive, mysterious and a bit wild with her hair out of place. She shrugged her shoulders and went for the bath.

As she slid her legs into the tub, Bethanna moaned at the perfect, soothing heat. There was not enough water to submerge her body, so by taking a small towel, she dunked it into the water and wrapped it over her shoulders. She shut her eyes, and tried to relax, hearing occasional noises throughout the inn. In small circular paths, she began to use the soap.

The room felt about as private as could be, given the circumstances of an inn, and up the wall, parallel to the tub, was a two-foot long glass window for lighting and venting. Outside, the height of the window was well above eight feet from the ground, but because of careful stacking of a remote pile of firewood, it was within an easy four feet. Standing on this pile was the builder himself, Stephan.

He had been patient to discover the weekly tub rounds fell on Friday. The window held a perfect view of the small room as his face reflected the bouncing lamplight near the tub. His breath fogged the window, and he moved to another position to clean the haze with his sleeve. Seeing her clearly from his perch above the tub, she filled every promise of his fertile imagination. His lust found new proportions at the sight of her nakedness and he mumbled pleasantries that the two of them could enjoy.

Bethanna hummed as she sat up and removed the wet towel from her shoulders. Her skin glowed, shiny and firm as she rinsed clean. Changing position, she lifted her weight onto her knees and bent down, soaking her hair completely.

Stephan chuckled at the conquering stature he enjoyed over the pretty young girl bathing below. To him, the intrusion was justified. Bethanna was not warming up to him like most females. His cute humor and charming smile made not the least impression on her, even after his best efforts, which usually need not be many. To compensate, he enticed Darlene into a secret union in his room, but still could not shake Bethanna's rejection. Soon he thought of other ways to know her, and in a pinch, this was the best, most intimate way, he assumed.

While he gazed upon Bethanna's flesh and warmed to the view, the cold night reminded him that even though he was a strong man, he still felt the elements. He shivered and smelled future snow in the air. Below in the tub, Bethanna toweled her hair and Stephan guessed that the show would end soon, but not the fun.

He began to step down the pile, bending at the knees and feeling his way. He slipped and hit the wood with his butt. A heavy boot hit the wall and inside, Bethanna jumped. She looked up to the window; a light fog covered the outside of it near the middle.

There was nothing that represented a threat from the sound outside; perhaps one of Hinchel's ladders fell from a gust of wind. She wrung out her hair, got out of the tub and patted herself with a towel. She gave the mirror one more try, and liked the cleaner reflection. Her wetted hair darkened her looks and the effect pleased her. "The bad Bethanna," she said, turning to see her rear and back. She let her hair lay wild on her shoulders and put on her robe. Opening the door, she jumped when Stephan appeared.

"Hello, Beth, a kiss goodnight before we part?" he asked. Blocking the doorway, Stephan grabbed Bethanna's robe by the sash.

She gripped his hand, tugged at his arm. "Please, cousin. We are not even proper friends yet."

Her attempt at polite sarcasm tickled Stephan. He reached for her hair. "That's not my fault," he said. "Your beauty is a magical thing, Beth. It has bewitched me, and only your touch can break the spell." He smiled, pulled her hand up and kissed it.

Bethanna pulled away. "No, stop this!" She shivered at his cold touch.

Stephan put his hand to her mouth. "Shhh, you are aware of it, aren't you?"

She shook her head as his hand covered her low, muffled response. "Whaf?"

"The spell you cast, with your eyes, your hair, your walk. It holds all men in a rapturous torture they would be happy to suffer until death." His hand moved down to her throat. He gently squeezed. "But I don't want to wait for death and I think you don't either."

Bethanna's eyes widened and she froze. His hand was indeed ice cold, like the outside. She remembered the fog at the window, the noise. *It was him out there!* She raised her hands and Stephan's grip tightened while she pushed against a hard wall of muscle under his cold coat.

He leaned in and kissed her forehead. "See, that was not the devil's touch." He smiled. "I'm not the devil, Beth. But I do burn, like any other man who is rejected far too often by a lady he wants. Why don't you let me touch you?" His hand moved away from her throat, down to her cleavage and breast.

Bethanna yelped and slapped his hand away. "You have spied on me!"

He laughed and checked the hallway door to the kitchen a few yards away. Nobody stirred. "Why can't I see your lovely skin? You saw *me* through that window, remember?"

Bethanna shuddered and gasped. "How did…"

"Yes, my dear, I saw someone sneaking a look at us. I thought it was strange to see Uncle's team and wagon hitched at Darlene's fence, so I doubled back and looked in on you both, eating and chatting on her couch. I was surprised like you, when Uncle introduced us, but I can hide my excitements, you can't." Stepping into the room, he forced her back. "What did you think, what did you feel staring at us in the thrill of passion? You see, we're even now, you have seen my body, and I yours. So now that we're acquainted…. " He swung the door shut and moved at her. "Did you dream of me?"

Bethanna backed away slowly towards the corner. There was something coming to her, not terror but a stunning realization of her advantage. She smiled a little and reached behind her to pick up the lantern. "Let me turn up the light if you want to see me."

Stephan's face brightened, sensing a final victory and great pleasure. Bethanna turned the wick screw and killed the light. She grabbed the handle and swung the lantern wildly through the dark space until it smashed into Stephan's body.

In the kitchen and out into the family parlor, a muffled crash of shattering glass stirred Hinchel, sitting in his favorite armchair. He popped up and stood, quickly taking his pipe from his mouth. "What in all saints, is that?"

Verna put down her book. "Wolves again?" she asked.

Upon entering the room with candles aglow, Hinchel discovered Stephan sitting on the floor of the washroom with a sleeve to his bloody head. Verna patched up her son as Hinchel lectured him about tomfoolery in the house. "I do not feel like putting out a fire tonight. You want to be an officer? You must be more careful."

Stephan said nothing about Bethanna, played stupid and decided not to mess with the rough mountain girl for now. As he drank Verna's hot tea at the large table, he realized his best chance at her had failed. As a matter of simple observance, he knew Bethanna was different, and to succeed with her he would need different tactics and most definitely, a change of place, away from the influence of her family—too many favorable conditions to ask for at the present time.

Not long after Stephan had tried to molest her, Bethanna sat on her bed and toweled her hair. "We will have to leave earlier than expected."

Darlene, lying under cozy blankets, raised her head, "Why?"

"Well, I think it is very hard for Stephan to be here with you and me."

Darlene frowned. "Why? Did he say something to you, about me?"

"No." Bethanna hesitated, unsure how to portray what had happened in the tub room. *What would Darlene think of her lover now? She must hear the truth.* "Nothing about you, but about me and what he wanted from me."

"No." Darlene sat up. "Did he touch you? I will let Hinchel know and we will see about Mr. Trouble!"

"No, Darlene. We must be wise, say nothing and keep it to ourselves. You see, Hinchel would never believe us about his son. He is too proud, and Stephan is the talker. He will fool him if he has to."

Darlene fell back into her bed, sighed heavily. "Oh, the foolish men."

The room went dark as Bethanna blew out the candles on the small table between the beds. She wrapped up in her quilts, rolled over and looked at Darlene's silhouette against the moon-lit window. "Why are some men's words so different than others? I know that I have heard kind words from a man, received a kiss, and they still linger over me, like a sweet smell."

"Well, my girl, whatever they say, men always want the same thing. Perhaps some just use more direct ways of getting at the point."

"I see," Bethanna said. "But I can't imagine every man is like that, is he?"

"Most."

"My God."

"Yes, quite the stunner I presume. Sorry, dear. Good night."

Bethanna shook her head. She yawned and listened to the wind outside. She thought she heard a horse clatter away from the yard, then fade down the street.

On that horse, Stephan rode through the cold wind, his head throbbing under the bandage Verna had wrapped for him. After a short ride, he would numb the pain with whiskey, beer, or gin, perhaps all. On the east side of town, The Signal Tavern was the popular place for cavalrymen from the outlying units patrolling the roads. Rude jokes, dirty songs, and dancing carried the revelers away to distraction. The night often ended in drunken fights with artillery privates, who boasted of their "big guns."

Indeed upon his arrival, Stephan poured a few drinks down and listened to the debauching of those friends who make up bar mates but inside his mind, within that soft throb at his temple, Bethanna's glowing body danced and twisted, dappled with water like wet leaves in the rain, and now, it was further away than ever. His anger, usually quick to dissipate, remained locked deep, weighted by depression and now more than anything, rejection.

Stephan carried on through the motions of frivolity, induced by the liquor trance that controls one to lose control, a wicked spin that takes memory and banishes feelings, hurts and torturous wants. He moved about the bar flirting and laying down propositions like a lawyer giving away calling cards.

He danced with Julia, a small plump blonde, with large breasts and big eyes. And upstairs, as she lay under him in bed, accepting all of his frustrated gifts, his life seemed as empty as the whiskey bottle on the floor.

* * *

Major Vogal Gurtag,

Nov. 12, 1862

Dear Brother Hinchel,

I write to you from the house of a gentleman here in Kentucky, close to the town of Barboursville. My host is the father of one of my lieutenants and good Union man. I am detached from my unit for a short time, as I have traveled to fetch my wife.

The family here is very generous and has put Hertha in a nice room facing a lovely park, where she can watch the horses run. She always wanted horses, and I know they have cheered her. She is in better health now, but was in very bad straights when I found her alone and starving in our house.

I am sure Bethanna told you about our village and the plunder there. I saw it myself and it disheartened me so. To see such scenes of pitiful waste, animals rotting in the open, burnt dwellings that have only seen happiness. I may never go back, though I still have the house for the time being, and my land. What will it be with no one to tend it?

The doctor said Hertha had not eaten well for weeks and she was in danger of dying. I am thankful that Bethanna wrote me and tremendously glad she moved her sister to your house. To find my family scattered and hurt has always been my fear. Now it has come to pass. *I know, thanks to you, and with God's care, finally they are all safe.*

I assume that Bethanna and Mirra are doing well and are being useful at your inn? I miss them greatly so please give them all my love. I know they have grown and given a good account of their upbringing and morals. Wish Bethanna a belated birthday. Eighteen now and an adult, I can't imagine. Much time will pass before my homecoming, so please give her and Mirra my love, hug them both, tell them with all truth, that I am very proud.

As for my recent duties, I have been repairing damage done by Bragg's foray into Kentucky; it is such a mess and there is no time to fix it all. I am being called farther west, to help move supplies. More of the same, I am sure. But I wish not to waste words on it. I am fine in my work.

Good wishes to Verna, your boys and your business.

God bless,

Your brother, Vogal.

Thanks to Vogal's letter, the timing was perfect to announce the big news.

Telling Hinchel and Verna turned out to be easier than the girls thought. Darlene began. "I am going home to be with my parents in Chattanooga and Bethanna, being a trusted friend, will be a welcomed part of my recovery." She explained that the time she suffered alone in the country had been detrimental to her overall health, but now with Bethanna to help, she could make the move in a truly Christian way.

It was perfectly clear to Hinchel that this was good. He lit his pipe at the head of the large table, comfortable and settled. "The girls will be happy there; too many sad memories here for Darlene. I can see this now," he said.

Verna agreed with her husband's conclusions and gave Bethanna her blessings. "God will go with you, teaching you and protecting you."

Bethanna sipped her coffee, satisfied. She noticed Stephan was gone and it pleased her that she could present her and Darlene's plan without him listening in. He had not even come home the last two nights and Hinchel never said anything about it. They were used to his ways.

"The letter from Vogal is very heartening, yes?" Hinchel noted. "Your mother is safe now, so you can ease your mind, Bethanna."

"Yes, uncle. And I feel like I am free to go."

"That you are, my dear. You are an adult now with a responsibility," He said, toasting her with his smoky pipe.

"In our journey, there is a mission, a spiritual purpose and a calling," Bethanna said.

Verna retrieved a small book from the shelf, and presented it to Bethanna. "I think you should have this. It's a New Testament, the works of Jesus and his disciples. It will guide your path."

Bethanna stood and hugged her aunt. "I have been truly blessed here Tante. I know the Lord has already moved ahead, and awaits my first steps."

Reserved and not very happy about the move, Mirra was surprised that her sister would leave the security of the inn, although in the last few weeks, she saw Bethanna as a woman untied and free to follow her heart. The trip was a bold move that took courage to see through and Mirra knew that Bethanna's love for Jon was indeed strong. Still, she did not see the reasons to run off and find him in the unknown, war-torn country. "You wouldn't be doing this if mother were here," she told her sister in secret.

Mirra had the safest spot in the whole war and she was not leaving it. The inn could serve both sides. Hinchel was a deacon, an officer on the city's Business Council, and Verna had many friends throughout the town's church community. Mirra downplayed Bethanna's warning to her about Stephan's rude hands, "In five days his regiment moves west. Because you will be gone, he will not come back."

With her pet cats and new girlfriends, Mirra had plenty to keep her happy, but to Bethanna there was still something underneath her sister's freckled smiles that spoke of sadness or a restraint of happiness. Bethanna understood that look of family worry.

Bethanna hugged her. "I know that Mama frightened you. But she is a good person, only broken by grief, and in time she may be whole again."

"Not with the war, not soon."

"You are well and blessed to be here. Take time with Verna, she will teach you how to forgive, for she has forgiven Mother for her sins against the family."

Mirra held fast to her, saddened for the first time at their separation, perhaps for a very long one, for she knew that finding this soldier would take her sister far, far away.

With the blessing and prayers of her aunt, uncle and sister, Bethanna would set out on her great journey.

* * *

CHAPTER 22 ★

The passenger car, once a bright and ornate coach, now appeared as a dirty worn out reminder of past pleasures, holiday excursions and affordable living. Without regular care and replacement, the red leather seats turned brown with overuse and the wood panels lost their oily shine. The car's wheels clacked down the wavy, overused track at a safe 10 miles per hour, required by the engineers for reaction time in case of obstructions.

Thankfully, a small stove burned warmly at the head of the car, its output sufficient enough to battle the cold winds beyond the curtains and cracked glass windows. Bethanna and Darlene sat on a broken spring seat that for their comfort had been covered with old blankets. They looked out the window at a battered land and witnessed a big, wide world, foreboding and in trouble. The rails snaked through rough fields, once thick with cotton or corn, now only barrens that waited for seeds and the money to buy them. The pale-gray sky brought out the bright copper of the dead grass and stark brown landscape that with every mile, changed and widened as the hills spread out. Evergreens followed the streams into the high ground and in the fields and swales, tall empty oaks and pecan trees reached for each other with extended, branchy fingers.

The farther the train took them away from Stephan, the better they felt. For her own part, Bethanna could not abide another day near him and feared while under his unceasing pressure, he would have his way, with force. His eager passion was something to be wary of, now that she had seen it firsthand. From that day on, it must be foremost in her mind that she walked a clear path and he represented a stumbling block in the way, perhaps a test she had to pass before her mission could proceed.

The only man she thought of romantically was Jon. This thought was peculiar at first, after she left the valley, but in the time away from him, her fondness proved to be love, and like Darlene said, the first love is the strongest. This she felt when her heart warmed at the thought of him and his admiration of her, even his outright efforts to kill for her. His will to live for her would be just as strong. She thought on it and meditated for a time. *Yes, he will live for me, fight for me. The same I must do for him.*

Out there in the Tennessee hills, Jon faced danger and she would find him, to warn him or to help him in some way she knew not. As the thought filled her mind, the enormity of this task began to show itself for the first time. Out of a swarming sea of thousands, she must find one man, whose connection to her seemed overpowering, but inexplicable. Her decision to leave Hertha had led her here, somewhere on the Tennessee & Georgia line, heading south to Chattanooga—over 100 miles from anywhere she had ever been in her life.

She wondered about this strange and perilous land, its many fears, traps and desperate souls. Did she possess the heart to enter it, and the sense to survive? It was a bit too late to ask that now. The doubt made her angry and she clinched her fist against it. She would not ask such questions again. *Why test the will of God and doubt the purpose of my mission?* she thought. It was useless to do so and she vowed never to do it again. Encouraged, she took out Jon's poetry book and turned to a poem she had made her favorite called "All Joyous in the Realms of Day," by Tennyson, of course.

All joyous in the realms of day,

The radiant angels sing,

In incorruptible array,
Before the eternal king,

Who, hymn'd by archangelic tongues,
In majesty and might,
The subject of ten thousand songs,
Sits veil'd in circling light.

Surely, she thought, this man had seen his own vision of heaven, so well described in seven verses. It was good to know that Jon had read it too and perhaps found encouragement in the lofty words. He must miss his book of poems and for that reason she smiled, knowing that if anything, she had to find him to return his book.

Hours and hours passed with delays, passenger pickup, freight loads and track difficulty. When the train reached the small Calhoun depot, the porter announced a stop for the night. He explained that the track up ahead needed inspection and with such a long leg ahead, it was better to refuel there and travel in the morning light.

Along with the female passengers, Bethanna and Darlene were directed to a church for their shared and anticipated comfort. After a dinner of lima beans and sweet potatoes, they enjoyed a fire in the stove and scripture reading from the pastor. Sleeping on a church pew did not bother Bethanna at all. She felt safe.

When the train entered solid Confederate territory the next morning, the time schedule remained true and the closer to Chattanooga, the better the rail service performed. Around noon, the train rolled into the Cleveland Junction, only 20 miles from their destination. On the loading platform, Bethanna walked and stretched her back. Her mood had lightened when the sun peeked through the clouds for the first time during the long journey. In the sunlight, she noticed the subtle work around her as work parties attended the train.

Men with oil cans and grease tubes lubed the locomotive's wheels, and above, a team loaded wood into the tender. Ahead on a siding, a northbound engine received water from the round elevated tank via a long spout. Calling out instructions, the workmen spoke words Bethanna had never heard: "injector," "lever," "rocker," "sand dome" and "ash pan." Without much notice from passengers, the men worked steadily and spoke their special rail-yard language, which, after a few minutes of eavesdropping, Bethanna ignored for want of definitions.

Darlene approached and dusted off her trim black traveling coat. "I am going inside to look for anyone civilized enough to serve hot tea."

Bethanna approved and watched Darlene walk to the small depot office. Before she entered, five gray-clad cavalrymen greeted her politely as they noticed her mourning dress. The men did the same as they passed Bethanna and she curtsied. The squad loaded their equipment into a cattle car and then in quick succession, they pulled each other through the open door. The well-dressed troopers joked and teased each other in light spirits, and appeared nowhere near defeat, like Hinchel had said. She thought of Jon and in instant realization, knew he had been on this very platform. *Yes, the Army had traveled this way and his brigade had surely seen this railway before me. Jon leads the way, but to where?*

She walked to the end of the ramp and looked down the run of track heading westward into a misty forest. *Where are you now, my love?*

* * *

Sliding the cattle car door wide open, Jon Lyhton squinted as the bright morning sun bathed him and the platoon in warmth.

Crowded onto their train, the men had grown restless for space, air, and comfort during the cold night. Now with the door open and the hay dust clear, the men inhaled a new breath of rejuvenation in the crisp sunny air, blowing steadily into their faces.

The troop-train rolled smoothly northward on the Nashville & Chattanooga line, after a short stop to refuel in Tullahoma. Cheered to be near home again and closer to the enemy, the energized platoon dove into conversation, and not just idle soldier talk, but real strategic opinions about what they will do against the Yankee Army in Nashville.

Jon stood against the door beam and listened to Sgt. Hillford's theory on Northern overconfidence. "Wait a second; you see, they think that all their scientific knowledge makes them superior fighters…bull crap, I say!"

Lawsen briefed several men on the chief duty of the regiment, which he said was to liberate the women of Nashville from under the scourge of Yankee soldiers. "What do you think those ugly mutts will do when they see our soft white roses? They will think nothing of spoiling them, just to rub it in our faces. No gents, never should we allow them to get nary a glimpse!"

The point caused many to agree, aggressively and in much colorful language. Jon figured they could fuel themselves for the rest of the war with such vehemence. With pride, Jon beamed at his friends as they sat on hay bales in a tight circle. His pals, fighting and living as hardened soldiers, sure had changed while in the Army. The cheery ones like Cawley and the Daniel brothers turned into angry and quiet killers during combat, and the loudmouths, like Martello and Lawsen, who laughed in battle, became serious afterward as they lived under the war's specter of death, often introspective for the first time in their foolhardy lives. They cared deeply for things, where before they had taken completely for granted the peace of their parents' idyllic homes.

Now, used to a soldier's grim work, they had charged the enemy's guns, fought battles, and buried their dead.

Jon listened to the humorous chatter as long as he could, until his thoughts turned to the passing land, like on a big rolling, painted screen. The hills and farms of middle Tennessee were trimmed in long fences and golden haystacks, freshly cut during recent harvests. The sight took his mind away and back to the valley, back to Bethanna.

Such time had passed now between them that her face was not perfect in his mind, but her voice was clear, with its soft accent and comforting pitch. He thought of the moment when she defended her mother. Her strong tone had chiseled the image into his mind and as he touched his breast pocket to feel her letter over his heart, he sighed at her sweet memory. She was far away, hidden from harm at her uncle's inn. In the letter, she had tried to find him amid the wrecked Army and her efforts warmed his heart toward her even more. He enjoyed the outlet that their new correspondence offered.

Now, moving to the front, he expected many changes. He made one already when he picked up a new Springfield rifle at Tazewell. Resupplied in Knoxville and Chattanooga, the brigade acquired new Enfield rifles-the latest in British weapon technology. They fired a .577 caliber slug accurately up to 1,000 yards. Most of the men had updated weapons, new accoutrements and to their delight, uniforms.

Upon his arrival in Chattanooga, and waiting for him in the month-old mail, was a package from home. In a humorous ceremony conducted by Lieutenant Weston, Jon cut the twine and in the wrapper lay a new infantry coat with blue trim and corporal stripes. Two pairs of new socks fell from the package, along with a letter, telling how Jon's father, along with other businessmen, had organized a donation for Tennessee's troops, and that the new coat was a small gift for his efforts. Like many products in the South, the manufacture of this coat had been in parts. It began with imported wool from England, smuggled in rolls through the Union blockade and then transferred by river or rail to the small factories and shops throughout the South, where it was cut and sewn into whatever pattern the state required.

Regional codes varied, rendering differences in style and color. The gray wool dye often failed, especially in the west, and a tan color called butternut evolved from the imperfection. Jon's coat was exactly this type, but with foresight, his mother had sewn in a flannel liner, replaced the buttons with the fancy CSA-style die stamped, and wrapped the cuffs in blue, denoting infantry. In a few days, a new addition would grace the arm; the third stripe for his new rank of sergeant.

For leadership and inspirational élan, Weston wrote up Jon for a promotion. The request passed immediately and Jon replaced a sergeant put out of action by illness on the long march to Knoxville, after the Kentucky campaign in October. Lawsen was moved up accordingly to the rank of Corporal. The promotions trickled down from the top after Colonel Rains was made a Brigadier General, Lt. Colonel Gordon the full Colonel, and Major Thedford filled Gordon's place as Lt. Colonel.

Jon's new buttons gleamed in the sunlight flashing through the trees, and with his eyes closed he let the bright ray heat up his face. Under him, the train rolled over wavy tracks and high trestles as it carried General Bragg's troops northwest, to the Army's new staging ground, the town of Murfreesboro.

* * *

J.B. Lyhton,

December 21, 1862

Dear Mother and Father;

Thank you so much for you recent letters and news from home. Did you receive my thanks for the coat? It is a grand garment and the men say that the buttons are first-rate, worthy of an officer, as they say I am sure to be one. I pray the war ends before such an occurrence.

As you may have heard, the brigade of General Rains has been deployed in the defensive line near Murfreesboro. I am very close to home and I feel like walking north on those tracks like I used to do in my youth, so long ago.

We reside in a small town, a very quiet and uneventful place (I cannot write where), which to my amazement maintains a decent but small library. I apologize for my woeful absence of letters in the past month. We have been on the move from the eastern department, through Chattanooga, to this place. Father, the travel is as perilous as the fighting. I have survived both occurrences thanks to Mother's ardent prayers.

The fall weather is unkind to the soldier, but we have many pleasantries here in our station. There are friendly folks who cook for us and plan a great holiday for the brigade. Seeing children again in large numbers cheers me greatly, and I regard with warm feelings my two sisters at Christmas time. Tell them their big Jonny misses them and sends kisses.

The Army is ready, Father, and that is all I dare say, in case this note passes through unfriendly eyes. I am a sergeant now, and responsible for 20 men of my own. The battle ahead is sure to be a very tough contest, but the regiment has seen some shooting in our day and passed the test with great skill. We are righteously led by our fearless General Rains and have the confidence in our cause. Tell Mother I am calm and have no fear of death or of the challenge ahead. Freeing Nashville is the clear mission on everyone's heart and in all our conversations.

I am very sorry I cannot write more. This letter may be the last you hear from me until the post resumes, assuming we clear the way home. I have no doubt we can be victorious. Do not tremble for me, dear parents, God will lead me home, or reunite us in heaven.

Merry Christmas and Happy New Year to all,

Much love, your son,

Jon Braddock Lyhton

Chapter 23 ★

Stones River Battlefield
January 1st, 1863

Jon awoke to the loud clatter of horses stampeding by on the narrow road, 20 yards away. In a daze, he stared at the blurry forms as they disappeared behind thick trees. He discerned their existence by the smell of the animals. For a while, he sat, rubbing his eyes and his head, dumbly thinking of where he could be.

Unable to think and too tired to care, he had fallen asleep against a tree. Then, with a jolt, he awoke to his predicament. *I'm wanted.*

I can't just march blindly into camp; I have to get to Weston. What if they're waiting for me? How long have I been asleep, all day? I can't tell what time it is, there's no sky.

The tremors of distant artillery forced him off the ground. He checked his gear, wondering if any passerby thought he was dead and took something. *All there.*

A long column of troops jogged up the road. By now, units were being shifted, reinforced and properly aligned for a renewed attack, or defense. He would have to walk back to the regiment and disappear into the mass of soldiers. That was his only choice.

Jon followed the road south, but did not walk directly on the road. He reached a large open field and in the distance he saw the first Confederate flag since yesterday afternoon. It hung lifeless, like a small red handkerchief off in the distance, but the sight of it put a spark in his step. *This has to be the 11ᵗʰ.*

The regiment looked in good order, resting in long lines behind stone and rail fences. Ready all night for counterattacks, they had slept in their lines. There were no tents, only those for some of the higher officers behind the formations. Jon took a wide path towards the flank, avoiding the front lines. Perhaps, he thought, if he could get in from the rear and mill about, find Weston and get settled into the lines, this whole thing will… *Ah, it's all foolish dreaming now. They know my name. If the Arkansas men were looking for me, surely my officers know. God, what are they thinking of me now?*

A soldier stopped Jon in his long steps. "Halt, what's your business?"

This was the 11ᵗʰ Tennessee, the man on picket duty being from D Company. Private Hale Daniel, brother of Sheldon Daniel, wounded at Taldorf, and dead at the rocky fence line, just 100 yards away.

"Hale! Am I glad to see you." They shook hands, patted arms.

"J.B., so glad you're back, thought you took it bad up there with the skirmishers!"

"Ever so close it was, my friend."

"I've been told by the lieutenant to be on the watch for you; he's real concerned."

"Yeah, so am I," Jon said, looking towards the officers' tents.

"Just go ahead and find your way through. If he's not in his tent, then he's at Captain Binns' tent. Hey, J.B., I'm glad you're here, some boys may never come back, y'a know?"

Jon nodded. He shook Hale's hand and walked on, relieved that Weston had not told the men anything about him. He had no heart to share the news of Hale's dead brother, not now. When the fight was done, he will know where to find him, and tell him then.

Jon left the picket behind and marched through high brown grass, rocks, and then down a low slope toward a group of tents set under a cedar break. Something caught his attention near a line of wagons. He saw Weston standing behind the last one, talking with Dr. Larkin. The doctor seemed over-animated and hard pressed to explain something, his voice reaching Jon's ears. Jon pulled his hat down and jogged towards the scene. Hanging back until the loading was done, he approached Lieutenant Weston and the doctor when the others left the area.

Jon pulled up near the wagon horses to overhear Dr. Larkin. He could see the man's face, un-slept and full of sad overwork. Larkin always sported a clean face but here, his three-day beard, spotted with gray, lent unflattering age. Jon listened to the doctor's words.

"He is not going to make it, I am sorry. But a wound like that cannot be closed; there is no skin left to suture." Larkin paced, rubbing his sore arms, bloodied sleeves rolled up. "I know triage, lieutenant, and this man's a goner. Sorry, but after today I think I have seen plenty like him. All day sir, I have been cutting and throwing used parts of men into a pile. The North Carolina surgeon is wounded and I am taking on his work. I am using infantrymen as nurses to hold down legs. I am at the end sir, the end of my wits. No, I cannot spare any one to accompany your dying man into town! You go! There is little time I can waste." Larkin pointed to the medical tent beyond the grove, overrun, and spilling bodies out into the cold rain. "I pity them all, Lieutenant, but there is no time to comfort them. That's in God's hands." The doctor marched off, his bloodied apron dragging the ground.

Jon jumped around the covered wagon. "Jeff!"

Weston turned and could not hide his shock. "Holy Christ, Jon!" His face was finger-painted with blood, and smeared in such away it reminded Jon of Indian war paint. Jon reacted. "Are you hurt, Jeff?"

"No, it's not my blood." Weston looked around. "Come here." He pulled Jon behind the ambulance. "Where were you?"

"Lost out in that hell of a forest. I think our own boys shot at me more than the Yankees. Where did the regiment go?"

"We held on to the edge of the woods for a while, then back-tracked at nightfall, just a few hundred yards. I thought you were missing for good. Very glad to see you."

"Same here, my friend. How is the regiment? What's the count?'

Weston rubbed his face, smearing the blood prints. "Well, we lost a few, up to 60 wounded that we know of. Fifteen missing and we counted eight dead outright."

Jon shook his head. "Lots of wounded to look after. Count one more dead."

"Who?"

"Sheldon. Took it up there where the artillery beat us and never let up."

"Does Hale know?" Weston asked.

"Couldn't tell him." Jon pulled the I.D. badge from his pocket. "Here is the proof. You'll need it. The body is unfamiliar."

Weston nodded. He brought out his handkerchief and licked it, wiping the remaining blood from his face. "Well Jon, do you know that we lost General Rains?"

Jon stiffened. "God, no. I heard rumors from the field."

"Yes, killed by a shot to the heart—the only way a man such as he could be ended. Colonel Gordon is wounded but safe, and sure to recover. Lieutenant Colonel Vance commands the brigade now. He has been very steady, where some have not been. We lost our steam, Jon, when Rains went down. The fight raged on, the men did their best to shun emotion and carry on with their duty. I saw some weep like children when they heard the news, while others seethed with white-hot anger, fighting with inhuman energy. I think I refused to believe he was really dead." Weston paused. He slapped Jon's arm. "My God, I'm glad you're here, but you may not be so glad, you are charged..."

"Yes, I've heard the latest."

"Is it true, this charge of murder? A warrant has been passed...."

"I killed someone last night, but there's no way to know who. I even back-tracked to find a body, nothing."

"Well, for some reason this man's brother and captain are accusing you. Look, we need time. I've been thinking this through, Jon. You have to go into town; it's the safest place. We are in a thick fight here. Once the battle is continued, they can't look for you. Just sit this out and stay in town. After this fight, then perhaps things may change, you may have a chance for self-defense. Here, get on the cart and help poor Lawsen."

Weston stepped up on the back of the ambulance and looked inside. "You hang on there. We'll send Jon with you, please hang on," he begged. Jon looked into the wagon and his soul split in two. Dr. Larkin had been talking about Lawsen, *a goner.*

Lawsen's eyes failed to find Jon, his lips pleaded in silent prayer. A torn blood-soaked coat revealed an open rip in his chest, from the right collarbone to below the breastbone. A pale-gray hand reached out. "J.B.?"

"A shell fragment," said Weston, his face wincing. "He was out there all night."

Jon hesitated. All night? So was I. Out there, killing our own.

Stopping his whirlwind mind, Jon zeroed in on his comrade. Lawsen motioned with his hand for Jon to come near. He climbed into the dank, foul smelling wagon and leaned into Lawsen's face. His voice, a cold murmur, spoke to him, "J.B., don't let me die... alone."

Jon shuddered as his face wrinkled with sadness. He saw certain death in Lawsen's pale eyes and with sympathy, he gently positioned his friend's head and shoulders onto his lap, providing the broken man with some sort of body-warm comfort. Jon looked at Weston. The lieutenant gripped Jon's arm and begged. "You will go, then?"

Wagons of every sort jammed the Wilkinson Pike—ox carts, hay wagons, captured Union ambulances—anything to carry bodies, each containing its own sad tragedy of war. Surrounding this long train was the spectral presence of thousands of stragglers and walking wounded, those men who had run out of ammo, purpose, or patience, joined those who were running out of blood and life, mostly time.

In the bouncing wagon, Jon noticed that the other two men were from the 11th. Recognizing features proved difficult with their faces blackened by gunpowder. After some study, he knew one was Private Dabney, a man who had worked for his father years ago preparing stockyards for the incoming cattle. His arm was severely fractured and he moaned with each shock from the jumping wheels. Dabney scraped at his coat pocket, but was unable to get his good hand into it. Jon reached over and pulled out a small tarnished flask. The sight of it made them both smile faintly.

Jon opened the flask and handed it to Dabney, who sipped the last of its contents. He exhaled, smiled and nodded. "Thanks, Sergeant Lyhton."

Jon rested his hand under Lawsen's head and face. The skin felt cold and wet. His stiff hair was encrusted with a day's worth of muddy soil, gritty and clotted.

Lawsen's mouth moved again and Jon leaned down to listen. "Tell me about the regiment, J.B., it's all going from me," he whispered.

Jon's throat caught, unable to talk. He took a deep breath, coughed, and found the voice to describe the many characters in the platoon, all the fights and laughs throughout the year and the bravery at Tazewell. "We were truly heroes that day amid that damn cannon fire."

Jon's face grew slick with tears, as he sounded off the trials and funny tales of their camp life together, fist fights, jokes, and the officers' nicknames. His tone turned poetic and he slipped into his old self, the well-read boy with a bright tale to tell.

The Taldorf valley came alive again, its wind blowing into the trees, curling around the church and settling onto their friendly camp. The fish raced down the stream and all was perfect again in the mind of his dying friend. A smile crossed Lawsen's gray face when Jon described how he read to Bethanna on the hilltop, how she fell asleep, how she touched his heart with her grace and beauty.

As Jon relived vivid memories of passionate days, he didn't notice that the other two men had been distracted from their pain as well. Dabney looked at his friend and they chuckled while Jon animated Cawley's naive ways, and bad German.

Jon went on talking and deep inside, realized that here in this bloody ambulance was his finest moment, a most stunning contrast to his recent crimes. He felt Lawsen's breathing shorten and stutter. With shots of breath, Lawsen whispered, "I will gladly enter, Lord." Then, in a second, he was dead.

Jon felt the body loosen in his grasp, but he would not let the sight of death choke off his words. He held the dead man's face with a tender hand and continued his stories with a smooth flow. Inside his mind, accepting the assured fate of a murderer, he resigned himself to death. If the innocent Lawsen suffered, surely he, as a guilty man would not escape earthly wrath. The evidence around him proved that the war was going to butcher them all, today or another day, and that reality in itself, was as fair as it got.

As long as he could die like this, he could accept his fate, because he knew from Lawsen that there was a heaven. The fear of death was gone, but to die alone would not do. He delivered mercy to Lawsen and in a thought, which formed and sounded almost as a prayer, he asked for the same favor.

Coming into Murfreesboro, the wagon train slowed to a crawl and Jon wondered how the bleeding men lived through the long minutes of delay. No organized method of dispersal existed, only a quiet rush of medical personnel trying to handle the overflow. Jon dismounted the ambulance and two young hospital stewards reached for Lawsen. Jon interrupted them, "Please gentlemen, look to the living," he said, as he pointed to Dabney.

As the men helped Dabney onto a bloodied litter, he said, amid his moans, "Much obliged to you, Lyhton."

Jon patted the man's hand. "Sure thing, Richard."

The two litter bearers carted him into the warehouse across the street. Jon looked around and saw that every structure on the block had been designated as a hospital of sorts, or at least a place to keep wounded men out of the weather.

"This man got a name?" asked one of the stewards.

Jon gazed at him and blinked. He was pointing at Lawsen's body.

"He's got no I.D. badge, no papers, nothing." the steward said, searching the corpse.

Jon found a pencil in his haversack. He searched the area and tore a scrap of paper from a recruitment advertisement hanging in pieces from a fence. Taking care to be legible, he wrote:

Paul G. Lawsen, Nashville, Tenn.
Hero of Cumberland Gap, Tazewell, and Murfreesboro.

The steward read the words and nodded. Making a hole in the paper's corner, he attached it to a button on Lawsen's shirt. "That will do," he said, as he signaled three men on the sidewalk. Two slaves and a civilian carried Lawsen's body to a grassy lot near the warehouse and laid it next to row of corpses, which Jon could see, stretched out for many yards.

Jon stood in the road as two more bodies were stacked like rail ties next to Lawsen.

His comrade no longer needed comfort, and after seeing the dead pile up, Jon turned away to view the hectic street, cluttered with a maze of wagons, bodies and orderlies who failed to keep order. A queer masque took place around him, like a circular dance the wounded entered and the dead were removed, the women moaned and the doctors yelled. It sounded like the final doom of the world. *If the battlefield didn't humble you, this place will.*

In a building dilemma, there would be only so many surgeons and medics to attend the thousands pilling up in and around the town. Another catastrophe was in the works. *Had not the Army prepared for such things? We cannot continue the battle with such losses. What did they think, that no one would be hurt, attacking head-on into lines of cannon and muskets?* The resulting calamity aggravated him.

Jon walked over to the ambulance seconds before it pulled away and retrieved his rifle. He didn't remember taking it with him. Lieutenant Weston must have put it there. Quickly inspecting the wagon, Jon figured that Weston had kept Lawsen's personal things, after Dr. Larkin gave up. Feeling a bit more complete, he slung the rifle over his shoulder and walked down a clear street leading to the center of town.

In morose irony, a visual cruelty nagged at Jon's moral senses. Boughs of holly, pine and chestnut wreaths adorned the doors of shops and nearby apartments. Candles trimmed the window dressings and a Christmas tree stood tall in the center of town a few blocks distant, where the square had filled with the drifting sounds of midnight carols only a week prior.

As even Jon could attest, Christmas was bright for the Army and the inhabitants of Murfreesboro. Being free from harassment, there was plenty of food for the soldiers during their fall preparations. General Bragg had proven himself a worthy supply strategist, garnering the proper roads and routes to speedily move materiel from several quarters of his military department. Generals Forrest and Wheeler's cavalry units raided the Union supply lines so thoroughly that the Confederates were afforded a more pleasant yuletide than their enemy.

At that time, during the Army's respite, the 11th Tennessee was transferred to the division of John P. McCown and assigned to the right wing, twelve miles east of Murfreesboro near the town of Readyville. The soldiers enjoyed a splendid holiday dinner—a large slice of turkey, bread, hot cider, cabbage, and carrots. Although rationed to the finest degree of measurement, it was still more than anyone had expected. With the decor, songs and general Christmas spirit abounding, the troops felt like home was very close indeed.

Even in such doleful surroundings, a slight relief settled over him that he was some distance from the battlefield. Not that he feared the fight, but for the time, there was substantial distance between Riles and himself. The fact that Lieutenant Weston knew of the incident brought a sting of shame to his heart, but in Weston's eyes, he found no condemnation.

There wasn't much reason to worry over Riles now. Jon grasped the bloodstained blue coat, tied to his bedroll. The winter chill again pierced his bones. There was little action to warm him now and in a glance, he noticed soldiers close by who had adorned the same garment, captured from the overrun Union camps. Their method of procurement was not like his. He put on the overcoat, cursed in a low growl and moved on.

Walking into the town square, he stopped at the 15-foot Frazier fir, decorated with all the trimmings that Southerners could offer, from popcorn garland to painted eggshells and the patriotic ribbons of the Confederate states. One thought prevailed; home. How wonderful the house must smell at this hour on New Year's Day, complete with turkey, perhaps lamb, sweet potatoes and pumpkin bread, beans of every sort, and the pine boughs that his mother loved to set on the window sills—all blending into a once-a-year, fragrant delight.

The large tree drooped. Wet and rained on for three days, it had lost most of its trimmings and classic shape. The sagging evergreen was not unlike the Confederate hopes at the present time.

Jon's thoughts turned to the regiment and his heart ached for Lawsen. He worried about the men, his suffering friends. He then wondered if others from the platoon were here. With some renewed purpose, he decided to look for any of the regiment's wounded. *Yes, Lieutenant Weston will appreciate that. Any information about the men may at least give the lieutenant some sort of accounting. Who else was here to do it?*

After a time questioning the orderlies and walking wounded, Jon found a medic who knew of a wounded man from the Eufaula Light Artillery, the same unit that was attached to Rain's brigade. This clue led him back to the street where he entered town, and then into the warehouse. In the badly lit crowded space, he followed the medic through a maze of wounded bodies strewn about on the floor.

The only natural light filtered through opaque windows high above the beams overhead. Directed by a steward, they found their way with lantern light, back into a corner of the building and stopped behind a young man assisting the wounded corporal of artillery with his rations.

Jon squatted down next to the young helper, whose uniform was trimmed in the red piping of the artillery.

"Please pardon the interruption, but perhaps you could help me."

The young man turned around and revealed a friendly, relaxed, almost womanly smile. "How can I be of service?" he said.

Jon appreciated his politeness. "I am sent by my lieutenant to ascertain the loss of our company and as you know, this will be a search in the haystack for a few needles. But if this gentleman here, being from my very brigade, could possibly answer a few brief questions, I would be most obliged,"

The young assistant reached and shook Jon's hand with a firm, true grip. He held it. "This is the higher duty of the soldier and I applaud you for it, sir. I am Private William Charles, Semple's Alabama battery."

"Good to know you, I'm Sergeant Lyhton, 11th Tennessee."

William directed Jon over to the side of the wounded man. "This is my friend and relation from Eufaula, Alabama, Mr. Max Lucas," he said.

Max smiled, reaching for Jon's hand. "Pleasure to make your acquaintance. Please pardon my stature." He said, tapping the ground with his other mummy-wrapped hand.

"Indeed, you have my humblest sympathies for recovery. I would like to ask if you have seen any brigade men, Rains' men, especially from the 11th, pass through here, or anywhere, for that matter?"

Max thought for a moment, resting his eyes momentarily on William, then back to Jon. His face, boyish and freckled, winced at the pain in his hands, then brightened. "Yes, I believe when I was dragged in, literally, mind you, there being no litters here for some time during the night previous, a man or two from the 11th had accompanied me on the very same rickety wagon, which in its own part, tried to kill us as soundly as the Yankees."

Jon winced. "I can sympathize. Where, do you think they could be now?"

"In this very space. But of course, if they required surgeries, I do not know. Then they could be scattered beyond this room or I fear, on a heap somewhere. Please forgive my indelicate speech," Max said.

"There must be thousands coming into town every hour. Well, I have a job then. I thank you, Corporal Lucas, for your time. May I give you some ration of jerky?"

Max gladly accepted the barter, chewing, as the other two stood.

William, presenting the same pleasant smile as before, said, "He's a brave boy, sure to get well and rally to the guns again. For as Wordsworth described the soldier, -This is the Happy Warrior, this is he -That every man at arms should wish to be."

Jon reeled in pleasant surprise and smiled. "You have the poet's blood?"

"Yes, and bad, I must admit."

"No, no, never bad my friend, for that is what makes us human and amid this grave state we find ourselves in today. It makes us sane."

"Well put, Mr. Lyhton." William smiled down at Max. "We have another ally."

Max stopped his chewing, grinned. "*Entendu!* We salute you, sir."

William gestured to Max. "My friend here seems to be in a state of grace and faring better than I had hoped. I could leave him for a while to help you, Mr. Lyhton, to find your friends, for I know the unsettling anguish that afflicts the soul when you know not of your companions. I believe half of the Army is here just for that exact purpose, to find a suffering friend."

Jon looked around and nodded in agreement. "That would do me fine, then. Two is better than one."

"Then I am your man!" William stated. "Please call me 'Will', as my friends do."

"'Will' it is. Then to you, I am Jon."

Searching with their single lantern, the new friends gazed into forlorn faces and horrid wounds while they crossed the warehouse floor. Quietly, they asked those who could speak, for some did not have parts of their mouths, if they were from the 11th. Most of the men yelled their reply, being deafened from hours of rifles and blasting shells.

A man pulled Jon's arm. "Can I help you locate someone?"

Jon turned to see a young man in a dark frock coat, clean and pressed, with the chaplain's collar. "You see, I've been here for some time and could know of them," he said.

The pastor was a tall fellow, slim, with dark eyebrows and goatee. His eyes were a strong gray and his beard was as black as his hair, which was uniquely marked by a short white streak above the forehead. He held a bucket and rag for cooling hot fever. On closer inspection, Jon saw that he wore the Union blue uniform.

Jon drew back and then recovered. "Who are you?"

"Chaplain Patrick Lovejoy, 77th Pennsylvania." Besides being rather clean and tall, Lovejoy was unbothered. He did not slouch or carry himself about in confused angst. His eyes had a confident weight in them but his brow furrowed, perhaps from buried humiliation, for he was captured. Married, but not yet a father at 26, he was a young pastor, fervent in his beliefs. However, he was quite humbled by Army life and unimpressed with his ineffectual calling of ministry to soldiers, or "the mobs" as he called them in his letters home, which by this time had grown very rare. "So whom do you seek?"

"Men from the 11th Tennessee," Jon said. After some time, they found a man from the 29th North Carolina, a regiment in line with his during the fight.

The young soldier spoke to Jon, "We were pulled off the field together, that one there, over there." He pointed to a dark corner area.

Excited, Jon called to Will. "There, in the corner."

The three walked over to the dark space. Jon bent in and the lantern lit up the man's face. "Martello!" he said, kneeling in.

Martello responded to the sound of Jon's voice, moving his head in the direction of it. "J.B., you there? Don't go, Jonny!" he moaned. Jon inspected his friend and saw a bandage on his right elbow and another near the same shoulder. Above his right ear blood soaked the hair. He had no blanket and his bare feet were exposed and ice cold.

"I'm right here, now you don't fret." Jon grasped Martello's left hand. The grip was loose and Jon felt little strength in it. He looked at Will, who nodded and walked off with the young chaplain, leaving the two alone. "Leo, what happened? I lost everyone after the cannons, remember?"

"That's what finally got me." Martello said weakly. "Shell hit us in the woods. Rocks flying into us, got me bad. Water, got some?"

Jon slapped his canteen, there was none left. "I'll get you some. You need something on your feet too." Jon thought for a few seconds. He took off the Union overcoat, and laid it over Martello. "This will do much better, but I'm going to get you something for your feet; you'll catch pneumonia if uncovered very long."

"Sure, Jonny." He smiled. "Told ya you'd need one of these coats, didn't I?"

"Sure did. You were right Leo. Glad I listened to you. Now your set up quite well."

Jon found his way out of the building and passed Will and the chaplain at the door. "Jon, this Reverend Lovejoy is a most intriguing man, I must tell," Will said.

Jon glanced at the Yank. "Can you get Martello some water?" Lovejoy nodded. "I can."

Jon pulled Will away. "How did that Yank get here?"

"He was caught in the morning attack, never had a chance."

"Well, I guess any Yank prisoner is a good one. Let us look now for my friend's comfort."

They both set about searching the hospital tents for any spare socks or shoes. An orderly in a bloody apron accosted them rudely. "Scavenging already?"

Jon frowned. "Absolutely not, sir, beg pardon. But we're looking for any spare socks or shoes for a friend."

"Ask him!" he said, pointing to another assistant.

A nurse, who was cleaning gore from a set of surgeon's tools, pointed to a wagon containing cut off legs and arms, ready for burial or burning. "Plenty over there," he said.

Jon's stomach wrenched. He looked at Will and the young man flinched at the sight of so many ragged, shot up limbs. "You don't have to do this, Will, it is my chore."

"It is every one's chore, Jon Lyhton," Will said, with obvious pride.

The two walked slowly over to the wagon. Three bucket-loads of limbs rotted in the open air. Jon looked around and found a stick. Using it to lift with, he tried to identify any useful foot ware. Not much remained, as the medics removed them for amputation. Jon turned away as he pressed the stick into the soft, rotten flesh and separated the fresh cutaways.

Finding, near the bottom of the stack, some colder stiffened legs, Jon saw a foot with a useable sock. He had to hold it with one hand and pull the sock off with the other. Crusty and stiff, it peeled away with much effort.

"This is absolutely putrescent," said Will, holding his nose. "There's got to be something better."

"Well, there's nothing this close, may as well use it. Let's find another. Look, a split shoe lying there. That will do!" He pointed to the bottom of the wagon.

Will noticed its size. "That one may be too big."

When they returned to Martello, he had already begun to shiver. William put the lantern down between his shaking bare feet to warm them. Jon prepared the socks and shoes. "Forgive me friend if these aren't first rate, but it's what we could find, just don't ask me where I got them."

Martello forced a smile, "Ain't that what we say 'bout most of our forage, Jonny?"

"That's right, Marti."

"Hey, Jonny."

"What."

"I saw Lawsen take it." Emotion caught his voice. "Bad, too. He's not alive, is he?" Martello, waiting for Jon's response, raised his head.

Jon stopped his work. He couldn't look him in the face. "I recon not."

Martello dropped his head back into the hay. He began to sniffle.

Jon felt the tremor of loss once again move in his soul. He completed the dressing in silence and allowed Will to comfort the weeping Martello, which he did quite effectively with a steady stream of psalms straight from memory.

Save me oh God, by your name; vindicate me by your might,
Hear my prayer oh God; listen to the words of my mouth,

Strangers are attacking me; ruthless men seek my life,
Men without regard for God.
Surely God is my help, The Lord is the one who sustains me.

Jon sat motionless and stared into the flickering lantern.

For he has delivered me from all my troubles.
And my eyes have looked in triumph on my foes.

Satisfied, William said, "Rest now, young warrior, be content in thy duty, and know that the Lord holds you now."

Martello grasped his hand. "Bless your kindness," he said. "I know you're a man of deep faith and I have not been. At this time, I must pray for the Lord to forgive me, for if I should die… without it."

Will responded to the fear in Martello's eyes. "Now there, don't fear for a second. Rest in the Lord, for he is closer than you think."

At this, Jon interrupted. "Shouldn't we get the reverend?"

Will searched the dark building and concern fell over his usually light demeanor. He saw the Yankee chaplain consoling a man who had suffered amputation to both lower legs. "It may be the only thing we can do at this time."

Patrick Lovejoy knelt on the hay-strewn floor amid the wounded of his enemies and prayed for the forgiveness of a brave child of God who, at this time of uncertain mortality knew where the path of righteousness was to be found. And in the finding, there was reward. Lovejoy opened the small, thick prayer book of the Episcopal Church.

Blessed is he whose transgressions are forgiven,
whose sins are covered.
Blessed is the man whose sin the Lord

does not count against him,
And in whose spirit is no deceit.

Jon swallowed hard. He clinched the sleeve of his blue coat. The words pricked him, but how nice they sounded, even in a Northern accent. Will, too, smiled at the rarity.

They stayed with Martello for some time, gave him more water and salt pork. He did not fade like they expected, but stayed alert to eat, until after some time he fell asleep, snoring.

Next to them, a man died in the last vision of life, seeing his loved ones in a private hazy dream and biding them a stuttered goodbye.

Jon sat quietly listening to the prayers for the dead, patiently read by the chaplain from his prayer book. A numbing pall fell into Jon's heart as the ethereal phrases confirmed the finality of death and the assurance of the everlasting. Both of his good friends and partners had been struck that day, Lawsen dead, now Martello… Sheldon Daniel, too. He wanted to cry, but couldn't.

When Jon and Will exited the warehouse, the day had receded into full dusk. The activity on the streets remained heavy but somber, and most civilians had moved indoors. A group of women carrying baskets met with a strong rebuke from an officer of guards. "More ambulance wagons are coming, you are in the way!" he shouted. As the carts rolled through the fog, the sight drew an audible sigh from Will. Jon figured that even the buoyant William T. Charles was now faltering at the continuous sights of wounds and death.

"I do not mean to disparage, but it is hard to conjure such faith as you do during times as these?" Jon motioned to the filling litters.

"It is at these times when I ask, how can one not believe?" asked Will.

"Because of this," Jon said, again pointing to the sprawling wounded. "Such tragedy as this."

"It is precisely why we need the Almighty, because of our forlorn state of spiritual loss. It is pitiful, I agree, that men must fight with such fantastic butchery, but the state exists and only sin could have created it." In a moment, Will regained his light expression. "There is hope for us Jon, that is all." He shrugged his shoulders and smiled.

Jon wished for that to be true for his friends. As for him, whatever forms his relief or redemption came in, he needed to see it soon.

The two walked quietly through the town. Jon had been here years before, when his father had taken him on train rides south. He recognized nothing from his memory, it being dark. And with the debris of the broken Army everywhere, it was not a town, only the reaper's collection area full of blood and crying women.

Once again, like the Perryville retreat, the Army was a shambles. How can the commander take great care to prepare his troops with supply and relentless drill, and then not show the same attention during the battle? It was a brazen folly that any decent man would regard as unnecessary and immoral.

Will suggested they would have to find a place to sleep, perhaps a barn or such shelter to keep them out of the renewing rain and dropping temperatures. "I can drudge up something capital, let me talk to these gents." Will pointed to three nearby sergeants belonging to the medical branch. He approached them and collected a few options on where they could stay. Jon sat down on a curbside and watched.

The young William Charles worked them good. Jon gladly let him assert his verbal talents, for his own energy had waned. Across the street, he noticed the group of women that had been run off by the rude officer. Two were older, one younger. A pair of them stepped up on the sidewalk to peer into a window. A bright lantern on the doorpost illuminated them and Jon's vision blurred as he stared into the glow. He distinguished the young lady's form and in a quick blink, thought she resembled Bethanna. He squinted to be sure. Sure of what, he didn't know. He knew that his eyes were sleepy and weak.

The girl had her hair up, wrapped in a scarf, with a few blond tresses hanging lazily. Her long, dark coat hid her size but when she moved, it seemed familiar. For a daring second he thought of approaching her, if only for a brief look, even at a stranger, to revive the fading memory of dear Bethanna. Jon shook his head. "Wouldn't that be lovely?" he said, falling into a chuckle. "What would I do if she were here?"

The fact that she was far away in Taldorf actually reassured him. For dealing with this chaos and mad murder should not be her lot, but his. He did not want to see it played out where they meet in such a place, where she would see what soldiers really do. Perhaps, if she begged him, he would decide to resign this foolish duty of battle. Or worse, in a rush of paranoia he thought, she would see the coat, ask of its origin, then the blood. He must lie to her too, and that will be worse than anything.

He looked at the girl through the frosty light and stood up. He stepped into the street. *If only to feel her eyes upon me, that could be nice.*

"Hey Jon, the deed is done," William called. Jon stopped and looked at her a last time and then he followed his new friend. They would be staying the night with the three sergeants, sleeping in a blacksmith's shed, owned by a father of one of them.

Inside the shed, a hot stove heated water and biscuits. The luxuries restored some humanity to the two young men, and eased the stress of the last few hours. Bedded down on horse blankets, Will and Jon counted their blessings as they divided the last flaky roll. They discussed the battle thus far, the successful attack and the stiff Yankee resistance at the center of the line.

"That night was God-awful as any I'd ever seen," claimed Will.

Jon nodded in agreement as he nibbled his last morsel.

Will continued, "As you probably know, there could be no fires that night and it was deadly cold. My pal Bob and I had sunk ourselves into the artillery's elevation ditch. Using cornstalks as bedding, we found this a satisfactory place until a giant fat man, whose identity we never learned, came lying on top of us. This rude behavior offset us gentleman in the artillery and in an instant, Bob threatened the man with his Bowie, but the bull did not move. We soon realized that he kept us quite warm with his mass, so we endured it and had a suitable, if not smelly, sleep."

Jon smiled at the story. Will asked him about his night. Jon hesitated. "About the same, cold and miserable." For a moment, Jon felt he could confess the killing of Bertram to Will, a Christian man, and someone detached from the situation. But in proper scope, perhaps the whole tangled mess was just too much to dump on a one-time acquaintance. He spoke nothing of it. Changing the subject, he asked, "You've seen this land around here and where I am from. What about you?"

Will smiled. "I hail from the river lands of middle Alabama. A small hamlet east of Montgomery called Mount Meigs."

Will's home sounded lovely indeed. He described a tight-knit community of planters and farmers, and how the cotton fields sprawled over a gentle land spotted with large magnolias and pecan trees. He listed the families that dwelled there: Lucas, Raoul, Taylor, and Burch. Even the houses had charm with names like Ingleside, Longwood, Rose Hill, and his Uncle's home place, Chantilly, named after Napoleon's summerhouse.

"Do you have a beau?" asked Jon. "I presume you do from your outgoing, altruistic nature."

"Now that you ask, of course I do." Will seemed to surprise himself. "I look on her fondly and when I think of home and she is foremost in my mind. Her name is Florence Burch, a lovely, dark-haired girl. I've known her for years and only recently, after some gentle nudging from her mother, we have been close." Will leaned back, rested his hands behind his head. "Oh how the feelings grow when one is separated from such amorous potential. I think we will marry."

Jon smiled, understanding the result of separation.

The sound of horses in the street kept them awake for a short time until, at last, the two rolled over to sleep—Will, with visions of Chantilly and the fair Florence Burch fading into his dreams, and Jon, with the unshakeable visions of his dead friends, and Riles' grating voice of judgment echoing into the fog of the restless night.

* * *

Almost as an afterthought to a stagnant day, or to give his men something constructive to do, Union General Crittenden saw a chance to secure the Army's left flank and to threaten Bragg's open right flank. He ordered Colonel Price and his five-regiment brigade to cross Stones River at McFadden's Ford and to occupy the hill adjacent.

Colonel Price executed the maneuver in the early hours of January 2nd, in total darkness. Sentries from out-posted Confederate cavalry gave up the position in a brief skirmish and with this single deployment, the battle of Stones River would be allowed to continue another day to its fateful, bloody end.

* * *

CHAPTER 24★

JANUARY 2ND, 1863

The long silence of New Year's Day drew both opposing commanders into a lull and fostered the belief that neither one wanted to continue the momentous battle. All morning, reports flowed through the headquarters of both sides as their cavalry scouts shared the same conclusion—the enemy is disorganized and moving away from the front. Actually, both armies had stayed in position, while sending their wounded in long wagon trains to the rear.

Maneuvers on the dark morning of January 2nd had been short but profound. The reports of Union infantry on the south side of the river astonished General Bragg. They sat there on a hill, taken without much effort, and observed the Confederate actions at their leisure. Bragg directed General Breckinridge to survey the danger. With the darkness hampering this effort, his scouts could not determine the strength of the Union infantry.

Once dawn lighted the scene, a larger force was assembled to reconnoiter the Union lines on the rise. General Breckinridge overlooked the advance himself as the artillery kept up steady fire over the river to cover the exposed sections of infantry. The gray-and-butternut troops swept forward over an old cornfield and into open ground converging on the forward Federal lines, spread out around an abandoned farm.

The Yanks retreated and then countered. They occupied the farm buildings long enough to set them ablaze, and rendered them useless to enemy sharpshooters. The duel continued with the skirmish lines moving and probing for advantage in the foggy drizzle.

General John C. Breckinridge sat astride his horse. Tall, erect in the saddle and uniformed to perfection, he cut the model figure of a commander in the field. Known to be fierce in combat but sensitive to emotion, his wide expressive eyes emoted strength and a glint of genius. Crossing his face, a long mustache gave him a distinguished, political look. This was not happenstance. Having served in earlier state and national legislature seats, his political career peaked in 1856 when he was elected vice president of the United States under Buchanan. Now a Major General, his loyalty to his new country and native Kentucky was undying, as was that of his subordinate, Brigadier General Roger Hanson, who had taken command of the Kentucky brigade upon Breckinridge's promotion to division commander.

Hanson, riding next to Breckinridge, scoured the fields for clues to the enemy's weakness. To his left, the river snaked through clear terrain. To his right lay broken, hilly ground, peppered with thick stands of trees. To his center-front, a rolling field, checkered with fences and small groves, sprawled forward to the Federal position. The field was clear below the partially wooded hill where the Yankees rested.

"This open stretch of ground," Hanson said, pointing beyond the burning farmhouses, "is their one sure advantage." He looked at Breckinridge, who nodded and lifted his glasses to view the hill, almost a 1,000 yards distant.

Hanson trusted Breckinridge implicitly, knowing that he was a Kentuckian above all and whatever the circumstances, he would lead with character. The famed Kentucky brigade was known more for its disposition than perhaps the hard fighting spirit it displayed at Shiloh. The men were out of sorts at times over the fact that Union forces occupied their home state. For this, the men were called the "Orphan Brigade."

An aide interrupted General Breckinridge's thoughts. "Pardon, sir. At General Bragg's request, you are to meet him at his headquarters immediately, sir." General Breckinridge cased his binoculars, pulled his gauntlets tight and bid his subordinate farewell. "Well, Roger, can you imagine what the old man wants now?"

Hanson and his aides saluted as they watched Breckinridge ride away, followed by his staff. He knew there would be trouble with Bragg today even though he had no idea what would be discussed between them. There didn't have to be any special circumstances for this. Bragg held a grudge against the Kentuckians, Hanson was sure of it.

The story of Bragg and the Kentuckians was no secret, as the sad facts had circulated amongst the Army. A private in the 6th Kentucky regiment named Asa Lewis had been executed under Bragg's direct order. The tragedy started when Lewis' 12-month enlistment expired. An edict was passed by the state requiring three-year extended service, but since the private did not re-enlist, he thought his service was over. He desired to return home and help his newly widowed mother.

Returned by a bounty hunter and placed in high arrest, the catch for Asa was that he had been caught for desertion once before and let go with a harsh warning. Bragg had not the temperament for this behavior and keeping with his strict discipline, handed down a sentence of death.

Hanson was ordered to carry out the execution under Breckinridge's direct supervision. Both commanders were moved close to illness as they watched the young man die at the muzzles of a firing squad. Hanson would never recover from the sight, which took place on the 26th of December, only seven days prior to the fight at Stones River.

In all circumstances, fighting was nothing new to Roger Hanson. He had been a soldier in the war with Mexico, an adventurer and a politician, and now a general in the service of his new country, and as he observed the Yankee position atop the hill, he thought of how foolish it had been for Bragg to ignore such strategic ground.

* * *

Jon and Will awoke late, and with no real urgency, cleaned up best they could with what little water was available. Will attempted a dry shave with his fine bone-handled razor and to Jon's surprise, pulled off the feat remarkably well.

"I'll pass," said Jon, rubbing his two-month-old beard.

Returning to the warehouse, Jon and Will looked in on their respective pals and were pleased to find Martello and Will's cousin, Max Lucas, eating rations donated by the townsfolk.

Thankfully, more was done to comfort the wounded, as pails of hot embers warmed the large room and two aides served water rations. The midday passed while Jon and Will wrote letters for their friends, and for other men who needed assistance. Outside, the rain soaked the streets, the town, and every exposed soldier waiting for battle.

At 2:30 in the afternoon, low moans of artillery emanated from north of the town. Will knew the resonance instantly as that of Napoleon cannons. "There is something afoot."

Jon reacted also, "Sounds like more than probing fire. It's concentrated, large."

"I fear my battery is involved and I am woefully absent!" claimed Will. He said a rushed, but polite, farewell to his wounded cousin and rushed out of the warehouse.

Martello smiled with Max, "Sure is an eager boy." he said.

Jon stood, and looked to follow Will.

"Go ahead," said Martello. "Jonny, go with your friend, and here, take this coat. You will need this out in the rainy cold."

"But that's for you."

"I am well to do now. It's warmer in here, and the attendants are regular, please take it."

Jon followed Will into the streets and chuckled at the private's sense of urgency. "I don't think General Bragg has much in store for us today. But if you're concerned, we can go see what's cooking." Jon draped the coat over his shoulders and slung his rifle. "Let's go see."

By the time they reached the edge of town, the cannons had ceased. Familiar pungent smoke drifted on the wind. "It's still a far ways off, but does it ever carry in this cold, wet air," Will noted.

Jon rubbed his neck. "You figure we're about to get into it again?"

"Sure sounds like it," said Will, squinting to see the origins of the smoke. "I think we should move in that general direction. Perhaps we will both be needed."

Jon agreed and made a quick assessment of his gear. He had ten rounds left and plenty of caps. From the weight of his haversack, he had little food, perhaps some jerky or hardtack.

The two men marched up the Nashville Turnpike and passed a line of troops headed to the river, whether to cross over or just to see what the fighting was about, no one could know. Jon saw something peculiar and pointed, just as Will noticed it.

Small groups of men veered off the road towards a gate. At the entrance, they greeted comrades and entered an abandoned barnyard. Maybe, Jon thought, they were assembling for an assault, but there was little urgency in their steps.

"What the hell now?" said Jon, slowing his walk to observe the gathering.

Will stepped forward to investigate, then he turned and smiled with his usual distinction. "Let's go to church!"

Before Jon could think, Will led him by the elbow down towards the gate. Jon hesitated. "Is that what they're doing? No, I'll just wait out here."

Will pulled back. "What?" He scanned Jon's face and saw his unease. "Look, I'll go. If you want, join in later. For some of us, this may be the last chance for spiritual communion, on account of that shelling earlier." Will entered the gate and searched for a space on the makeshift plank pews.

Jon saw a group of rugged teamsters huddled around a fire near the gate. *Perhaps I could stand there, get warm and hear the message without going into the church area,* he thought. A sudden worry occurred to him that he should go back to the regiment and tell Lieutenant Weston about Martello, and Lawsen. *No, I must wait it out, like he said.*

Jon remained outside the gate and looked into the corral. As he witnessed during his youth, church served his generation well, creating community, Christian respect and charity, but now as the war progressed into more horrendous displays of human barbarism, the men around him had searched for meaning to it, perhaps just a reason, even just an excuse.

Like all the men, Jon witnessed the revivals that had broken out in the Army after the devastating losses at Shiloh. Some of the ministers and heads of government took the troop's religious passions for a sign, meaning that God had favored their struggle for independence and their fight against Yankee secularism.

But the common soldier knew better. It was, as Sgt. Hillford had interpreted, really God saying, "Hey boys, come back to me, because this here war is going to get a lot worse before it's over."

Jon stepped to the fire and spread his stiff fingers in the heat plume. The hot coals hissed as raindrops fell onto them. It was another miserable day, gray, wet, and freezing.

"Ya look awful blue there, boy, some belief, or hope maybe… ya might need?" inquired a man close to Jon. He turned and saw an older sergeant who was chewing something and sitting with his back to the fence.

Jon nodded and said, "I guess."

A song broke out in the yard, "Nearer My God to Thee", and those who knew the tune hummed or sang immediately. Jon noticed the preacher moving behind a long, wooden crate turned up on its end for a pulpit. Then he saw someone familiar. The name popped into his head. Patrick Lovejoy. "How could anyone forget that name?" he mumbled. Lovejoy sat on the front bench with a few Yankee prisoners in tow. Then the preacher started.

The message spread into the cold silent air and fell onto the men like warm sun. Soldiers without shoes or long coats, shivered from hunger and lack of sleep, and patiently listened to the lesson. The preacher, a captain, did not sound like a man out in the cold, but spoke in a smooth, paced fashion, distinguishing him as a genuine reverend.

He read from his bible about King David and God's promises for victory over his enemies and how David had strayed from the Lord, whom he had praised in song as a young shepherd. Jon clearly heard the next line.

"For you see, though King David sinned, with murder and deceit, there was still forgiveness in God's heart for his chosen warrior. Therefore, as we fight for our earthly causes, rest in the peace that God has fought and won our victory over death. His promise to David is now the same to us; to be delivered from the ultimate wrath of sin, which is death."

Jon felt the weight of his secret deed upon him. *How can God see us and love us?* He fought the pain, but could not kill the sadness of it all. In his spirit he mourned, for himself, for Bertram, and for his friends.

After an introduction by the chaplain, three black mess stewards and a company vocal trio stepped forward to sing. The soft chorus of "River Jordan" described a soul crossing the river with Jesus and how his dearly departed mother welcomed him to the other side, on the "shore of love, place of peace."

Knowing that they may die soon, men were moved to tears and prayer by the poetic lyrics and sweet melody. Jon had avoided the "last chances," as the services were recently nicknamed, not because of a fear of religion or the rejection of its moral and spiritual edicts, but because he knew where he stood, or thought he did.

His family practiced the Episcopalian tradition, passed from Jack's parents in Baltimore. Jon's faith was more like a handed-down suit, very nice and appreciated, taken out and worn on occasion. Since he had grown up and especially now during the war, he took hold in a belief that there was no great manipulation of man's will, that man's destiny was truly self-ordained.

God was the Lord of war, and the Prince of Peace and everything else in between—all the menial concerns of man's daily struggle—amounted to chickens in the dirt. This inert belief had just about cemented itself until last August, when Bethanna had scratched open his spirit, exposed it, and fed it with tenderness. Months later, her influence persisted. Earlier, when Jon had described the Taldorf valley during Lawsen's death, her attributes, faith, kindness, and hope, filled that wretched wagon. Now, those virtues struggled for existence during this bleak hour.

Trying to find hope in the most hopeless time, he began to see something clearly. If there was hope for the dying or future

---

dead, then there had to be a solution to his own act of murder. His heart softened and realizing that he may have to answer for his wayward deeds, he said bitterly in a desperate whisper, "God? What should I do?"

He thought hard about Bertram. *Should I turn myself in?* He could not expect mercy from God if he did not come to terms with own actions. He wanted mercy. His soul cried for it. In his struggle, he was crying, not noticing the tears on his dirty cheeks. He would have to face justice. Yes, return to the regiment and surrender to the military tribunal's justice.

But, he thought, surely in the vast battle, other instances of mistaken identity, perhaps more deliberate than his, existed. *I was attacked unawares, in total darkness! Wasn't I correct in my actions? Military justice would mean dishonor if it were found out that I did, indeed, and without hesitation, murder for material gain. It could be derived as such. Father would be horrified...Mother.*

Riles will surely pull every bit of wool out of the story until he had his revenge, right or wrong. The swift court of man, in a time of war, may not see him as a soldier trying to survive, but as a roving brigand, looking for booty from his own confused and shaken ranks. Riles could make it such.

He found the human side confusing and growing more so, but Jon could see that God's judgment was clear. *Atonement brings mercy.* He would have to find a way to make up for Bertram; some sort of sacrifice for the taking of another's life. What it would be, he did not yet know.

A pat on the back broke his thoughts and he jumped. Cawley laughed.

"My friend!" Jon hugged him, like a long lost little brother. Jon looked down to where the sergeant was sitting. A younger man was there instead.

* * *

CHAPTER 25 ★

Carrying a bucket of warm soup, Bethanna stepped carefully between the wounded men and doled out servings with a ladle. She did her best to keep strong amid the carnage of the great battle. Earlier that morning, distant but clear artillery duels had alarmed her, and as she mentally prepared for more casualties, worried questions from the poor men under her care overwhelmed her; are the Yankees moving in for the kill? Could they have run over our force so easily? She did not know, for the news coming in changed with the hour.

Meanwhile, she felt safe in the house of God. The Murfreesboro Methodist Church gave its sanctuary for recovering wounded as their oak pews became stained with their sacrificial blood. Bethanna had mopped up bucket-loads in the last two days.

It had been a full three days since she stepped off the train from Chattanooga. She had missed Christmas with the troops and now the quaint holly-trimmed town of Murfreesboro stood frozen, battle-shocked. Her heart dropped lower than ever as the ghastly effects of war filled her eyes and mind with images she never thought possible—piles of dead men, lines of wounded waiting untreated in the cold rain, the savagery of amputation, all impacted her emotions and then her actions. The true meaning of her journey fell on her like the cold, sharp rain; *you must give yourself to the care of the hurt and be the Lord's witness in this place of hell.* Being here now, she could easily see why she had to leave Darlene.

In Chattanooga, the widow had settled into her new life of church-school and attempted run-ins with the older businessmen bachelors. Darlene had adapted well in the few weeks since taking up residence at her father's house. She fit in with her mother's clique, often taking long walks with new girlfriends and stepping into a more elevated society. Adorned with new dresses and hats, her cheerfulness returned, accompanied by newfound confidence, which made her father proud again and her mother show her off.

Darlene insisted that Bethanna join her circle of influence. "Two beauties are better than one. We can keep many callers, Beth, a blonde and a brunette, what a team we will make. But you need some refining, my dear, some powder, perhaps a tightening of the waist."

Bethanna quickly figured out that she could never be a *refined lady*, wearing French fashion, or an imitation thereof. Though the temptation seemed a fairy tale, Chattanooga was not the perfect place for it. Still very much a cow town and railhead, the polite society was very tight, small and closed to her, a Germanic farm girl. For the first time, she felt like an oddity. The notion did not offend her as much as Darlene's constant prodding.

Still though, the great ridges and hills reminded her of home, and when she shared a desire to climb the tall, dominant Lookout Mountain, Darlene almost spun out of her hoopskirt. "Ladies do not speak about such things! We take the carriage."

After that, Bethanna knew where her path led, to the west, Jon and his Army. Disappointed, she had discovered that his brigade was not there in Chattanooga. Again, the Army moved ahead of her and she had to wait for the right time to continue her mission, which to her seemed a mighty task that only the Lord could finish.

One scrap of news was clear. Bragg's Army of Tennessee was concentrating near Murfreesboro to stop any future movements of the Yanks out of Nashville. There were plenty of supplies to keep the troops in good spirits heading into the week of Christmas and many relatives visited the Army during the holidays, evidently, the perfect time for her to go. It had happened almost as an accident that Bethanna ended up on a train chugging its way towards a battlefront.

On her trips to the Chattanooga depot, she waited for word on the outgoing trains, as the scheduling proved unreliable. In the office, she witnessed families waiting for news, or letters from troops. One day, she was dropping off donated home-spun blankets when she overheard a clerk ask an elderly couple a simple question, "Are you relatives of the deceased?"

They answered yes.

Before long, the clerk handed the older couple a special passage to Wartrace to retrieve their son's body. He had died in recent cavalry action south of Nashville fighting under General Forest. Bethanna shuffled in behind them and approached the desk. "Sir, I must ask you. What should I do, if the soldier I know has not died yet?"

The man stared through his gold-framed spectacles. He thought for a moment and came to life suddenly. "Oh, you mean someone *is* dying!" he asked.

Bethanna shuddered at the horror. "God forbid, I hope not yet!" She became downcast and fearful. Her youth and tenderness pried at the clerk's heart.

"Now dear, I am so sorry. Is it...?"

"Yes, he is my only love. He is in danger. I must go to him!" she begged.

The clerk had seen it before; a young wife traveling to her dying husband. If it were at all possible, under the eyes of God and man, they must reunite and declare their last devotions to each other before, in a pitied moment, the young man dies of his wounds.

To the experienced clerk, the signs could not have been any clearer. Immediately, he secured her a ticket and told her the next train for Tullahoma/ Murfreesboro was due in the morning.

Darlene became emotional as Bethanna explained that she could no longer stay in Chattanooga and that she missed the inn and her sister. She had fulfilled her mission to its fruitful end, now there was nothing here she knew or desired. "You are still my great friend, and we will write, promise me."

Darlene cried for a time and they sat together as Bethanna prayed blessings on a woman that had hardly known any.

On the morning train, everything was done for her comfort. A stooped man too old to fight, dressed in the dingy red coat of the rail steward, led Bethanna to a comfortable seat, perhaps the only one without holes in it. She carried no baggage with her, only her canvass bag, which held personal items and Jon's book of poems, plus the New Testament that Aunt Verna gave her. As the train cut through the wind and cold, she had plenty to read and inspire her. Obviously at that time, she could never predict what she would need the inspiration for.

Arriving in Wartrace for more passengers, the train stopped to pick up mail and water. Bethanna remained seated, contented to read about Jesus raising Lazarus from the dead. Out the window, she saw the older couple walk up to the casket of their dead son. There were more boxes there, near the platform. Many sons to bury. Bethanna prayed, "Lord, raise them, also, into heaven."

Looking in from the doorway, the kindly old steward checked in on her while she waited patiently and gazed out the window at the waiting passengers. She did not want for anything and he left her alone. The old man hoped fondly that the young lady would not find a coffin at the end of her journey.

Bethanna's comfort and ease proved to her that she was being led and protected. Because of this, a look of calm purpose overtook her face. Besides, she was in all sense of the word a woman now, and that's how she appeared as she rode the train to the front, to her love. She heard raised voices outside and saw three men arguing with a porter. In a moment, she could tell they were not allowed to board the train. A blessed feeling overtook her, as she appreciated her seat, honestly gained.

Although close to untruth, she was glad that she did not have to lie to get it. Apparently, the Chattanooga desk clerk was moved to action by God's hand and by her claims of a dying love, a story not far from truth as her vision showed. But she had to lie to Darlene and that did not come as hard as she thought it would. It was good to have a close girlfriend, but Darlene would never understand the spiritual nature of her quest and never allow her to run off towards the front without quickly alarming her parents.

The train out of Chattanooga ran into delays due to Army priorities, often when supplies and men passed by while civilian traffic waited on remote sidings. At some point north, the Army assembled with terrific speed as all loose ends were tied before a clash with the enemy, expected very soon. After three days, she finally made it to Murfreesboro.

Yet again, she was crushed to find Jon's brigade stationed at Readyville a few miles away and that civilian movements had been restricted upon eminent action. She found shelter at the church and made herself useful to the staff there. She waited, stomach in knots, as the troops converged north of town to begin their deadly New Year's dance. As the massive Army moved into history and took Jon with it, she could not shake her vision—the flames, the flag and death waiting.

The Methodist Church pews had filled with bandaged bodies, and each one possessed a different kind of wound and a stirring tale to go with it. The only way to stand the noxious sights and smells was to find a higher meaning in the difficult job. *After all,* she thought, looking around at the ornate decor of God's house, *everything has a higher meaning.*

A man reached for her dark blue dress and Bethanna gave him gulps of bean soup. She went on to the next patient, who could not eat with his head completely wrapped, except a spot for his nostrils. His dirty hair stood up like stiff, muddy grass above the hasty field dressing. With her fingers, she separated the bandage and spooned the soup in for the hungry soldier. "Careful," she said. "It's hot."

Her young female voice startled the patient. Accustomed to the male stewards or the older ladies, he hesitated and cowered in mild embarrassment. He looked like a young man, with his light frame and full hair, but his hands were older, or used to hard work.

She saw his obvious discomfort. "Please, if you are able, you must eat something while we have it. I have waited a long time to help you brave men. It is my honor to care for you." Bethanna's tact relaxed the blind and mute soldier. She had spoken to him personally, perhaps a more meaningful treatment, at the time. The wrapped head nodded. He sat back and took more helpings.

Then on impulse, she thought that the man before her could be Jon. "Is your name, Jon?" she asked.

The head shook slowly. She thought over the question of his name. "Sorry, that was rude of me. I was looking for someone earlier."

The soldier opened his lapel like a street salesman and pointed inside his coat. She looked at the inside pocket liner and saw the name, "Cale A. Walkins," written on a leather patch.

"Cale. Nice to meet you, I am Beth." She reached for his hand, and gently took it. "I am glad to meet you, sir."

Cale nodded and pointed to himself, relating the same. She let the soldier hold her hand a short time. He felt her fingers, enjoying the soft feel of a girl's skin, and patted her palms.

"Yes, I am a young one. Everyone here is older and I am not allowed to treat the patients medically, due to my age, so the older nurses have said. They assigned me to pass out what food there is to the wounded men here. I know the Lord has..."

Before she could finish, one of the older women nurses slapped the pew rail. "Feed the others, missy."

"Sorry, Cale, I must do my job. I will bring you more food later."

Cale nodded again, patting her hand, and if he could talk, she figured he would be that kind of person that never stops. Bethanna continued her path among the pews and scanned every patient, as she thought Jon might be suffering among them. Every young man showed a little bit of him and if he lay amid this crowd, she worried if the face she admired many weeks ago will be unrecognized and more horribly, w*ill he know me in his delirious state?*

She chased this fear from her soul with a mumbled prayer and then headed over to where three wounded men chatted near the choir loft. Sporting various arm and hand wounds, the men were fine enough to stand and sort bandages from strips of donated clothing.

She approached with her pail of steaming soup and they welcomed the meal with cautious glances. She hesitated at their hesitation.

"Sorry, miss, you just don't know what is getting cooked around here." One of them said. His right arm was wrapped from the elbow to his wrist.

"This is fresh bean soup with bacon, God's truth" she said.

The men dug out their tin cups and dipped into the pail. Surprising Bethanna, they slurped the soup as fast as they could without too much rude noise. They looked at their new hostess and her youth intrigued them. One of them, a young man with a thin, dark beard, spoke. "You're a kind and fair girl, do you attend church here?" He gestured with his cup at the surroundings.

"I came from far away to look for someone, but that is an effort larger than I can bear. So I am moved by the Lord to help those who are hurt." Bethanna gave him another scoop from her bucket. "I am glad to see you are helping, too," she said.

Her tale touched him. "Eh, who ya looking for?" he asked.

Bethanna's eyes brightened for a second and she smiled. "Do you know of the 11th Tennessee regiment? He is with them."

"Tennessee? Uh... I'm an Arkansas man myself, so are my two ugly chums here. But I recall that brigade, where the 11th is attached lost their commander in the first assault, couple days ago. Rains I believe his name was. Too bad, too, young man, very inspirin'."

Bethanna touched her chin and her face winced as she recognized Jon's commander. "It must have been a horrid battle." A short daydream flashed in her mind about the close combat and Jon's place near this dying General Rains. She refused to be drawn by the vision and in seconds, cast it away.

One of the other men spoke up. "I'm Hodges, pardon the manners, eh, and this is Private Mullibey and Corporal Sanderson." They nodded to Bethanna.

Being older and more outgoing, Hodges, a private, seemed to outrank the corporal. Bethanna bounced glances between the men as they took more from her soup pail. Sanderson was young, maybe 24, with dark brown eyes and hair, and had a thick beard. Most soldiers had them.

The other, Mullibey, had brown eyes, dark hair and pointed goatee, which balanced his narrow face. He seemed friendly and in little discomfort from his forearm wound.

Hodges, dipping in for his third cup of soup, continued his battle talk. "And yes'um, it was the damndest place I ever hit in my life. Our brigade kicked them Yanks for most of the mornin' but they dug in on the highway. We drove into them and got plain clobbered."

"I am grateful you lived through such a thing," she said.

The men nodded, bobbing their heads as they chewed and swallowed. "Plenty of those poor fellas' didn't, though," Hodges said.

The group was quiet for a moment. Bethanna felt an obligation to encourage them from thoughts of despondency. "Please continue your much-needed work." She motioned to the rag pile. "I'll be back for those within the hour and we shall talk again."

Polite farewells followed her down the red-carpeted isle. As she exited the sanctuary for the church's kitchen, the low rumble of artillery rolled through the air. She hurried her steps.

* * *

Upon finding his sergeant and best buddy— J.B. Lyhton— Private Cawley, in his utter gladness, cried a little. He tried very hard to disguise his sobs with laughter, but he sounded more like a fiendish old woman than a happy friend. "I knew you'd be alive!" He backed off, stood at rare attention and saluted Jon.

Returning the salute, Jon shared the sentiment. He laughed. It was nice to be so missed. "I knew you'd be alive, too, Private Cawley, the tiger you are."

The two stood by the fire as the troops filed out of the stockyard. Jon noticed more men coming into the area. As Cawley explained his duty mission from Weston, Jon nodded and smiled, proud for Cawley. Soon, Jon noticed that another service had started.

The Reverend Lovejoy led a Christian song and he looked at Jon, nodded as he sung.

Jon looked back to Cawley. "This ain't Sunday, is it?" he asked.

"Nope. It's a Friday, Sergeant"

"Then what, pray tell, can be going on with the faithful today?"

Cawley shrugged his shoulders. He and Jon looked around like lost children at a crowded fair. A few moments later, they saw a regimental-size line of troops curving down the road and beyond them, more troops. This was no large church service.

"This is big," Jon said. "Only before battle do we assemble in such numbers." He felt a shiver go through his body. "Were gonna' hit'em!" Looking around at the gathering ranks, he spotted the artillerist, Will Charles, standing with a group of men that seemed to be good friends. Will saw him too and brought his pals over to meet Jon and Cawley at the fire. "Jon, who is your friend? I am pleased to meet a friend of a new friend." He properly introduced himself to Cawley. Then he introduced his mates. "Lyhton, Cawley, this is our proud and honorable Lieutenant Pollard."

The young officer shook their hands and his wavy hair bounced behind his ears.

"And these are our pals, Bob Hails and Charley Holt. Bob, who's famous for his Bowie knife antics, of course," said Pollard.

Jon chuckled, knowing the story. "Great to meet you all. Mr. Charles here has proven Alabamians to be an industrious folk. He scrambled up decent shelter for me last night."

Lieutenant Pollard laughed. "Yes, we are familiar with his instant, fireside arrangements. His boyish grin has done him well, endearing him to several local hostesses. Eggnog and ham last week, was it?"

Will shrugged. "Yes, I am guilty, but I always include a friend."

Jon raised a hand. "I can attest to that."

"I'm doubly glad you waited and listened to the message, Jon," Will said, deflecting the attention. "I think that it was a providential thing for me too, because I have just heard from Lieutenant Pollard here that Semple's guns have been divided again. Pollard's section will be put into action. Unfortunately, my half, under my old schoolmate Lieutenant Goldthwaite, is stationed apart from them. Looks like I am to be excluded from this business to come."

"What business is that?" asked Jon, eager to know.

Lieutenant Pollard spoke up. "These men are all Kentuckians, from Roger Hanson's brigade. There has been an order given to the men of Breckinridge's division, to prepare for attack. Our Napoleons will be heard again."

"Can you believe that it's not over?" Will mused.

"I can't believe it's taking so long to end. This action *might* be providential, dear Will." Jon patted the young man on the shoulder. "Your guns have chance to give those Yanks some hell!"

Will smiled. "I can only hope to do my duty as ordered. Hell? I do not now about."

Cawley spit on the ground. "Yep, that's what they need, some hell."

The men laughed and soon quieted, knowing that the Yankees gave hell in equal measure. Will, put a hand to his heart. "I must bid you a hasty farewell, Jon Lyhton and Private Cawley. Please take care, both of you, my prayers and hopes go with you!"

"And to you, my poetical friend. Glory to Alabama today and for you all."

Jon shook his hand, as did Cawley. They wished his friends Godspeed and watched them run up the lane towards the Nashville Turnpike. "Cawley, there walks a true servant," Jon proclaimed.

Jon and Cawley kept warm at the fire while they looked over the Kentucky troops. Jon fell into deep thoughts about the coming action; *Breckinridge and Hanson, too. That means Preston's men are there. The 20th Tennessee is with Preston and so is Elias.*

Thoughts began to fly through his mind, scenes from his life, his father and mother, how they reared him, taught him. Then he thought of Cassie, his little sister. Her life was just beginning amid this storm of war that would ravage her world. If only he could make it go away, as he had done with her typical toddler troubles.

His childhood came into mind with foggy memories growing more vivid. There was something there, deep in his heart that forced its way forward with surprising clarity. Then it struck him. *There is a way, extreme though it is. A way to find mercy for me and perhaps another, if I could get there in time. It may not totally complete the process. There is still something else to do.*

Jon felt tremors underfoot. Everyone heard it and like a fold of startled sheep, the troops raised their heads. The low moans of cannon fire rumbled through the earth and rebounded in the atmosphere. It had started again and its resonance was broader than before. More guns meant more troops. *This was big, indeed. Perhaps Breckinridge's whole division will be hurled at the Yankees. Was it enough?*

Jon arose, standing a bit taller than he had in days. "I have to go," he said.

Cawley looked up at him and smiled. "Where we goin'?" he asked.

"No, not we…me. I have to go hash something out," Jon said, looking off into the distance.

Patrick Lovejoy walked amongst his enemies unmolested, and even as a "vile Yankee" felt quite welcomed as a counselor of the Lord. Beating his arms against the cold, he approached Jon, recognizing him from earlier in the day.

"Hello, remember me?" he said.

Jon nodded and managed an aloof smile.

"It seems the battle is to resume; be thankful you're not a Kentuckian," Lovejoy gestured to the troops walking away from the yard.

Jon's smile faded. "And if I were?"

Lovejoy's sharp eyebrows dipped. "Well, because they seem to have been selected for action. I was wondering about your welfare, that's all." Lovejoy shrugged, as he crossed his arms.

"I see," said Jon, lifting his chin. "I think that today, I wish I were a Kentuckian, for they will have the distinct honor of sweeping away the remnants of a beaten Army. I only wish we all could be in on it."

The young chaplain accepted Jon's prideful boast with an easy smile. "I must remember my place here is to be a shepherd not a strategist." Refining his original thought, he said, "I only hoped that you wouldn't share the same fate as your friends. Or even more important, that if you do, there is a knowledge of, and opportunity for redemption."

Jon squinted at the reverend. He rubbed his beard. "That's something that I may be working on."

Cawley yawned. Jon looked at him. "Private, go over yonder and get prayed over."

"Yessir." Cawley gladly walked through the fence gate and joined a short line of ragged men, soon to be thrown in front of the enemy.

Lovejoy smiled, observing Cawley's servitude. He returned to his serious tone.

"Is there anything that you would like to confess?" Lovejoy said. He waited.

Jon found it hard to move. He had never faced such a question, at such a time. "I think that the Lord will hear my confession soon enough." Jon felt ashamed of his fear.

"God is always listening," Lovejoy said, as if he knew what the confession would be, only waiting on Jon to confirm it.

Jon stared at the ground, past the blood stains on his coat. "If there was a murder, for survival, and a friend was mistakenly killed."

Lovejoy leaned in. "There is still hope. Whatever the deed, God will forgive."

Jon rubbed his beard. "But how can there be no punishment?"

Lovejoy's eyes searched, as if scanning a large, inner library. "There may be, if found to be worthy of punishment. It is only right. Is this killer accused by anyone?"

One name lit up his eyes, Riles! Jon raised his head but said nothing. The two stared at each other for only seconds and Lovejoy seemed to know all, as his gaze changed from mild curiosity to surprise.

Jon turned away slowly. "I have to make it right."

"Man's judgment is a harsher thing than God's," said Lovejoy, holding Jon's arm.

Jon turned back around, his face souring. "That's what I have feared. There is no man that can judge as God does, with mercy. But I am at the mercy of men."

He left the chaplain and went to fetch Cawley, who had received his blessing and waited at the fire. "Cawley, listen, I'm going." He held the shorter man by the shoulders, as if to brace him. "You go to the lieutenant and tell him Lawsen is dead. Martello is wounded and in town. I have to see to some urgent business. I don't know when I'll be back."

Cawley's face flushed. "Dead? Martello wounded?"

"There are just some things that work out strange for some folks and sometimes for others, it's too late to fix 'em." Jon's voice broke with emotion and his eyes grew wet. "I'm not that great soldier you might think I am. In fact today, I may be the worst of us all. After what I've seen today, I can't accept that fact any longer. You're a good man, Cawley, much better than me. I know you'll make me proud and earn a promotion soon. Now run directly to the lieutenant!"

There was finality in Jon's tone. Something did not sound right to Cawley. He grabbed Jon's blue overcoat; he did not understand. "What do you mean? You're the best damn soldier I ever knowed, you're my friend, and without you, I'd be runnin' inta trees!" In desperate clamor, he pulled at the coat's shoulder cape. "Where ya goin'? You can't leave us." One of the brass buttons on the greatcoat tore off.

Jon pushed his anguished friend away. "You go to them, Cawley! That's an order, Private!"

Cawley reacted to the command, and then resisted it. "No, Jonny… you can't."

Jon pointed to the button. "You keep that…remember me, Lawsen and Martello, too. You remember the Gap and Tazewell. The 11ᵗʰ forever!"

The doom in Jon's words scared Cawley and he broke under the shock. His efforts to hide the misery failed and he choked on short, coughing sobs. Clutching the little button like a valuable coin, he backed away slowly. Then out of anger, he turned and fled. But in his sorrow and blinding tears, he ran toward town, not the regiment. What good would it do to return to the 11ᵗʰ without his best buddy, and a hero's welcome for finding Sergeant Lyhton?

After a long time jogging, Cawley slowed and began to walk. From a rise in the land, he viewed the town a mile distant and stood alone. With trepidation, he turned around and witnessed, in broad scope, Hanson's Kentuckians moving up the south face of Wayne's Hill. Breckinridge's division spread across the hill and eastward, as artillery caissons unlimbered for additional support.

In the midst of this, Cawley had not the nerve to run off like Jon and seek whatever it was that nagged his heart or spirit. Jon's mind was too broad for him to figure. A deep person of great knowledge, Jon surely knows what he is doing, but he usually pulled his favorite private along to help. Not this time, in the worst of times.

Cawley needed a brother; his twin had died at age twelve and getting along was hard for him, until the 11th, and Jon's great ways of encouragement, like a brother's. It was known to him, that on his own, he proved very slow and stupid. With Jon to guide him, he felt smart enough to perform whatever duty there was to do. Their hurtful and sudden separation would surely doom him. Gazing in fear at the marching lines, he whispered a trembling, "Goodbye."

* * *

The concerned Chaplain Lovejoy had seen Jon's dismissal of Cawley and followed shortly, catching him by the arm. "I will only say it once. Whatever your crime, you walk amongst criminals here and God will forgive you, if you plead to him. Do not walk away."

"I'm not walking away from anything, in fact, I'm facing my judgment, be it life or death."

Jon stomped off and blended into the marching lines.

After finding no more energy for the effort, Lovejoy turned and headed for town; he was cold, hungry, and in the way. The assault was building around him like Gideon's legions from bible times, except, in his view, not so anointed. Quite the opposite he feared, as they would be cast into a bitter furnace and wasted on martial whims of Southern planters. He did not want to witness it.

When he enlisted, the only thing he wanted to see was the slaves freed, the masters punished, and God's great blessing continue for the United States. But a horrid thing appeared that no one had thought over—something called combat—a woeful devil that devoured all causes, morals, and high and mighty sermons.

Damned the sermons that led me here, into a stinking field on a stinking road towards a stinking town. Damned the men who fouled their senate seats satisfied with the Southern compromises, those idiotic deals that continued the black sins and never moved towards abolition. Shortsighted fools and cowards afraid to fight for what they preached. Never again, not me, by God. I am through with the whole lot of 'em. And those at home, what do they want? Letters, notes, sentiments from the glorious field? Nothing I have to say anymore. It is rather all disastrous and defused of hope. Why and what is there to convey? How do I lie to them, why begin to?

Evolving from a devout realist to a cynic, then to something worse, Lovejoy was now a preacher who has lost faith in man, seeing him unworthy of God's glorious message. Lovejoy's war had changed him, and that war was not physical.

As sure as he told Jon, God was the ultimate judge and mistakenly, Lovejoy had assumed that mantel over several months of stagnant war. He witnessed man's fall in the pit of every sin and vice available to a soldier, as his friends became wild with excess, violence, and revenge.

And the enemy, too, was the same, as before him marched the slaver's lamb of sacrifice lined up to accept the hellfire and brimstone, soon to be falling from the gray sky and decimating their mortal numbers. It occurred to him that with all of his faith and belief, training and religion, he was a man of God walking with them, condemned in hell. Although true, he could not equate himself with the demon soldiers, slashing, shooting and taking souls.

He arrived to the out skirts of Murfreesboro and thought of his previous duty, praying for the wounded. If he cannot make this hell any better for himself, then he will try for the suffering ones. Acting out faith was better than preaching it. By God's grace, he had done some good for the suffering and that's what he must continue to do, or stop and go insane.

* * *

CHAPTER 26★

Dropping like thunder, the rumble of distant artillery reverberated off the low clouds over the town of Murfreesboro and into the church where Bethanna tended the Confederate wounded. She looked up from her work and tried to distinguish the range of the guns. A wounded soldier taking his late lunch said it was "our guns." There were more now, firing incessantly. The low thumps distracted her momentarily and she tried not to show a nervous face.

It was almost 3:00 in the afternoon. Bethanna patiently worked with two widows who had stayed to look after the church with their faithful reverend. "Now is not the time to leave the house of God," he had said to them. The widowed women agreed, having nowhere else to go. These women had seen suffering in their lives and were fit to serve as nurses, but the last two days' carnage dwarfed their past experiences into things of idle chatter. A great calamity had befallen their sanctuary and their town. It would stamp their lives forever with nightmares.

Bethanna found out from the widows that younger women like her could not be good nurses, due to their youthful appeal to the troops. "It is better for the motherly, older women to bathe a man than the younger, more distracting girl, you see?" one of them said to Bethanna during their small lunch. Put that way, she now understood why she was given her specific duties.

Despite her limits, Bethanna's strength of faith impressed the small church group and they gave her liberal access to the men most of the day. She seemed to know what to say to the frightened boys, who were no older than she was. Sometimes just a smile would put them at ease or more often, a prayer. At times, the natural summons of death ignored the holy surroundings.

When the litter-men came to cart away a corpse, Bethanna prayed for the man's soul and after she grew used to this scene, she could not help but think that a church was a great place for the men to meet the Lord in life or death.

As they had done several times, the nurses sent the swifter Bethanna to the surgeon's tents to fetch the sulfur for the cleansing buckets. Adorning her cape and hood, she ran with careful abandon, through the puddled streets, determined in her mission.

Located in the stable yard of a local hotel, the main medical tent was an elongated square, with a high-pitched top and solid plank sides. She entered a large canvass-flap door and saw the doctors standing around a bloody mess on the surgeon's table. Bethanna shuddered and pulled up. To her shock, the battered body moved with life, but the doctors surrounding him did nothing, bewildered and exhausted.

Bethanna asked a steward about the sulfur. He gave her a tin box from a crate. She put it in her canvas bag and was about to leave, when she looked at one of the doctors. He was shaking his head at the patient. "Is there nothing to be done for him?" she asked.

"No, girl, nothing. I'm in wonder that he's lived this long. I'd say he needs a priest, soon as possible."

Another doctor spoke. "He's full of laudanum. He may not understand a priest." The surgeon wiped his bloody hands on a used rag.

Bethanna steeled herself. The call rang in her ears—a prayer for mercy. She approached the table and tried to concentrate on the man's face. The scene was overpowering. Most of his clothes and upper torso were discernible, but everything else was cut and broken. Amazingly, the man's face was clear except for his gaping, bloody mouth. His head turned left and right, as if he were looking for something. His black beard grew to a point and he had a wild look in his eyes, and with more study, he reminded Bethanna of some pictures she had seen of the devil.

"What is your name, soldier?" asked Bethanna. The man did not answer, only raised his head and coughed, gurgled and vomited blood on his chest.

Bethanna clamped her eyes shut, then turned away. The doctor raised the soldier's hat to his eyes and read from the leather band inside. "Private Riles Mullibey, 4th Arkansas."

Bethanna repeated the last name. "Mullibey?" Her eyes widened. "I have heard this name, not but an hour ago." She thought for a moment and remembered the group of men in the choir loft. She looked down at Riles' bloody form. "Do you have a brother?" She said forcibly into his ear. The man's eyes grew large and he reached for her, bloodying her arm with a slick stripe. Bethanna reeled with fright.

A lanky soldier stepped out from the shadowed corner behind the doctors. His face was white, woebegone. "Please missy, if this man's brother is alive or dead, he must know it for himself, now, without delay." Stokes shut his eyes, looked down.

Bethanna felt the Lord's compassion and without speaking, bolted for the door. She would provide the last good thing this man would ever see. She ran, like she used to run in the valley. She ran in the rain as she and Jon had done to escape the downpour on top of the ridge. *A chance for grace.*

She threw open the church doors and ran down the aisle to the choir loft. The young man was sitting lazily, reading the bible. He looked like his brother. "Mr. Mullibey!"

Bertram dropped the bible in surprise and as he arose, bumped his knee on the pew brace. "Ouch! What?"

"Come now, there's no time! Your brother is dying!" she yelled, heaving for breath.

Bethanna waited at the tent flap while Bertram entered. As he did, he tried to define the dark-red mass on the table. The doctors backed away from the dying body. It resembled some half-skinned animal, cornered and fighting for every breath. Bertram stared at the face. "Riles?" Then he looked away. "Jesus, mercy."

Stokes approached Bertram and the two greeted each other with affirming embraces. "He thinks you are missing or murdered," said Stokes. "He must see you, if he is to die in peace."

Bertram approached his brother with fear. He looked on his shredded form and then into his eyes. They were filled with the same rage as had always occupied them.

Riles held up his head and gazed at the hazy figure before him. *It was himself, no, it was a spirit. Was it his spirit?*

Then the blurry form spoke. "It's me, Bertram." Riles' vision cleared enough to see that it was his brother and when he inhaled to speak, a wet, croaky voice passed over his slick, bloody lips. "You haunt me now, do you, Brother?"

Stokes could no longer hold back his tears. He wept for joy and sadness. Bertram was found and Riles, in the worse way, was lost.

They had found Riles Mullibey during a delay in the morning skirmish and artillery duel. He had been scouting near the front line when his contingent was enveloped by cannon fire. Thinking he would die very slowly and having pity, the survivors dragged him on a wooden board for a mile, where then he could be given proper burial. But he was too angry to die. In his demented state, he repeated a name and called to his dead brother. The bewildered troops loaded him into an available ambulance, amazed that he was still breathing.

Riles reached for Bertram, gripping his brother's hand in a soft seal of blood. "If I can feel you, I'm closer to hell than I thought."

"Don't say that, Riles!" Bertram begged. "I am alive, see?" Outside, Bethanna heard the unrepentant tones coming from Riles' bloody mouth. Her heart broke for the angry man. A tear came. The poor younger brother would not see his sibling off to a better place. She searched for a proper prayer, none came. Then she saw an answer.

Look now... the priest is here," Bethanna announced, entering the tent.

"Damned reverend has a blue coat; don't serve me none!" Riles yelled.

Patrick Lovejoy removed his blue uniform coat and winced at the ravaged body. Digging into his black leather bag, he tried to find his prayer book before he fainted flat away, or perhaps vomited. "Ah, here it is." he said.

"Let your soul confess, to receive the grace and mercy of God," Lovejoy said, becoming sickly, turning gray. Rarely had he seen life remain in such a gory form.

He read, "Oh blessed Lord, the father of mercies and the God of all comfort, we beseech thee look down in pity upon this thy afflicted servant...Thou writest bitter things against him and makest him possess his former iniquities; thy wrath layest hard upon him, as his soul is full of trouble."

Riles recoiled in fear. "You tell this spirit of my brother to leave at once."

Lovejoy looked at the doctor.

"There is so little morphine," said the surgeon. "we must use it on cases who's chances are better. This man's pain has turned to madness."

As Riles quivered, the spasms pumped blood out of numerous openings in his flesh, created by shrapnel and protruding bone shards. Lovejoy hesitated, closed his eyes and waited for the shaking to settle.

"Riles, I'm alive, I'm real, see." Bertram touched his brother's face.

Riles screamed. "Leave me!" In a fright, he put a broken, stumped hand over his face, hiding it from some unseen, private terror. Bertram pulled away, as did Lovejoy.

Riles went on, his voice turning frail. "I'm so sorry, brother, so sorry I let you go! Please, don't punish me!"

A frothy wheezing came from his broken chest as he drew a huge breath. Once again, his face contorted with wild anger, then he shouted. His words rang into every soul present.

"Jonny Lyhton done ya! Jonny Lyhton killed ya! You're dead! Dead!"

The phrase stabbed Bethanna's soul like an icy knife. All the heat left her body and she shivered under Riles' wide, crazy glare. Hell had just attacked her.

Lovejoy froze. His eyes moved back and forth on a triangular line among Riles, Bertram and Bethanna, and in thought, he attempted to calculate the unlikely collision of souls; Jon Lyhton and his victim Bertram, his dying brother, and the unknown girl, who reacted emotionally to Jon's name.

Bethanna, pushed by desperate anger, rushed to Riles and with two hands grabbed his bloody arms. "Why do you condemn him? Why have you named him?"

The dying man starred at her, his bloody mouth giving the world one last smile, that smile of smug satisfaction which Jon had seen and loathed. Bethanna let go of him and as she backed away from the table, she saw in his dry, dying eyes, great pleasure in the suffering of her loved one. She covered her mouth and shuddered in the presence of pure evil.

They all watched Riles as he stared at his brother, Bertram. Fearing his journey into the unknown abyss that awaited him, he gagged hard on his last breath. Darkness enclosed his vision and cut off the world forever.

After his death, a word was said.

"Surely, the Lord loved even him."

Lovejoy looked at Bethanna. She had said it.

* * *

CHAPTER 27★

The order to attack the heights was given that afternoon and because of the hard fighting his brigade suffered on the battle's first day General Breckinridge hardly believed the words coming from Bragg's mouth. "Attack, using the artillery and cavalry in support."

Breckinridge politely mentioned that he had just scouted the strong position and deemed the ground perilous, guarded by tight infantry formations crowning the hill. He added that his left flank was vulnerable, in plain view of the Union artillery across the river.

Bragg continued to argue his case for the attack. "General Polk can strike the center once again and lend artillery support, but the Kentuckians must first clear the hill to our right. It is the only way."

General Breckinridge protested again, more notably about the lack of cover for his troops approaching the high ground, but to no avail. Bragg indicated his desire to take the position, a weaker and outnumbered one, and to attack in two hours, at 4:00.

Upon returning to his subordinates at headquarters, Breckinridge gave them the news. The order was not acceptable to most of them, especially Roger Hanson. "Since his failure in Kentucky, he has always blamed the good people of that state. How dare that old man test the courage of the brigade with a foolhardy, idiotic order such as this! I will ride out and face that beast with a pistol and eight paces!" Hanson darted for the door and his division commander closely followed. "No, Roger, wait!"

Hanson turned in the doorway. "You will have to arrest me, John!"

Breckinridge faced him. "That, I can do. And Bragg will have his way."

Hanson paused, his face soured in deep thought.

"How much good can you do me under restraints?" Breckinridge added. "He can make a fool of us or we can make a fool of him."

General Hanson's regimental commanders agreed, as one by one, they offered their hands in trust and loyalty. Hanson could only react as a gentleman. He shook their hands, accepted their oaths. Calmed, he strode to the center of the room and said, "Then if we fight, what is your plan, General Breckinridge?"

Having quelled the mounting insubordination toward Bragg amongst the Kentucky officers, Breckinridge breathed easier and signaled his adjutant to bring the map. "Gentlemen, the attack will put us at great risk in the open, but in the enemy's strength, I think I have found a weakness."

Despite the suddenness of, and insinuation behind the order, Breckinridge had accepted it as a dutiful soldier and by late afternoon, tried his best to plan the most effective assault. The orders where passed out to the brigade commanders:

"The attack will commence at 4:00, the late hour will give the Federals little daylight to mount an effective counter attack."

* * *

Lieutenant Elias Ambersaile of the 20th Tennessee jabbed his hand into his overcoat and pulled out a gold pocket watch. It was 3:30 in the afternoon. He replaced the watch and inspected the line of troops sitting in the wet, icy grass. The men loaded their muskets or wrote final letters. Elias pulled his pistol, an old Massachusetts Adams revolver, and checked it one more time. He holstered it and buttoned the strap. There wasn't much left to do since their arrival in line. About an hour before, the 20ᵗʰ Tennessee had crossed the river with their brigade, Preston's, and were directed to the east of Wayne's Hill. The eminence overlooked the entire field on which the future contest would shortly be held, and on it, General Breckinridge made his last-minute adjustments.

Elias saw the guns of Robertson's Florida battery relocate for closer support, and hastily unlimber for preliminary action. The horse teams were led away to the rear, saved for future transport when the guns will be moved closer to the Union lines.

Elias studied the action around him, his amber eyes prideful and eager. A short, trimmed beard framed his round face, centered with a large nose, red from the cold. He scratched it and over his hand, in the middle distance, an odd sight drew his attention.

A lone soldier walked randomly through the kneeling troops and approached the line. He was an infantryman with a musket and dirty blue overcoat. His brown slouch hat turned up with a motion from his head and Elias looked into familiar eyes.

"You, who are you?" He asked thinking the man was from his own regiment.

"I am Jon Lyhton, your cousin, from Nashville."

Elias stared at the dirty face. He walked around the man to his left, then inspected closer. "Jonny Lyhton?" He was different, older, thinner, but it could be. "Yes, I believe it is you." He looked him square in the eyes and clapped his hands. "By rights, it is. What in the devil has brought you here?"

"Not the devil, I hope," Jon said. "Before I join the attack, there are some things we need to settle between us."

Elias cocked his head. "You want to do…what?"

"Can we talk, away from the men?" Jon asked.

Elias led Jon over to a stand of hard, leafless oaks. "Is this some timely joke from my cousin, someone I haven't seen in months?"

His suspicion came off as repugnance. It surprised them both.

"It's a matter of making things right," Jon said, "if we come together as old friends, perhaps we can. It is our one last chance."

"Fancy that, then." Elias laughed. He noticed that Jon didn't fall into the humor. After he settled down, he studied his old playmate and discovered that Jon's timing annoyed him. Jon was a distant memory and one that hurt presently, now that he was reminded of it. He frowned and stiffened.

"Go find your regiment, Jon. Besides, it's against the code of conduct to join another unit without permission. Do you have authorization?" He shrugged and turned to leave.

"I'm joining the attack, even if you refuse me."

"What?" Elias said, turning back to him. Inspecting, he moved in closer. "Why bother at all? By the look of you, I'd say you've done enough. What are you doing here?"

"It's time, Elias, that we make the past over. You put blood on my hands. I was a little boy who became a killer. Did I sin? I don't know, but I was led to it. You left me to die at the hands of that wicked man. You have to answer for that."

Elias squinted. "You marched all the way out here for this?" He stepped back and rubbed his head. "If you want to blame me, I guess you can, but I was a brazen and woeful youth and it has benefited me since. Am I beholden to the sins of childhood?" He crossed his arms. "But if I remember, you ignored me for years, Johnny, and never gave me a proper moment to repair things betwixt us."

Jon chewed on the fact like it was bad bread. He nodded. "You're right."

Elias was intrigued, but needed more. "Interesting, go on."

Jon spoke with grave surety. "True then, I deserted a friend who needed me. Though you brought trouble, you didn't deserve to be shunned for life; for that, I have always suffered. Please forgive me, if such a thing can be asked now."

The schism had left them both scarred. They had carried the wounds underneath the façade of adulthood, like secret snakes hiding and waiting for the perfect time to strike the spirit and infect it with fear, guilt, unworthiness, and unbelief.

"This has troubled you, too?" asked Elias. He never imagined. He never asked. There was too much growing up to do and plenty of years to bury the horrors of youth with the thrill of adolescence, that time when all he did was try to make up to a young girl with a broken heart; one that *he* broke. As two old friends now in the Army, their reconciliation made sense at this time, but to Elias, Jon's problem seemed much deeper than an old hurt. "Jonny, you're right. I think we can forgive each other. Tell me, what has caused ..."

In a sudden roar, the Confederate artillery opened up, close and loud. Their shots whined over the long space and landed on the top of the distant hill, where smoky flowers sprouted among the waiting Yankees. Near Elias and Jon, the huddled Confederate infantry fidgeted in nervous expectation. "This is not your fight, Jon! Don't do it!" Elias begged.

"Like hell it's not!" Jon shouted back over the pounding guns. "I'm between dishonor and death, my friend, accused of a crime that is beyond trial. I will show God my heart and he will judge. There is much at stake, my soul, my name, but above all, Elias, my home!" He held up his rifle. "But as long as I have this, I might go home again! Don't you want to go home again, Elias, home to your Sally, to your land?"

At Jon's vigorous gesture, Elias fell silent. A snag in his throat blocked speech and he swallowed hard. He managed a meager, "Yes." It was always Jon's gift to inspire with words, but something in his eyes shone brighter. Some new spirit had taken hold in him.

Elias wanted to go home, and home was just a few miles away, beyond Stones River. He looked to the northwest, up the railway tracks leading to his childhood playground.

"Right over there!" yelled Jon.

Elias clutched Jon by the sleeve. "There is nothing between us now and I am glad of it! You're a good man for coming to me, Jonny!" He paused, fighting the lump in his throat. "If you choose to charge with me, my old friend, then I will be honored to have you in the ranks!"

"I choose it, without permission, of course!"

"Hell, Jonny, I'm a lieutenant, I'll write up a temporary transfer so you will have no issues with your brigade. Soldiers get caught in bad places all the time!" Elias walked Jon over to meet his men and he introduced him. "Men, this is my cousin from Nashville, Jon B. Lyhton, who has sworn to fight for Tennessee. He is our guest today."

Some of the men chuckled at Elias' humor and greeted Jon with handshakes. He recognized a few familiar faces from town and made sure to say hello, a gesture which eased his mind and made him comfortable. His name was familiar to some, thanks to his father's political reputation and years of good business.

With Elias in front leading the platoon, Jon took his place in the ranks, shoulder to shoulder with his native Tennesseans and men of the Nashville surrounds. They stood at attention and were ordered to fix bayonets, spiking their lines with the pointed teeth of steel.

So it was decided. Jon put himself at the mercy of the Almighty and the Yankees. If he passes through this sacrificial deed, then the innocence he craves will be his. *If I die, then God will take me as a forgiven man.*

Jon looked out into the fields, spotted by tree clumps and broken fences, and out further, the area cleared of obstruction where high grass waited, ripe for trampling. The hill stood 1,000 yards distant, in a partially wooded area, and fogged with steady rain and mystery. On the top, Yankee flags moved about to signal the last-second maneuvering of regiments. *Move 'em all you like. I believe nothing will stop us now.*

Looking to the near left, Semple's Alabama battery roared away, sending in an announcement of the artillery's passionate belief in the cause. Lieutenant Pollard yelled orders to reload, while the crew sponged and cleared the guns for another turn. Jon was glad that young William Charles had been assigned to the opposite flank. He had plenty to live for, a lovely belle, a good name, and a future without dishonor.

In the lines, soldiers prepared, and stuffed cotton, wool, or anything into their ears as the noise grew into a painful din. Jon stood tall, holding his rifle and marveling at the smoke curling around the cannoneers like protective tails of dragons. The bronze beasts breathed fire and spit iron as their wheels cut the earth in recoil. The sounds and sights calmed him and he fell into poetic thought...*All is made right now. By God and man, it is. At last I will be redeemed for my misdeed. There will be honor in it.*

The Army is in perfect order and insults the enemy. Generals Hanson and Breckinridge stand there on the rise and fear not death, nor the death of a thousand of their men. We can move forward now, with all the confidence of our country and the pride of our veterans. Yes, we can run over this field, up that hill, and then home. Home. I wish that, Lord, I do.

Jon looked over the regiment; they were men from his locality.

These men have spent too many lonely nights away from their homes, families, and livelihoods. Today I will live, or die, with Tennesseans.

We will all make it right again, oh Lord, I will. Lord, your will be done. Death stings me not, nor does regret. Only one tear shall I

*shed. For you, my dear Bethanna, I did truly love. Did I ever tell you
my true feelings, which have grown more in absence than in our short
time together? It is good that you remember me as a bright lad and a
hero than a murderer. I should have seen your purpose, your warnings
for me. Oh dearest, do not love me as I was. But you will know what
I did here this day. You, and the country will know.*

At this thought, he pulled out her letter from his inside pocket
and decided to look upon her soft handwriting one last time.

Dearest Jon,

> *I am moved to write you by the compassion of the Holy
> Spirit. My heart aches, as I have heard of the Army's sufferings
> from the long march and I pray for your safety. I attempted to
> find you in the camps and I failed with much illness. Now I hear
> of your regiment moving and I do not know where. To remember
> you often, I read your poetry book and find that it is comforting,
> like being near you.*

> *Have peace, my dearest, for I am here in Knoxville, at
> Hinchel's Inn. He is my uncle. Mirra and I are safe, away from
> Taldorf and the raiders. Here, I attend the prayer meetings, where
> we talk of God and his love in Jesus. He showed me a vision.
> Please be aware of the danger you face. I believe you will see a
> great battle and be tested by Satan. Be on guard and pray for
> God's good judgment. You protected me, so now I must protect
> you in what little ways I can.*

> *I am not a great poet, but I will try to say things right. Jon,
> you must know that my love for you is true and because of you, I
> know what it means to love. I was a girl in the valley and now I
> am a woman who loves you. Many times a day, I think of your
> words, your care, and your kiss. Please write me when you can,*

that I may not only dream of these things, but hear them again, from your heart. God bless you and keep you.

Forever I am yours, with faith,

Bethanna

Jon lay down his rifle and took off the blue overcoat. He tossed it aside.

* * *

CHARGE OF BRECKINRIDGE'S DIVISION

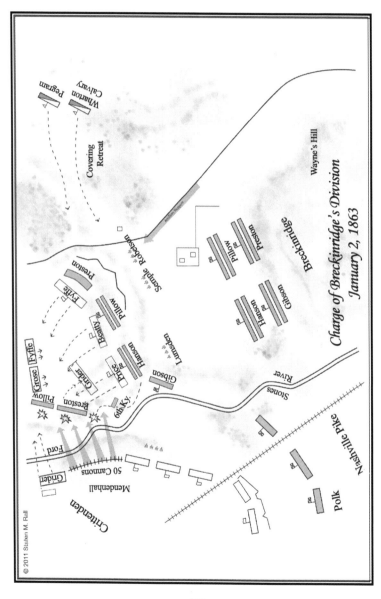

CHAPTER 28 ★

Private William Charles stood on the west bank of Stones River and gazed in wide fascination at the grand spectacle taking shape before him. On the rise opposite his position, neatly packed lines of men marched to the smart taps of drums. His heart was in the action though he was physically removed from it. Semple's artillery battery had once again been divided, as it was on the first day of battle, and Will, feeling a bit cast off but lucky, was anxious over the fate of his friends.

Hanson's Kentuckians moved with precision up to the top of Wayne's Hill. Fluttering over the lines in the gray haze were their distinct flags of blue, emblazoned with blood-red Christian crosses, filled with white stars. Will witnessed General Hanson, stately and proud, attending his command mounted on his horse. He rode down the line to their flank and gazed across the river, inspecting the Federal line of fire to his front. His horse jaunted to and fro, as an expectant boxer waiting for the first of many rounds. General Hanson held the beast in check as he gave directions to waiting couriers.

Smoke from the previous cannon fire blended with the low clouds. This unnatural fog drifted over General Hanson's troops and down the slope of Wayne's Hill, eventually to catch in the trees and settle on to the river. The troops were shrouded momentarily in a ghost-land world, hidden from Will's sight. As the cloud enveloped him, he waved at the thick smoke—sulfuric, acrid. Then he heard the signal gun fire from the far side of the hill; one single note to start the orchestra.

When the smoke had cleared, Hanson and his troops were gone, having started down the hill to the plain. An artillery unit moved in behind them and began to unlimber. From the distance at which Will observed, the guns were moved with such precise ease, as a boy shifts his playthings into the most dramatic posture.

Soon the battery resounded with the familiar commands, shouted by officers and answered by the gun crews. Will jumped at the first blasts of the massed cannons. It surprised him. He laughed at himself, having been mesmerized at the beauty of precision, set amid the languid haze.

In a clear and heightened state of mind, he remembered Wordsworth.

> Forever, and to noble deeds give birth,
> Or he must fall to sleep without his fame,
> And leave a dead, unprofitable name-
> Finds comfort in himself and in his cause
> And, while the mortal mist is gathering, draws
> His breath in confidence of heaven's applause:
> This is the happy Warrior; this is He
> That every man in arms should wish to be.

* * *

Bertram did not understand his dying brother's last outcry. He looked at Bethanna, her hands shaking, bloody. Chaplain Lovejoy, in a fretful trance, stared alternately at all present. Stokes turned away from his dead comrade, cleared tears from his eyes and addressed Bethanna.

"'Tis a sad way to leave earth, cursing a name as Mr. Lyhton's. But you, ma'am, know the name?"

"Yes, I do know Jon Lyhton" she said.

The name brought Lovejoy into the urgent moment. He recalled the sad figure of Jon walking away to atone for his secret murder and there was nothing to stop it. He stood gaping, speechless at the unrepentant, loathsome Riles, who had twisted Jon's conscience into suicide. He hesitated to speak, seeing Bethanna's distress. But the name was aired, and he felt for the girl. "I have seen him," he confessed, some color returning to his face. "this very afternoon. A Tennessee man, sandy-brown hair, greenish eyes?"

"Yes!" Bethanna stepped to him quickly. "Where? In God's name, where is he now?"

"I saw him at a prayer service out near the lines. The men, they... " he stopped.

"Thank the Lord in Heaven." Bethanna crossed herself, though it was not in the correct order. Riles' blood on her hands alerted her to something, that almost went over her head.

"Why does this man," she pointed to Riles, "accuse Jon of, killing *him*?" She then pointed to Bertram.

Bertram frowned. He looked at Stokes. "You thought I was killed by this Jon man?"

Stokes shook his head. "No sonny, Riles did. He thought this Lyhton fella did it. Riles had some suspicion about him drudged up in his mind. But since you're here, that would mean Mr. Lyhton ain't so guilty like Riles thought." He rubbed his long mustache. "Poor fella, Riles had him on the scare pretty good too, I'm afraid."

"How scared, exactly?" Lovejoy asked.

Stokes looked at the dead Riles. "Enough to put the fear into him that he would be a hunted man. We even got the captain loose over it for a time, till the shellin' started. I suppose he deserves quite an apology for such a badgerin'."

"Apology?" Lovejoy almost laughed. "This will need more than just an apology. A man's soul and life are about to be forfeit for this mishap, this cruel mistake."

Bethanna did not like the chaplain's certainty. "What do you mean, soul and life?"

"Well, I believe there has been a grave misunderstanding in Jon's mind, eh… and it has taken over his whole being. He spoke to me of this situation like a crime and being guilty of a murder. He gave the impression that the case was not his. I suspected it was; now we all see that it was *he* that needed help. I think because of this guilt, he has gone and done something drastic to make up for it." Lovejoy paused, and then was sure of his gut feeling. "I believe that he will sacrifice himself on the battlefield."

Bethanna stared at him. "But, you cannot know this is true."

Lovejoy spoke of the planned attack, the Kentuckians, Tennesseans, and Mississippians at the prayer meeting. He ushered the others out of the tent as more patients were brought in and Riles' body was taken away. Before they walked out, the stewards asked Bertram if he wanted the remains. He said no, for a reason.

When Bertram left the hospital tent, the smell of open bodies lingered in his nostrils and his brother's blood ran from his fingertips. He shook and burst out in weeping. He cried for the sad sudden loss of his brother, while soaking in a strange, guilty relief. He was free.

Riles had overindulged his role as older brother and caretaker. There was not a step Bertram didn't make that Riles did not fuss over. In the Army together, there was no room to stand out and become an individual. It was always "little brother Bert." With this sort of moniker, he could not excel or fail without the voice of big brother Riles telling how he did it.

Bertram was smart and perfectly capable of concrete thought, so one night he decided to leave his shackled existence. In the confusion after the battle, while Stokes, Riles and Charlie were at the campfire, he ran off to scavenge, or so he said. Actually, he worked his way to the rear and headed for Murfreesboro.

Perhaps Riles would never find him. What better place to go missing than a dark battlefield, where lost soldiers are never seen again. Maybe the officers would list him as missing. He wanted to fight—he even liked the Army—but not with his oppressive brother. Even the shame of desertion was better than living in a sibling's prison, formed over years of capitulation to the other's iron will. Luckily, he was wounded during his night escape when he fell flat on exposed rocks and badly cut his arm in several places. Joining the long lines of wounded was a better option than he had hoped for.

It was over now. He stood in the muddy street a free spirit, but somewhat of an orphan with no place to go. The rain blended in with his tears and washed the blood from his hand. Riles was angry, mad till the end. That's what hurt Bertram more than anything.

Despite his brother's unflinching hatred, he saw a hope forming, an unexpected good. In his very last breath, Riles had cursed, but perhaps saved this Jon person. Bertram decided that his brother's damnations would not win out. He wanted to make it right. Because of Riles' rash actions, a man needed to be saved and if he could save Jon Lyhton, perhaps he could do something worthy for himself, and help this love-torn girl. For it was too late for Riles.

Stokes, joyful that one of the Mullibey brothers still lived, took off for regimental head-quarters with Bertram's statement and a signature from one of the Doctors about Riles.

Standing in the rain like stranded passengers, Chaplain Lovejoy, Bethanna, and Bertram waited for the answer to drop out of the pale sky, each one juggling the past few moments around in their heads in shock and in silence. The same question loomed over them, overwhelming their small roles in the world and in the life of Jon Lyhton. *How do you save someone from death?*

Lovejoy motioned them over to the raised sidewalk. A pair of wagons cut the mud behind them. The chaplain strained for wisdom, something to rattle his mind, but there came no brilliant solution. "There is nothing in my soul that compels me. I can only pray for Jon, as we all should. He is in God's gracious hands."

Bethanna frowned under her hood. She felt, for the first time, anger toward God. She stifled it, but it lingered, because she could not feel or sense the outcome of this cruelty Jon was entangled in. *What about my faith, Lord, has it counted for nothing? How could I come this far and fail?* But now, there was nothing she could do.

The vibrations of a new bombardment rolled under their feet, heavier and longer than the others that morning. Bethanna's eyes glazed over in fear. "My God, it has begun."

She walked away from the men, towards the church. Lovejoy and Bertram looked on as she staggered slightly, almost drunk with confusion.

"She has been a good servant here," said Bertram. "Pity she has to suffer this."

Lovejoy nodded. "It's sad that the two did not meet here as the Army prepared. Now, I doubt if they will again." They walked slowly, following Bethanna to the church.

Bethanna reached the arched doorway and ducked inside. Under her wool hood, she began to tremble as the vibrations of cannons unnerved her. Her lips shook with fear at the low ominous booms, which to her, sounded like the opening of hell. Its ravenous maw would swallow the earth, the troops and all hopes. It was not stopping; the attack will go forward.

Inches away from her face, the rain fell in a long, thin waterfall from the roof. The fast stream blurred her vision. She went cold inside and could feel Jon's soul being torn away from hers. "Jon?"

She said, in a foggy whisper. "Please, Lord, have mercy on him."
Again, the rumble of the guns echoed in the doorway. She shook
her head, denying their destructive power. "No," her voice rose in
anger. "You cannot take him!"

Bringing her hands up, she saw Riles' blood and gasped. She
washed her fingers in the icy run off, cleaning away the red stains
as the steady drone of rain entranced her. She began to listen and
in the downpour, she heard an odd sound. She walked through
the waterfall to the sidewalk and stood, staring out into the
street, straining to hear. It was singing—no, different than that—
familiar and growing in intensity. No one else around seemed to
hear it. Glancing quickly at Bertram and the chaplain, she saw no
reaction from them.

Lifting her hood, she walked into the street, the rain wetting
her hair and face. She heard distinctly, the sound from her vision,
thousands of men screaming as they ran into battle. Death was
winning, Satan triumphant.

She covered her ears with her hands and collapsed to her
knees. "Lord, why must I hear him die?" she cried to heaven. A
few yards away, a man was surprised by her outburst and when
he saw the face of the young lady, he drew a breath and stopped
short. He ran to her. Cawley lifted Bethanna from the mud.

* * *

The Kentucky Orphans stepped off into the rolling fields.
To their right marched the Tennessee brigade of General Gideon
Pillow. Second in line from the left, followed Colonel Randall
Gibson's brigade of consolidated Louisiana regiments and the
32nd Alabama.

On the right marched General Preston's troops consisting of
three Florida regiments, the 1st, 3rd and 4th, then the 60th North
Carolina. On the right flank of this brigade, marching into

uncertainty, was the 20th Tennessee. Five thousand infantry, plus the artillerists, had stepped onto the field of honor and blood.

The 20th regiment and the whole brigade moved as one man, steady, determined and immovable from its straight course. Jon had a perfect view from his place on the extreme right and rear of the formation. The distant blue flags of the Kentuckians anchored the left flank, now nearing the curving river. His heart leapt at the bravery of Hanson's men. At the very apex of danger, the "Venerable blood of Boone" marched into history once again.

Long sweeping lines of infantry, half a mile wide, barely fit into human view. Jon had to turn his head to take it all in. Each line, ornate with battle flags, stretched into long human walls, fenced with the steel of bayonets. Drums tapped out the cadence of step. A nearby drummer picked up the beat, and the martial air grew thick with the sound of thousands of footfalls pounding the subservient earth.

To the front, Jon saw the colors of another Tennessee regiment, the 18th, in line with Pillow's brigade, leading the way to the enemy. To the right, he heard the musket and pistol pops of General Wharton's cavalry skirmishing with the enemy's exposed flank.

The Confederate grand advance brought expected attention from the enemy; cannon balls and rifled shells were sent out to greet them, noted by the sure whine of incoming rounds. Jon gripped his gun and prepared for the hell to proceed. His mind cleared, as if his thoughts were erased from a slate board. He freed his memory and his conscience, and could not see the past, even if he wanted to. It was gone. No yesterday, only now; smoke and war. To go home or die, that was all.

The voluminous troop columns, loud cheers, and sweeping tide of men lifted Jon's spirit up and out into the openness of the field. All was resonant in purpose, history, and glory. He felt suspended now by the great will of God that had moved so mightily in the scriptures, calling men to great causes, forcing time to cease and chariots to descend. The feeling seemed to be worth death. Even now, he felt immunity from its sting. Or, if killed, then he was honored to be stricken from such a holy tide, if that's what God willed.

The death began in earnest as the Union gunners across the river unleashed their iron ammunition, cutting into the Confederate lines at an oblique angle. Hissing balls flew through the sky, over the river and into Breckinridge's division, slashing men from their positions, cutting them away forever from the day's final roll. Some went down in piles as rifled cannon shells struck the lines. Others left the earthly life without even a yell, as they were thumped randomly out of line by a bouncing round shot.

Jon heard the order for the quick step. The rattle of the drum ramped up into his heart, pounding into his ears with the falling shells. He jogged, keeping pace with Elias and the colors. There where obstacles. Soldiers hopped over broken fences, rock walls and bodies, like children jumping into hopscotch squares. More incoming shells crashed in.

Blasting into the 20th, two rifled shells rammed the ground, tearing earth and men with shards of iron. Jon stammered and fell. His head seemed to crack from the bangs. Ten or so men went down, most ripped apart, some wounded. Jon shot up and ran back into place, cursing the screaming shells. The gap filled, renewing order again as the troops held fast in tight lines. Surviving the test so far, Jon growled with satisfaction. He looked ahead up the gentle rise, where the Yanks waited to fire their hot bullets. How patient they were, and strangely quiet.

General Hanson's men moved ahead on the left and ran into terrible cannon fire. The arc of the river cramped their formations and compacted the left flank into an unwieldy mass. Overlapped and out of position, some regiments stalled. A major of the 2nd

Kentucky acted quickly. He reformed his regiment into columns and relieved some of the tangle. The trailing reserve did the same.

The Confederates had covered more than half of the dangerous ground that lay before their enemies. There was no sign of the complete slaughter that had haunted Breckinridge's mind as he was planning the assault. He rode out behind the center of the line and peered through his binoculars. His eyes, wide with excitement, flashed with the confidence of his men.

"They're gonna' do it! That's it, Roger, up and over man! Old Flintlock will carry the day!" His chest ached with the burdensome stress of command. *Will they falter at the top? God no, not after such bravery.* He ordered the reserve artillery forward. "All batteries up behind the assault!"

Closer and closer the gray and butternut troops came, reaching the gradual rise of the hill. Hanson led his men into a shallow swale, shielding them from the direct line of fire. The terrain feature allowed them to pull up to within a 150 yards of the enemy's position, un-harassed.

Up on the slope, the Union troops waited with an ever-increasing sense of peril. For most of the day, they had shivered in the chilled breeze and rain, stagnant in their positions. The rebels' blood was hot from their jog through constant cannon fire. The high ground favored the Union men but for once, the Confederates had the rare advantage of numbers. The Union artillery across the river had not depleted or stalled the strength of the attack and now the long lines of Confederates were enveloping the base of the hill, like a rising tidal wave ready to strike. The men in blue could only hope to out-gun them all. Then, the shelling from across the river stopped.

Most of the Confederate units had moved in behind the eminence of the rise so that the Union gunners could not see their clear targets. Fearing they would rain iron on their own men, the artillery was quickly halted. The Yanks on the hill braced. One of the units, directly in the path of Hanson's brigade, was the 8th Kentucky, a Federal unit from The Bluegrass State. The irony was not lost on them as their fellow statesmen marched straight at their lines.

With the Yankee artillery no longer thundering in, the Confederates double-timed their advance. Bugle calls rang and the officers yelled; the order of "charge" came from every officer and private. A searing scream overtook everything and men became furious with the rebel yell. The Orphan brigade rushed to the Union line.

A command echoed through the blue ranks, "Rise, aim." Three regiments rose and leveled their long muskets. "Fire!" A swath of lead tore into Hanson's men, shattering skulls and opening flesh. The officers rallied and pressed their men forward. The Confederates closed so fast that the Yanks could not manage another precise volley. The lines clashed in a gross blend of metal, bone, and yelling pain.

On the Confederate right flank, General Pillow's troops had now come within 200 yards of the Federal lines, which overlapped his far right flank, creating a dangerous enfilading position.

Col. Thomas Smith, commanding the 20th Tennessee, was ordered forward to cover the overlap. Moving smoothly to the front, the regiment pitched forward with the 18th in echelon.

Jon saw volley after volley spewing down the Union lines. To his left, the 18th Tennessee marched bravely under the sights of the blue troops, who stood firm behind a rail fence. The Yanks let loose a torrent of smoke and crackling flame. Lead slapped into bodies, men screamed their last words. The regiment stalled and took cover by lying flat on the hillside.

A Yankee regiment, posted near the road crossing the face of the hill, stood and fired into the 20th. The direct blast staggered them. Many troops went down unhurt, if only to avoid the open line of fire. From the ground, someone grabbed Jon's ankle and begged to be carried away from the murder. Jon attempted to stand but the badly wounded man tripped him. He landed on the blasted head of a dead lieutenant, and the corpse's face cracked in half like an over-ripe melon. Jon shouted in anger as he tried to right himself, but his foot slipped on the man's brains and he landed a knee in the wet, warm ooze. He yelled and bolted for the colors.

Elias jogged over to Jon. "Both of my sergeants are down. You're it! Follow my lead. The men will stay with us!" The regimental colors were brought up and the young Colonel Smith, only twenty-two years old, shouted to the nearby companies, "Give them one good volley and they will break! At the ready!"

The men stood against the hail of lead. Methodically and with care, they cocked their weapons. At the order, "Fire by rank," the front line kneeled and readied. "Fire!" 250 guns blazed, covering the slope with white smoke. "Rear rank, ready!" Jon held his aim steady on the hazy blue line. "Fire!"

Another 220 rifles rocked the hillside. Jon heard the results of their work. Screams and panicked yells echoed through the thick, white smoke. The Yanks answered with another sheet of lead and for the next few minutes, the two sides fired into each other with drill-like coldness. The 20th stepped forward with every volley, moving closer to the Yanks up the slope.

Most of the Union shots flew overhead, except the one that hit Colonel Smith. He fell to his knees, like a man punched in the gut. Elias ran to him. In severe pain, Smith tried to reclaim his feet. "Sir, stay down!" Elias yelled.

Smith stood anyway, his hip bleeding. "No! The men must charge *now*, we have the advantage *now*!" The colonel limped, crutching himself with his sword's blade. "We have to charge!

Look, the 18th is starting forward. We must move with them and secure this flank!"

The colors went down and the troops gasped in shock. The color barer had knelt to repair a tie on the staff and with great relief from the men, he stood up again ready to proceed. With the flag waving high, the regiment, from the center out, stood up, arising like hundreds of dead men coming alive with revenge, shouting, cursing, and proclaiming the day of salvation at hand.

Jon, too, cast forth his lot. "This is our ground by rights! Behold the invader and make him yield!" Some men repeated the words and fell in around the animated speaker, stabbing the air with pointed bayonets.

Colonel Smith, swaying with failing energy, yelled, "Now, forward with speed!" The troops regained their previous momentum and in a crowded mob, ran straight at the fence line.

The rebel gun smoke had drifted into the Yankees' faces and when they heard the screams from the other side of the opaque cloud, they stiffened, realizing that they had not stopped the advance. Through the swirling, foggy doom, a single red flag could be seen rushing at them, and hundreds of yelling faces breaking through the smoky veil. The shocked Federals fell away from the fence one by one, and then all together, they ran.

Jon reached the fence and paused, unsure of how to maneuver it. Then, like a wave, the whole regiment slammed into the posts and rails so that men and wood crashed to the ground in a cracking heap. Scrambling up, they moved on. Bullets ripped and whined around Jon's head, but he did not notice the danger. He joined Elias and the two led a contingent to the crest of the hill.

There, they witnessed a massive collision with the Union lines. Pitched battle crowned the top of the hill, like the white-hot steaming rim of hell itself. Jon reloaded and rapidly scanned the area. To the right, Hanson's men were trampling over a broad, tree-capped ridge sloping sharply out of view down to the river. To his front, the hill fell gently, covered in places by rocks and trees, into which, part of the routed Federal brigade had retreated.

The 20th Tennessee had little time to rest as the officers reformed the ranks and started their movement down the backside of the ridge, towards the river and the rattled Yankees. During this short lull, Jon finally noticed that his hat had been shot off and his haversack sported three bullet holes.

* * *

Witnessing this melee atop the hill was a newly commissioned lieutenant, assigned to the cavalry units of General John A. Wharton, stationed on the far right. His eyes widened at the spectacle arrayed before him, a large panorama of desperate charges and killing.

Lines of men, gangs, and mobs assailed the wooded heights while smoking shot fell into the trees from the supporting cannons. Decorated flags dipped in and out of the shrouded view. "Dear God, now they are into it," Stephan Gurtag said, captivated.

Like every green trooper new to battle, Stephan's last few days had been a brutal introduction to large-scale slaughter, inhuman suffering, and the cost of soldiering. On the first day, Wharton's men had maintained the left flank to the north and ran into hard resistance from dismounted Yankee horsemen protecting the Nashville Pike.

Colonel Parker's 23rd Tennessee battalion punched their way through to a line of supply wagons and Stephan's unit led the raid, making swift work of the guards. His horsemen rode freely through the Federal rear and terrorized the retreating troops, while Cleburne's division overran their scattered front.

Stephan relished the victory that evening as the cavalry enjoyed Yankee pickled herring, coffee, and fresh peas for dinner.

Their camps were located far from the enemy and the joy of warm fires cheered them, while their infantry brothers suffered in line and froze. Stephan led an early morning watch detail, but did not mind the duty, on a full stomach.

The second day of battle brought little action for him. Cavalry units scouted and surveyed the enemy in the dead spaces between skirmishes. That day, General Wheeler ordered Wharton's men to the far right of the field, over the river and beyond Breckinridge's command. Along with Pegram's cavalry brigade, they guarded the extreme right flank and pushed back any probing by the Yankee pickets.

Now, near the embattled hill, Stephan witnessed the final assault and he had no mad desire to join it. He spurred his horse and rode to the command group gathered near a grove. There, he found Colonel Parker at ease and smoking a cigar astride his black horse. Stephan saluted. "Sir, are we to support the attack?"

Parker raised an eyebrow. "I have no direct orders from Breckinridge. I have no direct orders from General Wharton, only to cover Preston's flank, there on the right. Now they are mostly out of sight and shrouded. I won't ride into that confused wrangle without full knowledge of the situation. So, Lieutenant, we shall stay here."

"Absolutely, sir." Stephan admired the colonel for his leadership, and his willingness to protect his men, even unto protestations. Yet, around Parker there lay sadness, not over war, but other things, that if one listened, could find out. Stephan listened and learned.

Bronn C. Parker, thirty-four years old, lean and aristocratic, was a Knoxville lawyer before the war and ran for a Senate seat in the new Confederate Congress. He suddenly withdrew his candidacy when Tennessee was threatened by the unstable border-states Missouri, Kentucky, and West Virginia. He joined the cavalry and drilled the new recruits so well that he was promoted to captain.

Parker drank on occasion, frequently alone, but never during the fighting. Many of his men said that he never fully accepted the death of his lovely child bride. As the story goes, a nineteen year old Belle approached Parker after a church service and swore herself to the morale of the gallant Southern cavaliers. The gesture touched him so deeply that he called on the young woman frequently and soon openly courted her, with the adoring parents' permission. They were married in three months and lived as a popular couple until March of 1862, when she died giving birth. The son lived.

Sad were the days and nights for many a man away from family, and without his wife and home, the time was even sadder still, as the case for Colonel Parker, a lesson Stephan paid close attention to. Darlene could have been his loving wife, but he had turned her into a whore. There was still his cousin, Bethanna, in Knoxville. This thought burned his heart, and he knew she was the right choice; challenging, but right.

The guns blazed from a nearby battery and Stephan thought he saw the Confederate infantry breaking through over the rise.

* * *

In the church, Bethanna paced, impatient. Her question to Cawley was direct and he bent under the pressure of her steel gaze. "He's out there fighting. I'm sure of it," he said. Kicking his leather brogans together, he sat uneasily on the front pew.

"Explain why you allowed this to happen?" She asked sharply.

"Uh, cause he's the sergeant."

Bethanna shook her head, dissatisfied with the answer. Bertram stood over the sheepish Cawley and patted his shoulder. "Can you tell this is sure information?"

"Yep," he said. "I know when Jon gives me orders, he's serious."

Lovejoy interjected, "I'm sure it is true."

The choir loft floor creaked as he stepped down. "He has been convicted of sin, even though, by all obvious facts, a sin he did not commit. In his mind, he is guilty. If this is something he has not dealt with before, then it's an overwhelming, oppressive feeling."

"What do you think it has done to him?" Bethanna asked.

Lovejoy rested against the loft rail and thought. "It could crush his will to live. Yes, could be so. But he does have a spirit of repentance and sacrifice, which is good," he said, nodding to himself.

Surprising them all, Bethanna slapped a pew arm. "Repentance? Sacrifice? For what! You are talking like this is ending very nicely, like it is over now!" She approached the chaplain. "There is something of the devil in this! He has been cruelly assaulted by evil and you want to be contented with sacrifice? Do you know him? Have you felt his kindness? How could you judge?" Her eyes glistened wet. "I have seen how he leads his men." She motioned to Cawley, who was working up his own tears. "I have seen his bravery and strength. What do you know?"

Lovejoy frowned. "Then if he is filled with such merit, he will be welcomed in heaven, what else can we do or say?"

Bethanna bit her lip and lifted her face to him, her eyes wide with fierce emotion. She took a breath and said, "Do you have no pity, man of God?"

Her words twisted Lovejoy. He raised his voice. "I took pity when he asked me to bless his dying friend! I took pity when he did not confess to God, but Jon Lyhton did not show any for himself, or anyone else, when he left on his...errand!"

Bethanna gasped. She stared at Lovejoy's reddish face.

The chaplain regretted his outburst, but it had to be said and with authority. "He has misunderstandings about what God wants. Jon has placed himself under God's judgment now."

Bethanna put a hand to her heart, the other to her head. She turned away, walked to the dark mahogany alter and fought the urge to break down. Closing her eyes, she breathed deeply to relax her tensed body.

Cawley, well into his grief, mumbled under his sniffing.

Lovejoy crossed his arms and hung his head down.

Like curious cats, a few soldiers heard the exchange and raised their heads to view the verbal combatants. It was the only interesting thing that had happened all day and recognizing Bethanna's voice, Cale scratched his spiky hair and waited for the discussion to continue. Wrapped in bandages, his eyeless, mummy-like visage looked around casually.

Shaking her head, Bethanna reeled inside. She was angry now. Not at God but at her own weakness of faith, a faith that had brought her here, over hundreds of miles. It was no small miracle that Riles named Jon. God had not failed her. She looked up into the church windows. A stained glass Madonna looked down at her dead son as she held him in her arms. "Reverend, you might understand God's judgment, his mercy and love, but you do not understand mine. I will go to him."

Lovejoy cocked his head, eyes wide. "Excuse me?"

She continued, "If God wants Jon, then I will surrender him, but not before he sees my face. I will find him."

"I'll take you," Bertram said, standing quickly. "I have to undo what my brother has done. If there is any way to reach him, I will try."

"I'll go, too!" yelled Cawley, standing and thumping a foot on the wood floor.

Bethanna walked to Cawley and wiped his teary cheeks. "You are so faithful to him. I love that." She embraced the shorter man.

Lovejoy stepped over to Bethanna. He went to pull her arm, but held back. In a voice of sadness he said, "It will break your heart."

He donned his kepi and overcoat, nodded to the men, and left. Standing outside, he leaned his back hard against the stone wall in frustration. The battle echoed through the low, gray sky and he thought how brave and foolish Bethanna was. He did not like to set his will against the young girl, for her devotion moved him, and her heart was indeed beautiful while his was estranged from such mercy.

Bethanna's strong emotional pleas reminded him of a woman's sensitivity and how his wife had the same devotion to him, and now he had tossed away that devotion because of self-isolation. How she must be distressed and hurt, not knowing about him, never a word for many weeks. Still, she did not come looking for him, all the way from Pennsylvania. That would be ridiculous.

What kind of love moves a girl to a battlefield? Indeed, her devotion spoke some good of Jon. He must be worth it and although he walks now under a very dark cloud, he clearly sees his error and aims to correct it, spiritually. Yes, looking in Jon's eyes, Lovejoy saw a ray of genius, if only darkened by his guilt. That guilt itself spoke well for Jon, also. But in all practicality, a man admitting murder on a battlefield was akin to a groom confessing lust on his wedding night: both extremes fell under legal precedent.

Before the chaplain returned to the wounded, he decided to make up for his errors and write a fast telegram to his family, to be sent after the battle when the Union lines were re-established, hopefully. He walked into the muddy street, with the battle droning in the distance like stacked thunder and a high-toned sound like waves crashing.

* * *

CHAPTER 29 ★

The noise atop the small hill had swelled to a deafening roar as the 8th Kentucky Federals grappled with the Southern men from their own state. In a crowded hand-to-hand, point-blank fight, muskets went off into faces, bayonets stabbed, and men fell underfoot, where they were caught in a perpetual trample. General Hanson's second line charged units of the adjoining Union regiment, the 51st Ohio, and they broke. Thus the Union 8th Kentucky lost its flank, and the whole lot began to run down the opposite slope toward the river.

The men of the 9th Kentucky regiment were stationed in reserve, directly in route of the fleeing blue troops. They stood stoic with two other regiments as the routed right flank passed through their lines. Then before they knew it, Hanson's whole brigade came down upon them.

A new clash echoed up the river as the combatants poured bullets into each other at devastating range. Massive clouds of low rolling smoke covered the field and the middle ground became a cauldron of steaming flame, bravery, and mayhem. The Yankees took the worst of it. Fire from up the slope rained down on them from several directions.

At this same time, a detachment of Hanson's men, the 6th Kentucky, had skirted a small bluff on the riverside of the hill and popped out on the Yank's extreme right. When these troops opened up with a storm of lead, the blue lines faltered. The fierce battle for Kentucky was being fought here, on a 100-yard wide expanse of ground on the east bank of Stones River.

An unexpected victory was in plain sight. With one Union brigade routed and another about to crack, General Hanson saw the possibility before him. His men pressed every inch of the lines, and soon McFadden's Ford would be in their control. They had only to cross the river and take the entire Yankee Army from the rear. Jubilant, and riding close to the action, he drew in a proud breath at the marvelous spectacle.

Union cannoneers noted the retreat of their fellows and fired at the newly exposed Confederate ranks on the opposite bank. Their shells exploded into the Orphan brigade, and General Hanson pushed his men forward. His horse traversed the slope, galloping from one detachment to another as he carried his master into the heart of battle. Two close explosions jarred the beast and Hanson felt his leg burn at the thigh. Another round landed nearby, knocking over his horse and landing him hard on the earth.

Swarming around the fallen brigadier, panicked aides and staff officers yelled to relocate the stricken Hanson to the safe side of the ridge. "Nothing is safe here!" yelled one man. "To the trees!" shouted another as he freed Hanson from his bleeding horse. Staff officers carried the stunned general to a copse of trees, just out of sight of the Union cannons. Seeing the commotion, General Breckinridge rode up to examine the gathering and grew pale at the sight of his wounded subordinate. He dismounted and stood over the fading Hanson. "Roger, steady goes it. Let them treat you, please."

Hanson sat up and saluted. "Treat me for what?" he said, down-playing the mortal wound. "Tell Bragg, Kentucky has led the way." He dropped his arm. Blood pooled on his torn leg and he looked at the spreading stain, embarrassed, as if he had spilled coffee on himself. Breckinridge, too emotional for controlled response, gripped hands with Hanson. He smiled sadly and left the scene despondent.

Charging into mortal history, the 20th Tennessee chased down two more regiments of Union infantry. Jon threw himself headlong into the human wave, encircling the unsupported 23rd Kentucky Federal troops and the 24th Ohio. Without artillery support on the far side of the hill, the isolated Yankees where doomed to suffer under the coordinated assault of General Preston's massed brigade.

Popping out of the tree line, the 20th Tennessee crashed into the waiting Federals, who went into them hand to hand. Jon waited for a clear shot, but in a blur, he saw a lone Yank running wildly straight at him through the mixed troops. With no hesitation, Jon brought his rifle butt down and bashed the man's temple, sending him toppling over to the ground. Without pause, Jon bayoneted him. The act recharged his heart with more adrenaline.

Elias emptied his pistol into the faces of three men and at a young man, almost a boy, pelting him right in the nose. The boy in blue fell over backwards as his feet flew up. Jon and his Nashville chums sliced, kicked, and punched in the close combat, a short but filthy melee.

The men from Ohio stood it as long as humanly possible, which at this stage, no human should have been standing. The blue troops retreated and tried to reorganize, reload, and bring an effective volley to bear on their pursuers, but the 20th gave them no time.

A running fight turned into a rout and Jon fired a shot into the back of a fleeing Yank. The man fell, writhing in agony, his hands tugging at the copper-tinted grass. Jon stood over him and patiently reloaded as the dying man bled out. The victim's face retained the expression of the shock and unbelief of his horrid ending.

The artillery batteries of Lumsden, Robertson and Semple, who had been stationed behind the infantry, climbed the contested hill and unlimbered on the crest to support the troops below. Lieutenant Pollard sighted the first shot from the Semple's battery. "Fire!"

The canister shot landed amongst the fleeing Yankees scurrying across the river.

"I'm sure that Holt, Will, and Joe Goode are biting mad for missing this!" Pollard shouted to a private clearing the vent. They shared a smile as the other guns blasted away.

With the way clear, the 20th Tennessee and the rest of Preston's brigade pushed northwest to the river. Elias and Jon moved together, both of them black to the pores from nonstop action. The powder, sweat, blood, and small bits of human tissue blasted onto their coats, made them appear demonic, as some form of beast not yet known to the journals of science or the annals of war. The regiment cleared a lightly wooded area and in their immediate front appeared the river ford, crowded with splashing Federals. The way was open and the iron hot. Some of Hanson's men were standing in the river, shooting the panicked Yanks like trapped ducks.

"Look, Jon!" yelled Elias. "The whole goddamn lot!"

"All in one big boodle, too!" Jon said.

At this point in the fight, the enlisted men took over from the generals. Intoxicated by victory, individual units, platoons, battalions, and regimental size formations piled up on the riverbanks. There was one place to go. With all the precision of a yard full of mice, the gray troops dashed into the cold, knee-deep water and splashed their way over, firing and yelling to the enemy's side.

Jon ran out from under the sparse trees and blended into what was now a flowing mob. A few steps away, Elias pointed to the riverbank, and shouted, "There is our way, Jonny!"

It seemed the enemy had vanished and there was nothing more to do but clear the Nashville Pike, only a short jog west from the river.

Merging into the blended mass of troops were units from Preston's Florida Regiments. Jon followed a two-flag color guard and ran with them, until in clap of flame the men were hurled in all directions, wounded and killed. One flag was picked up instantly and raised high. Jon stopped and waited for assigned men to raise the other grounded flag. None came. He reached down and grasped the wood shaft. A swell of pride surged through him as he lifted the noble colors overhead. At the same time, he dropped his rifle, as if in an instant, the weapon had been made obsolete. Re-gripping the staff in both hands, he waved it in a circle, which exposed the full battle flag to the troops running wild around him.

Soldiers clustered near the visible rally point and Jon could see a shudder of awe rise in the prideful men. With the flag in his grasp, he was a million times more powerful. Now at last, his full soul poured out—the evil, hate, bitterness and love, regret too—all the damn sin of a lifetime came through his blood and possessed him wholly.

Nothing was too sick, perverse or unreal to ever shake him now. He was facing the reaper and taunting him. He yelled incoherently in a crazed, hoarse voice of revenge as his eyes flashed wide with terror, and all the majesty of victory raked his flesh in the tingling burn of life. Upon his knightly, bearded face shone the bright hope of youth and the red anger of a righteous saint. He yelled, "Come on home boys! Come on home!"

A wild yelp ensued and with a run, the whole mob went tearing off for the riverbank. In the confused, piecemeal charges, Jon and

Elias didn't notice that most of the 20th had reorganized to the right and marched on in some semblance of order.

This did not matter to the two reunited friends. They were the only soldiers on the field at this point. Bounding down the bluff to the river, their boyhood energy had returned, as it did with most of the pursuing rebels.

Union chief of artillery Captain John Mendenhall did not see it coming. The clear and sweeping destruction of the Federal positions across McFadden's Ford had been so swift and thorough that there was no time to organize any effective infantry stand. What he did see, prior to the engagement, was that by adding cannons to his position, his massed guns could protect the Union left on the extreme and hold any assault if it got out of hand. This one had. After retreating across the river, the routed Yanks were congregating under the trees on the slope, like ducklings seeking shelter.

To Mendenhall, positioned on a low ridge with his guns, there was no better opportunity than now. With his own infantry out of the way, and the opposite riverbank and hillside teeming with rebel infantry, he gave the order. Fifty-five guns boomed in order down the line in a beautiful thunderous symphony.

It may have been music to the huddled masses in blue, but for the rebels, the barrage crashed in like disharmonious bedlam, sending water and man parts skyward from the shallow river.

A complete shattering of the earth and soil surrounded the Southern forces as they froze in abject terror and surprise. At the peak of their victorious charge, they had become the most perfectly clear targets in military history as they flew and twisted into the air. Jon was just about to wade into the river when the abrupt bombing began. He fell to the ground, shielding his face from the bursting shells. Elias, too, skidded to a halt and dove down.

The very air moved around them, side to side, as the rounds landed on the bank. Jon peeked through his armpit and saw the whole hillside covered in smoke and exploding dirt. Two thousand confused and stammered men ran about with no direct leadership. He tried to find Elias and forcing himself to his knees, he looked for the flag. To lose it now would be a sin beyond all pardon. To his relief, a retreating soldier had scooped it off the ground. The boy waved it proudly, taunting the Yankee artillerists. Around this inspirational sight, Jon witnessed his fellow troops re-crossing the river in panic.

Elias yelled at the crowd running by him, "Hold you men, hold!" But it was impossible to hold against dropping iron. Jon punched Elias' arm, getting his attention in the crushing din. "Is that our own guns?"

Elias read Jon's lips and nodded. "I think so, maybe we ran under their range!"

Within seconds, it made no difference; the two were caught up in the mad rush to the rear. Up the peppered slope they ran, with the hundreds who had moments before conquered the ground with resounding victory.

Jon ran with the tide and then he stopped, falling in with some men standing fast with Confederate colors. Forming a line, they prepared to fire into a sure counterattack. He felt ashamed at having no weapon. The line disappeared with a flash of flame and smoke. Two bodies slammed into Jon and knocked him hard to the ground.

To his amazement, he wasn't hurt, but blood leaked from his ears. He shook his head, peered through the smoke and saw the men, cut up like dead hogs, heaped in piles. Oddly, the wounded men underneath dug themselves out from under their dead comrades and continued running. A man dove over him into a shallow ditch. It was Captain Hargis from the 20th, a local man from town. Jon pulled at his coat. "Where's the regiment?" he yelled.

Hargis looked confused, his face wet with tears. "Nowhere! Nowhere!"

Jon saw Elias laying a few yards down the hill. He was hurt, maybe dead. His leg was bleeding and his face bruised and head cut. Jon ducked and waited. He looked again for signs of life. Elias kicked his good leg. He was alive. *I won't leave you—never again—we will die together.*

Jon ran amid the incoming drop of iron shells and landed next to Elias. A load of fresh earth sprayed upon them. Yelling, mad, cursing troops ran past them. *So this is the end. This is how we end.* Jon rolled his friend over and pulled his arm up onto one shoulder.

"I knew it," said Elias. "You did come for me, you did!" Elias reached for him and Jon lifted his stricken friend up to his feet and helped him towards the trees on the top of the hill.

Another blast sent them down. Elias screamed. Jon dragged the wounded body over the ground, low and quick, into the trees at last, but not much safer. Falling cannon rounds shattered tree trunks, as shards of jagged splints slashed the fleeing troops from all directions.

Behind the two friends, a large plume of smoke engulfed the hill. Even without the sun, it cast a dark shadow over the land, as the earth erupted from the bombardment. Jon stared at the gross cloud, rising like a fire-pit devil, forming on the surface of the earth's crust and preparing to choke everyone to death.

How, he wondered, *can the enemy rally with such ferocity after our decisive blow?* Jon saw the hazy view of hundreds of men rushing by, running down the slope and returning to the fields from which they came. The Confederate artillery had taken a heavy beating. Dead gunners lay next to their abandoned caissons. Horse-pulled limbers rushed away to preserve their precious and un-replaceable guns, if horses were still living. There were some men in Semple's battery yelling at each other and dragging a dead officer. "Take Pollard's body, take him back!"

Pollard? The name was familiar to Jon. *Yes, Will Charles' hometown friend.* He'd just met him less than an hour ago. Attempting to focus, Jon's eyes burned as he viewed the artillerymen. The pain of bruising and fatigue overtook his cold wet skin. He sat against a torn tree and watched the world end. Elias looked very weak from his leg wound, a slashing fragment cut mid-thigh. Jon took Elias' belt and strapped the leg, slowing the blood. *I can't leave you. Not out here, in this lost and defeated space. I will carry you on.*

Jon stood, lifting Elias up at his shoulder. He wobbled, unsure of his own strength, but he persisted. They walked and rested while the Army retreated around them.

Through the mad scramble, they reached the road with the flattened fence. The waste of the South lay strewn over the hill and fields as bodies crawled, shook, or lay stiffening. The survivors walked like dejected, jilted schoolboys leaving a rained-out festival. Into this scene dropped random shells, insulting and wasted. Then a great cry arose behind the fleeing hoard. Jon turned to see who had cheered. *Was it the reforming of the division? Re-enforcements from Bragg?*

It was none of these. As Jon raised his eyes, he saw crowning the hill, a solid belt of blue. Fresh Union regiments joined those who had been routed, and they prepared to charge the confused mass of rebels. Eager to return the favor, the Yanks shot hot lead into the backs of running Southern troops.

Any organized Confederates turned to harass the advancing enemy, loading and firing in slow, military order. Those rebels who had no weapons could only turn to face the enemy and curse Yankeedom in general with hastened oaths.

From the east, beyond the right flank, Jon heard horses pounding the ground. "God no, we'll be taken for sure."

The flags of General Wharton's cavalry burst through the smoke and dismounted troopers began to deploy, covering the retreat. More mounted units rode up the hill to shock the new Union lines. They maneuvered in small bands and sniped at the blue troops with their pistols and carbines, in Indian fashion, making themselves hard targets.

With the extra relief from Wharton, Jon concentrated on moving to some sort of sheltered area. He pulled his feet through mud patches, losing a shoe to the spongy ground. The time dragged on and the slow pace created a sure dread around his escape. It played a sharp contrast to their grand charge, when the harsh details of action flashed by Jon so quickly, in a matter of seconds. Treading onward, he helped Elias to a stand of oaks and lay him down. "Rest, friend."

Elias nodded with a brazen smile. "You're the boss, Jonny boy."

Breathing became difficult now for Jon, as his throat burned with hot thirst. An explosion rocked the area, followed by two more bursts. Jon dove down, thinking the Federals had brought their guns over the river in a mighty hurry. Looking up, he saw that a Confederate caisson had exploded and turned into a hissing, burning hulk.

A flag bearer ran past, followed by a company of infantry, moving up to stem the Union counter attack. Jon searched for a weapon and saw a rifle in the grass near a patch of dead men. He hurried over to it and discovered that a bodiless hand, white and frozen, gripped the stock and trigger. Jon preyed it away without a thought and the appendage dropped to the grass.

He loaded, grabbing a paper cartridge from his box, biting it open and emptying the powder into the barrel. He rammed the bullet down. Priming the weapon with a cap, he half-cocked it.

This small resistance would not stop the vengeful Yanks, he knew. But it would end him, and since there was no victory, no hope of returning home, it was good to die.

He ran out into the open, chasing the colors, which were labeled in white letters of the 4th Florida. Only about forty men of their effective force remained in the area and Jon fell into their line. A captain with drawn sword and bandaged head shouted orders out in front, "Prepare to fire." The men halted. Jon's vision blurred, but with determination he worked his eyes over the gun's sight, searching for a definite target. A blue haze lingered at the end of his barrel. Men began to fall around him.

Like a thin string, a black line appeared over the terrain as a random cannonball bounced at full speed and then crashed into the captain's body, splitting it and splashing the line of men with his guts. The captain lay partially severed, shrieking.

Jon wiped his face, spitting out the gore from his mouth. He looked up and over to the other men. They stared at something in the grass. He froze when he saw the cannon ball, still intact, its fuse burning. The men stood shocked, waiting for the expected blast. Jon looked away. He closed his eyes, and in that slow moment before death, did not feel scared, only horribly alone.

Jon's vision went black as his body lurched in the shockwave.

* * *

CHAPTER 30 ★

In a farmer's wagon, hastily converted into an ambulance, Bethanna held fast to a leather grip hanging overhead, which helped steady her in the bouncing cart, but hurt her wrist with a continuous pull. The ride was rougher than she expected as she sat most uncomfortably on an overturned bucket. With the other hand, she held two lanterns between her feet. More supplies lay in a burlap sack on the ambulance litter. Without judgment, she appreciated the talents of Cawley and Bertram in scavenging the needed equipment. It amazed her with such a large Army, how much troops had to do on their own. Their rummaging skills served them well.

Stealing glances out of the canvas flap, she saw pale smoke floating by in broken clouds. Moving ever closer to the battlefield, her heart began to surge and beat with new excitement as the wagon neared the sure dark pit of war. It would be a horrid thing and there was only one way to prepare for it. She released a simple plea,

> Lord, you are the mighty warrior,
> you go before me and clear the way.
> Let your light find Jon this day, Lord.
> Give him up to mercy, oh God.
> Let him not suffer the final darkness if he leaves this place.
> Lord, accept him, he is worthy of it. Amen.

Bertram drove the team of two horses from the bench and maintained an even gait. Cawley sat next to him eying the increasing haze—part smoke, part twilight fog—forming over the adjacent fields. In the distance could be seen a large, storm-like cloud, hovering over the trees. By the sound of it, the battlefield was very near. Bertram stopped the cart, it settled and they heard the pounding of guns and felt the shock of artillery under their seats.

Bethanna rested her arms in the still cart, rubbing them. She shuddered when the cart jumped forward. Bertram turned off the northbound Lebanon Pike and onto a road, heading west. The battle din droned louder as the wagon traveled a narrow farmer's road around a small rise and there, sounds of individual reports and explosions were heard distinctly from the crackle of small arms fire, which had dissipated in the last few minutes.

Bertram looked at Cawley, sizing him up. "That rifle loaded?"

"Yep."

Bertram nodded. "Good. Never know what we'll find out here."

After some time on the road, the first real signs of disaster began to show through the smoke. Clumps of men, dragging other men with them, became visible in the waning light. The echoing voices of the lost and dejected soldiers bounced around the lone cart creaking down the worn path, cutting into shrouded fields and smoky forests.

Cawley shivered as the ghastly moans drifted into the dark-blue cast scene. He checked his rifle again, hoisted it. "Look, the men are retreating, scattered all over."

Bertram pulled at the reigns and turned the horses slightly right, towards a barn located near a thicket of oak and cedar. The building was empty, stripped of many boards, but still functional. Bertram told Cawley to guard Bethanna while he walked up a short rise beyond the trees to have a look. Cawley pulled the cart into the dark barn. Bethanna crawled out, rubbing her bottom.

From the small ridge, Bertram gazed over the field, sprawling west towards the river. The sight made him gasp. Scattered remnants of the retreating Army crawled over their own dead to reach the safety of Wayne's Hill. There was not much of a Union presence visible to him, but a firefight was going on somewhere. So much smoke covered the area it was hard to see anything at a great distance. *Where can we start to look for Jon? Surely he is dead with all of this open slaughter. Even so, we must try.*

He saw in the open field a large fire burning, and in the flames, the debris of artillery wagons. To his immediate right, about 140 yards, was a clump of trees extending out into the trampled grass. Bertram figured they could use the trees as cover, search the near field and then find their way back to the barn, again using the trees as their pathway. "But night is dropping fast," he said, rubbing his chin.

He returned to the barn and explained to Bethanna and Cawley the lay of the land, and the obvious repulse of their assault. There was a moment of silence as they accepted the news. "We can wait until dark, which is almost here. Or head out now, search locally over that rise, then try again at dawn."

"We can't take the chance of leaving him out there all night," said Cawley.

"He is right," Bethanna said. "We brought lanterns and water. We must go now."

"That's another thing." He looked over his shoulder to where he viewed the contested fields. Bertram paused, touched Bethanna's arm. "I ain't so sure you should be out there, Miss Beth. This looks about as worse as any killin' I ever saw."

After a moment's thought, Bethanna said. "I understand you. But if he hears my voice, he will know me. I must believe this."

* * *

In a perfect flash of orange and white, Elias had seen the blast knock the line of men down like a row of pins and send them in high directions. He saw Jon fall with the rest of them, but he would not leave his old friend and cousin alone, because Jon had come to him, made peace, and did not leave him on that flaming hilltop. There was courage in Jon's act of forgiveness and of admitting fault. Elias had never shown such courage and in that moment when Jon had forgiven him, Elias' soul never felt weaker, or more hopeful for renewal.

Elias pushed himself away from the tree trunk and began to crawl, pulling himself forward with handfuls of grass towards the smoking hole in the ground. "Jonny!"

* * *

At the edge of the misty tree line, three wanderers appeared hesitant and small against the dark woods. Here, like on a barren shore, the safety of the trunks gave way to the plains of death, a fogged opaque abyss, moaning with pain. Night had fallen and in a short time the freeze was expected. The lanterns were lit; two small lights to find one man amid the wreckage.

Into the plain stepped the trio, single file and slowly walking, attentive to their glances and careful in their steps. The lanterns swayed over the scattered wounded, pouring a dim light onto their sullen features and the fixed stares of the dead. In the air, the searchers pitched soft addresses to the stiffened fallen.

"Jon. Jon Lyhton. Jon, that you?"

Some moaned in reply, answering to anyone who would call to them. Cawley was out front, being Jon's friend, familiar with his looks. He walked over to every groaning body, but shook his head. "Nope."

Wounds were intensely grievous and open. In the freezing air, skin and muscle contracted and cramped, doubling the pain for many. Until their limbs froze, the agony would persist. The further into the field, the worse the carnage grew and a whimper arose from behind Cawley and Bertram. It was Bethanna.

She stared down to her feet as she tried to avoid the unknown horrors that only soldiers know, and never tell those who can't understand. "Lord...why?"

"Miss Beth, give me your scarf there." She did, and Bertram tied it to his belt. "Hold tight to this here and shut your eyes if you want. Walk close to me and keep calling for Jonny."

Trailing close to Bertram like a blind beggar, Bethanna held the tied scarf. Although walking with her eyes shut, the gruesome images shot into her mind as another cry rose up from the frozen plain. "Please, let us help some of them."

"I'm sorry, Miss Beth, but we will be here all night if we do," Bertram said.

She knew it was true. "Jon?" she cried.

Cawley realized that they were nearing a burring pile of debris and if he could feed it, perhaps it would cast a stronger glow over the area. "Hey, Bert."

Bertram answered and walked up next to Cawley with Bethanna bumping into him. "We could stoke this fire and use it as a hub. Ya know, go out and come back, keep warm for hours."

The two men agreed and with girl in tow, walked on towards the fire's promise.

Pitching the splintered fragments of the caisson wheels and limber into the coals, the fire roared into new life. Bethanna sat and watched. Warm and tired, she gazed into the large flames, her eyes burning and watering at the fresh heat. Around them, the field glowed orange, illuminating a dozen more dead and wounded. Her nose filled with the bitter smell of gun smoke, burnt grass, and a foul stench tracing in the wind, reminiscent of cow guts.

Cawley and Bertram gave in to the pitiful pleas of the men. With mutual agreement they proceeded to drag in a few of the casualties that were still living. Bethanna gave them water. "Do you know Jon Lyhton?" she would ask them. No one said yes.

Cawley began the search again as he and Bertram took opposite sides of the fire, combing the outer extremity of the glow; beyond that, it was pitch black. They could see other fires, just dots of light through the mist or the bobbing of lanterns out in the plain.

A smattering of distant gunfire surprised Bethanna. She stood, wondering if the blue troops would come out of the blackness. An urgent fear shot through her that perhaps the fighting will resume, with lines of troops charging and trampling the maimed, and her. She walked to the edge of the firelight and called out again, this time louder. Her voice rang clear and sharp like she was calling to Mirra in the rushing wind of the valley.

Jon's name reverberated away into the shadows. She looked at the white, dead faces on the ground, their dry eyes blinking from the fire's flickering glow. Most of the corpses were posed with stiffened arms and rigid, clawed fingers, like wooded statues. She looked away from them, afraid that one will be Jon.

Reaching the border of light and dark, she repeated her call, "Jon! Jon Lyhton! She lengthened the words, "Johhhhn Lyyyhton!" The ground crunched under her feet as she moved around the edge of light. Her voice strained as each desperate yell echoed after the last. A gentle cold rain began to fall and with it, her hopes. Tears swelled in her eyes.

When Jon heard her voice, the faint call sounded like someone yelling through a dense wood. He struggled to see where the voice came from, but was not able to see in the dark place he laid, unless he could somehow awaken into his body again. He was leaving it, sensing that the world was no more.

Piercing the darkness, Bethanna's voice became clearer and he saw a small, misty light appear. *A dream?* A presence drew near. He felt her spirit pulling at his. He could smell her, *Bethanna. Is it really you?* He felt himself smile in the warmth of the dream.

A clear shout awoke him, opening his eyes. A cold breeze blew over his face and he felt the movement of his beard. He laid in the dark, wet grass of the field, covered in blood, gritty gore and black powder. The icy rain struck his face, a sign of the real moment, out in the living world. He took in a deep breath and smelled the rain again like it was the first time he had breathed. He was alive.

Bethanna stood still under the rain's patter. She listened, staring into the darkness, and in it she saw the gray smoke floating by, slithering like a living creature. It was a monstrous thing standing in the way of her and Jon like a hideous demon that guarded death's wide gates, and at the foot of the demon laid these many battle dead claimed for his master. From their moans and pleas, she heard, and interpreted Satan's audible laugh, as the doleful noise grew in her ears from human to inhuman. "Stop it!" she yelled, pressing her hood to her ears. Kneeling in exasperation, she tried to breathe, her eyes closed and she concentrated on her mission, God and his strength.

Hearing her outcry, Bertram approached her, held her arm. "Please don't give up, Miss Beth." He helped her up. "You're doing so well, try this 'a way." He pointed to another wall of dark night. She straightened herself, wiped her eyes and took a deep breath. Again she called.

Jon heard the voice again, so bright and clear, full of emotion, desperate, loving. He noticed, for the first time, a weight held him down and he rose up to see what it was. Elias had found him and fell onto his body, keeping him warm.

"Elias?" Jon patted his arms and pushed at him

Elias awoke, groggy. "What? Jon, you're alive! Where are we?" Lifting himself from Jon, he shuddered in pain and fell away. "Oh, that's bad, Jonny. Can't move my leg!"

Jon rolled over onto his elbows and moaned in pain, his voice hoarse and damaged. "I hear her." He sucked air into his sore lungs and his throat burned. Searching the ground with his hands, he felt for something to aid him to his feet. He found his rifle, or someone's. Struggling, he pulled up on it and tested his legs. The right one stabbed him with pain, stinging with every movement. *Shrapnel.* His hands were numbed from the bitter cold and he rubbed and shook them.

Elias pulled at Jon. "There...is help, at that fire. I can't walk, Jonny. Can you?"

Jon attempted to talk, but there was pain in his efforts. "I'll... try."

Through the drizzle, he saw the firelight a good 60 yards away. It seemed the same light he saw laying on the ground. He used the rifle for a crutch and moved slowly towards the fire and Bethanna's voice; hopefully it *was* she, and not his imagination fuelled by madness. If she was a dream, then that would be very nice, but disappointing.

If it were heaven or imagination, there would not be the tremendous pain in his leg. He still could not see clearly, so he took a moment to wipe the captain's dried blood from his eyes. Hobbling closer and closer to the fire, he squinted, seeing blurry figures near it and then, someone calling his name, perhaps a man this time, not Bethanna after all.

Jon reached the light and a warm tingle touched his face. He spoke out, but only a raspy cry came from his wounded throat. He clutched it and felt a gash near the base of his neck.

At the animal sound, Bertram wheeled about and saw a man tottering and holding out a hand as he crutched himself on a rifle.

He walked cautiously toward the needy soldier.

Jon froze. With a jolt of recognition, he brought up his rifle and realized he had been fooled. Even with the blur of his eyes, he was staring into the familiar face of the taunting and evil Riles.

God could see the justice in it; a chance to go beyond sacrifice of one's self, all the way to eliminating true and terrible evil. God had brought him through the battle, judged him innocent, and now Riles, if dead, would be unable to overturn the verdict. There was a good chance that the rifle was loaded, as the men around him never fired before the cannon ball exploded. He clicked the hammer back and raised the gun to his chest. In his delirium, the target moved and then doubled, shifting back and forth.

Bertram put up his hands and called out, "Cawley, help! Over here, got a wild one!"

Confusion arose in Jon's mind. *How did Cawley get mixed up with this devil?* Jon tried his voice again, grunting and finding a chord. "You have the gall to come... for me now?"

Bertram stared at the muzzle, awaiting the blast of flame. "Cawley, help!" He backed away as the stranger limped nearer. "Hey there mister, wait! Now wait! Settle down, I ain't here to hurtcha'."

Stepping forward, Cawley raised his musket and dropped his sight on the haggard soldier, who had lost his mind and threatened his new friend. "I got 'em Bert."

Bertram waved his hand out, gesturing to the darkness. "Just looking for a friend out here mister."

Jon could almost laugh at the statement. "A friend? You?" He felt his bad leg give way and he hit the ground. Supporting his weight with the rifle butt, he pushed up and knelt on his good knee. The pain overtook him and soon he'd pass out or be dead. Now was the time, before Riles had a chance. He checked the gun. Ready. "Prepare to be judged, as you have judged."

When he lifted the rifle, he could see behind Riles the figure of a woman rushing at them. He aimed. Down the barrel he saw her, as she pulled away her hood and revealed a head of blond hair. His mind tangled and could not fathom what was before him. Then her voice filled the cold air. "Do not shoot! We are friends!"

"Bethanna?" Jon said, widening his eyes, trying to find a clear image of her. He gasped for air. "Riles will kill you!" He pointed the gun barrel at Bertram, who raised his hands again.

When Bethanna heard the thin, bearded stranger say her name, she knew. *Jon.*

She recognized what was happening. The resemblance of the brothers had struck her as astonishing. She ran to them. "Jon, Jon. Yes, it's me. Look, Riles has died; this is his brother, Bertram!"

Jon staggered, "What?"

"Yeah, see." Bertram took off his hat. Jon could not differentiate the man's looks in his fragile state but the voice was indeed separate, pleasant and not like Riles at all. He would know Riles' indignant rasp in any dark cave.

Jon's gun barrel dropped and a heavy breath of relief came from the three searchers. Bethanna rushed to Jon and hugged him, she kissed his face, tasting the sting of bitter gun- powder, blood and burnt earth. "My God, you would have killed him," she said.

"I thought I already did…." Jon collapsed to the ground.

"Don't speak; you'll hurt your voice. You have a cut, it's swollen badly." Bethanna turned to the others, "We must move him to the barn."

Cawley ran to Jon and knelt, crying, "He's alive, he's alive! Oh Lordy. I'm 'a going to church every Sunday, and Wednesday prayers, stoppin' cards and chew…"

Jon grabbed Bethanna, "No, wait, please. My good cousin Elias is out there." He pointed into the dark void.

Cawley sprang up. "Jonny! I'll go get'im for ya."

* * *

CHAPTER 31 ★

During the night, Jon went home. Not in any near reality, but in his hallucinations, caused by a dose of morphine. Mother and Father with young sisters Cassandra and Eliza waited for him at the front door. A large homecoming dinner sat spread out on the wide table, fixed just the way he remembered. Even the smell of fresh food and vegetables forced the realism of it. As quickly as this scene came, it left, replaced by tremors of battle.

He bucked and kicked as his feverish night in the barn dragged on. The lumbering ghosts of Rains, Lawsen, and all the battle dead chased him over the fields of defeat. The devil himself, Riles, dressed in a bloodied overcoat, lit fire to flags, corpses and the living maimed. Then he re-lived the sudden, stark scene of his last fight.

He was staring at the hissing cannonball, exactly thirteen feet away. Before it blew, two men had stepped between it and Jon. They were in the short process of getting away from it, when, as the ball burst into sharp chunks, these men absorbed most of the iron shards. A flying piece of rifle butt hit Jon in the neck as his left leg took direct shrapnel. The falling artillery cleared the area of any remaining Confederates eager to reform and brave it out. Night fell and the Yanks scurried back to the hill where they had started the day.

The barn glowed with the cast light of a fire set in the center of the wide dirt floor. Bertram opened the high-load doors in the loft to let the smoke out. He climbed down and walked over to the fire. Bethanna sat next to the ambulance litter, on which Jon lay. He was wrapped up, warm and asleep.

"Finally," Bertram said. He checked on Elias as he lay sleeping, after some food and freshly dressed wounds.

"Look, the doctor sleeps, too." Bethanna gestured with a nod to the man curled up in the corner.

Bertram huffed. "He snores like a bear. Guess he couldn't wait for his pay."

During his surgery, Jon had been agitated, struggling against the pain and pressure of the procedure. The physician removed two pieces of iron from his leg. To Bethanna, the fact that a doctor had been found at all was a miracle. And it was, thanks to some frantic behavior by Cawley to lure the tired surgeon away from the nearby camps of Wharton's cavalry.

Jon's friend had guaranteed the medical man a warm place to stay and a bottle of something special if he would help his wounded captain and his adjutant, Elias. Somehow, during the operation the doctor never asked about Jon's rank, only assumed that he had better get it right, or else.

During the operation, Cawley headed for the cavalry camps to find a bottle of spirits and by 3:30 in the morning, he came trotting up tired and dead-eyed on one of the ambulance horses.

Bertram, well rested and awake, held the rifle that had been aimed at him by Jon. He called out to Cawley, "Who goes there?"

From atop the horse he heard, "You know darned well who it is! Me, Cawley!"

Bertram laughed then smirked, "Don't get yer britches up. Hey, our good doctor is cutting logs back there, so I guess we might have a go with that whiskey."

Bethanna's nursing instincts awoke and she washed Jon's dirty face with a wet cloth. He had considerable bruising on his throat near the gash. The doctor sewed it up easily and she finished the work with a compress and bandage. Besides the distress of battle, she noticed that Jon's looks had changed. Perhaps it was the full beard. He looked older, thinner.

Her face had changed too, and mostly in the last few hours. She smiled openly for the first time in months as she celebrated. "Lord, your miracles never end."

When Jon woke up a few hours later, he saw that face, stressed and tired, but strong and still lovely. "It was you, after all," he said, his voice raspy. "I thought the delirium had overtaken me last night. Like a dream, I left my body."

"It was I calling. I knew you would hear me. I never gave up," she said.

Jon winced from pain and touched his wrapped throat. "You saved me. But how did you get here?"

Bethanna touched his forehead with the cool cloth. She leaned down close to him and kissed his face. "I could not save you alone. Bertram and Cawley helped, too."

"Yes, they did." He admired her kind eyes. "You believed, so you did it."

"Yes, I trusted God's will and his vision to me," she said.

Under such care and in the presence of her again, Jon knew he had fallen.

"I have not believed so strongly. I…should be ashamed," he said, turning his head away.

"Why do you say that?" she asked, taking his hand.

Jon shook his head. "Your letter warned me and I failed to see it. Out there on the field, I thought I knew God's will, but seeing the end of our victory, I gave up on everything good that I loved. I wanted to leave it." Thinking a moment, he said, "But Bertram is alive, how amazing. Truly, I never would have lived if you weren't here. It was your voice that woke me, that saved me."

"You are strong. Someone would have found you, Jon. Now we are both together." She placed his hand to her face. "We must know that our Lord has brought us here, through many trials…." Her cheeks blushed. "…and our love, too."

Jon looked to her again. "Yes, we do love each other, don't we?"

"Yes, my dear, we do."

"Because you are here, I believe it is true. You have proven God to me." Jon could not speak any more and rested. His head spun warmly as his body processed the morphine—a fortunate aide that the cavalry surgeons had plenty of.

"I know a safer place where to move you. We will leave soon." Bethanna let Jon drift into more needed sleep. She cleaned his coat as best she could and set it to dry near the fire. Worn out, she fell asleep next to Jon.

Cawley remembered his recent oath to God. "Now I did swear against cards and chew, but I don't remember that I ever mentioned drinkin' in that list, did I?"

Bertram uncorked the doctor's pay. "I never heard a word about drink. Here." As the two heroes dowsed the battle's fury from their minds, they joked, giggled, and became best friends.

* * *

The contest of armies along the banks of Stones River ended in a tactical draw, but as the Confederates vacated the field, they left the Union as victors. General Rosecrans cabled Washington of his great New Year's victory and announced his total command of the road to Nashville.

That evening, he took mass in the Catholic tradition and said prayers for his dead and dying, in full knowledge that many of them still lay out in the cold. He received a cable from a grateful President Lincoln, stating how the victory had saved the sagging morale of a nation faced with the recent defeat at Fredericksburg, Virginia, while General Lee still held all roads to Richmond.

On the 3rd of January, Confederate cavalry scouts reported that Federal reinforcements had taken up positions in the Union line and that trains had delivered supplies and ammo into the Union camps. Any further action by the Confederates would be heavily repulsed and only repeat the efforts by Hanson and Breckinridge. Bragg organized a methodical and orderly retreat for the evening of the 3rd.

Using what equipage he had left in wagons and rail cars, Bragg directed his three corps to their locations around the new headquarters in Tullahoma, but not before making sure that this defeat was the fault of others. Soon after the battle, he demanded reports from his commanders and began to pass blame before receiving them. He did not bother asking General Breckinridge for an account of his action near McFadden's Ford, nor did he interview him afterwards. Because of this, the enmity between the two men would quickly grow into hatred.

Such command politics had to wait, for the Army was not in a safe position after the battle. Thousands of wounded soldiers needed care or transportation and many more languished on the field or in the shelter of trees for long hours, unattended. Both sides cared for enemy wounded, as lines had shifted, especially over the hills where Breckinridge's division made its assaults.

The appalling scenes of carnage, wagon loads of broken, bloody men numbed the small town of Murfreesboro and moved citizens to compassion. Placed in churches, schools, and public buildings, some casualties were hometown boys and used these places in younger, brighter days.

The men who received the warm care of a family to see them to health were fortunate. Even with all their kindness, a disquieting pall settled over the streets as the townsfolk were caught in a death zone and the impending doom of desolation. Their protectors would soon leave them to the wilds of the Bluecoat masses.

* * *

Although much safer than the exposed barn, in a few hours, the Methodist church would eventually be a home of prisoners. Bethanna did not want to be caught behind the enemy lines, a situation that she never worried about before. The Northern Army was only another force to be driven and smashed, killed and wounded, same as any other army, but now if that army kept her from Jon and her mission to him, then yes, they were the enemy.

Bertram rushed into the church and found Bethanna where he had left her, watching over Jon. She stood to meet him. "Is Elias safe, where did they take him?"

"I followed the orderlies to the rail yard, where they are collecting wounded for transport. Elias was placed aboard a medical car." He pointed at Jon. "I think we could do the same for Jonny here, if we move with haste."

The rails led due south, through Wartrace and directly to Tullahoma. This, indeed, was the only sure way to safety and her aunt Mirrasane. She could make Jon a safe place to recover and perhaps escape the war. But, then she thought, *Escape? Never.*

She knelt down to Jon lying under the dark-stained pulpit. "There are trains coming and going. We need to take one south to Tullahoma, where you can rest and get well, without the threat of disease and crowded hospitals."

Jon smiled, painfully. "That is fine with me...." His throat still swollen, he chose to spare his voice on occasion. He reached for Bethanna and she grasped his hand.

Her touch, still surreal in the aftermath of battle, was better than he could remember, a soft hand, strong now and assured. He did not know, in his drifting state of mind, how she had come to be here in a battle, after existing only as a memory tucked away in some love letter.

And what about that love? It was unlike the deepest dreams he ever had of a woman loving him. Their love had been built on the unfamiliar foundation of equality, in a time when the man saved himself. Yes, he had saved her once and she, with more faith and bravery, had saved him now. Here in this holy place, he could see her as a bride, lovely in white, welcomed by family and sanctified by God.

The church had filled to capacity, every row and pew taken as beds, the carpets long removed for storage. Moans of pain echoed from the crowded pews onto the stone and wood walls, up high into the vaulted ceiling and onto the stained-glass ears of saints.

Cawley had returned to the regiment, by Jon's order, of course. Jon had put it a good way. "Private, go report to the captain and lieutenant, that I and Martello are safe. Only return if ordered."

Bertram hovered nearby. He walked in occasionally, checking on Jon and Bethanna, then out into the cold day to smoke or help with the wounded escaping in long wagon trains. He thought as a couple, they were very sanguine and in such surroundings, inspiring. Jon was, indeed, a brave soldier, perhaps overwrought in his action, but dedicated to higher morals. Together at last, the sight of them made sense, and Bertram liked their story and his part in its continuance. He wanted to see it through.

Other stories were passed among soldiers, proving they had survived the most terrible struggle ever witnessed by small town boys. Stories about men they knew and tales about the great heroes of the battle who, dead or alive, lay in the town's public places.

One such man, Colonel Bratton of the 24th Tennessee, had his leg shattered by a large artillery fragment, which sliced through his horse, then gashed his other leg.

In the charge of Breckinridge's division, Semple's Alabama battery lost half its men. Exposed in the open during the Federal's counterattack, most of the wounded became prisoners as they lay helpless on the retaken hill.

The body of General Rains, after being carried from the field, was placed in a fine black coffin. The troops passed by the funeral wagon and mourned openly, reluctant to release such a valiant soul to the hereafter, and to legend.

The respectful scene turned horribly tragic as the young general's sister was shown the dark casket and collapsed in pitiful screams, unwilling to take comfort from her relatives. Her dress became muddied as she beat the earth and cursed its claim on her hero.

Her tortured cries echoed into the church and silenced the wounded for a short moment. The sounds taught Bethanna what true sorrow can be and she felt a chill deep inside her. She held Jon's hand while the wailing touched a new level of pain, so close and personal, a woman mourning. She prayed against the awful spirits of death that pervaded the air.

A woman stepped through the crowded space and the hem of her dress, dirty and bloodstained, brushed against Bethanna, gaining her attention. The lady bent down to her. "You are such a good servant, my girl, praying, and working. I have seen your comfort here, and you make us proud." Genuine kindness showed in her round, pretty face, her eyes red from recent tears.

Bethanna thanked her. Moving on, the lady consoled the soldiers and prayed for them. She had a regal charm about her, and remained calm amid the chaotic activity. Bethanna wished for that kind of spirit. It must come with age, she thought.

Bertram stepped through the masses and sat next to Jon. He opened a rag, which contained pork and crackers, a typical soldier's repast, but welcomed by his two new friends. They ate quickly.

"Thank you, Mr. Mullibey," Bethanna said, stuffing her mouth.
"Call me Bert."

The three looked at the charming woman tending a wounded man on a table, near an alcove. The patient seemed to know her. "I wonder who she is," Bertram said.

A man lying behind Bethanna sat up on his elbows and spoke. "She is the general's wife, Mary Breckinridge. These are as much her boys as the General's."

Jon leaned up and observed her. She did not seem to care about her clothes or the neatness she was used to, and went about her work with determined devotion, like a mother. She did not have to endure the awful scene but chose to share in the suffering. Jon's thoughts turned to his mother and what news she must be hearing now of the large battle and their losses, of General Rains and his tragic death. *What must they be thinking about their boy?*

Bethanna asked the man who Mrs. Breckinridge was helping.

"She attends the dying General Hanson. They brought him in during the early night. He is my commander. We all love Mrs. Breckinridge and have much devotion to her—the 4th Kentucky that is. The white stars that grace our flags are silk from one of her eloquent dresses, and we proudly fight for her as if she were with us on the field. Now, you can see her faithfulness to us."

The group looked over and admired her as she put a cool cloth to General Hanson's head and spoke unknown, comforting words. The symbolism of Mary rang true for Bethanna. She realized that she was remarkably obedient in her mission and saw her own value in these difficult circumstances.

Having strong faith, Bethanna knew that all things work to the glory of the Lord; however, not always how people think or want. It became true, indeed, that the war around her was as much a spiritual battle as physical one, costing souls as well as lives, forcing people of faith to act on faith, and men of honor to act on honor. Both shared the fearful cost, or a final victory.

In Mary Breckinridge, Bethanna saw both the cost of love and its reward displayed in her actions towards the dying man. As the commanding general's wife, she was making her grand charge into death's face and winning like no other brigade had done. Surely, as her femininity adorned the silk stars of the brigade's flags, she commanded the soldiers to stand and secure Southern womanhood or die in their attempt.

The Kentuckians had charged under her orders as surely as if she had raised a sword aloft and directed the men herself. Her total commitment was no less than her husband's, and took valorous bravery. Obviously, her battle continued long after the fight, as did the general's.

The soldiers changed then, in Bethanna's sight, from pitiful, foolish boys running mad with fright, power, fear and hatred, into men spattered with honor, protectors of heritage and homes, their wives and girls, sons, and lands. She had seen men like these not long ago; her father, Saul, and Carl—men who were not standing still, but facing life's toils. She could see in the sad, disappointed faces of the wounded, that it was not hate that moved men into such awful action and death, but love was the eminent reason; the most impassioned, desperate, and unbound love for all that they drew from life. But did this love blind them? Did this love convince both sides to war with each other? There was no doubt. She looked on Jon and his comrades with new clarity.

* * *

"I'll find a way on." Bertram patted Jon's arm as he broke away to search for space aboard one of the passenger cars. Not much like a free-for-all, but very near, the loading of patients tended to be disorganized as the town began to bleed away divisions, regiments, and wandering soldiers. The station platform crawled with movement as litter bearers lifted and sorted men into neat lines. Nurses and men with white hats or coats, scurried about with water pails or spare blankets. But above the motion, rang the ever-present drone of voices, coughing, wailing and moaning of injured men.

Heading south, lines of Army wagons passed on the opposite side of the train and Bertram slipped between them. "Jesus, what a mess." He could see more railcars being readied on the sidings, lined up and connected in anticipation of another engine arriving soon. "They will fill that one, too."

He looked down the tracks and counted eleven cars, mixed cattle and passengers. Jumping up to a doorway and grabbing the handrail, he looked in to see empty seats filling up fast. To his relief, bunks had been added for the stacking of litters.

Bertram ran down the track and checked every car for space. Alas, through a window, in a blue flash, he saw something familiar. He doubled back and lifted himself up at the door. Chaplain Patrick Lovejoy sat with three Confederate officers, his prayer book open as he read.

One captain was missing an arm and his coat was tied off at the bloody elbow. Quite relaxed, he sat up straight and calm, like a church deacon at Eucharist.

The other officers leaned forward, following the text. He closed the book and the group seemed well relieved with their blessing as they shook hands.

Bertram shifted around the seats and tapped Lovejoy's shoulder. The chaplain turned and reeled, like he had seen some past stranger who offended him once, and then with a gleam, he smiled. "Well, I'll be...blessed."

"Pastor, can you help me with a patient? Got to get him on this here train car."

Lovejoy raised an eyebrow. "I have been doing that all morning son, eh…I am done here now."

"No, you're not," said Bertram, pulling the chaplain by his sleeve. "Bethanna found Jon. He's got a bum leg and can't walk very well."

Lovejoy's eyebrows twisted in wonderment. His face brightened. "You found him?" He grabbed Bertram's arms. "That's incredible, my God. How did you ever…?"

Bertram had no time for explanations, though he did enjoy the chaplain's shocked expression. "Later, Reverend. Eh, can you save this bench? Yeah, and that bunk over there, good man? Just sit yourself down and reserve this one, right here." He pushed Lovejoy onto the leather bench seat and the Yankee easily sat. "Gladly."

Lovejoy looked out the window over his left shoulder and saw Bertram appear, running back onto the wide loading platform. He knelt near a couple, a man with a heavily bandaged leg, in filthy butternut and hatless. The girl, obviously Bethanna, had on her wool cape with the hood pulled over her head. She had a carry bag strapped around her shoulder.

Bertram gathered the two and with much effort, began to move Jon toward the train through the twisted lines of writhing men. After much time, they appeared at the doorway.

Lovejoy reached out a hand and Jon took it blindly while stepping on the foot-rail with his good leg. Bethanna and Bertram pushed him up and he yelped.

"Sorry," they said, in sincere unison.

Jon looked up and instantly reacted. "You again?"

"Yes, me again." Lovejoy helped him limp down the aisle to the bunk. "But I am shocked to see you. I'm awfully glad you did not disappoint her."

Jon sat on the bunk, looking into Lovejoy's eyes. He did not get the chaplain's statement, but agreed with it in kind. "'Tis a good thing."

Bethanna removed her hood and was pleasantly surprised to see Lovejoy. She elbowed Bertram. "You did not say *he* was here. You should have said something."

Bertram pointed to Jon. "Well, not sure how he would react. Just a hunch."

Jon lay back on the canvass bed, grateful for a softer place to rest. His face winced at the pain in his leg and he groaned. Bethanna put a blanket on him. "I hope the railroad is clear." she said. "There is nothing we can do now but wait on the actions of others."

Lovejoy stood back, witnessing a miracle in the flesh, three miracles in one and not without fantastic irony, strange twists, and the nerve of a brave girl. "This is almost too funny. You three…," he laughed.

Bethanna smiled, she knew.

Bertram smirked and chuckled.

Jon raised his head. "What's wrong with you, Lovejoy?"

Bertram moved in to explain. "You see, Jon, we met this here chaplain, and he told us you went off on a suicide mission of sorts. 'Course, you had noble motivations, thinking me dead and all."

Bethanna then explained the meeting of Lovejoy and how Riles said Jon's name and the discovery of Bertram. "The Reverend here made us aware of your intentions to join the battle. If not for him, we would have never known where you were," she said.

Jon stared at Lovejoy. "Thank you, sir, I owe you my gratitude. I am very glad that you spoke up, even after the way I ignored you." He stretched his throat. "And may I say that there can be hope for the Yankee nation yet."

Lovejoy nodded and replied, "Well, maybe." Frankly, he did not know about hope. Perhaps he had been taught recently by

Bethanna's persistence and now Jon's will. He shook Jon's hand without hesitation.

Bethanna crossed her arms and addressed Lovejoy. "And I forgive you reverend for your disbelief earlier. Now you have seen our faith at work, do not ever doubt it again."

Lovejoy nodded, put his hands together and said, "I should dare not…around you."

Bethanna motioned to a seat. "Please join us and we can all be together."

"No, as much as I enjoy all of you, I cannot stay. I must go into town and be collected by my friends shortly. The best thing for me is to care for my wounded comrades. But I must say, I have been awakened here amongst you rebs, it has been …" He raised his dark eyebrows. "…a revelation."

Lovejoy shook their hands. "May God protect you all, as he has done so mightily." He recited a benediction, blessing them with official churchdom.

To his surprise, Bethanna stood and hugged him, her cheek touching his face. She pulled him tightly and said, "God bless you and may we meet again in peaceful days."

Lovejoy quietly walked away, turned and looked at them from the door, then left the train. Horsemen rode by and he waited for them to clear. There were more horses coming, so he quickly jogged around the car to overstep the coupling. Feeling tears in his eyes, the sentiment was overpowering. He had not been touched by a female in a year, and the pureness of Bethanna's spirit bathed him with lightness, much like his wife, when they were together.

He walked into the town, known only to him as the wreck cast before him. There had been nothing untouched by the troops, from the public buildings to the houses. Bloodied walkways led Lovejoy back through a ravaged church garden littered with ripped clothes and used bandages. Tables and doors used for speedy operations lay awash in blood.

He took a pew in the sanctuary for a time and watched soldiers who could walk prepare to be moved. Under the cross and steeple, a weight lifted. He had seen miracles granted, he had survived and treated the rebels as friends, obeying Jesus. *Love your enemies.* Soon, the Northern troops would take the town and reunite him with his unit, and then he would have to make a decision to fight on or leave the Army. He didn't want to have a faulty state of mind over his duty, but he wrestled within because at the moment, he wanted so much to go home, run into the arms of his wife and love her. Even in this war, Jon's miracle had proved such love exists and Bethanna, touched by God, had believed and obeyed. Tears flowed down the chaplain's face in awe and humility.

Jon looked out of the window at the cavalrymen passing the train. Taking orders from a young officer, the horsemen formed their lines in the muddy yard adjacent to the rails. The officer looked strong and in no way affected by the last three days. He addressed his superior and saluted. It seemed that they were not finished with the battle, and Jon felt a pang of sympathy for the rear guards. "Thank God we still have such able forces."

Standing over Jon, Bethanna looked through the wet pane, taking note of the gray troopers. She thought of Carl's dead body, his mottled and wormy uniform, trimmed in the yellow piping of the cavalry. "Yes, they are brave to fight on." She rested her hands, holding Jon's hands, and continued to observe the action out the spotty window.

Stephan's men rode past the waiting train and began to gather in the open lot. His detachment had been chosen as Colonel Parker's new escort because they met great success in the recent battle. After meeting with General Wheeler south of the overcrowded rail depot, Parker loaded his wounded, refreshed his horses, and began to collect his troops at the edge of town.

Stephan rode over to Colonel Parker, who gave the last assignments to his orderlies. "Lieutenant Gurtag, stay close. This rain will fog out all of our formations and those of the enemy. I don't want us separated."

"Absolutely, sir, the escort is ready at your command."

"Very well." Colonel Parker took the lead. His horsemen turned their mounts and formed two neat columns to begin their trot toward the Nashville Pike. Stephan looked at the train as the whistle echoed and the engine built up steam, fogging the air with clouds of vapor. The smokestack billowed, tossing out black balls of soot and ash. He would get no comforting ride south, and that was fine. He did not mind the duty of saving Bragg's rear, someone had to do it and why not the cavalry. Forest and Wheeler were already famous for it.

There would be time for rest later, when the troops settled into winter quarters. The cavalry will be needed to guard the flanks, spy on the enemy, and secure communications. Stephan was glad to be on a horse, out in the open, not to be huddled amongst the infantry all winter waiting on disease.

A bright idea came to him, of how he could pass the coldest months at the ranch of his aunt Mirrasane in Tullahoma. She would gladly welcome him in as a nephew and a soldier. With a crack of the reigns, his horse turned and darted for a position near the front of the column.

* * *

CHAPTER 32★

After an hour of delays, the train pulled away in the late morning and carried the shattered remains of a once formidable Army southward through a bleak land. Marching along the nearby roads, the troops and horse-soldiers that had gallantly faced terror, shock and shell, left behind a good third of their force north of Murfreesboro. Their morale crushed, each man dragged himself further from the defeat and closer to unknown hardships in the days to come.

From aboard the train, Jon looked at the bedraggled formations through hazy glass as he lay on his swaying bunk. Somewhere in that retreat was the 11th, Lieutenant Weston, and men he led. Not surprisingly, Jon longed to be with them, to help encourage and rebuild the unit. Now, on the train, he realized his great fortune and present destiny. Jon turned and saw Bethanna sitting across the aisle faithfully watching him. Because he wasn't alone, he smiled.

She, too, shared his joy, and she reached for him. Their hands clasped over the walking space. Her affection remained strong in her grip and in her eyes.

Jon held them in his gaze, so clear and familiar, welcoming. Surely, she had been directed by God to come all this way just to find him. The thought could not be taken as a whole, only appreciated in the small steps it took to complete such a task. He felt her warm hand, and wanted it always.

"Bethanna, come close."

She stood and leaned over him. "Yes, my dear?"

"I thought I'd never see you again, but you were never very far away."

Jon struggled against his swollen throat. "Please know that you were with me, even though I had lost you, for a time."

He reached into his coat and revealed Bethanna's letter, dirtied and frayed. "Here are your tender words that sustained me with love and care."

Her eyes brightened. "I forgot all about that letter." She took the paper and read it. "Yes, words from a girl that could not find you, and I was very afraid for you."

Bethanna remembered something and reached into the bag on her seat.

She pulled out Jon's poetry book. "Here, I've read them all."

"By Lord, you saved it?" Jon smiled as he took the familiar book like a first-time gift. "I get the thought that you really care for me."

She picked up his jocular tone and smiled. "You know better than to think that."

Bertram observed, appreciating their romantic, paper connections. Sitting near the door, he leaned against the bulkhead and watched the land go by in jumpy, short streaks. He had given up his seat to an older woman. Her twin sons were wounded and one died not long after the battle on the first day. The surviving son had been strapped to a litter just in front of Jon.

As for Bertram, his job was not complete. He wanted to make sure the sweet couple made it to the safety of Bethanna's aunt. This duty was only small payment for Riles horrid actions against a good man. What was more egregious—one man killing for self-defense or a man being falsely accused? Secretly, he carried the debt with some pride, knowing he would make it right.

The train crept through the rising land, over a long east-west barrier called the Highland Rim, and then through a gap which led to an area locally known as The Barrens, a flat plateau that precedes the foothills of the Cumberland Range. The train pulled onto a siding at the town of Wartrace to wait out a northbound hospital train. From there, the trip seemed to slow as the cars clacked over buckles in the worn track. Coming upon a high bridge, Bethanna could not look as she hid her eyes from the gorge, and the rocky stream below. She did not breathe easier when overhearing a wounded man describing the next bridge over the Duck River, and how it was taller, and longer. He also noted a storm approaching, and within minutes the train had glided under the low line of clouds. The inside of the train car became a dark room, shadowed in places and offering only silhouettes to identify the people aboard. The storm hit suddenly, buffeting the car with showers, wind, and lightning flashes. Under the rushing winds and swaying railcar, the affect became sea sickening to Bethanna, as she stood next to Jon's bunk and held his hands. Unused to rail travel, and running on three days of little sleep, she became weak-kneed when a wave of nausea shot through her head.

Jon heard her moan and he sat up, seeking her face in the darkened car. A streak of lightning flashed, revealing Bethanna's ill features. He put his arms around her and she leaned into his grasp. "Yes, quite a rough way to go. Hold on."

"We are so close to safety, Jon, so close."

"I know, my love. We'll make it."

Thunder cracked overhead, the train jolted, slowing abruptly before taking on the Duck River crossing. From the window, Bethanna saw the engine approaching the bridge at a slight curve, leading to the narrow trestle, now a hazy line heading into sheets of rain.

"Jon, hold me tight!"

"I will, my dear. I am holding you always."

Bethanna faced him, her eyes tired and dark.

"Look at me," Jon said. "These are the last miles, the last journey for us. It will be over soon."

Suspended over a rushing river, full of recent rains, the train pushed its way through the storm and across the deep chasm. The howling wind fought every angle of the square cars and whistled into window seams and door jams. Cars rocked side to side, and to those aboard, it seemed only a moment before they would be hurled into the gorge. Seconds dragged on as the danger increased with every new gust. Jon searched for Bertram. He found him standing flat against the back of the car, arms out, eyes wide with excitement and a perverse smile on his lips. The pose alarmed Jon, only because Bertram resembled Riles, and in a fast blur, he seemed to change from one brother to the other. Jon blamed the sudden hallucination on the last trace of morphine.

To Bethanna, the pounding storm resembled the battle that she had heard on her cart ride to the front. But this was no battle of men. It was another kind. She looked at Jon, fixed on his eyes and said, "Whatever happens, the Lord will hold us."

In a shudder, the train landed on solid earth, and cheer of relief escaped those who were cognizant of their surroundings.

Jon counted the seconds between the lightning flashes and soon the gap widened. "You see, the storm is moving away." Listening to the spattering rain, Bethanna laid her head on Jon's shoulder. He rubbed her back and some sense of equilibrium returned to her. The car ride steadied and her breathing eased.

"I'm sorry, have tried to be strong but…"

"You are very strong and brave." said Jon. "But you have to rest dear. Please sit for a while, I'll rest too. "

Bertram noticed her discomfort and offered his canteen to Bethanna. The water helped to ease her dizziness and thirst, which until now, she had not been fully aware. Exhausted, she took her seat and rested her head so she could see Jon. In a few minutes she closed her eyes and began to drift into an instant, hard sleep. Like a dream, the storm passed away and left behind low clouds, fog banks and muddy crossroads that bogged down army wagons. The train rolled deep into the Barrens, away from the battle zone and past the fog to a place of unknown comfort, and expected welcome.

Startled momentarily, Bethanna awoke from her deep sleep next to the older woman, who was snoring. Around her, the train still moved safely onward. Checking behind her, she found Bertram asleep on the floor, leaning up against the bulkhead. She was relieved to see Jon sleeping, too. To ease her mind, she read verses from Acts in her Testament about the Disciples of Jesus and their step into ministry. She felt a kinship with the men who accepted the Holy Spirit, and faced endless trials to share God's word, though she did not think herself equal to their sainthood. In a while, she noticed Jon was awake and looking out the window.

Bethanna moved to him, kissed his cheek, and then felt his face. "Your head is still too warm. Did you sleep?"

"A little," he said. "You slept too, I can tell." Jon sat up, felt his throat and tried his leg muscle, which was still painful, but thankfully not bleeding through his bandage. Ahead of him in bunks, men suffered in various ways, some alone, others with friends or mothers to ease their souls. For him, there was Bethanna, the girl from a place left behind, most surely, forever. His heart swelled with a gratefulness he'd never known. He lifted Bethanna's hand and kissed it.

Within the dark car, the pair found intimacy with ease, as Bethanna kissed Jon's forehead and met his eyes with hers.

Jon smoothed her hair from her cheek and his fingers brushed her lips. He laid the loose strands behind her ear, and when he clutched her face, she relaxed into his warm palm, gave him control and fell into him. Jon found her lips expectant. He kissed them softly, discovering a rare but familiar place that he knew and missed badly. Her very breath was spirit, pure and healing.

She took his lips and formed to his kiss. A quick rush of heat to her head slowed the sensation, making sweet and wonderful his every move on her mouth. She allowed him to deepen his soft stroke, tasting her for the first time, and she knowing him. Joy filled them both as Jon released her.

Drawing breath, she kissed him again, as if the first never happened. He had kissed her in the valley and it was not a dream. Yes, he kissed her, but so hurriedly and long ago. She was a girl then in the reverend's cellar, when the surprising caress had changed her heart. Bethanna had sealed a bond with him and she knew that nothing would break it, not the generals with their orders, not the war, nor death.

"There it is. We made it!" someone said aloud.

Bethanna looked outside and saw the growing limits of Tullahoma – barns, fences, country houses, and people. "Thank you, Lord, for our deliverance, and our love." She kissed Jon's cheek.

The gloomy sky had lingered above them during the last mile, until for the first time in weeks, the sun knifed its way through the clouds in brilliant golden blades, slashing away the gray overcast. Bethanna sighed audibly, smiling at the glorious light.

THE END

ORDER OF COMMAND ★

BATTLE OF TAZEWELL
AUGUST 6, 1862

DEPARTMENT OF EAST TENNESSEE

CONFEDERATE STATES
GENERAL CARTER L. STEVENSON

Colonel James E. Rains' Brigade
11th Tennessee
42nd Georgia
3rd Georgia Battalion
29th North Carolina

Yeizer's Georgia Battery, "Charokee Artillery"
Eufala Battery (Alabama)

* * *

Colonel Thomas H. Taylor's Brigade
23rd Alabama
46th Alabama
29th Tennessee
3rd Tennessee Cavalry

Rhett artillery

* * *

UNITED STATES
GENERAL GEORGE MORGAN

Colonel John DeCourcy (26th Brigade on detachment)
  16th Ohio (Major Kershner)
  14th Kentucky-(Col. Cochran)
  22nd Kentucky
  42nd Ohio
Foster's Wisconsin Battery

* * *

STONES RIVER
ACTION OF JANUARY 2, 1863

UNITED STATES,
ARMY OF THE CUMBERLAND
MAJ. GENERAL WILLIAM S. ROSECRANS, COMMANDING

Major General Thomas L. Crittenden -
Commander, Left Wing (McFadden's Ford)
  2nd Division–Brig. General John M. Palmer
    3rd Brigade – Col. William Grosse (Detached)
  3rd Division – Colonel Samuel Beatty
    1st Brigade – Col. Benjamin Grider
    2nd Brigade – Col. James Fyffe
    3rd Brigade – Col. Samuel Price

Chief of Artillery – Major John J. Mendenhall

* * *